SHORT-STRAW BRIDE

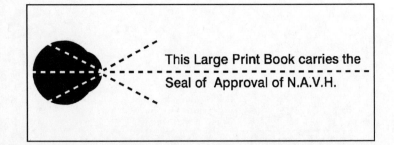

This Large Print Book carries the
Seal of Approval of N.A.V.H.

SHORT-STRAW BRIDE

KAREN WITEMEYER

THORNDIKE PRESS
A part of Gale, Cengage Learning

Detroit • New York • San Francisco • New Haven, Conn • Waterville, Maine • London

GALE
CENGAGE Learning®

LIBRARY OF CONGRESS CATALOGING-IN-PUBLICATION DATA

Witemeyer, Karen.
   Short-straw bride / by Karen Witemeyer.
      pages ; cm. — (Thorndike Press large print Christian romance)
   ISBN 978-1-4104-5156-9 (hardcover) — ISBN 1-4104-5156-9 (hardcover) 1.
Texas—History—1846-1950—Fiction. 2. Large type books. I. Title.
PS3623.I864S56 2012b
813'.6—dc23   2012026798

Published in 2012 by arrangement with Bethany House Publishers, a division of Baker Publishing Group.

Printed in the United States of America
1 2 3 4 5 6 7 16 15 14 13 12

To Gloria and Beth
my eagle-eyed critique partners
and beloved friends.

You strengthen my stories,
encourage my heart,
and corral my characters
when they get out of hand.
Thanks for walking this road with me.

Bear ye one another's burdens, and so
fulfill the law of Christ.

GALATIANS 6:2

PROLOGUE

Anderson County, Texas — 1870

Ten-year-old Meredith Hayes balled her hands into fists as she faced her tormentor. "Hiram Ellis! Give me back my lunch bucket this instant!"

"Oh, I'm sorry, Meri. Did you want this?" His voice dripped sarcasm as he dangled the small pail in front of her.

She lunged for it, but her hands met only air as the older boy snatched it away and tossed it over her head to his snickering brother. Meredith ricocheted between the two, never quite fast enough to get more than a finger on the tin.

Why was she always the one to get picked on? Meredith stomped her foot in frustration. She thought she'd gotten enough of a lead today after school, but Hiram must have been watching for her. He'd had it out for her ever since her family moved to the area last spring. Probably because the land they bought used to belong to his best friend's family.

"Meri, Meri, quite contrary," Hiram sang in a ridiculously high-pitched voice, skipping in a circle around her and swinging the lunch bucket back and forth. A group of girls came around the bend and stopped to giggle behind their hands. Meredith asked for help, but they just stood there smirking and whispering behind their schoolbooks. Even Anna Leigh, her desk mate and the one girl Meredith thought a friend. Angry tears pooled in her eyes, but Meredith blinked them away. She'd not let Hiram win.

"You're a bully, Hiram Ellis."

"Yeah?" Hiram stopped skipping and glared at Meredith. "Well, you're a carpet-bagger's daughter."

"My papa's not a carpetbagger. He's a teacher, just like your sister."

Hiram's face scrunched up like a pumpkin that had started to rot. "My sister teaches white kids. Not good-for-nothin' darkies."

Meredith raised her chin and repeated the words she'd heard her father say countless times. "They're freedmen. And they have just as much right to learn as you do."

"If those *freedmen* were still slaves, like they oughta be, Joey Gordon's pa wouldn'ta

10

been killed by Yankees, and Joey would still be here." Hiram glowered and strode toward her, his boots pounding into the earth. Meredith instinctively retreated a step before she remembered she wasn't afraid of him.

"You want this stupid tin back?" Hiram growled out the question as he halted a couple of feet in front of her. "Go fetch!"

He sprinted to the edge of the road and hurled the pail through a thick stand of pine trees. Meredith watched it fly, wondering why God thought it fair to give a mean-tempered boy such a strong throwing arm.

The bucket clipped a tree limb and disappeared over a small rise. A hollow clang echoed through the pines followed by a series of quieter thunks as it tumbled down the back side of the hill.

Meredith winced. Mama was going to skin her alive for bringing her pail home dented and busted. The only thing worse would be not bringing it home at all.

Meredith glared at Hiram and trudged forward.

"Meri, no!" Anna Leigh ran up and clutched Meredith's arm. "You can't. That's Archer land."

Archer land? Meredith looked around to get her bearings and swallowed hard as recognition dawned. Anna Leigh was right.

"No one steps on Archer land. Not if they value their life." Anna Leigh shook her head, eyeing the trees as if their branches might reach down and snatch her off the ground. "Just let it go, Meri." She backed away, tugging on Meredith's arm. But when Meredith made no move to follow, Anna Leigh released her with a heavy sigh.

It couldn't be as bad as all that. Could it? Meredith gazed through the pines, to the small hill that hid her lunch bucket. Her heart thumped against her ribs. It wasn't very far. If she ran, she could get her tin and be back before the Archers even knew she'd been there. Then again, everyone in Anderson County knew the Archer boys were trigger happy and plumb loco, to boot. What if one of them was hiding out there somewhere, just waiting for her?

"I hear they got bloodthirsty hounds that can sniff you out the minute your foot steps off the road." Hiram spoke in a low, husky voice. "Dogs that'd sooner gnaw your leg off than look at you."

Meredith told herself to pay him no mind. He was only trying to scare her. But she couldn't quite banish the image of a big black dog barreling down on her, teeth bared.

"You know Seth Winston . . . and his hand?"

Meredith didn't turn around, but she nodded. The man ran a store near her father's school. He only had three fingers on his right hand.

"Travis Archer shot them two fingers clean off when Winston tried to pay a call after old man Archer died. Woulda done worse if Winston hadn't hightailed it outta there as fast as he did. And don't think you'd be safe just 'cause you're a girl. They peppered Miss Elvira's buggy with buckshot when she came to collect the young ones to take them to the homes she'd found for them. Nearly put her eye out."

"At least . . ." Meredith's throat seemed to close. She forced a little cough and tried again. "At least they weren't hurt too bad."

"Only because they escaped." Hiram came up beside her and spoke directly into her ear. "Five other men weren't so lucky. They came out here at different times, each with hopes of buying the Archer spread. None of them were ever seen again." Hiram paused, and Meredith couldn't fight off the shivers his words provoked. "Their bodies are probably buried somewhere out there."

Something rustled just beyond the pines. Meredith jumped.

Hiram laughed.

She should go home. Just leave the pail and go home. Mama would understand . . . but she'd be disappointed.

"I dare you," Hiram said, finally drawing Meredith's attention. "I dare you to go after that tin."

"Don't do it, Meri," Anna Leigh begged.

"Oh, she won't. She's too scared." Hiram's cocky grin resurrected Meredith's pride.

Crossing her thin arms over her chest, she glared up at him. "I'll get it. Just see if I don't."

The girls behind her gasped, and even Hiram looked a bit uneasy, which only served to bolster Meredith's determination. She marched to the tree line, turned back for one last triumphant glance at the stunned Ellis boys, and dashed off in the direction the pail had disappeared. Her shoes crunched on fallen pine needles and twigs as she ran, her breath echoing loudly in her ears as she huffed up the hill.

She stopped at the top and clutched her aching side as she scanned the ground for her lunch bucket. Something shiny glinted in the sunlight down and to the left. Meredith smiled and hurried forward. *This isn't so tough.*

Her fingers closed around the handle of

the battered tin, but when she turned to head back, the hill blocked her view of the road. Suddenly feeling very isolated, she bit her lip as forest noises echoed around her. A twig snap to her left. A rustle to her right. Then from somewhere in the distance behind her, a dog barked.

The Archer hounds!

Meredith fled, scrambling up the hill. But the sandy soil was too loose. Her feet kept slipping. She clawed at the ground with her fingers, to no avail.

Another bark sounded. Closer this time.

Meredith gave up on the hill and just started running away from the barking. The slope gradually lessened, and she spotted a flat section up ahead where the pines turned back toward the road. Aiming for the opening, she veered between the trees.

As she looked up to gauge how close she was to the road, her right foot hit something metallic. A loud crack rent the air a second before a pair of steel jaws snapped closed on her leg.

"Good girl, Sadie." Travis Archer folded his wiry adolescent frame as he hunkered down and stroked the half-grown pointer. "We might turn you into a huntin' dog yet."

She still barked too much when she got

excited, frightening off the game, but she'd successfully pointed a rabbit and held when he called *whoa,* so even though the hare scurried away before he could get in position to shoot, Travis was proud of the pup's progress.

"Let's try again, girl. Maybe we'll find some quail for you to flush. Jim's getting tired of fixin' squirrel mea—"

An agonized scream cut Travis off and raised the hair on his arms. He hadn't heard a cry like that since his mother died birthin' Neill.

Sadie barked and took off like a shot. Travis called for her to stop, but the pup ignored his command and ran west — toward the road. Snatching up his rifle, he gave chase. If a new threat had wandered onto Archer land, he'd do everything in his power to protect his brothers.

The barking intensified, and it sounded as if Sadie had stopped. Travis slowed his pace and brought his rifle into position against his shoulder. It wouldn't be the first time some greedy land grabber tried to draw him out, thinking four boys were easy pickings. He might not be full grown, but he was man enough to defend what was his. No one was going to drive him and his brothers out. No one.

Travis wove through the narrow pines, catching a glimpse of Sadie's black coat. He recognized the spot. It was one of several places he'd hidden coyote traps. He'd posted warning signs, but some idiots were too cocky for their own good. Hardening himself against any pity he might feel for the interloper, Travis fingered the trigger on his rifle and stepped around the last tree that stood between him and his target.

"Hands where I can see 'em, mister, or I'll put a bullet in . . ." The threat died on his lips.

A girl?

Horror swept over him, loosening his grip on the rifle. The barrel dipped toward the ground.

"D-don't shoot. P-p-please." The girl turned liquid blue eyes on him. "I didn't m-m-mean any harm." Her tearstained face stabbed him with guilt as she bravely tried to swallow her sobs.

"I ain't gonna shoot you." Travis relaxed his stance and set the weapon aside. "See?" He held his palms out and took a cautious step toward the girl sitting sideways beneath the tree. "I thought you were someone else. I ain't gonna hurt you." Although judging by the blood staining the edge of her ruffled pantalets, he already had.

"W-what about your d-dog?" She eyed Sadie as if the pup were some kind of hell-hound.

"Sadie, heel." The pointer quit barking and padded over to Travis's side. He motioned for her to stay, then gingerly approached the frightened girl. "I'm gonna get that trap off your leg. All right?"

She sucked in her bottom lip, her eyes widening as he approached, but she nodded, and something inside Travis uncoiled. He'd no idea what he would've done if she'd gone all hysterical on him. Thankfully, this gal seemed to have a decent head on her shoulders. Travis smiled at her and turned his attention to the trap.

His stomach roiled. The thing was clamped above the ankle of her right leg. She whimpered a bit when he reached for the spring mechanisms on either side of the trap, no doubt anticipating more pain. The metal chain clanked as she moved.

"Try to keep still," he instructed. "Even when the trap opens, don't pull yourself free. Wait for me to help you. Your leg might be broken, and we don't want to do anything to make it worse. Understand?"

Another brave little nod.

Travis grabbed the release springs and was

about to compress them when the girl spoke.

"Can I . . . hold on to you?"

Closing his eyes for a second, Travis swallowed, then gave a nod of his own. "Sure, kid."

Her hands circled his neck as he bent over her, and she leaned her head against his shoulder.

He cleared his throat. "Ready?"

The side of her face rubbed against his upper arm. "Mm-hmm."

Travis pressed the spring levers with a firm, steady pressure until the trap's jaw released. Once it clicked back into its open position, he gently removed her foot from the trap.

"I need to check your leg to see how bad it is." Her arms still around his neck, Travis rotated her until her back brushed the tree trunk. "Rest here."

He eased away from her hold and lifted the edge of her pantalets a few inches up her shin. The skin had been broken, and there was a deep indentation where the steel had clamped her leg, but she'd had the good sense to keep still, so the bleeding was minimal. There seemed to be swelling and discoloration around the indentation, though, and that worried Travis.

"Can you move your foot?"

The girl flexed her foot and immediately hissed in pain. "It hurts." Her voice broke on a muted sob.

"Just be still, then." Travis gritted his teeth. Probably a fracture. "I'm gonna look for some sticks to splint your leg with, and then I'll get you home. All right? Don't worry."

On his deathbed, his father had made him swear never to leave Archer land, to protect it and his younger brothers at all cost. And Travis had done exactly that for the last two years. But today, he was going to have to break his promise. He had to make things right with this little girl. Had to get her home.

Travis stood and scoured the ground for splint-worthy sticks while silently vowing that, before he went home, he'd spring every stinking trap on his property. No way was he going to run the risk of something like this happening again. He'd thought that any troublemakers who found themselves snagged would be able to free themselves with a minimum of fuss and leave with a sore leg to remind them not to return. The traps were too small to do significant damage to a man's leg, especially through the thick boots most of them wore. But a child?

20

A *girl?* Travis never even considered such a scenario.

By the time he made his way back to the tree, the girl had composed herself. "What's your name?" he asked, thinking to distract her as he fit the splint to her leg.

"Meredith."

He pulled a handkerchief from his pocket and tied it firmly around the sticks just below her knee. "I'm Travis."

"*You're* Travis?" She said it with such disbelief that he stopped what he was doing to stare at her. She blushed and stammered. "I just . . . uh . . . thought you'd be meaner or bigger or . . . or something."

Travis shook his head and chuckled softly. "That's exactly what I want people to think. Me and my brothers are safer that way."

He looked around for something else to use to tie the bottom of the splint. Finding nothing, he took out his pocket knife and used the point to tear a hole in the seam at his left shoulder. Then he yanked until the sleeve pulled free and slid it down over his hand. He knelt back down and fastened it into place around her ankle.

"You know what you could do for me, Meredith?"

"What?"

He made sure the knot was tight, then

smiled up at his patient. "When you get back and your friends start asking you questions, make me sound as big and mean as possible. The fact that I helped you get home can be our secret. Okay?"

Her eyes glowed with something besides pain, and she actually smiled. The weight dragging on his conscience lightened.

"Grab onto my neck again — I'm going to pick you up." Travis shifted to her side and maneuvered an arm under her knees.

"Wait! I need my tin."

He pulled back. "Your what?"

"My lunch tin. Hiram threw it into the trees. That's why I came onto your land in the first place. I can't go back without it." She twisted and tried to reach behind her.

"Hold still," Travis barked, not wanting her to hurt herself. "I'll fetch it." He grabbed the beat-up pail and handed it to her. Meredith cradled it to her middle, and Travis decided that if he ever met this Hiram person, he'd find another pail and give the numskull a wallop or two upside the head.

Travis slid his arms around Meredith and lifted her from the ground. The little warrior never cried out, just tightened her grip on his neck as he pushed to his feet. He examined the ground for the smoothest

22

path to the road, even when it meant going out of his way. It was crazy, really — this urge to protect her. He'd spent the two years since his father died building barriers to keep the outside world out. But when this slip of a girl looked at him with trust blazing in her bright blue eyes, all he could think about was protecting the one piece of the outside world that had found a way in.

When he made it to the border of his property, Travis halted and inhaled a deep breath as his gaze tilted up toward heaven.

Sorry, Pa. I gotta do it.

Then, with a prayer for his brothers' safety resounding in his mind, he leaned forward and stepped off Archer land.

1

Palestine, Texas — 1882

"I don't think I can do it, Cass." Meredith peered up at her cousin through the reflection in the vanity mirror.

Cassandra pulled the hairpin from her mouth and secured another section of Meredith's braided chignon. "Do what?"

"Marry a man who wants me only for the land I can bring him."

"How do you know that's all he wants?" Cassandra leaned down until her face was level with Meredith's and winked at her in the mirror. "If you ask me, the man seems rather smitten, paying calls on you every Saturday night for the last month."

Calls where he spent more time discussing the lumber industry with her uncle than conversing with her. Wouldn't a man who was smitten spend his time talking to the woman he hoped to marry rather than her guardian?

Meredith sighed and turned to face her younger cousin. "I know I should be thrilled. Uncle Everett has told me again and again that Roy Mitchell is an excellent catch, and your mama nearly swooned when she found out he'd proposed. But something doesn't feel right."

"Maybe that's because saying yes would mean letting go of a girlhood dream."

Meredith squirmed under her cousin's knowing look. Cassandra was the only person Meredith had ever told about her infatuation with Travis Archer. An infatuation based on a single encounter. It was silly, really. What girl would dream about a young man whose hunting trap had nearly taken off her leg? Yet something about Travis Archer had left a permanent impression upon her heart.

Cassandra understood that.

During holidays and family visits, the two cousins used to huddle together beneath the covers of Cassandra's bed and spin romantic tales of the heroes who would valiantly rescue them from rockslides and stampeding cattle and even a polar bear or two when they were feeling particularly inventive. Meredith's hero always wore Travis Archer's face. Even now, she couldn't stop herself from imagining what he must look like twelve years later. He'd been handsome as a youth. What would he look like as a man?

Standing abruptly and moving to the open wardrobe where she could riffle through her dresses instead of looking at her cousin, Meredith mentally crammed Travis back into the past, where he belonged.

"Goodness, Cass. I'm far too sensible to hold on to a bunch of silly daydreams. I put those thoughts from my mind years ago."

Cassandra reached around her and took down the rose-colored dress Meredith only wore for special occasions. "You might have put Travis from your mind, but I think he still claims a piece of your heart."

Meredith reluctantly accepted the polonaise and matching skirt and laid them on the bed. But instead of removing her wrapper to dress, she hugged her arms around her waist and flopped onto the mattress. "You're right."

And where did that leave her? She hadn't seen the man once since that day. It was doubtful he even remembered her. If he did, the memory was probably a vague recollection of some scrawny kid who'd gotten caught trespassing. Not exactly a vision to inspire romantic feelings. Besides, none of the Archers ever stepped foot off their land.

Waiting for Travis would be about as fruit-ful as waiting for a snowstorm in July.

"Give Mr. Mitchell a chance, Meri. Maybe he's the kind of man who doesn't know how to express his feelings." Cassandra sat beside her on the bed and patted her knee. "It'll be just the two of you today at lunch. Papa won't be around to distract him with business talk. Get to know him. You might be surprised by what he can offer you."

Meredith glanced sideways at her cousin, a grin tugging at the corner of her mouth. "You know . . . I'm supposed to be the wise one here, not you."

"I may be three years younger," Cassandra said with a wink, "but that doesn't mean I don't know a thing or two about men."

"I can't argue with that. You've probably collected more courting experience in the past two years than I've had in the last five." Meredith smiled and nudged her cousin with her shoulder. "Look at the way Freddie Garrett follows you around."

"Freddie Garrett's barely fifteen, you goose. He doesn't count." Cassandra grabbed a pillow and swatted Meredith on the chin. Meredith, of course, had to retali-ate. The two dodged and giggled until their sides ached so much they had to stop.

"I think you're going to have to fix my

hair," Meredith said as she blew a loose strand off her forehead. The ornery thing fell right back across the bridge of her nose, which set the two girls to laughing again.

Cassandra gained her feet first. "Come on," she said between chuckles. "Let's get you dressed, and I'll see what I can do about your hair."

Twenty minutes later, dressed in her best polonaise with her hair artfully rearranged, Meredith stood by the window looking out over the street. Her cousin had kissed her cheek and wished her well a few minutes ago and left her to gather her thoughts before her suitor arrived. The only problem was, her thoughts were so scattered, Meredith was sure she'd never pull them together in time.

Roy Mitchell had many admirable traits. He was ambitious and prosperous, and would certainly support a wife in fine style. His dark hair and eyes were handsome to look upon, and his manners were impeccable. Yet he stirred no strong feelings in her. And as far as she could tell, she stirred none in him.

What am I to do, Lord? Do I marry Roy and hope that affection comes, or do you have someone else in mind for me? Please make your will clear to me.

A brisk knock sounded on the door, but before Meredith could answer, her aunt swept into the room, her brows lifted in a scrutinizing arch. "I'm glad to see you had the good sense to dress for the occasion."

Meredith bit her tongue. After living with the disapproving woman for several years, she'd learned to speak as little as possible during their private . . . discussions.

"Come here, child, and turn around so I can see you."

Trying to ignore the *child* remark, Meredith did as instructed while her aunt clicked her tongue and sighed like a martyr who had been given a heavy cross to bear.

"Can you do nothing more to disguise that awful limp? We can't have Mr. Mitchell second-guessing his offer before the engagement is official. I've already done all I can to ensure you every advantage. Cassandra has strict instructions not to enter the parlor while he's here. Don't want the man drawing unfavorable comparisons, do we?"

Aunt Noreen narrowed her gaze, as if she could sense Meredith's inner doubt. "You'd best not do anything to sabotage this proposal," she said, shaking her finger under Meredith's nose. "Everett and I have too much riding on this for you to dillydally around. The man expects an answer today.

30

And that answer had better be yes."

When Meredith had asked God for guidance, she'd never expected him to shove it down her throat with a dose of her aunt's less-than-flattering opinions. Was this really the answer she sought? Was God speaking through Aunt Noreen, or was Aunt Noreen just spouting her own agenda? Meredith didn't mind rebelling against her aunt, but rebelling against God was another matter entirely.

Needing to get away from the waving finger in order to think straight, Meredith stepped over to the wardrobe to collect her shawl, exaggerating her limp as she went. When Aunt Noreen moaned, Meredith smiled. She knew it was petty of her, but she refused to let the woman browbeat her without striking back at least a little.

In reality, the hitch in her gait was barely noticeable except on those days when she overexerted herself. Years ago, the doctor had explained that the bone damage she'd sustained from the steel trap had hindered the completion of normal growth in her right leg, eventually causing it to be slightly shorter than her left. With custom-made shoes that added half an inch of height to the right heel, she got along without much trouble. Unfortunately, Aunt Noreen tended to see mountains where the rest of the world saw only molehills, especially when it came to Meredith's shortcomings.

Wrapping her ivory shawl around her shoulders, Meredith stared at the silky fringe instead of her aunt as she cautiously ventured into the conversation. "Papa always encouraged me to choose a husband with utmost care since the bond would last for life. I aim to follow his advice. Roy Mitchell has many fine qualities, but I need more time to get to know him before I can make this decision with confidence." She glanced up and found scowl lines furrowing Aunt Noreen's brow. "Today's luncheon will certainly help me achieve those ends," Meredith hurried to add.

"More time?" The woman sounded as if the words were choking her.

Aunt Noreen eyed the open doorway and prowled three steps closer to Meredith. "Did I ask for more time when your father requested lodgings for you in my home so that you could attend the Palestine Female Institute five years ago?" she hissed. "No. And two years after that, when your father's dealings with those . . . those *Negros* finally resulted in the end I predicted, did not Everett and I give you a permanent home?"

Meredith swallowed hard, trying to fight

the memories of the fever that had taken first her papa and then her mother. They hadn't allowed her to come home, too afraid she'd catch the sickness. She'd tried to go to them anyway, but when her father refused to unbar the door and gazed at her through the front window, palm pressed to the glass, sunken eyes silently pleading with her to leave, she'd had no choice. She returned to her aunt and uncle's house and wept in Cassie's arms.

"My food has fed you," Aunt Noreen muttered, bring Meredith back to the present. "Your uncle's income has provided a roof over your head. You've been given more than enough *time*."

Noreen sniffed and crossed her arms, looking uncomfortable as her focus jumped to the doorway before returning to Meredith. "You might not be aware, but your uncle's business has experienced some setbacks in the last few years. We need the stability that a connection with Roy Mitchell would provide. He's promised to partner with Everett once his land deal goes through. All his lumber will be cut exclusively by the Hayes mill. But the deal hinges on your marriage. No marriage, no partnership."

Because Roy Mitchell needed her land —

the land her father had left in her uncle's care, intending that he restore it to Meredith when she married or turned twenty-five.

"Would you jeopardize Cassandra's future simply because you're unsure of your feelings?"

Meredith blinked. If she refused Roy Mitchell's proposal, *would* she be hurting Cassandra?

Footsteps echoed in the hall outside the room for a moment before Cassandra's smiling face appeared in the doorway.

"Papa sent me to fetch you, Meri. Your suitor's here."

Aunt Noreen gave her a pointed look and nudged her toward the door. "Go on, now. Let's not keep Mr. Mitchell waiting."

As Meredith stepped into the hall, Cassie's eager smile, so full of innocence and romantic dreams, lit up her face. Guilt pricked at Meredith like a row of sewing pins protruding through her corset seam.

Cassandra deserved the best, and if marrying Roy would provide her cousin that opportunity, perhaps Meredith should make the sacrifice.

Yet when she entered the parlor and Roy walked toward her, she couldn't quite stem the quivers of panic that convulsed in her stomach.

Lord, I asked for guidance, and so far everything seems to point me toward marrying Roy. But if you have another plan, any other plan, I'd gladly consider it.

Roy extended his arm to her, and Meredith fought for a polite smile as she slid her hand into its expected place.

2

By the time Meredith finished her slice of chocolate cake, she'd given up on finding common ground with Roy Mitchell. After the soup, she'd asked him what he enjoyed doing in his free time, and he'd answered that he was fond of traveling. This perked her up initially, until his description of a recent trip to Houston turned into a quarter hour of rambling about the area's booming lumber industry.

Then, when the waiter arrived with their entrées, blessedly interrupting the *Ode to the Big Thicket's Virgin Pine,* Meredith slipped in a question about what he liked to read. Roy smiled and confidently assured her that he much preferred to experience things firsthand rather than read someone else's view on the subject.

"For example," he said as he leaned across the table in obvious enthusiasm, "I've made careful study of the lands here on the edge

36

of the Piney Woods. Acres of forest stand virtually untouched, just waiting for the right man with the right vision to capitalize on the opportunity. Reading books only teaches a person about the past. I'm a man who looks to the future."

He went on to describe how his forward thinking led him to line up a handful of investors to supply capital for the manpower and equipment he'd need to expand his small logging operation. All he lacked were a few parcels of land that would allow him direct access to the railroad. And those he would soon have in his possession.

Desperate by the dessert course, Meredith broke all the etiquette rules her mother had taught her and asked about religion, questioning Roy about the role he expected God to play in his expansion plans. The man chuckled and offered some sort of platitude about God helping those who helped themselves before he tucked into his apple pie.

The meal could not have left her more disheartened. She supposed Roy was simply attempting to convince her of his ability to provide for a wife, but what he'd succeeded in doing instead was paint a dreary picture of the two of them sitting on a porch, staring at a field of tree stumps with no fodder for conversation because all the virgin pines were gone.

"Are you ready to go, my dear?"

Meredith blinked. "Oh . . . yes." She dabbed her lips with her napkin and smiled up at Roy as he hurried around the table to assist her with her chair. "Thank you for a lovely meal. I don't often get to eat in such elegant surroundings."

"That will change once we're married. As my wife, you'll dine in the finest establishments in the state. Houston, San Antonio, even the capital."

"Mmmm." Meredith couldn't seem to vocalize anything more committal as Roy helped her on with her shawl and escorted her from the hotel dining room.

The two strolled down the boardwalk in front of the International Hotel in silence, and for the first time since leaving her uncle's house, Meredith relaxed. Maybe being with Roy wasn't so bad after all. His firm grip steadied her uneven gait, and the people they passed didn't look through her as they usually did. Men tipped their hats and women gazed at her with new respect. Being on Roy Mitchell's arm apparently made her a person worth noticing.

But did it make her the person she wanted to be?

A hat in the milliner's window caught

Meredith's eye, and she slowed. Ever the gentleman, Roy steered her closer to the shop, but she found it nearly impossible to concentrate on the bonnet, for she could feel him scrutinizing her face.

"Have you given much thought to my proposal, Miss Hayes?"

Meredith's stomach lurched. *Not yet.* She wasn't ready.

He released her arm and placed his palm in the small of her back. "I confess, I have thought of little else," he murmured.

The warmth of his hand penetrated her clothing, but the intimate touch left her chilled.

Lord, I need a sign here. A hint. Anything.

"Mr. Mitchell?"

Roy's hand fell away from her back as he turned to face the burly man approaching him from the street. "Now's not a good time, Barkley."

"I'm sorry to interrupt, sir, but it's important."

Roy held his hand out to Meredith, and she took it, letting him drag her to his side. "Nothing could be more important than what I'm doing right now."

What he was doing right now was pressing her for an answer she was unprepared to give. Mr. Barkley's interruption could not have pleased her more.

"I don't mind, Roy," she said. "Truly."

Roy patted her hand. "Nonsense. I'm sure whatever Barkley has to say can wait until after I see you home."

"But he says it's important," she insisted, praying he'd do the unchivalrous thing for once. "I'd hate to be the cause of a delay that ended up hurting your business ventures."

Roy hesitated. He glanced back to where Mr. Barkley stood shifting his weight from foot to foot. "Can it wait an hour?"

"You . . . ah . . . you said you wanted to be informed the minute Wheeler returned with an answer, boss." The man finally looked Roy directly in the eye, and a silent message seemed to pass between them. "He's back."

Meredith held her breath as Roy battled with himself over which course to choose. Then he squeezed her hand, and she knew she'd been granted a reprieve.

"I'm sorry, my dear, but this really is an urgent matter. I promise not to be long."

"Take as much time as you need." Meredith slipped her hand from his loose hold and wandered back toward the shop window. "I wanted to examine the new bonnets more closely anyway."

40

Roy favored her with an appreciative grin and gestured for Mr. Barkley to meet him at the end of the boardwalk. The two met at the edge of the milliner's shop and ducked into the alley that stretched alongside.

Meredith had just set her mind to figuring out a way to postpone responding to Roy's proposal when the man's voice echoed back to her from around the corner.

"He's back from the Archer spread already? That doesn't bode well."

The Archer spread? As in *Travis* Archer? Meredith strained to hear more, but Roy's voice faded as he walked deeper into the alley.

Meredith ambled down to the far end of the display window, careful to keep her eyes on the hats while diverting all her focus to her ears. A wagon rolled past, harness jangling and horse hooves clomping, making her want to scream in frustration as the men's words got lost in the din. Giving up on the hats, Meredith moved to the building's corner and pressed her shoulder against the brick, getting as close as she dared without being seen. Thankfully, the noisy wagon turned down an adjacent street, and she could finally catch pieces of the conversation again.

". . . can't be convinced to sell?"

"Wheeler offered him twice what the property's worth . . . man threatened to shoot . . . ain't selling, boss."

". . . connects the northern properties to the railroad. . . . my investors will pull out. I have to . . . one way or another."

"I thought . . . Hayes spread, too."

"That's in the bag. You . . . that crippled gal was hanging on to me. I'll have my . . . deed before the month is out. No, Archer . . . only serious obstacle."

Meredith sucked in an outraged breath. *Crippled gal?* Of all the nerve. If he thought he was going to get his greedy hands on her father's legacy that easily, he couldn't be more wrong. Why, she had half a mind to —

". . . issue my threat?"

Threat? What threat? Meredith shoved aside her indignation and fixed her attention back on the men in the alley.

"Yep. Wheeler warned . . . didn't sell there'd be consequences."

"Good. Burn. . . . tonight. Target the barn. Then . . . offer half the previous price to take . . . off their hands."

Meredith gasped. Roy had just ordered an act of arson with the same nonchalance as he'd ordered their beefsteak at the hotel.

God had given her a sign, all right, and it clearly read *Stay Out!*

But what about Travis? Fires could be deadly. She had to do something to help him.

One set of footsteps echoed in retreat while a second grew louder. Meredith lunged awkwardly back to the window, her pulse throbbing.

"Have you decided which you like best?" Roy came up beside her, once again the solicitous gentleman. Revulsion crept over her, but Meredith forced herself not to shy away.

She wanted to spit on him or slap him or shove him off the boardwalk and into the mud where he belonged, but she couldn't do any of those things without tipping him off that she had overheard his plans. So she smiled instead, vowing to beat him at his own game.

"I'm leaning toward the blue one with the flowers. What do you think of it?"

"I think it would look lovely on you. But then, you have a way of making everything lovely." He smiled and lifted a finger to stroke her cheek.

Meredith's stomach roiled.

"Oh dear." She quickly covered her mouth with one hand and her stomach with the other, thanking God for the excuse to cut their time together short. "I think something

43

from lunch may not be agreeing with me."
That something being Roy Mitchell.

An impatient frown darkened Roy's face
before he quickly replaced it with a look of
concern. "Would you like to sit and rest for
a moment? There's a bench outside the
drugstore across the street."

"No. I think I should lie down." She
hunched herself over and added a quiet
moan for good measure. "Can you take me
home, please?"

"Are you sure?"

Meredith nodded vigorously, keeping her
hand over her mouth.

"Very well."

Roy took her arm and helped her navigate
the three blocks back to her uncle's house.
When they reached the front gate, however,
he used his grip to slow her to a halt.

"I'm so sorry to have ruined our afternoon," she blurted, not wanting to give him
the chance to ask her anything. Besides, the
longer she thought about what he planned
for Travis, the more ill she truly became.
She looked up at the brick house, longing
for the escape it promised.

"Meredith, darling," Roy said, turning her
to face him, "please, just tell me that I can
move ahead with our wedding plans."

The idea was so nauseating, Meredith

didn't have to prevaricate. Her stomach began to heave all on its own. Roy must have seen the truth in her face as she bent forward, for his eyes widened and he quickly stepped back. Meredith covered her mouth and ran for the house.

"I'll come by later this evening," Roy called after her, but Meredith didn't slow until she was safely inside.

The kitchen stood empty, so Meredith made her way to the sink pump, hoping that a glass of cool water would help settle her stomach. She needed to calm her body so her mind could focus on how to help Travis. If Roy's henchmen planned to strike tonight, that left her precious little time to strategize. The Archer ranch was a good two and a half hours' ride to the north. A well-conditioned horse could possibly shave thirty minutes off that time, but that still left her less than an hour to implement a course of action.

"Mercy me, Miss Meri. You look like someone done wrung you out and hung you up to dry. You all right?" Eliza, the cook Meredith's aunt employed, strode into the room cradling a selection of carrots, onions, and potatoes in her upturned apron.

Meredith managed a wan smile. "I'm not feeling well, I'm afraid. Is Uncle Everett back from Neches yet? I need to speak with him."

Not for the first time, Meredith longed for her own father's counsel instead of her uncle's. She missed the days of occasionally riding beside him in the buggy out to the freedmen's school he continued to run even after the Freedmen's Bureau shut down — missed the talks they had, the dreams they shared.

Papa would've known what to do about Roy and Travis. But Papa was gone.

Eliza dropped the vegetables into a wash pan with a cascade of thumps, then shook her apron out over the dry sink. "Master Hayes told me not to expect him till suppertime."

Meredith's shoulders sagged. Suppertime would be too late.

"Miss Meri, you better go up to bed and rest some. You're looking right peak-ed."

"I don't need —" Meredith stopped herself as she recalled Roy's promise to return. "Well, maybe I will." She'd not want to face her aunt, either. "In fact, with my stomach as unsettled as it is, I'll probably forgo dinner tonight. Would you mind asking Aunt Noreen not to wake me?"

"Of course, child. You go rest."

Why was it when Aunt Noreen called her

a child she felt degraded, but when Eliza did it, she felt nurtured? Meredith set her half-empty glass on the table, the churning in her abdomen finally beginning to subside.

"And in case ya get hungry later," Eliza said, pointing to the cookstove, "I'll leave some of my stew broth on the warmer. You just sneak on down here and help yourself. Ya hear?"

Meredith smiled and, on impulse, hugged the older woman. Eliza flapped her hands and shooed her away, embarrassed by the display of affection. "Go on with ya, now."

Meredith climbed the stairs and closed herself in her room. At least Aunt Noreen would not be home to pester her. She and Cassandra always paid their social calls on Tuesday afternoons. Usually Meredith accompanied them, but Roy's luncheon invitation had taken precedence over the weekly torture of censorious glances and nose sniffing that Aunt Noreen and her friends enjoyed while expounding their ponderous opinions. Unfortunately, that meant Meredith wouldn't be able to confide in Cassandra, either. That left only one person she could think of who might be willing and able to help her.

Changing out of her fancy polonaise, Meredith pulled a more practical dress out of her wardrobe and buttoned herself up into her favorite dark green calico. Just in case anyone should look in on her, she lumped an extra quilt under her covers to make it appear she was sleeping, then tiptoed down the stairs and slipped quietly out the back door.

Meredith chose an indirect route to Courthouse Square, studiously avoiding any avenues where her aunt might be visiting. She hurried down Market Street until she reached the jail, then circled around to the north and entered the sheriff's office.

The man lounging behind the desk bolted upright, dropping his booted feet from the corner of the desktop to the floor. He braced his palms on the arms of his chair to boost himself up until his eyes met hers. Then he promptly slouched right back into his negligent pose.

"Well, if it ain't Meri Hayes. Come to ask me to the church social?"

Hiram Ellis. Of all the rotten luck. The fellow was just as obnoxious grown as he'd been as a kid.

"I'm looking for Sheriff Randall." Meredith ignored Hiram's cocky smirk and glanced around the office as if he were beneath her notice. "Do you know where I might find him?"

"Still as contrary as ever, I see." Hiram slowly rose to his feet, puffing out his chest as if to emphasize the deputy's star pinned to his coat. "The sheriff's transportin' a prisoner over to Rusk County to stand trial, so it looks like you're stuck with me, darlin'."

Could this day get any worse? Hiram Ellis was the last person she'd trust with her troubles. But then, they weren't *her* troubles. Travis Archer and his brothers were the ones in danger. A spark and an unruly gust of wind could easily set their home ablaze, killing them in their beds.

Meredith gritted her teeth. If Hiram was her only choice, so be it.

"I overheard a threatening conversation today." Reluctant to reveal Roy's part in the scheme due to his connection with her uncle's business, she kept the account as anonymous as possible. "Two men were discussing Travis Archer's land and how he refused to sell. One man ordered the other to set the Archers' barn on fire in an effort to convince him to reconsider."

Hiram leaned a hip against the edge of the desk. "So what do you want me to do about it? It ain't no crime to run off at the mouth. You probably didn't hear them right anyhow. How close were you to these two

49

fellers?"

"Around the corner," Meredith admitted, "but I heard them clearly enough. And I can assure you, this was no idle talk. It was menacing and authoritative. You have to ride out to the Archers' place and keep this terrible thing from happening. At the very least, warn Mr. Archer that trouble is headed his way."

Hiram shook his head. "I ain't riding all the way out there on the say-so of some woman who can't be sure of what she heard. You always were the kind to get all worked up about one thing or another for no good reason. Besides, I gotta stay here and protect the good citizens of Palestine while the sheriff's gone. We can talk to Archer when Randall gets back."

"By then it will be too late!"

Hiram just shrugged. "I'll make a note in the log book that you came by to make a report. That's the best I can do."

Of all the lazy, arrogant, self-aggrandizing men she'd ever had the misfortune to meet, Hiram Ellis sat at the top of the list.

As Meredith marched out of the sheriff's office, one thing became exceedingly clear. If there was to be any hope of getting a warning to Travis Archer in time, she was going to have to deliver it herself.

3

A half hour later, Meredith penned a note to her cousin.

Cass,

I need your help. Roy Mitchell is not the gentleman he pretends to be. With my own ears, I heard him order the burning of Travis Archer's barn because the man refused to sell his land. Thankfully, Roy doesn't know I overheard him. However, he's planning to call tonight, and I need you to tell him I am feeling poorly and have retired early, since I'll be on my way to warn Travis.

Tomorrow you can tell Uncle Everett that I decided to visit the old homestead, for that is what I plan to do right after stopping by the Archer place. I will stay out there a few days, cleaning and preparing the house for winter, and return to town by the end of the week.

I'm sorry to put you in an awkward spot, but Roy's men are headed to the Archer place tonight, so there's no time to delay. I know you'll understand.

She signed her name at the bottom, knowing Cassandra would cover for her. There was no one she trusted more. Yet when she returned, nothing would be the same. Rejecting Roy's proposal meant sabotaging the Hayes family business. Her aunt would resent her more than she already did, and Uncle Everett's disappointment would be hard to bear. Perhaps it was a good thing she was spending a few days at the old house. She might very well be taking up residence there again soon.

With a sigh, Meredith folded the ivory paper and walked down the hall to her cousin's room. She tucked the note into the basket that held Cassandra's hair ribbons, a place where her cousin would be sure to find it but one that would make the note inconspicuous to others. Then she retrieved the small leather valise she'd packed with a spare dress, sleeping gown, and necessary toiletries and slipped out the back to where she'd tied her horse.

The man on duty at the livery where she boarded Ginger had been kind enough to saddle the animal for her, and Meredith had already tucked a few days' provisions into the saddlebags, so all she had left to do now was mount up and go. Yet as she gazed back at the redbrick building that had been her home since losing her parents, an odd reluctance filled her. It was almost as if she were saying good-bye.

But then the image of a young man with sun-kissed brown hair and compassionate eyes lured her back to her mission. She would find a way to warn Travis Archer and deal with the repercussions later. She owed him that much.

The sun had started to streak the sky orange by the time Meredith reached the turnoff to Travis's property. Losing light and warmth in the shadows of the trees, she shivered beneath her cloak as she urged Ginger from the main road onto the little-used path that wound through the Archer pines.

Several yards in, a wooden gate rose from the brush to bar her way. Two hand-painted signs nailed to the top slat of the gate glared up at her. The one on the left read *Trespassers will be shot on sight.* And the second wasn't much friendlier. *To conduct business, fire two shots and wait.*

The Archers certainly weren't long on

hospitality, but what really concerned her was the padlock that held the gate secure. With barbed wire stretching out on either side as far as she could see, it would be impossible to get Ginger through. And with no gun, she had no way to summon any of the Archers to her position.

For the first time since she'd left Palestine, urgency gave way to uncertainty. She'd known Travis and his brothers were reclusive, but by the look of things, they were downright hostile when it came to outsiders. They obviously wanted no news or visits from the outside world.

But they had no idea of the menace waiting to strike.

Meredith inhaled a deliberate breath and dismounted. She'd come this far. She might as well see it through. With trembling hands, she secured Ginger's reins around the gate post and stroked the mare's neck.

"I'll be back soon. I'm just going to deliver a message. It won't take long. You'll be fine."

Ginger reached her head down to nibble at some grass, apparently unperturbed at the prospect of being left alone. But as Meredith hiked up her skirt and wedged her left foot onto the bottom slat of the gate, the confidence she'd projected into that little speech evaporated.

She scaled the gate quickly and paused at the top to swing her leg over. Closing her eyes for a moment, she straddled the gate and whispered a quick prayer.

"Please don't let them shoot me."

Then before she could talk herself out of it, she scrambled down the far side and started walking.

The last time she'd trespassed on Archer land, she'd ended up with a broken leg and a nasty scar. Last time she'd had an excuse, and there'd been no fences. This time she didn't have the innocence of childhood to protect her. Was Travis still the kindhearted man she remembered, the one who hid his tender side behind a harsh reputation and a wall of secrecy, or had he hardened into the unyielding, coldhearted man people thought him to be?

Meredith shoved that last thought aside. She refused to believe it. She'd seen his heart that day. Travis might put up a ruthless front, but gentleness was too ingrained in his character to disappear over time.

But just to be safe, she walked with her arms angled away from her sides, palms facing forward, to present herself in as unthreatening a manner as possible. No point in putting her theory to the test if she didn't have to.

The smell of woodsmoke tickled her nose, and Meredith's heart skittered. The house must be close. An odd-sounding birdcall echoed somewhere in the distance off to her left. Her head swiveled in that direction. Then another bird answered from up ahead of her to the right. A chill passed over her. In all her years in Anderson County, she'd never heard a bird that sounded quite like those surrounding her. Then again, she'd been in town for quite some time. Perhaps she'd forgotten.

The trees began to thin, and Meredith spotted a clearing ahead. She picked up her pace, anxious to have her errand over and done. But before she took more than a dozen steps, four men emerged from the woods and surrounded her, each pointing a rifle directly at her chest.

What in blue blazes was a woman doing waltzing onto Archer land at the brink of dark?

From his vantage point behind her, Travis couldn't see much of her face, so he had no way of judging her intelligence. But anyone crazy enough to come onto Archer land without an invitation was sure to be unpredictable, and he wasn't taking any chances.

The woman kept her hands a healthy

distance from her sides, and he could see her fingers quivering. Yet despite her obvious nervousness, she stared at each of his brothers in turn and even twisted around to examine Neill and finally . . .

Travis raised his head from sighting down the rifle as shock radiated through him. Those eyes. Such a vivid blue. It was as if he'd seen them before. But that was impossible. Females didn't exactly pay them calls on a regular basis.

Clearing his throat, he readjusted his rifle. "We don't cotton to trespassers around here, lady. You best skedaddle back the way you came."

"I will. But not until I say my piece." She pivoted to face him fully, her lashes lowering for just a moment before she aimed her gaze directly at him again.

Even knowing what was coming didn't stop the jolt from ricocheting through his chest when those piercing eyes latched onto him.

"I came to warn you, Travis."

Travis? She knew who he was? Most folks meeting the Archers all at once had no way of knowing him from Crockett or Jim. Yet she said his name with the confidence of recognition.

He squinted at her. "Look, lady. I don't

know what kind of game you're playing, but I want no part of it."

"This is no game. Please, Travis. Just listen."

"You know this gal, Trav?"

Out of the corner of his eye, he saw his youngest brother start to lower his rifle. "Hush up, Neill, and hold your line." The kid obeyed without question, firming up his grip.

"The man who wants to buy your land is sending men out here tonight to persuade you to change your mind. They plan to set fire to the place while you sleep and force you to accept the next offer in order to recoup your losses."

Her announcement closed around Travis's heart like a vise that slowly began to tighten. Why wouldn't people just let them alone? Whether it was the do-gooders fourteen years ago who thought they knew best and attempted to take his brothers off to some orphanage, or the string of men who came after, trying to take advantage of a green kid with prime land, he was sick to death of people interfering in his affairs.

There was plenty of other land to be had, after all — although none of the available acreage had a house and outbuildings already built or a creek that didn't run dry in the summer. The more honorable vultures had sought to buy him out at a price far below market value, assuming he was too inexperienced to know the difference. The less honorable ones tried to take the land by force.

He still shuddered every time he thought of that bullet in Jim's shoulder — the one Crockett dug out, holed up in the cellar, while Travis drove the rest of the attackers from their land. Jim had been a pup at fifteen. Crockett, seventeen. And nine-year-old Neill had been the only one left to stand guard. They'd almost lost Jim to the fever afterward, but in the end, God had spared his life.

And now, according to this woman, another round was about to begin.

Travis glanced at each of his brothers. Being well trained, none had dropped his guard, but he could sense their wariness, hear the questions hanging unspoken in the air.

"Please, Travis. You have to believe me," the woman pled. "You and your brothers are in danger."

"Look, lady," Travis ground out between clenched teeth, "I don't know what you're up to, but I do know that if someone was planning to attack us, they sure as shootin' wouldn't go around announcing that fact to the general public. That tells me that if what you're saying is true, you're a part of it somehow, and I can't trust you."

Pain flashed in the woman's eyes, but she quickly blinked it away before jutting out her chin. "The man my aunt and uncle want me to marry is the one who wants to buy your land. While in his company earlier today, I chanced to overhear a private conversation between him and one of his subordinates. I was horrified by what I heard and knew I had to warn you. After your kindness to me, I couldn't stand by and do nothing."

Travis drew back. "What *kindness?* I've never even seen you before." Yet the familiarity that continued to stir at the edge of his consciousness made him question the accuracy of that statement.

"But you have." The crazy woman actually took a step closer to him, completely ignoring the rifle he was still pointing at her chest. "I was a trespasser then, too, only a much younger one."

She reached for something in her skirts, and he cocked his weapon. "Don't move, lady. I don't want to hurt you."

"I know."

Instead of shrinking away from him, her

eyes held his, filled to the brim with . . . trust? That made no sense. Maybe the woman *was* crazy.

"You told me it was all an act on the day you helped me. Do you remember? After you freed me from that trap and splinted my leg, you made me promise not to tell anyone about how you were helping me. Said it would be safer for your brothers if everyone continued to believe you a mean-hearted, trigger-happy fiend. I kept that promise. And now I'm back to return the kindness you extended to me twelve years ago."

She reached for her skirts again, and heaven help him, all he did was lower his rifle barrel so he could watch her better. He remembered that girl and those abominable traps. How brave she'd been. How trusting. But this couldn't be her, could it? Surely time hadn't passed so quickly. She'd been just a child. This woman couldn't be the same person.

Travis fought his reaction to her and regained his stance. "This is some kind of trick — some way for you to worm into my good graces so your fiancé can step in and steal my land."

Her eyes narrowed. "This is no trick, and that man will never be my fiancé." She tugged on her skirts again. "I can prove who I am, Travis, if you'll just give me the chance." She lowered her gaze to somewhere near the ground. "Look at my leg."

He might be a recluse, but even he knew what she asked wasn't proper. But apparently Neill was too young to have any qualms.

"Ah, that little scar ain't nothin'. Jim's is better."

A quiet growl rumbled out of Jim, but Crockett actually laughed. Travis turned a glare on the man to his left. Crockett swallowed his mirth.

Fed up with this girl's shenanigans, Travis finally glanced down at her ankle, at the small amount of skin exposed above the top of her shoe and below her hem. Sure enough, a thin scar marred the pale flesh there.

In a flash, he was seventeen again, tending her wound, and carrying the little girl in his arms all the way to her home. He'd thought of her often — wondering what became of her. Travis examined her face again. Her hair was a little darker now, but a few golden streaks remained, evidence of the towheaded girl he'd met so long ago. Her vivid blue eyes cut through him just as they had back then, when they'd been full of tears. The curves she sported now were definitely new, but the determination and bravery he remembered clung to her bearing like a grass burr to a pant leg.

That scrawny little kid had grown into a right handsome woman.

Travis lowered his weapon. "Good to see you again, Meredith."

4

He *did* remember. Even her name. Meredith couldn't hold back the grin that begged for release.

"So, brother . . . how come you never told us about your little friend, here?" The teasing drawl from the man at Travis's left drew Meredith's attention. He deliberately looked from her to Travis and back again. Then he winked. She couldn't believe it. Biting her lip to keep her embarrassment in check as well as to keep from smiling too wide, she dropped her gaze to the ground.

"Shut up, Crockett," Travis grumbled as he stalked forward to take her arm. "It was a long time ago." His grip was gentle but exerted enough force to propel her toward the clearing. "She wandered off the road and stepped into one of those traps we used to have set up. I freed her, splinted up her leg, and took her home. End of story."

As they rounded the last stand of trees,

the house came into view off to the right. The snug cabin with its trail of smoke curling up from the stone chimney beckoned Meredith with an earnest welcome completely at odds with the rifle-wielding foursome who had met her on the path.

"Wait a minute." Crockett jogged around them and planted himself in front of her.

Travis tried to maneuver around his brother, but the quick change of direction gave Meredith no time to compensate for her weaker leg. She stumbled a bit, her limp becoming more pronounced. Travis frowned down at her leg as he drew her to a halt.

"Did you say you took her home? You actually left our land?"

"Her leg was broken. What did you expect me to do?" Travis demanded. "Leave her for the coyotes?"

"Of course not. It's just . . ." Crockett stood there staring at him, the incredulous look on his face almost comical. "I never thought you'd cross that line."

"It was one time. Don't make more of it than it is."

Good advice for her, too, Meredith realized as Travis shouldered past Crockett and continued escorting her across the clearing. The fact that Travis had kept their meeting a secret from his brothers didn't mean something private and personal existed between them. Most likely, all it meant was that he didn't want to give them an excuse to follow his example and venture too far from home. Allowing the warmth expanding all too rapidly inside her to cloud her judgment would indeed be foolish.

Too bad his hand felt so good on her arm and his solid presence at her side confirmed all those heroic imaginings she'd indulged in as a young girl. It made sensibility far less attractive.

A horse whinnied somewhere behind the house, though, and reason returned as she recalled Ginger tied up at the gate. Coupling that with Travis's comment about the coyotes, Meredith knew her errand had taken too long already.

Before he could haul her up to the covered porch that stretched the length of the log house, Meredith tugged her elbow free and stepped a couple of paces away from the steps. "Thank you for offering the hospitality of your home, but I really should be on my way. I left my horse tied at your gate, and she tends to get restless if left alone too long."

Travis's gaze bore into her. Gone was the compassion she'd experienced as a child. And the gratitude she'd expected to see was nowhere in evidence, either. The only thing glimmering in those greenish-brown eyes of his was steely determination.

"I'm not bringing you to the house to offer you hospitality, Meredith." Travis closed the distance between them with one long stride. "I'm bringing you here so that you can tell us everything you know about this former fiancé of yours and his plans for our ranch."

"But . . ." Meredith looked from brother to brother. Even the teasing Crockett looked implacable. "I've already told you all I know," she insisted.

The Archers surrounded her once again and started herding her like a stray cow. Before she knew it, she was up the porch steps and through the front door.

This was not how things were supposed to go. The heroic Travis of her dreams would never dictate to her in such a way.

"It's nearly dark. I really have to go. It's not proper for me to be here." Her protests fell on deaf ears as they drove her toward the kitchen. Warmth from the stove permeated the air along with the smell of some kind of roasted meat.

Travis pulled out a chair from the kitchen table and glared at her until she sat down. He set his gun against the wall and leaned close to her face, one hand on the table, one on the back of her chair. "I'm sorry, Meredith, but I can't take any chances. Protecting my brothers and my land always comes first with me. Always." His words rang with righteous conviction, leaving little room for argument. "You'll stay here and answer my questions until I'm satisfied that I've gotten all I can from you."

Meredith's temper flared, although she didn't know if she was more upset about being coerced to stay or about her hero acting in such an unchivalrous manner. "So it's to be an inquisition."

"A friendly one. I promise." He smiled, and for a moment, the hardness in his face relaxed and a touch of kindness leaked through. But all too quickly, he shut it off. "I wouldn't worry about propriety if I were you. I'm guessing no one knows you're here, so your reputation is in no danger."

"My cousin knows." The argument was weak, even to her own ears, and probably accomplished as much good in changing his mind as sticking her tongue out at him would have, but she couldn't stand to leave his smug assumption unchallenged.

"Your cousin, huh? Well, I doubt a family member would risk tarnishing your good name."

Heavy footsteps clomped around behind her as the other brothers made their way to the table. She didn't feel threatened by them, but having four men tower over her in a confined space didn't exactly boost her confidence, either. Travis must have noticed her unease, for he lowered himself into a nearby chair and gently touched her shoulder.

"You have nothing to fear from us, Meredith. You have my word." Her gaze locked with his, and something passed between them. A remembered bond from that childhood encounter? She wasn't sure, but she was certain she could trust him.

She sat a little straighter and lifted her chin. "What about my horse?"

Travis smiled and turned to the youngest Archer. "Fetch the lady's horse, Neill."

The boy was standing by the stove and had a spoonful of beans halfway to his mouth. Undeterred, he jabbed the spoon between his lips and talked around the mouthful as he dropped the spoon back into the pot. Meredith cringed.

"I don't want to miss all the discussin', Trav. The horse'll keep."

"If you hurry, you might make it back before we eat all the vittles."

"Eat the . . . ? You wouldn't dare!" Neill

scowled, then shot an anxious look toward the stove. Meredith ducked her head to hide her smile. Amazing how much sway food could hold over a young man's decisions.

Travis shrugged. "We have a guest, which means less to go around. Might be slim pickin's if you dally."

Neill growled low in his throat, like a cornered animal, and after aiming a final glare at Travis, he snatched up his gun from where it stood propped against the wall and stomped out of the room.

Travis shook his head and smiled at the kid's back, his affection obvious despite his firmness in dealing with him. But as he turned his attention to Meredith, his smile faded, leaving nothing but stoic resolve lingering in his gaze.

As if by silent cue, Crockett and the other brother who had yet to speak lowered themselves into chairs across from where she and Travis sat and stared her down. Meredith instinctively shrank away from them and edged closer to Travis.

"What do they plan to target?" Travis hardened himself against the surge of protectiveness that rose in his chest as Meredith leaned toward him, her cloak brushing his arm. He hated being so brusque, but it was imperative that he learn everything possible about his attackers. And quickly. The woman might be privy to valuable insight or a clue to his enemy's scheme without even being aware of its significance. Such knowledge could prove vital when it came to defending his home. This was no time to go soft.

"Meredith?"

She looked past him to the doorway, and for a moment, he thought she might bolt, but then the level-headedness he remembered from twelve years ago reasserted itself. She folded her hands together atop the table in a serene prayerlike pose and kept her attention riveted on them while she spoke.

"The barn."

It made sense. They'd already put up most of their winter stores. The hayloft and corncrib were full, and with the nights getting so cold lately, a lot of their stock was sheltered there. Losing the barn would cripple them during the winter. Not that it would convince him to sell. Nothing could do that.

"How many men are coming?" Crockett probed.

"I don't know."

Travis tried coming at the question from

the back door. "How many men does this fiancé of yours have working for him?"

Meredith's head swiveled around, her blue eyes shooting sparks. "He is *not* my fiancé — never was. And I'd appreciate it if you'd quit referring to him as such."

Travis held up his hands in apology. "All right."

She inhaled slowly and refocused on her hands. "The man's name is Roy Mitchell, and I have no idea how many men work for him. He owns a logging company, so I imagine there are a good number in his employ."

And they'd be physical men, too. Comfortable in the woods. Not a bunch of city-bred dandies. Travis tapped his thumb against the pine tabletop as his mind spun.

Crockett cleared his throat. "We'll have to move the stock out."

Travis nodded his agreement. "But we can't just leave them all in the paddock. If Mitchell's men get close enough to see that the stock are safe, they might suspect we're on to them and burn the house instead."

"We could tether the draft horses down by the creek."

"Good idea, Jim. Being near the water will help calm them if fire does break out." Travis tipped his head up to stare at a rafter in

72

the ceiling, the ordinary view helping him concentrate. "Each of us can keep a saddled mount near our position when we set up a perimeter. That will help spare the tack, the horses, and give us a way to chase the vermin off."

"What about the mule?" Crockett asked. "You know how cranky Samson gets at night. If we try to take him down to the creek bed, he'll bray his fool head off and give away his position."

Travis nodded. Old Samson was as cantankerous as they came. If he wasn't in his stall come dark, he'd pull a tantrum worse than Neill used to at bath time. "I guess we better leave him in the paddock. Maybe if we keep Jochebed tied out there, too, it'll keep him calm." The milk cow occupied the stall next to Samson, so having her close might soothe him. Then again, it might just endanger their milk supply. But he didn't see as he had much choice. "Two animals outside the barn shouldn't draw much suspicion."

"And the fodder?" Crockett asked. "I was thinking we could store the contents of the corncrib in the shed." He turned to Jim. "If that's all right with you."

The shed was Jim's domain, a workshop for the furniture he made from the walnut, pine, and oak that grew on their land. He was as protective of that space as a squirrel was with a cache of nuts. But he nodded acquiescence, as Travis knew he would. Family needs came first.

"I'll clear out a space."

"Good." With each solution they generated, Travis regained a piece of the control he'd lost when he'd learned of the pending attack. His confidence growing, he posed the last issue. "What about the hay? Any ideas of where to store it?"

The smokehouse was too small, as were any of the other outbuildings. And if they stacked it in the open, it would prove an easy target for a lit torch. Travis looked to Crockett and then to Jim, but his brother's faces were as blank as his mind. Silence stretched around the table. The control restored to him was once again slipping from his grasp.

"The hay wagons that deliver to the liveries in town are always heaped to the sky. Why don't you load as much as you can into your wagon and drive it down to the creek bed or into the woods somewhere? You can cover it with a tarp for added protection."

Three pairs of Archer eyes turned to stare at the female in their midst — a female they had all but forgotten was there. At least Travis had. But looking at her now, he couldn't quite fathom how that could've happened.

"It's a good idea," Crockett said.

Travis was about to agree when pounding hooves echoed from the yard. In an instant, he was on his feet, rifle in hand. He felt his brothers behind him as he dashed down the hall.

5

Travis sighted down the barrel of his Winchester. A rider on an unfamiliar white-and-chestnut paint thundered toward the porch. Travis released a nervous breath and steadied his aim. The dimness of twilight made it difficult to distinguish features, so he went for the high-percentage shot and drew a bead on the man's chest. But as he moved his finger to the trigger, a sense of recognition registered. The rider had a very familiar posture. Travis jerked the Winchester away from his shoulder, his heart thumping with the dread of what could have happened.

Neill pulled up short of the porch and leapt from the horse's back before the paint had fully stopped. "I ain't too late for supper, am I?"

Travis stormed down the steps and shoved his kid brother hard enough to land his butt in the dirt. "What were you thinking, riding in here without giving the signal? I could have shot you!"

The shocked look on Neill's face gave way to one of abashment. "Sorry, Trav. I thought you'd know it was me, since you sent me to fetch Miss Meredith's horse."

"Did you forget we were expecting other visitors tonight? Unwelcome visitors?" Travis extended his hand to his brother and yanked him to his feet. "With the poor light and you on a strange mount, for a minute there, I thought you were one of them. You gotta think with more than your belly, Neill."

"I'll do better next time. I swear."

Travis gripped the boy's shoulder and offered reassurance with a squeeze. "I know you will. You're an Archer."

"Jim," Travis called up to the man waiting on the porch with Crockett, "dish up the vittles. We can't afford for this boy to be distracted. We got too much work to get done."

Neill's ready smile reappeared, and the tension in Travis's gut relaxed. A little.

As Jim led the way back into the house, Travis hung back and scanned the darkening woods, wondering from which direction trouble would strike.

Lord, I'd be obliged if you'd get us through this night in one piece.

■ ■ ■ ■

Watching the Archer brothers eat was like watching a twister blow through the room. Meredith sat with her elbows tucked close to her side, afraid to do more than occasionally raise her fork to her mouth for fear of being rammed by a reaching arm or thumped by a tossed biscuit. The venison steak was overdone, the beans gluey, and the biscuits were dry as unbuttered toast, yet the Archers attacked their food like a pack of dogs fighting over a fresh kill. No one spoke. They just ate.

Well, not all of them. The one called Jim slowed down enough to glare at her over his dish and grunt as he chomped down on what must have been a particularly tough piece of venison, giving her the distinct impression that he held her responsible for the condition of the food. Which was probably true. Her arrival *had* delayed their supper. And with the threat of Roy's men so imminent, she supposed haste was more important than decorum. Still, it was a bit unnerving to be surrounded by such ravenous appetites. Therefore, when Travis pushed away from the table and started giving orders not five minutes after the meal had begun, Meredith found herself as much relieved as amazed.

"Jim, you're in charge of the corncrib. Crockett, bring the wagon around and get started on the hay. We won't be able to get it all, but we should be able to save a decent portion. I'll give you a hand as soon as I fill Neill in on what to do with the stock."

A chorus of chair legs scraping against floorboards echoed in response as each of the Archer brothers stuffed final bites into their mouths and rose to follow Travis. Not one of them spared her so much as a glance, all of their faces set in grim lines.

Feeling left out, Meredith jumped to her feet. "What can I do?"

Travis pivoted, quickly scanning her from head to toe, hesitating ever so briefly on her weak leg. "Stay in the house. As soon as this is over, I'll see you home." And with that, his long strides carried him away from her and out into the night.

Meredith chased him down and grabbed his arm from behind. "I can help, Travis."

The dark brown vest Travis wore flapped open as he spun to face her. "This isn't your fight. Just stay in the house and keep your head down. You don't know your way around out here, and it'll only slow me down to answer your questions."

Even though he didn't say it, she could easily imagine what he was thinking. That telling glance in the kitchen had said it all. He believed her to be weak. A liability.

Meredith made no further protest as Travis left her to jog over to the barn, but as she made her way back to the house, she vowed to prove to him that she was more than just a girl with a limp. She was smart and strong and capable, and any man who thought different needed his opinion adjusted.

She charged through the front door and down the hall to the kitchen. A table full of dirty dishes and a stove covered in food splatter called out a defiant challenge. Meredith narrowed her gaze and stripped out of her cloak. Rolling up her sleeves, she moved to the table and started stacking dirty plates and utensils. It might not be the most glamorous of jobs, but she'd have their kitchen shinier than a new copper kettle by the time those thick-headed Archers returned.

Besides, her mind did some of its best work while her hands were in dishwater. And she had some serious thinking to do. The men were focused on saving the contents of the barn, but they'd really taken no time to strategize ways to protect the barn itself. That would be up to her.

Once the dishes were done and the stove scoured, Meredith set about enacting phase one of her newly hatched plan. First, she pulled out every stockpot, bucket, and washtub she could find. Then she searched the cupboards for medical supplies. She prayed Travis and his brothers would escape injury, but she'd make sure things were ready just in case. Next, she dug through the bedrooms, gathering old blankets. There was more than one way to fight fire, and she aimed to have as many weapons at her disposal as possible.

Meredith piled the blankets in the largest washtub and threaded her arm through the handles of three buckets. Then, with the *cling-clang* of the tin pails bouncing against her hip, she hefted the washtub and headed for the back door she'd discovered in a small room off the kitchen. She scanned the yard, squinting against the dark shadows, until she found a shape that fit what she was looking for. Squaring her shoulders, she made her way to the edge of the paddock.

The men had been busy. The mule and milk cow were already in the corral along with four fully outfitted saddle horses, and she saw the back of the wagon from around the corner of the barn. Male voices called to one another from within the structure, and Meredith guessed they were finishing up the hay. She'd need to hurry if she wanted to be back in the house by the time the men came in to get their coats before they headed out.

Meredith grasped the pump handle and worked it until water gushed from the spout into the horse trough beside the paddock fence. She filled the trough to the brim so it would be easy to refill the buckets quickly should the need arise. Then she filled the washtub and each of the pails. She stacked the blankets beneath the trough to protect them from the wind and returned to the house for the stockpots. When she finished, an entire line of vessels stood ready to extinguish and douse. Meredith nodded in satisfaction and headed back to the kitchen.

From the window, she could barely make out the dark outlines of the trough and bucket line she'd put together, but knowing it was there filled her with a sense of accomplishment. It was odd, really, the protectiveness that welled in her whenever she thought of the barn burning. She'd been on Archer land less than two hours, but a strange sense of belonging flowed through her when she looked out over the yard.

"I know your men are coming, Roy," she

whispered to the darkness, "but I'm going to fight you with everything I've got."

The sound of the front door opening and the heavy thumping of booted feet turned Meredith's attention away from the window. Wrapping a dish towel around her hand, she grabbed the coffeepot she'd put on earlier and started pouring the steaming brew into cups.

As the coffee worked its way up the sides of the fourth cup, Meredith became aware of a complete lack of sound coming from the men. She tipped back the pot and cautiously glanced up. All four Archers stood bunched in the doorway staring at her as if they'd never seen a woman pour coffee before.

"I thought you'd like something to warm your insides before you set out. The night will be cold, and there's no telling how long you'll be out there." She smiled as she fought to control the nervous tickle in her stomach.

Finally Travis stepped forward and accepted a cup from her. "Thanks." His gaze met hers, and a warmth that had nothing to do with coffee penetrated her.

Meredith ducked her head and grabbed another cup, handing coffee to Crockett, Jim, and then Neill. Each man murmured his thanks and dipped his head in deference, but none of them inspired the same quivery feelings as their brother.

Careful, Meredith. You're going home after this. Don't be leaving your heart behind with a reclusive cowboy whose life has no room for you.

"I brought Sadie to keep you company while we're out." Travis gave a low whistle and a big black dog pushed her way past the Archer legs blocking the doorway. Her nails clicked against the wood floor, and her stiff gait stirred Meredith's sympathy. At a motion from Travis, the animal padded over to Meredith and sat down.

"This is Sadie? The ferocious pup I thought was going to chew me to a pulp?" Meredith grinned at the slightly arthritic dog and bent to pat her head. Sadie's tail swished across the floor in friendly response. "Now that I'm bigger and you're older, you're not nearly as frightening."

"Frightening? Sadie?" Neill scoffed. "She's just a retired bird dog. Who'd be afraid of *her?*"

"Neill." Travis spoke the name like a warning.

Meredith laughed softly. "That's all right." She hunkered down and rubbed the dog more thoroughly along her neck and sides.

"Anyone can tell that Sadie is a loyal, sweet-spirited animal. But to a ten-year-old girl with an overactive imagination, who had stories of the vicious man-eating Archer hounds ringing in her ears, Sadie's enthusiasm was easily misinterpreted."

"Man-eating Archer hounds? What kind of nonsense —"

"Never mind about that, Neill." Travis cut off his question. "We have other issues to deal with. Grab your coat and mount up."

Neill complied, followed by Jim and Crockett, leaving Meredith alone in the kitchen with Travis. He shuffled his feet for a moment, then thunked his coffee cup down on the table. "Sadie might be old," he said, his gaze not quite meeting hers, "but she's a good watchdog. She'll bark if she hears anything, so keep her close at hand."

"I will." Giving Sadie a final pat, Meredith straightened.

Travis gripped the back of the chair nearest Meredith, his hands massaging the wood as if he wasn't sure what else to do with them. An odd gesture for a man who wore authority like a well-broken-in hat. The hint of vulnerability in his movements now made Meredith's pulse skip.

"Stay in the house," he said. "You'll be safe." His eyes finally met hers. "If anything

85

should happen to me, the boys have orders to see to your protection, so you don't have to worry about anything."

She lowered her lashes and peered back up at Travis. "Be careful."

He cleared his throat and looked away. "I will," he mumbled, then collected his coat from its hook and shoved his arms through the sleeves. "Oh, and, Meredith . . ."

"Yes?"

"Thanks."

As Travis strode out of the room, Meredith smiled. Whatever the night held, the trip to the Archer ranch was definitely worth it.

Each of the brothers set out on horseback to their assigned positions, needing the cover of the woods to conceal their presence. They had considered hiding out in the barn, but that would have given them only two vantage points instead of four. If Mitchell's men came in from the east or west, they'd be nearly impossible to spot. Out among the trees, he and his brothers stood a better chance at stopping the attackers before they drew close enough to the barn to toss a torch.

Besides, he wanted to keep an eye on the house, as well. And Meredith. He still couldn't believe she had come out to warn him. A pretty woman like that should have better things to do with her time than brave the den of a bunch of mangy men who'd lost touch with civilization years ago.

But she'd come. Because she felt beholden to him. Travis shook his head as he dismounted and pulled his rifle free of its scabbard. He'd noticed the woman favored her right leg, an injury he was no doubt responsible for, but instead of laying blame, she went out of her way to help him. Not your average female.

Not that he had much experience with females. He'd quit school after the eighth grade to run the ranch with his father, and a few years later he was raising his siblings on his own. Outside of a couple church socials he'd attended when he was fourteen, he had no experience with the fairer sex. That didn't mean he was too ignorant to recognize the effect of one, though.

Travis rubbed the stubble on his chin and frowned, wondering for the first time what kind of impression he'd made on her. She probably thought him half wild, pointing guns at innocent women and snapping out orders like a general. Yet when he and the boys had dragged in after clearing out the barn and found Meredith in a spotless kitchen, pouring hot coffee with a welcoming smile, his gut had tightened with longing. And he wasn't the only one suffering such a reaction. Crockett and Jim had felt it, too. He could tell by the strange tension radiating from them. Even Neill's youth had not kept him immune.

As Travis stared out into the darkness, watching for any movement that didn't belong, questions churned in his mind, distracting him. Would his reaction have been the same for any woman standing in his kitchen looking homey and inviting, or was it something specific about Meredith that kindled his appreciation and protective instincts?

Travis crossed his arms and leaned his shoulder against the trunk of a nearby tree. It was a shame she'd be leaving so soon. He would have enjoyed trying to figure that one out.

6

Meredith's chin jerked up from its resting place on her chest, and she blinked several times, trying to get her bearings. She stared into the darkness from her seat on the porch rocker but failed to see anything amiss. Rearranging the thick folds of her quilt cocoon, she burrowed into the coverlet and leaned the side of her head against the back of the rocking chair, allowing her eyes to slide closed once again.

A low growl resonated near her feet, culminating in a sharp bark.

Meredith's eyes flew open, and she bolted upright. "Did you hear something, Sadie?" she whispered. Meredith freed her arms from the quilt and reached for the old shotgun she'd found in the den.

Sadie lurched to her feet, her posture stiff, her ears pricked. Meredith rose, as well. Clutching the shotgun across her middle with trembling hands, she squinted into the night, trying desperately to make out the form of someone moving about where he didn't belong. But the barn was nothing more than a dark, hazy form against a landscape of black and gray.

Then a shadow separated itself from the others. And divided into two . . . no . . . three smaller silhouettes. Meredith's heart dropped to her stomach. Her pulse thrumming erratically, she inched her way to the porch railing. Had Travis and the others returned to check on things, or had Roy's men somehow reached the barn undetected?

While she debated with herself over what to do, a breeze ruffled the loose strands of hair around her face — a breeze that carried a familiar, cloying scent.

Kerosene!

Meredith darted off the covered porch and lifted the shotgun to her shoulder. Pointing the double barrels into the air, she braced herself for the recoil and pulled the trigger. The blast shattered the silence, its alarm echoing in the stillness.

That should bring the Archers down around their ears!

Meredith lowered the weapon, satisfaction filling her as the man-sized shadows around the barn began to scramble. Then an answering gunshot cracked. Meredith yelped as a bullet kicked up dust a foot in front of her. She darted back into the darkness of the covered porch and hunkered down behind the rocker she'd been dozing in moments earlier. Sadie followed, protectively flanking her right side.

"Good girl." Meredith grabbed the dog's neck and pulled her down behind the chair, too.

No longer concerned with stealth, Roy's men scurried around the barn with new urgency until one of them finally struck a match.

That tiny spark ignited a bonfire of dread in Meredith's chest. For it didn't stay tiny for long. It ignited a torch. Then a second. And a third.

Sadie barked despite Meredith's efforts to shush her. The mule in the paddock brayed and kicked against the fence with sharp thuds that carried all the way to the house. Meredith closed her eyes and prayed until the sound of hoofbeats descending upon the barn interrupted her pleas.

Travis!

A pair of horsemen emerged from the woods near the front of the barn, rifles drawn. Gunfire erupted and male shouts punctuated the air. Was one of the riders Travis? And where were the other brothers?

Were they on the far side of the barn, hidden from view? How many of Roy's men were over there? Meredith peered between the spindles of the chairback, her grip on Sadie tightening until the dog finally squirmed away. If only she could see what was happening!

Soon the other two brothers rode in, and the torches were discarded in the fray as guns and horses became more important. For a few minutes, Meredith believed the barn would be spared, but when Roy's men gained their mounts and scattered into the woods, and Travis and his brothers gave chase, the smell of smoke wafted back toward the house. A stronger odor than could be explained by a few smoldering torches lying in the dirt.

Meredith came out from behind the chair and cautiously made her way down the porch steps. With one barrel of her shotgun still loaded, she shouldered the weapon and stole across the yard. She scanned from the barn to the corral to the trees, checking for any man-sized movement. Just as she determined that all was clear, Sadie rushed past her, ducked under the lowest rail of the corral fence, and set to barking at the barn entrance.

Tightening her grip on the gun, Meredith

bit her lip and followed. "Anyone there?" she called.

The only answer came from the mule, Samson, which was still kicking up a fuss. The milk cow was nervous, too, sidestepping and moaning an occasional complaint. As Meredith strained to hear any evidence of a human threat, her ears picked out another sound altogether — a muffled crackling from within the barn.

Hurrying forward, Meredith straddled the bottom fence rail and squeezed her body through the opening between the slats, then ran to Sadie's side. A blast of heat hit her face when she crossed in front of the doorway.

Greedy flames were climbing the interior walls.

The thugs had lit the *inside* of the barn! Anger surged through Meredith's veins as she hiked up her skirts and sprinted to her bucket line. Travis and his brothers had no way of knowing that their barn was afire when they set off after Roy's men, so they'd be in no hurry to return. Capturing the men responsible would take precedence. Which left Meredith alone to fight the blaze.

In case Travis wasn't too far afield to hear a warning shot and grasp its meaning, Meredith fired the final shell from her shotgun and dropped the weapon on the far side of the trough. She grabbed two of the full pails she'd prepared earlier and walked as fast as she could without sloshing too much water over the edges.

"Of all the times to have an uneven gait," Meredith grumbled. The moment the words left her mouth, her right foot hit a divot in the earth and water splashed onto her shoe. With a grimace, she redirected her path but didn't slow her pace.

Once in the barn, she maneuvered to the east wall, where the fire seemed to be the strongest. She tossed the bucket contents onto the burning wood, rejoicing at the hiss of dying flames. But in an instant, new ones rose to take their place.

Meredith ran back to the trough. "Lord, help me make a difference. Please. It's not right for good men to suffer on a wicked man's whim."

Back and forth she ran. Dumping water over and over until the trough was nearly dry. Her arms felt like rubber, and her back screamed at her to stop. Her lungs burned from the smoke and heat, but she refused to quit.

Wiping a soot-covered arm across her brow, she turned away from the barn to inhale a deep breath of clean air. Then, ignoring the weariness that threatened to claim her, Meredith dropped a blanket into the trough and soaked up the last of the water. She'd beat out what flames she could, then refill the buckets at the pump. Surely the Archers would return soon.

Circling well out of the reach of Samson's hooves, Meredith trudged back into the barn and turned her attention to the west wall. She slapped at the flames with the wet blanket, but they seemed to tease her, dancing upward, out of her reach.

Then, as if a furnace door had suddenly swung wide, light flashed above Meredith's head and heat swooped down on her in a massive wave.

Lord, have mercy.

Fire had exploded across the hayloft.

Mitchell's men had escaped. Every last one of them. Travis glared at the cut wire that left a gaping hole in his boundary fence and ground his palm into the saddle horn. If it hadn't been so dark, things might have been different. But Archers knew better than to endanger a horse by racing over rough terrain at night.

Would there be another attempt? Without Meredith to warn them next time, Travis held little hope they'd be as successful in

95

thwarting Roy Mitchell's efforts.

"Look at the bright side — they didn't get the barn, and none of us were injured in the fray." Crockett's quiet statement seeped into Travis. He shifted his focus from the damaged fence to the three hale-and-hearty brothers congregated around him.

"You're right." Travis cleared his throat, buying time to squirrel away his own disappointment and muster a halfhearted smile for the boys. "Things could certainly be worse. With the way those bullets were flying, it's a miracle no blood was drawn."

"I still don't know how those skunks got past us in the first place," Neill groused. "I didn't fall asleep, Travis. I swear it!"

"I know you didn't, little brother. Don't sweat it. What's done is done." Travis nudged his chestnut gelding forward until he sat even with Neill. "There was too much ground for four men to monitor, and too little light to see more than a stone's throw in any direction. I knew going in that our best chance was to have them stumble onto one of us as they were coming in, since they expected us to be at the house, sleeping in our beds. But it wasn't meant to be."

"Speaking of sleeping in our beds . . ." Crockett tugged on the reins until his horse faced homeward. "I'm more than ready to do just that. Let's head back."

Travis nodded, his own energy giving way to weariness now that the danger had passed. "Lead the way."

They wound through the trees, sticking to the well-worn paths that would cause the horses the least amount of trouble. No one spoke, too exhausted and dispirited to do more than keep themselves upright in their saddles. But as they climbed the rise that led to home, Neill broke the silence.

"It's a good thing you got off that warning shot when you did, Trav, or we wouldn'ta had a chance of stoppin' 'em."

"Wasn't me." Travis reined his horse around a large rock, keeping his gaze trained on the ground in front of him. "I saw a muzzle flash near the house. My guess is that Meredith fired the shot."

"Meredith?" Disbelief tinged Neill's voice. "Didn't you tell her to stay in the house? What was she doin' out there, and where did she get a gun? You don't think she was helpin' 'em, do ya?"

"Of course she wasn't helping them," Travis snapped. "If she were, there'd be no point in making all that racket to bring us charging out of the woods like the cavalry, would there?" Travis bit back the rest of the words that sprang to his tongue, shocked at his vehement reaction. Neill didn't know Meredith. Shoot. None of them did, really. Including him. Questioning her loyalty was reasonable — more reasonable than blindly defending her character based on two encounters that totaled less than a day's worth of time in her company.

Travis grimaced. Was he really so susceptible to a pair of bright blue eyes and a pretty smile? He'd better get a grip on his reactions before he ended up doing something stupid.

"She probably found one of Pa's hunting guns," Crockett said. "The case in the den isn't lock—"

"Quiet!" Jim's sharp voice brought Travis's head up. "I smell smoke."

Smoke? Travis sniffed the air, and alarm gouged through him. He smelled it, too.

Had a spark from one of the fallen torches managed to catch? He'd not seen any evidence of fire when he signaled the boys to give chase. Had he left their home unprotected?

Had he left Meredith unprotected?

"Yah!" Digging his heels into his horse's flanks, Travis charged toward home.

7

As the trees thinned, the smell of smoke grew stronger and an eerie orange glow winked at him from between the pines. Travis tightened his grip on the reins and leaned low over the saddle, urging his mount to a pace that bordered on hazardous. So close to home, though, the ground was familiar, and Bexar responded without hesitation.

The barn came into view, and Travis gritted his teeth. The thing was glowing from within like a jack-o'-lantern, an occasional flicker of flame licking through the hayloft door to tickle the outer walls.

How could he have been so stupid? He hadn't even thought to check the interior of the barn before he went tearing off after Mitchell's men. He'd simply assumed he'd interrupted them in time. His thirst for justice had outweighed his common sense.

Travis reined his horse around to the side

of the barn closest to the trough pump and pulled up short. A host of empty pails, tubs, and even cooking pots lay scattered beside the trough, firelight gleaming across their tin surfaces.

Surely she wouldn't have . . .

Travis leapt from the saddle and scaled the corral fence. "Meredith!"

Sadie shot out of the barn and circled his legs, almost tripping him. She barked and dashed back toward the barn. Travis sprinted after her.

Thick, dark smoke hovered near the rafters, and the stench of burning wood and hay enveloped him. He squinted through the haze, searching the ground for any sign of Meredith. When he spotted a feminine figure battling the blaze along the west wall, relief hit him with such force his knees nearly buckled. Then anger stiffened his joints and propelled him toward the woman whose dark green dress had faded to a sooty gray.

"What do you think you're doing?" Travis snatched the damp blanket from Meredith's grip as she swung it behind her shoulder. The rag pulled free without any resistance. Her obvious exhaustion only heightened his ire. "I told you to wait at the house."

Meredith pivoted toward him and blinked

as if she couldn't quite understand what she was seeing. "Travis?" A spark of clarity flashed in her eyes before she launched herself at him, wrapping her arms around his waist. "Thank God you've come."

The contact was so unexpected, it nearly threw him off-balance. Travis didn't quite know what to do. He'd been shouting and scowling a second ago, and now he had a grateful female pressed up against him. How had that happened?

"I tried so hard, Travis. I really did." She tipped her face up to look at him. The soot smeared across her cheeks and forehead made the blue of her eyes even brighter. "I had the east wall put out and started on the west when the flames reached the loft. Do you think you can save it?"

"Don't know. The boys and I will try, though." He separated himself from her and took her hand. "We need to get you out of here first."

She stumbled along behind him as he steered her out to the corral. Crockett was already working the pump to fill the trough while Jim and Neill righted the buckets.

"The heart of the fire is in the loft," he called out to his brothers. "Do what you can, but don't put yourself at risk. If the roof catches, get out. We'll move to containment. Make sure the house doesn't catch."

Travis didn't release his grip on Meredith until he had her at the fence on the far side. "Go up to the house."

"I can help."

"No, Meredith! I don't want you anywhere near that fire." The very thought made him shiver despite the heat pouring out of the barn.

"I managed not to burn myself to a crisp for the thirty minutes it took you to get here." She crossed her arms and glared at him, her spunk reviving. "I think I can find a way to preserve that tradition a little longer."

"The answer's no." He turned his back on her and strode away, praying she'd obey. If she were one of his brothers, there'd have been no question. He was the head of the family, and his word was law. But she wasn't an Archer. And he had no idea how he'd handle her if a direct order didn't work.

She leapt past him and moved into his path, forcing him to halt. "Let me work the pump."

"You're too tired to lift the handle." Travis cut her off with a wave of his hand when she opened her mouth to protest. "I don't have time to argue. My barn's burning." He sidestepped her and resumed his long-legged pace. This time she let him go.

Travis and his brothers fought the blaze as best they could. With ladders inside and out, they doused the loft simultaneously from the barn's center as well as through the loft window, but it wasn't long before the fire reached the roof.

When Neill arrived with another pail of water, Travis waved him off. "Go help Jim and Crock outside." He shimmied down the ladder, his voice hoarse from the smoke, his face scalded like a cow's hide after branding. "I'll get the animals a safe distance away, then meet you there."

Neill nodded and jumped to obey, but the determination in his eyes dimmed. Even at seventeen, the boy could recognize defeat when he saw it. And Travis figured that was exactly what the kid saw when he looked into his big brother's face.

It killed him to lose twice in one night. The arsonists' escape had been hard enough to swallow, but believing the barn had been spared had made it tolerable. Now everything was sticking in his craw.

He pulled the ladder down, kicked dirt over the few flames that had taken root on the top rungs, and carried it outside. As he tossed it over the corral fence, cool air bathed his stinging face. He wanted nothing more than to close his eyes and relish the coolness, but all he could afford to do was cough some smoke out of his lungs and turn back to the task at hand.

Which apparently included scolding a certain hardheaded woman for not heeding his instructions. Meredith glared at him from where she stood pumping water into the trough, not a hint of apology in her demeanor. Travis stormed past her and worked the knot on Jochebed's lead line. "I thought I told you to go up to the house."

The pump arm creaked as she gave it a series of vigorous yanks, then fell silent as water gushed into the trough. "As I recall," she said, rubbing her palms into her skirt, "you never forbade me from working the pump. You simply expressed your doubts as to my ability to do so."

Travis's grip on the cow's rope tightened. "Don't play word games with me, Meredith. You knew what I meant."

"Did I?" She reached for a stew pot and dipped it into the trough. "Seems to me that a man who claims protecting his brothers and his land always comes first wouldn't be so quick to refuse able-bodied help just because that body happens to be female." She set the full pot on the ground and crossed her arms over her chest.

Travis's eyes followed the movement, noting the curves it accentuated. Yep. Definitely female. He wouldn't be arguing that point.

Crockett rounded the barn at a jog, an empty washtub banging against his leg. Meredith unclasped her arms and immediately returned to the pump.

Travis made no move to stop her, deciding it wasn't worth wasting more time or breath debating. Having her there *did* speed the process, and even though he still didn't like her being so close to the fire, she was probably in no immediate danger.

At least Jochebed obeyed him without question. More than eager to get away from the burning barn, the milk cow lumbered along beside him to the back side of the corral, where Travis removed the fence rails from their notches and set her free.

Next he went after Samson, but the old mule was too busy throwing a fit to recognize what was good for him.

"Enough of that," Travis reprimanded as he grabbed hold of the mule's halter and forced the animal's head down. Samson tried to jerk away, but Travis held firm, asserting his dominance until the animal calmed. "That's it. Settle down, now." Travis patted Samson's neck and slowly unfastened the hitching strap. At the same moment, a thunderous *pop!* exploded from within the barn.

Samson's eyes went wild, and with the sudden strength of his namesake, he wrenched free and tore across the corral. Travis gave chase in an effort to steer him toward the fence opening, but the old mule was either too blind to see the downed railings or too terror-stricken to comprehend their meaning. Instead, the fool beast raced straight into the barn.

Stunned, Travis stared at the entrance. What would possess him to run *into* the fire? Sure the cantankerous thing would run right back out, Travis braced his legs apart and prepared to make a grab for him. Only he never came. The old mule was probably standing in his stall — third one on the right, under the loft — too stubborn to leave.

"Stupid critter," Travis muttered under his breath. He had half a mind to leave him in there. Of course, he never could stomach the thought of any living creature suffering. Not when it was in his power to do something about it.

Digging his handkerchief out of his coat pocket, Travis marched up to the entrance. Heat flared against his skin. Steeling himself, he turned his head and sucked in two deep breaths, then tied the red bandanna over his nose and mouth.

"No, Travis!" Meredith's voice barely penetrated the roar of the fire. "Don't!"

But he didn't have a choice. The longer he waited, the more dangerous it would be. Ignoring her calls, he ran into the barn.

Travis lifted his arm to shield his face from the heat and his head from any debris that might fall as he made his way to Samson's stall.

Not daring to get near the mule's hooves, he entered the adjacent box and scaled the half wall near Samson's head. "Easy, boy." The mule shied, but Travis snatched the halter and yanked the animal's head around while pushing on his shoulder. "Back," he ordered. "Back."

Samson pinned his ears down and bit at Travis's arm. With a quick move of his elbow, Travis dodged the teeth and smacked the mule's neck with the flat of his hand. "Quit!"

The mule blinked and retreated a step, but Travis dragged the mule's head around until Samson faced the doorway leading to the corral. The fire raged directly overhead in the loft. Sweat and smoke stung his eyes and blurred his vision. Burning air scalded his throat, making it hard to breathe. If he didn't get the animal out soon, he'd be forced to leave him behind.

Travis tugged the mule forward and Samson actually complied. He'd only taken a handful of steps, however, when the loft floorboards gave way. Fiery debris plummeted. Planks of wood struck across his shoulders, and lit hay showered upon his back. Spooked but unharmed by the downfall, Samson brayed and pulled against Travis's hold, trying to retreat farther into the barn.

"No you don't. We aren't going through that again." Travis shook off what he could from his back and swatted Samson's neck a second time. The mule tossed his head, but obeyed. However, Travis had a new problem to contend with — a focused heat was radiating through the back of his coat, and he feared some of the flames from the debris had taken hold.

"Get up *now,* mule." Travis walked backward, tugging on Samson's halter with one hand while trying to undo his buttons with the other. He had to get that coat off.

The heat on his back grew painful, and panic made him clumsy. He arched away from the fabric clawing at him and was about to release Samson and tear the coat off with both hands when a gush of blessedly cool water hit him from behind.

"Thanks." Travis swiveled to see which brother had just saved his hide, only to find Meredith standing there, an empty stockpot in her hands. His gratitude evaporated.

"Get out of here!" he shouted.

The woman was as bad as Samson.

He tried to order her out again, but a chest-heavy cough blocked the words as it pummeled his ribs. It bent him forward, and Meredith took advantage of his weakened state. She dropped the pot and pulled something from under her arm as she rushed toward him. Clicking her tongue, she latched onto the opposite side of Samson's halter and tapped his hindquarters with the end of a long stick.

The mule hopped and kicked, but the movement carried him closer to the door, so Travis bit back his protest. They'd nearly made it outside when the roof collapsed. Twenty feet behind them, timber beams splintered the weakened loft floor and slammed into the ground of the barn with a deafening crash. Meredith screamed. Samson bucked and contorted. Meredith lost her hold on the halter and stumbled sideways. Travis strained to lead the animal away from her, but Samson finally grasped the danger the barn represented and kicked wildly for his freedom.

Travis released his grip on the halter. "Go!"

The panicked mule kicked out a final time and ran out to the corral.

Travis spun toward where he'd last seen Meredith, and a new terror twisted his gut. She lay crumpled on the hard ground.

"No." The whispered denial fell from his lips as he ran to her. He dropped to the ground and yanked his gloves from his hands. "Meredith?"

She gave no answer. Not even a moan. He reached beneath her head to support it as he hoisted her into his arms, his only thought to get her away from the fire. But something sticky wet his fingers.

Blood.

8

Travis gathered Meredith close to his chest and ran out of the barn. He didn't stop until he reached the pump. Neill was at the trough filling a pail. He straightened when he saw Travis approach.

"What happened?" His eyes roamed over Meredith's limp form, and beneath the soot, his face paled.

"Fetch Crockett." When Neill just stood and stared, Travis's voice sharpened. "Now!"

Neill flinched and dashed off, leaving his pail behind.

Cradling Meredith's head in the crook of his arm, Travis slowly knelt and lowered her to a dry patch of ground. He combed her hair from her face, and a feather-light stirring of air brushed against his palm. She was breathing.

"Thank you, God," Travis murmured.

He shrugged out of his coat, folded it

inside out, and gently cushioned her head with it. Careful of her wound, he angled her face so that the right side of her skull would take most of the weight, leaving the left side exposed for Crockett to examine.

She lay so still, it hurt to look at her.

This never should have happened. He should have let her leave as soon as she'd issued her warning. What had he been thinking, dragging her into this mess?

Desperate to do something — anything — to help her, Travis yanked the bandanna from around his neck and dipped it into the trough. Then, kneeling in the dirt beside her, he rinsed away the worst of the soot smears from her face, all the while praying for her eyes to open.

He was so focused on Meredith, he didn't realize his brothers had surrounded him until Crockett hunkered down and touched his shoulder.

Emotion clogged Travis's throat. He cleared it away with a rough cough. "I think the mule kicked her." He tilted her head to expose more of the bloodied area to Crockett's view. His brother was no doctor, but he was the closest they had. Ever since the day Jim had been shot, Crock had taken it upon himself to memorize the two medical books in his father's study, *Gunn's New*

Domestic Physician and *A Dictionary of Practical Medicine.* Travis just prayed there'd been something in those books that could help Meredith.

Crockett pulled off his gloves and probed the wound. Meredith moaned and thrashed her arms, but her eyes didn't open. Travis took her hand in his, wishing he could do more.

"She can feel the pain," Crockett observed. "That's a good sign. But I'm going to need to get her into the house, where the light is better, before I can tell you more."

Crockett made as if to pick her up, but Travis nudged him aside. "I'll carry her." His brother shot him an odd look. Travis ignored it. Meredith was injured because of him. She was his responsibility.

After pushing to his feet, he shifted Meredith's weight in his arms and turned to Jim and Neill. "The roof's gone, so let the barn burn itself out. Keep an eye on it, though, and don't let any sparks spread to the house or shed. Neill, when it's under control, fetch the draft horses and Miss Meredith's paint from the creek bed, and tie them up by the old lean-to behind the shed. Jim, take care of the barn. Oh, and one of you better keep watch in case Mitchell's men decide to return. I'll come spell you when I can."

"Take care of the girl," Jim said. "We'll handle things out here."

Travis nodded and strode toward the house.

Crockett had every lamp in the den blazing with light by the time Travis arrived. "Set her on the sofa," he said. "I need to wash out that wound and see if any bone has chipped or if the skull is dented from the blow."

Travis laid Meredith across the cushioned seat, arranging her head at the end nearest the lamp table where Crockett had piled several squares of toweling.

As Crockett moved in with basin and sponge, Travis backed away and paced the room's perimeter.

Why was it that every time Meredith's path crossed his, she ended up hurt? First her leg in one of his traps, and now her head kicked by his mule. Both were accidents, of course, yet Travis couldn't shake a growing sense of guilt. If he had made different decisions, neither would have happened.

He dipped his chin and rubbed the aching area above his eyes. *Help her recover, Lord. Please. Don't make her pay the price for my mistakes.*

Travis circled past the woodstove, his mother's rocking chair, and his father's bookshelf, and then found himself once again at the foot of the sofa. He studied Meredith's face. Her dark lashes lay delicately against her pale cheeks, fluttering slightly. Tiny frown lines puckered her forehead between her brows as Crockett probed her wound, and quiet whimpers vibrated in her throat. An insane urge to shove his brother away and spare her the pain of his invasion had Travis balling his hands into fists, but he restrained himself from interfering.

After several more minutes of cleaning and probing, Crockett finally set aside the washbasin and pushed to his feet. Travis met his eye, silently seeking answers.

"The bleeding has slowed, and she continues to react to the pain — both of which are good signs. The cuts are fairly minor and won't require stitching. I've treated them with salve. It's the impact to her head, not the abrasions, that I'm most worried about, but best I can tell, there are no skull fractures."

Travis acknowledged his brother's words with a slight dip of his chin, and then reached out to grip the back of the sofa, bracing himself for the rest of the news.

"The fact that she hasn't awakened could be a problem. There is no way to know the extent of the damage inside her skull. The only thing I can recommend is to make her as comfortable as possible. Let her rest and heal at her own pace."

At first, Travis said nothing, just silently absorbed the verdict. So much of his life revolved around controlling his environment. Control meant security. That's why Archers never left their land and why few people were ever granted permission to cross their property line. Control minimized risk. But all his efforts to minimize risk tonight had failed. Mitchell's men escaped, the barn burned, and Meredith — a woman whose only "crime" was trying to perform a good deed — lay unconscious on his mother's sofa, and there was nothing he could do to remedy the situation.

Travis pressed his fingers into the wood trim of the sofa back and straightened. "My room's closest," he said. "We'll put her in there. I can bunk with Neill."

"Someone should probably sit up with her until she regains consciousness." Crockett raised a brow and searched him with a look that seemed to ask more than one question. "I'd be happy to —"

"No. I'll do it." Travis bent and lifted Meredith from the sofa. "She came here because of me. It's only right that I be the one to tend her."

Crockett nodded, a slight smile curving his lips. Travis glared at him, uncomfortable with his brother's shrewd expression. Crockett's grin widened at his reaction, but he wisely said no more and, instead, strode down the hall to open the bedroom door and pull back the covers on the bed. Travis carried Meredith through the doorway and lowered her to the mattress.

"We should probably . . . um . . . try to make her more comfortable." Crockett glanced at Travis from the opposite side of the bed, his face reddening.

Travis took secret pleasure at his brother's discomfort until the meaning of his words settled into Travis's brain. His mouth suddenly dry, he looked from Crockett to Meredith and back to Crockett again.

"We can't —" He cleared his throat. His shirt collar seemed to be shrinking. There was no way he was going to undress her. Especially not with Crockett looking on.

"I'm not suggesting we do anything improper." Crockett blew out a heavy breath. "Well, not *too* improper. Aw . . . blast it, Travis. I'm trying to be practical here. Her breathing is shallow, and if we loosen her stays, that might help. That and taking off her shoes so she can rest better. That's all

I'm saying."

Shoes. He could handle shoes. Travis swallowed hard and moved to the end of the bed, where her feet hung off the side of the mattress. It was true that she didn't look very comfortable, her legs skewed at an odd angle. If he was lying there, he'd sure want his boots off. So why did he feel like the worst kind of cad when he touched her ankle?

"Throw the blanket over her legs," Travis ground out between clenched teeth. She'd shown them all the scar above her ankle when she first arrived, but that had been her choice. Neither he nor Crockett needed to see anything besides shoe leather now. Once the covers were in place, Travis waved Crockett over to his side of the bed. "Come help me with the other shoe." The faster they completed the task, the better.

They undid the laces and gently tugged off the shoes.

"Just like when Neill was a kid, right?" Crockett said.

"Right," Travis agreed. Only it didn't feel anything like putting Neill to bed when feminine wool stockings rubbed against his hands as he poked her toes under the covers. Nor was he able to picture Neill's sleepy little boy form when it came time to take care of the second order of business.

Travis looked to Crockett. His brother shrugged.

"It has to be done, Trav. She needs to be able to breathe freely. If you don't feel right about it, I'll do it."

He sure as shooting didn't feel right about it. But he felt even less right about letting anyone else do it.

Travis sat on the edge of the bed and reached for the buttons at Meredith's midsection. But before he touched one, he stopped. His eyes moved to her face. "Meredith," he said in a firm, loud voice. "Meredith, can you hear me?"

Her head shifted slightly on the pillow, but she gave no sign of waking.

"Meredith, I'm going to loosen your . . . ah . . . clothing to help you breathe. I swear that's all I'm doing. All right?"

She made a slight moaning sound, then quieted. He'd have to take that for permission. Setting his jaw and focusing strictly on the task that needed to be accomplished, he made quick work of the buttons on her bodice. Unfortunately, instead of the laces he expected to encounter, he uncovered another layer. Some white frilly thing offered up a second set of buttons. Travis bit back a groan but tackled the obstacle with businesslike precision. Finally, he found the stiff, boned corset he sought, but there were still no visible laces.

Why couldn't a woman just throw a shirt over her head like a man? This was ridiculous. At least there were metal fasteners of some sort running down the front.

"I swear, if there's another row of buttons under this, I'm gonna get my knife and cut her out," he grumbled under his breath. No wonder her breathing was shallow. She was wrapped up tighter than a roped calf at branding time.

However, the moment he unclasped the last fastener and the corset fell open to reveal another layer of white fabric, Meredith let out a sound that could only be described as a sigh. Her breathing deepened, and Travis's frustration melted away. He quickly drew the covers up to her chin.

"She'll rest easier now," Crockett said from behind him, "and that will give her the best chance to recover."

Travis nodded. Her recovery was more important than any awkwardness or embarrassment his actions might have caused. He just hoped she saw it the same way when she awoke.

9

Meredith rolled to her side and grimaced when pain throbbed behind her ear. She squeezed her eyes more tightly shut and gingerly rolled back the way she'd come, only to have something stiff jab her in the soft spot below her ribs. Had she fallen asleep reading again? She felt around for the book that must have worked its way under the covers, eager to remove the impediment and go back to sleep. However, when she extracted the poking object from beneath her, it felt nothing like a book and everything like a . . . corset? What was her corset doing in her bed? She always stored it carefully in her bureau drawer at night.

Cassandra had secretly given her the pink satin undergarment for her birthday last year, letting Aunt Noreen believe her gift had been nothing more extravagant than the package of stationery she'd presented at the family dinner that evening. But later she had taken Meredith's hand, dragged her upstairs to her room, and closed the door. Eyes twinkling with suppressed secrets, she had pulled a brown paper package from her wardrobe and presented it with giddy delight. The pink satin corset trimmed in white lace and covered with embroidered roses had been the most beautiful thing Meredith had ever seen. She treasured the garment and would never discard it haphazardly. So why was it in bed with her?

Meredith's mind flitted from dreamlike memories of her cousin to the puzzle of her present circumstance. Yet the more she tried to make sense of things, the more her head ached. Then another ache made itself known — the ache to use the chamber pot. Meredith swallowed a moan, hating to forfeit sleep. Maybe if she hurried, she could bury herself back into the covers before Aunt Noreen banged on the door.

Pressing her palms into the mattress, she started to lever herself up, but when she lifted her head from the pillow, stabbing shards ricocheted through her skull. She mewled and reached for her head.

"Easy now." A deep voice resonated near her ear. Strong hands supported her shoulders and propped a second pillow beneath her. "Are you awake, Meredith?" A warm fingertip drew a line across her forehead and gently smoothed back a piece of hair. "Please, God, let her wake," the voice murmured.

Meredith struggled to open her eyes, to make sense of the voice. It was familiar, masculine. Nothing like Uncle Everett, though.

Her lashes slowly separated. A face hovered over hers. She blinked, trying to bring it into focus. Craggy features, a strong jaw that seemed to tighten as she watched, and eyes . . . eyes that looked like home.

"Travis?" Her voice came out scratchy and cracked. "What are you doing in my room?"

Those eyes — not quite green, not quite brown — crinkled at the corners. "I'm not in your room, darlin'. You're in mine."

What? Maybe she was still dreaming. That would explain why Travis was here and why nothing was making a lick of sense. But the throbbing behind her ear seemed awfully real.

"My head hurts."

"You were kicked by a mule."

A mule? Meredith frowned. Uncle Everett didn't own a mule. Had she been injured at the livery fetching Ginger? And why was Travis grinning at her? Shouldn't he be more concerned?

"It's not very heroic of you to smile at my misfortune." *Really.* This was her dream after all. Her hero should be more solicitous. Of course, usually in her dreams, Travis rescued her before any injury occurred. The man was getting lax. She'd started to tell him so when he laid the back of his hand on her forehead as if feeling for fever. The gentle touch instantly dissolved her pique.

He removed his hand and met her gaze. "I'm smiling because I'm happy to see you awake. We've been worried about you."

"Awake?" Meredith scrunched her brows together until the throbbing around her skull forced her to relax. "Travis, you're not making any sense. I can't be awake. You only come to me when I'm dreaming. Although you're usually younger and . . . well . . . cleaner, and not so in need of a shave.

"But don't get me wrong," she hurried to assure him. It wouldn't do to insult her hero. "You're just as handsome as always. I don't even mind that you didn't save me this time. The important thing is that you're here."

She smiled at him, but his grin faded and frown lines appeared above his eyes.

"Don't you remember riding out here to warn me about Mitchell? The fire, Meredith. Remember the fire? You were fighting the blaze on your own until me and the boys returned."

Something important tugged on the hem of her memory, something she should know. Something Travis expected her to remember. Meredith grew uneasy under the intensity of his stare. He was disappointed in her. She could see it. Disappointed that she couldn't remember. She *had* to remember. Travis might leave her if she didn't. She didn't want him to leave.

Despite the pounding in her head, she searched deeper into the foggy recesses of her mind. Images flashed just out of reach. Flames. A line of pots. A gray blanket in her hand. The pieces jumbled in a confusing blur. Then she saw a building. Big. Open. Fire climbing its walls.

"A barn!" she cried triumphantly. "Your barn was on fire, and I was helping put it out. Right?" She found his hand and grabbed hold. "That's right, isn't it? See, you don't have to leave me, Travis. I can remember. I won't let you down. I promise."

Travis's face started to swim in front of her and her lashes grew too heavy to keep parted. Her fingers started to loosen their grip on his hand, too, and fear clutched her chest. He was leaving her!

"Don't go, Travis. Please." Her mouth

stumbled on the words as darkness descended over her again. "Don't leave me."

Then a firm, warm hand closed over the top of hers and held on with the strength she could no longer muster for herself. "I'm not going anywhere, Meredith. Go ahead and rest. I'll be here when you wake."

Peace settled over her then, and as she slipped back into the darkness, her spirit smiled.

Travis held Meredith's hand for several minutes and watched her sleep. Perhaps it was his imagination, but she seemed to be resting more peacefully now than she had before, as if knowing he was there actually brought her comfort. Then again, it probably wasn't *his* presence specifically that eased her. She hardly knew him, after all. Most likely she simply didn't want to be alone, and he was handy. Crockett or even Neill would have filled the bill equally well.

But, despite the logic of that observation, Travis couldn't quite shake the feeling that it didn't ring true. The things Meredith said during their brief, and thoroughly bizarre, conversation had sounded personal. So personal, they'd rattled him. And stirred an odd warmth in him, too.

Did she really dream about him?

Travis lowered himself back into the chair he'd placed at the side of the bed and slowly released Meredith's hand. He fingered his eyes, trying to massage the exhaustion out of them, then rubbed his palms down his face. Whiskers scratched his skin, eliciting a rueful chuckle.

She was right. He did need a shave.

A floorboard creaked in the hall, and Travis glanced up to find Crockett — barefooted, pants hastily donned, shirt untucked — standing in the doorway. "I thought I heard voices."

"You did." Travis pushed to his feet and waved him into the room. "Meredith woke a couple minutes ago. She was disoriented and confused, and most of what she said didn't add up." He turned his attention from his brother to the woman sleeping in his bed. "Thought she was at home in her own room and didn't recall the fire until I mentioned it. Even then, she seemed to have to dig real deep to muster any recollections."

Travis worked his jaw back and forth, trying to churn up enough courage to ask the question he was afraid to have answered. "You don't think her mind's been damaged, do you?"

"Not permanently, no." Crockett leaned

over the bed and felt Meredith's head for fever, just as Travis had done earlier, and pivoted to face him. "Confusion and memory loss are to be expected. Her brain took a hard knock. I wouldn't worry unless she fails to improve after a day or two."

"So she'll be staying with us for a while?"

"Yep." A defensive edge crept into Crockett's voice, as if he expected Travis to argue. "I don't want her out of bed until we're sure she's fully recovered. If we send her on her way too soon, she could succumb to a dizzy spell and fall off her horse or get disoriented and wander from the path only to get lost in the woods. I know you don't like having strangers here, Travis, but I'm going to have to insist."

"Meredith proved herself an ally last night," Travis conceded. "She can stay as long as is necessary."

He cleared his throat, afraid Crockett would sense how easy it was for him to break his own rules where Meredith was concerned. "But as soon as she's healthy, she has to go. I don't want a bunch of townsfolk poking around out here because one of their own is missing. It wouldn't do her any good, either, to be found alone on a ranch with four men." The last thing he wanted to do was cause Meredith more grief. He'd done enough of that already.

"Agreed." Crockett clapped him on the back. "Why don't you grab a few winks before the sun comes up. I'll sit with her for a while."

Travis shook his head. "No. I promised to be here when she woke, and I aim to keep my word." He scratched at his stubbly chin and caught a glimpse of himself in the mirror above his chest of drawers. *Haggard* was about as kind a description as could be applied to what he saw. *Filthy saddle bum* painted a truer picture. "I might take a few minutes to clean up a bit, though. I could stand a wash and some fresh clothes."

"Yes, you could." Crockett twisted his face into a look of mock disgust, then broke into a smile. "Go on." He pushed Travis toward the drawers that held clean trousers and shirts. "She probably won't wake for a couple hours. You got plenty of time to make yourself pretty."

Travis whipped off his sweat-stained shirt and hurled it directly at Crockett's head. The joker ducked, and the sound of his quiet laughter followed Travis down the hall.

The next time Meredith woke, the sun was well on its way across the sky. Travis had been dozing in the chair when her quiet moan stirred him. He shifted closer to the bed. Would she be more clearheaded this time?

"Don't move too fast," he warned as she rolled to her side and propped an elbow beneath her. "It'll make your head ache worse." He stilled her with a hand to her shoulder.

"Travis?" She blinked and struggled to fully open her eyes.

"I'm here, Meredith."

She smiled at him then, and the gesture did something funny to his insides. Not wanting to examine the phenomenon too closely, he cleared his throat and reached for the glass of water he'd brought in with him after cleaning up.

"Are you thirsty?"

Her eyes instantly lost their peaceful glow. She bit her bottom lip and gave her head a tiny shake. "You have to leave," she said in a wobbly voice.

"Leave? Why?" First she'd begged him to stay, and now she wanted him to go. Travis blew out a breath and ran his hand through his hair. The woman's confusion must be addling his own mind.

Her face flushed crimson, and her gaze dropped to somewhere below his chin. "I have to attend to . . . to personal business."

Her voice dipped so low at the end, he had to strain to hear her. Once he deciphered the words, however, an uncomfortable heat crept up his neck.

"Oh."

What in blue blazes was he supposed to do now? She could barely move about in the bed with the pain from her wound. How was she supposed to manage standing and walking about the room? What if she grew dizzy and fell?

Travis clenched his teeth. He'd get her up, but by Jove, she was going to have to find a way to accomplish the rest on her own. Heaven help her.

Without further discussion, Travis dragged the chamber pot from beneath the bed and set it beside the footboard so that Meredith could hang onto the carved bedpost for balance. He scanned the room for anything else that might be of help, and his eyes lit on the small bag Neill had retrieved from Meredith's horse last night. Without asking permission, Travis strode over to the bag and rummaged through it. Finding a white cotton nightgown, he draped it across the end of the bed, then dropped the bag on the floor nearby. That way she could reach it should she feel the need.

By the time he turned back to Meredith,

the woman had already pushed herself up to a sitting position and had her legs dangling over the side of the mattress. Deep lines furrowed her brow, and her left hand gingerly cupped the side of her head, but her chin was set and her back straight.

The woman had grit. If he hadn't learned that truth last night, watching her power through her pain this morning would've proved it.

Travis rushed to her side and wrapped an arm around her middle. Something pink and lacy winked at him from within the sheets. Recognizing the corset, he loosened his hold on Meredith in order to grab the frilly thing and flip it down to the far corner of the bed. Maybe if she found it with her other belongings, he'd get lucky and her confused mind would assume she'd taken it off herself.

Cinching his arm back around her ribs, Travis took her weight on himself and slowly raised her to her feet. "Easy now," he said. "I'll help you get to the end of the bed."

She leaned into his side as they moved slowly toward their goal, her left arm circling his waist. When they reached the bedpost, Meredith released him to grasp the oak column, and Travis found himself missing the contact. He maintained his grip another moment until certain she was secure. Finally, he slackened his hold and slipped his arm free.

"I'll be right outside the door." He ducked his head and shoved his thumbs beneath his suspender straps. "Call out if you need anything."

He couldn't quite bring himself to look at her with her dress half undone, but he heard her quiet "Thank you" as he strode to the doorway.

Once the door had been pulled closed behind him, he pressed his back into the wall and exhaled a long, slow breath.

Fifteen minutes later, Meredith called him back into the room. She'd managed to change and crawl back under the covers. Sitting with the blankets held up to her chin, she bit her lip and hid her eyes from him behind lowered lashes.

"I didn't want to bother you," she said softly, "but I couldn't reach all my hairpins. It hurt too much to twist my head back and forth."

Travis crossed the room and, lowering himself beside her, reached for the first pin he could see. She hissed a little when a tangled strand pulled painfully against her injured scalp. Travis scowled. His rancher's fingers were too thick for this. But who else was gonna do it? Setting his jaw, he reached for another pin. This time she didn't make a sound as he extracted the thin black wire. His confidence building, Travis searched for more. By the time he found the last one and added it to the pile next to his hip, Meredith's eyes had closed and her back slumped against his chest.

Travis eased her down to where her pillow waited. Scooping the discarded pins into his palm, he pushed to his feet only to have the bed groan at the loss of his weight. Meredith's lashes fluttered open.

"Travis?" she whispered, her voice groggy.

"Yes?"

"You're the best hero I ever dreamed up."

And in that moment, Travis wanted to be more to her than a dreamland hero left over from her childhood. He wanted to be her hero in truth.

But his wants never came first. His brothers, the land — those were what he swore to protect. And with Meredith's connection to Mitchell, he couldn't afford to indulge in selfish whims. No, when Meredith recovered, he'd see she got back where she belonged — far away from him.

10

Meredith drifted in and out of sleep most of the day. Each time she woke, she'd ask the same questions: Where was she? What happened? And each time, Travis gave her the same answers. Despite her continued memory trouble, however, her disorientation improved. No more talk of dreams or heroes, for which he was exceedingly grateful. If Crockett had overheard one of those statements, he'd never let Travis live it down. Besides, the less he thought about those early conversations, the better. He had no business trying to be someone's hero. He had enough to worry about.

Like the fact that someone was trying to drive him off his land. And because of that, he had no barn, only half the hay stores he'd need for winter, and an injured woman whose presence kept him in the house when he should be out helping his brothers build a temporary shelter for the stock. Travis paced over to the window and raised an arm to cushion his head as he leaned against the wall.

"I'm sorry about your barn, Travis." Meredith's soft voice settled over him like a comfortable, well-worn shirt. He turned and found she had bolstered herself on the extra pillows without his aid and was regarding him with remarkably clear eyes.

How had she so accurately deciphered his thoughts? He pasted on a smile, not wanting to burden her with his worries, and stepped away from the window. "It's nothing for you to be sorry about. The boys and I can build another."

"But it will cause you hardship. Perhaps if I had gotten here sooner . . ."

Travis's mouth hardened into a stern line. "None of the blame belongs on your shoulders, Meredith. Mitchell's the one responsible. Without your warning, things could've been a lot worse."

Travis dropped onto the bedside chair ready to scold some more, but it suddenly hit him that she hadn't asked him her usual questions. "Do you remember what happened?"

She started to shake her head but stopped with a wince. "Not really. I remember coming out here and helping fight the fire, but I

136

have no memory of you and the others returning or anything else from last night."

"Do you recall me explaining how you got injured?"

"Samson, right?"

He nodded, and she smiled like a pupil trying to impress her teacher. "You told me when I awakened a while ago."

"And four times before that." A true grin split his face. She was getting better. "I'm glad it finally sank in."

Her brows knit in bewilderment. "Four times? How long have I been . . ." She glanced down at the bed, as if only then recognizing the significance of where she was, and slid down on the pillows until the blankets came up to her chin.

So much for bypassing the awkwardness.

"It's nearly suppertime. I'll have Jim bring you some broth if you think you can manage eating."

"Suppertime?" she squeaked. "I was here all night and all day?"

"And you probably won't be leaving anytime soon." Judging by her horrified look, the prospect didn't exactly thrill her. Well, being chained to a sickroom when he had work to do wasn't his first choice, either. If he could deal with it, she sure as shootin' could, too.

"Look, Meredith. We have no choice in the matter. That lump on the side of your head ain't there for decoration. You're seriously hurt. Crockett knows what he's talking about when it comes to things like this, and he insists that you not leave until you've recovered to the point that there's no chance of you blacking out on the way home or growing so dizzy you fall off your horse. Until now, you couldn't even remember where you were. No way was I going to dump you outside my gate just because propriety said you shouldn't be here. Propriety wasn't kicked by a mule."

Travis sucked in a breath and reined in his temper. It was only natural for her to be alarmed. She was in her nightclothes in a strange man's bed. Any sane woman would protest. It only proved how delirious she'd truly been when she'd rambled on about him being handsome and the hero of her dreams. He should be thankful for the evidence that she was in her right mind again.

So why wouldn't that pang in his chest at the thought of her leaving go away?

"I understand." Meredith looked at him with those big eyes of hers and made an effort to clear the trepidation from her face. But when she bit her bottom lip, he knew she still harbored worries.

"I see our patient's awake again." Crockett leaned a shoulder against the doorjamb. His trousers and shirt were streaked with soot, but his face and hands glowed from a recent scrubbing. "How are you feeling, Meredith?"

"Stronger, thank you." Her lashes remained lowered, and her grip on the blankets tightened.

Travis moved to the foot of the bed to shield her from his brother's view. "She remembers things, too," he said. "Not everything, but enough that I don't have to repeat explanations."

"Well, that's good news." Crockett angled his head past Travis and projected his voice across the room. "Another couple days of rest, and you should be up and about."

Meredith's quiet moan was all the catalyst Travis needed. He strode to the doorway and, taking Crockett by the shoulders, manually pointed him toward the kitchen.

Crockett resisted, concern creeping into his voice. "Is she in pain?"

"Only if she moves." Travis strong-armed his brother into the hall. "Why don't you get her some of that soup Jim's heating up? She hasn't eaten since yesterday."

Crockett pulled out of Travis's hold and

turned on him. "What's wrong with you?" he hissed. "You're acting as if you think I'm going to hurt her or something."

"It's not that. It's just . . ." Travis let out a heavy breath. "She's not too pleased about having to prolong her stay, and your reminders aren't easing her worries none."

Crockett jutted his chin. "Well, she's going to have to get used to the idea, because I'm not letting her leave until I'm sure —"

"I already made that plain to her," Travis interrupted. "And she's coming around. She just needs some time to settle things in her mind." He glanced back toward the open doorway. "Meredith's tough. She'll weather whatever storm comes."

"She's got spunk. That's for sure."

Hearing the admiration in his brother's voice, Travis turned to scowl at him. "Just get the soup."

Crockett's gaze returned to the doorway to Meredith's room, giving Travis the distinct impression that the man remembered all too well what she looked like tucked up in bed.

He gave his brother a shove. "Get going."

"All right. All right." Crockett caught his balance and finally moved toward the kitchen. "I'll brew some willow bark tea, too. It'll help with her pain."

"Fine."

Travis marched back to his room and made a beeline for his chest of drawers. He grabbed the first shirt his hand touched and yanked it out of the drawer. His bootheels clomped against the wood floor, then muffled as he hit the rag rug at the side of the bed.

Meredith watched him, her brows slightly quirked.

"Arms up," he said as if she were a child and not a very beautiful, very grown woman. "Crock is gonna bring some tea and soup in a bit, and you won't be able to eat if you've got a death grip on those blankets." He scrunched the shirttails in his hands and stretched the unbuttoned neck hole wide. "Put this on. It'll cover you up and still allow you to eat."

She hesitated for a moment, then released the blankets and stuck her arm through the sleeve, her disgruntled expression making him smile.

With Meredith's condition no longer critical, Travis joined his brothers outside the following morning. He and Crockett split her care between them, and at her insistence, only checked in on her when a break in their work allowed it. Her head still pained her, though the willow bark seemed to take the sharpness away, but it was the dizziness that kept her in bed. He'd provided her with a book to read, Ballantyne's *The Wild Man of the West,* and while he doubted a less feminine book had ever been written, she'd assured him it helped pass the time.

Late that morning, Travis headed to the pump. It was his turn to look in on Meredith. He pulled off his work gloves, tucked them into his coat pocket, and ran his hands under the icy water streaming from the spout. Then he dampened his handkerchief and wiped the sweat from his brow. As he moved the cool cloth around to the back of his neck, two shots fired in close succession echoed from the direction of the road.

Company.

In a blink, he unfastened the protective loop on his holster, his fingers testing the freedom of his Colt. After Mitchell's attack, he and the boys had taken to wearing their gun belts even when close to the house.

"Neill, take position by the shed!" Travis yelled as he ran to the corral. He ducked through the fence and grabbed his saddle from where it lay slung over the top rails. He caught a glimpse of Jim running around the corner of the shed and called out for him to guard the road.

Crockett appeared at the corral with a horse blanket, and Travis whistled for his gelding. As the two worked in tandem to get the animal ready to ride, Travis ordered Crockett to see to Meredith's protection.

"She warned us Mitchell's man would return to make another offer after the fire. Things might get ugly when I spit in his face." Travis mounted, and Crockett moved to open the railings.

"I'll watch over her, Trav. Just keep your head out there."

He nodded to his brother and nudged Bexar into a run, his eyes only briefly touching on his bedroom window as he charged past the house.

11

Meredith shivered as a draft from the open window passed over her skin, yet her trembling had more to do with her concern over Travis than the cold. Crockett had assured her that his presence in her room was simply a precaution, but the rifle he held and the way he constantly scanned the trees outside as if searching for invaders did little to put her at ease.

What would Roy do when Travis still refused to sell? For he *would* refuse. She was certain of it. Would there be another fire? Would the house be targeted next? Or would Roy finally give up?

Please, Lord, let him give up.

But in her heart she knew he wouldn't. Roy's ambition ran nearly as deep as Travis's loyalty. Something drastic would have to occur before either man gave an inch.

Something drastic . . . Meredith's breath grew shallow.

"You don't think he's walking into a trap, do you?"

Crockett spared her the smallest of glances before turning back to his vigil. "Travis is smart. He'll assess the situation before revealing himself, and even then, he'll keep his gun trained on whoever's there. He can handle himself."

If Crockett was so confident of Travis's abilities, why was he clutching his rifle like a soldier about to be called to the front line?

"What if Roy sent more than one man? What if they lured him with their shots, then cut the fencing wire and caught him unaware? Someone should check on him. He's been gone too long."

"He's fine. Now hush." The gentle reprimand had the intended effect, but her fears must have been communicated at least a little, for when Crockett returned his attention to the window, he fidgeted with his rifle grip and shifted his stance three times before settling.

Meredith held her tongue, but her worries festered. She watched Crockett watch the yard. Every time his focus snapped to a new location, her breath caught.

Just when she thought she'd surely go mad from the waiting, a distinctive low birdcall drifted through the window — one she vaguely recalled hearing the afternoon she arrived. Crockett relaxed immediately and pivoted to wink at her. "I told you he was fine."

Thank you, Lord!

Meredith sagged against her pillows, relief bringing the sought-after comfort that had eluded her earlier. She grinned at Crockett, but before she could ask any questions, he slammed the window shut and strode out of the room, rifle in hand.

What did that mean? Was danger still afoot? Perhaps he was simply eager to greet his brother and hear the details of his encounter. *Hmmm . . .* She wanted to hear those details, too, and she doubted the Archers would make a point to share them with her. They were forever telling her not to worry. A rather bothersome trait, that.

Why did men think they had to protect women from reality? She didn't mind being protected from wild animals or murderous villains, but from the truth? Meredith made a face as she threw back the bedcovers. The more she knew about a situation, the less likely she was to worry, not the other way around. If she was to stay with the Archers another day or two, she needed to know what was going on.

Holding a steadying hand to her head, she

swiveled her legs to the edge of the bed and dangled them over the side. She blinked as the floor seemed to tilt forward and back and waited for the dizziness to pass. Grasping the top of the headboard, Meredith stood slowly, her bare toes digging into the rag rug to aid her balance. She still wore Travis's shirt over her nightdress, and it bunched uncomfortably at her waist. With her free hand, she tugged it down over her hips and untwisted the skirt of her sleeping gown before attempting to move.

A door slammed somewhere in the distance, and male voices poured into the house. Agitated male voices.

More curious and determined than ever, Meredith leaned her leg against the mattress and shuffled along the side of the bed, chilled air nipping at her ankles. If she could just make it as far as the doorway, she could listen in on whatever the Archers said when they congregated around the kitchen table.

Having reached the bedpost, she inhaled a deep breath, straightened her shoulders, and took her first unaided step. Her foot met the hardness of the wood floor and wobbled, but she found if she stared at the ground a few inches in front of her toes, the room didn't spin quite as much. She concentrated so hard on remaining upright, however, that she failed to hear the approaching footsteps until two pairs of boots appeared at the top edge of her vision.

An audible gasp sucked the air from the room. Meredith stilled.

"Heaven help us. You've ruined her."

Meredith jerked her head upright. "Uncle Everett?"

Pain shot through her skull at the too-fast motion. She staggered sideways, unable to maintain her equilibrium as the floor seemed to undulate beneath her. Then all at once she found herself braced against the firm wall of a man's chest. *Travis.* He caught her arms above the elbows and steadied her as she sagged into his safe harbor.

"You shouldn't be out of bed," he scolded in a soft voice, then promptly picked her up and delivered her back to the pillows.

"Good grief, man! Have you no shame?" Her uncle's voice followed her across the room. "You carry on with my niece in front of my very eyes?"

Horrified by her uncle's outburst, Meredith turned her face away from Travis as he set her down. Tension radiated through him as he released her, and when she found the nerve to look at him again, a muscle twitched at the edge of his jaw.

"She's injured, Hayes. Or don't you care

about that?" Travis ground out. "I thought I explained her condition quite thoroughly on the way here."

Uncle Everett stomped into the room, pulling his arms from his coat. Once he had the garment off, he stormed down the opposite side of the bed and forced it around Meredith's shoulders, drawing it closed under her chin.

"You failed to mention that her condition included a nightdress and a place in your bed!"

Travis leaned across the bed and grabbed Uncle Everett's wrist. "You insult her again with talk like that, and I'll throw you off my land with a buckshot escort."

The sound of a rifle cocking drew all eyes to the doorway. "Buckshot's too tame, Trav. I say we each carve out a piece of his hide with a .44." Crockett stood just inside the room, brandishing his Winchester. Jim and Neill flanked him on either side, hands hovering above their holsters.

Meredith diverted her gaze to the ceiling, wishing she could dissolve into the covers. Could her humiliation be any more complete?

Travis tossed her uncle's wrist away from him and straightened his stance to face the man squarely, arms crossed over his chest.

Uncle Everett straightened, too, though not until he'd done up three of the buttons on the coat he'd forced upon her. The two glared at each other for what seemed like an age before Uncle Everett finally looked at her and let out a hefty sigh.

"Meri. You've thrown everything away, girl. How could you be so foolhardy?" The disappointment in his eyes cut her to the quick.

"I had to warn them, Uncle Everett. You were away, the sheriff was gone, and the deputy just laughed off my concerns as if I didn't know what I was talking about. I had no choice but to come."

"You should've stayed at home and let the Archers take care of themselves. That's what they're best at." He aimed a pointed glance at Travis before taking a seat on the edge of the bed. "Ah, Meri. There'll be a high price to pay for this bit of foolishness." He patted her hand. "When I think of everything your aunt and I did to secure your match with Mitchell only to have you throw it all away on a crazy whim . . . Why, it breaks my heart. What would your papa say?"

"Papa would be proud that I followed my conscience." Meredith sat forward, indignation fueling her speech. "I want no part of Roy Mitchell, Uncle. He's the one behind the fire that destroyed the Archers' barn. I heard him give the order myself."

"Nonsense, girl. You misunderstood. Roy explained everything to me last evening."

Travis lurched forward. "You told him she was *here?*"

"Of course. As her betrothed, he had a right to know. The poor fellow feels dreadful about everything. He kept castigating himself for not noticing your upset and clearing up the confusion immediately. He is very concerned about you, my dear."

"He's concerned about my land, not me," Meredith grumbled under her breath. Uncle Everett didn't seem to hear, but Travis raised a brow at her before turning his attention back to her uncle.

"What exactly did you tell Mitchell about Meredith?"

"At first, nothing. After all, I had no idea where she was." He patted her hand once again, as if she were a child to be placated, then stood to address Travis, dismissing her from the conversation. "I arrived home for supper Tuesday night only to find my wife inconsolable. Cassie had told her Meredith was ill, but when Roy arrived to pay his respects, she went to fetch her anyhow. Noreen is very set on this match taking place. When she found our Meri missing . . .

well . . . she flew into a tizzy."

More likely a rage, Meredith thought as she pictured Aunt Noreen storming about the house.

"She questioned our daughter, Cassandra, until the girl admitted that Meri had gone to the old homestead. Noreen insisted that I fetch her back at first light. However, when I arrived at the place yesterday morning, I could find no evidence that she had been there. By the time I arrived home again, Noreen had scoured the house and found the note Meri left for Cassandra. Mitchell arrived soon after, and when Noreen showed him the note, he put the pieces together and explained the situation."

"Whatever he said was a lie," Meredith interjected. "The charred remains of the Archers' barn prove it."

"No, dear. They prove the villainy of one of his competitors." Uncle Everett pulled off his hat and set it on the corner of Travis's bureau with a nonchalance that made Meredith want to scream. "Roy explained how one of his men interrupted your time together, and how you must have overheard bits and pieces of his conversation and jumped to an inaccurate conclusion. He doesn't fault you, of course. He's too much of a gentleman. There was quite a bit of traffic on the road that day, I understand, and the noise surely interfered with your ability to decipher what was being said."

"I know what I heard." How could her uncle dismiss her intelligence and judgment so easily? Did he think she would risk her reputation and personal well-being if she wasn't sure?

"I fear you only know what you *thought* you heard." Though he smiled, condescension laced his tone. "Roy's man had come with news of a rumor regarding a large outfit from Houston. They planned to force him out of the bidding for local lumber by burning out those property owners who stood between him and the railroad. When the devastated owners were forced to sell, the Houston outfit would offer higher prices, thereby securing the necessary land. Roy would be out of the running. Needless to say, he was sickened by such under-handed tactics and intended to inform the sheriff as soon as the man returned.

"He even assured me he'd still marry you after your misadventure, but now that I see the extent of your ruin, I can't expect him to hold to that promise. A man in his position cannot afford to have such a scandal attached to his good name."

"You're wrong." Moisture gathered in her

eyes at her uncle's betrayal. He was her father's brother. Why did he believe Roy Mitchell's sly explanations over those of his own niece? She would expect such a turn from Aunt Noreen, but Uncle Everett had always been kind to her in his own negligent way. It didn't help that every time she looked at him, she saw features that reminded her of her father. "You want to believe Roy because he's promised to triple your business at the mill, but he's behind this attack. I'm certain of it."

She glanced from her uncle's shaking head to Travis's unreadable expression. Did *he* believe her? Somehow the thought that he might doubt her cut deeper than Uncle Everett's lack of faith.

"You wound me, Meri," her uncle said, putting his hand to his chest. "I would never put my own profit ahead of your well-being. In fact, I aim to do all that is within my power to rectify this mess you've gotten yourself into."

"There's nothing to rectify. I'll be well in a day or two and can return to town then." Not that she relished the idea of being back under Aunt Noreen's roof, but at least she could commiserate with her cousin.

"I'm afraid it's not that simple. When your aunt realized that this is where you must have spent the last two nights, she implored me not to bring you back into our home. Noreen is convinced that doing so would throw a shadow of scandal over Cassandra, hurting her prospects for a suitable marriage. I had hoped to calm her concerns with the truth of your circumstances, but if I tell her in what condition I found you . . . well . . . you know your aunt. I'd never hear the end of it." He gave her that haggard look, the one he wore whenever Aunt Noreen got a bee in her bonnet.

Meredith bit the inside of her cheek in a bid for control as her uncle's meaning sank into her brain. She was to be the sacrifice laid upon the altar to appease Aunt Noreen's wrath. Instead of standing up for his niece, Uncle Everett would do what he always did — take the path of least resistance.

"Word of your little . . . escapade . . . is bound to get out," he said, as if that excused his behavior. "These things always do. Noreen threatened to take Cassie away from me and move in with her sister if I don't bend to her wishes. I can't allow that to happen."

Meredith jutted out her chin. She had imagined such a scenario, although deep down she'd never truly believed it would come to pass. "I'll live at the homestead, then. The house is in fine condition —"

"No," Uncle Everett cut in. "I'd never be able to rest knowing you were out here alone. Your father entrusted me with your care, and I must see this through." He clasped his hands behind his back and rocked from heel to toe. "The way I see it, there's only one way to salvage this situation."

He looked pointedly at her, then scanned the rest of the room's occupants with a steely determination she'd never witnessed in him before. "You're going to have to marry one of the Archers."

12

"What?" Crockett, Jim, and Neill chorused the word as if it were one of the hymns they sang in the parlor on Sundays. But Travis said nothing. He wouldn't give Everett Hayes the satisfaction of knowing the pronouncement had rattled him.

Meredith, apparently, had no such compunction. "For heaven's sake, Uncle. You can't just foist me on them like an abandoned puppy. The Archers have been nothing but kind to me. They don't deserve such ill treatment from you."

Travis ground his teeth. Nothing but kind? They'd welcomed her at gunpoint and refused to let her leave after she warned them of the coming danger. Meredith was the kind one, not them. Shoot, his mule kicked her in the head.

And hearing her talk of herself in such unflattering terms, as if marriage to her would be a punishment to whomever found himself tied to the other end of the knot, riled him even more. He itched to hit something, preferably good ol' Uncle Everett, since the man made no effort to correct her assumptions.

"It can't be helped, Meri. It's the only honorable option. And if the Archers are honorable men —" the man stared meaningfully at Travis — "they'll take responsibility for you."

Travis felt more than saw his brothers step deeper into the room.

"Now you're *really* making me sound like an unwanted puppy," Meredith grumbled. Then she drew her legs up under her, and taking hold of the headboard for support, she turned her back on her uncle.

"Pay him no heed, Travis," she pled in a soft voice. His gaze moved to meet her bright blue eyes. "I have a perfectly good house on the land my father left me, and an allowance that will see to my needs. You don't have to give in to his bullying."

The thought of her living alone had his gut clenching. Wild animals, wilder men . . . He didn't want to think about what could happen. And what of Mitchell? He'd heard Meredith's comment about the man only being interested in her land. If she didn't marry him, to what lengths would he go to ensure she sold it to him? Would he burn her out, too? No, Meredith living alone was out of the question. It was the one thing he and Hayes agreed on.

Meredith's lower lip trembled slightly as he contemplated what course to take. She was a brave, fierce little thing, but vulnerable, too.

He gently chucked her under the chin. "Don't fret, pup. We'll figure something out."

Her nose wrinkled at the puppy reference, and he nearly laughed aloud at the resemblance. As he shared a smile with her, a strange urge burgeoned inside him — the urge to stroke her hair and tuck her into his chest as he would one of Sadie's pups. But he was certain the instant he touched her, puppies would be the furthest thing from his mind.

"Well, Archer?"

Travis hardened his expression as he returned his focus to Everett Hayes. The man was all bluster. He had no power in these negotiations, and he knew it — not when surrounded by four armed men. His only choice was to appeal to their sense of honor. Hayes wanted protection for his niece, Travis would give him credit for that, but he was too lily-livered to take care of it himself, letting his shrew of a wife kick Meredith out of his house. Meredith deserved better.

"I'll have a decision for you tomorrow. Come back then." Travis signaled to Crockett. His brother handed his rifle off to Jim and strode forward.

Hayes retreated toward the wall. "Tomorrow's not good enough, Archer! I demand —"

"You're in no position to demand anything," Travis snapped, his patience depleted. "My brother will show you to your horse."

"This way, Mr. Hayes." Crockett spoke through clenched teeth as he gripped the man's shoulder and firmly steered him toward the door.

Meredith's uncle grabbed for his hat as he dragged his feet and twisted his neck to glare at Travis. "What of my niece?"

"She's not well enough to travel. She stays with us."

The man frowned but offered no argument as Crockett shoved him out into the hall. "Mark my words, Archer." Hayes latched onto the doorframe, momentarily halting his exit. "I'll be back in the morning. And I'm bringing a preacher."

Travis said nothing, just stared the man

down until he finally released his hold on the wall and submitted to Crockett's not-so-gentle guidance.

"Travis?" Meredith's quiet voice drew his head around and had him fortifying his resolve. She might not like the way he'd treated her uncle, but courtesy could only be stretched so far. He refused to be polite to a man who would insult his own niece and try to fob her off on a virtual stranger. She should be grateful that he —

"My uncle will need his coat." Meredith undid the buttons and shrugged out of the heavy overcoat. Then she handed it up to him with a smile that offered no censure.

When he took the coat from her, she adjusted the too-long sleeves of his brown plaid shirt, the one he'd lent her the night before, and hugged her arms to her middle. She gave him a brief nod, and all he could think was that she had just removed herself from her uncle's protection and entrusted herself to his.

He stared at her a moment, then nodded in return.

"Neill." Travis pivoted away from Meredith. "See that Hayes gets his coat." He tossed the garment, and his kid brother snagged it out of the air. "Jim, follow our guest to the road. We wouldn't want him to

161

have a mishap on the way home."

Jim nodded, his expression assuring Travis there'd be no more surprises that day.

When the two men left, Travis turned back to Meredith a final time. Her eyelids were drooping, and her shoulders seemed to sag against the pillows. The strain of her uncle's visit had obviously depleted her strength.

"Get some sleep, Meri," he said, moving closer to the bed.

Meri. He liked the nickname. It reminded him of the young girl he'd encountered in the woods a dozen years ago, a girl with a brave spirit and trusting eyes, a girl who had grown into a woman of conviction and courage with a quiet beauty that awakened things in him he didn't quite understand.

Lifting the covers, he helped her lie down. "The boys and I will see to things."

She smiled sleepily. "I know."

He tucked the blankets around her, then crept out of the room and met Crockett on the porch. The two stood silently for several minutes as they watched Everett Hayes ride away, Neill at his side, Jim somewhere in the trees. Crockett never turned to face him, but Travis could hear his question before the words hit the air.

"You know one of us is gonna have to marry her, right?"

Travis inhaled a deep breath, prolonging the final moment before his world changed irrevocably. Then with a sigh, he let it go. "Yep."

All through dinner, Everett Hayes's demand hung over the Archer table like a boulder perched on an eroding precipice. No one spoke of it, as if fearful that doing so would bring a rockslide down on their heads, but everyone knew it was there.

Travis scraped the last of the rabbit stew from his bowl, mentally rehearsing how to relay his decision to his brothers.

As the oldest, it was his duty to do what was best for the family. It always had been. Therefore, he was the logical choice to marry Meredith. After all, it was because of him that she'd come to their land in the first place. None of his brothers should have to sacrifice his freedom for an unexpected bride just because —

"I'll do it." Crockett's proclamation slammed into Travis's carefully formulated rationale and shattered it like a stone hitting window glass.

Travis gulped down his mouthful of stew, his empty bowl thunking onto the table as he pierced his brother with a hard glare. "What do you mean, you'll do it?"

"I'll marry up with her." Crockett shrugged and glanced around the table, his palms turned upward before him. "What? She's decent enough to look at and handles herself well in a crisis. A man could do worse."

A man could do worse? *That* was his reasoning? Travis could just imagine the kind of husband Crock would make with that attitude. What was he thinking? There was no way —

"I'll wrestle you for her." Jim propped his elbow on the table, his open hand extended in challenge.

"Hold on!" Travis pushed out of his chair and braced his arms on the edge of the table next to Crockett, his heated blood pumping hard through his veins. "No one is going to wrestle over Meredith as if she were the last piece of Christmas pie. Show some sense. Besides, I've already decided that I'm the one to marry her. It's my fault she's here. She's my responsibility."

Instead of looking abashed, Jim quirked a cocky grin at him. " 'Fraid you'd lose to me, big brother?"

"I'd whip you any day of the week, *Bowie,* and you know it." Travis threw the despised name in Jim's face, ready to wrestle more than his arm if need be.

Jim kicked his chair out of the way and lurched to his feet, his face a thundercloud. The two squared off, hands fisted, eyes narrowed, the table the only thing separating them. Travis stepped around the barrier. Jim mirrored him, no longer his brother but a rival — a man who matched him in height, breadth, and most likely strength. Everything but experience.

And desire.

Yesterday he had come to grips with the idea of Meredith returning home to her uncle and perhaps marrying a druggist or banker someday, a man he didn't know and would never see. But there was no way he could stand to have her living in his house, belonging to one of his brothers. If an Archer was going to lay claim to her, by George, it was going to be him!

"You're not really gonna whup him, are you, Trav?" Neill's wide eyes came into focus at the edge of Travis's vision, and like a well-aimed snowball, the truth of what he was about to do slapped him in the face and left him cold.

Immediately, Travis relaxed his stance and opened his hands. "No, I . . ." Had he really been contemplating thrashing his own brother? His fingers trembled slightly as he lifted his hand to rub his jaw. "Sorry, Jim.

With everything that's happened lately, I suppose I'm a bit on edge."

Jim raised a skeptical brow, but Travis held his gaze without further apology. Finally, Jim nodded and bent to retrieve his chair. The tension in the room dissipated. Travis exhaled a long breath and returned to his seat.

"So how do you propose we decide which of the three of us gets her?" Crockett asked, dashing Travis's hopes that the others would simply accept his wishes.

"Three?" Neill piped up. "Don't be leavin' me outta the mix."

As if Crockett and Jim weren't bad enough.

Travis stared at his youngest brother, his left temple suddenly throbbing. "You're barely old enough to shave, Neill. You wouldn't know what to do with a wife."

"I'm as much a man as the rest of you." Neill sat forward with a confidence that demanded respect. "I do the same work, wear the same clothes. I ain't gonna be cheated outta my chance to have a gal of my own just 'cause I'm the youngest. Shoot. She might not even want an old geezer like you, Trav."

A chuckle erupted from Crockett, and

Travis shook his head, feeling older by the minute.

"The kid's got a point," Crockett said when his laughter subsided. "We don't exactly come into contact with marriage-able females on a regular basis out here. Who's to say how long it'll take the Lord to drop another one in our lap."

Travis leaned his forearms on the table, unable to argue the truth of that statement. "Any suggestions?"

Crockett rubbed his neck. Jim crossed his arms. Neill eyed the ceiling.

Travis glanced around the room for inspiration, as if the perfect idea might be hiding behind the coffeepot or under the stove. He needed some way to assuage his brothers while still ensuring Neill didn't end up as the groom. As the head of the family, he could simply claim first rights, but that could cause a rift. And the last thing they needed with Mitchell breathing down their necks was a lack of unity. No, there had to be a better way.

His gaze traveled over the cabinet that held his mother's dishes and drifted past the doorway to the bathing room. Something tickled his peripheral vision, and he looked back to the wall. A broom stood in the corner. Travis sat up straighter, a germ of an idea taking root. It would require some trickery, but he should be able to pull it off.

"Boys," he said, slapping his palms on the tabletop. "We're going to draw straws."

13

A loud crash awakened Meredith. Blinking, she eased herself to a sitting position and listened, trying to piece together what was happening.

The Archers were arguing about something in the kitchen. Something that had them quite upset. Meredith frowned and tossed back the covers. It probably had to do with her uncle's embarrassing demands. The whole episode came back to her with humiliating clarity. The only good thing about the entire encounter was that Uncle Everett had declared her no longer good enough for Roy Mitchell.

Never had she been so thankful to be found wanting. She just wished it hadn't hurt so much to hear him say so.

As Meredith stretched her toes toward the floor and reached for the headboard, the discussion in the kitchen escalated. She heard her name and something about

Christmas pie. She had no earthly idea what Christmas pie had to do with anything, but one thing was clear — the argument involved her.

Meredith frowned and hauled herself to her feet. This was not the Archers' problem to solve. It was hers. She never should have let Travis believe differently. She'd just been so weary when her uncle left, that handing over her burden for a time had been too comforting a prospect to resist.

Well, her energy had been restored, and it was time to reclaim ownership of the situation. Meredith stepped away from the bed, determination subduing her dizziness as she tottered across the room. Her heart might have fluttered at the thought of Travis becoming her husband, but what woman wanted her man forced to the altar? No. She'd have to find another way to deal with this mess.

As she reached the doorway, another thought brought her up short. If she didn't marry an Archer, would Uncle Everett make her marry Roy? Meredith inhaled a shaky breath and leaned her back against the wall.

If Roy coveted her land half as much as she thought he did, he'd waste no time convincing Uncle Everett that her sullied reputation meant nothing to him. He'd probably even offer to marry in all haste to minimize the scandal, further endearing himself to her aunt and uncle and blinding them to his true nature — a wolf hiding beneath a fancy wool overcoat.

Aunt Noreen would insist the marriage take place, and if Meredith proved incapable of swaying Uncle Everett from that course — a most likely prospect — she'd have no recourse but to flee. Away from Roy Mitchell's schemes. Away from her aunt's controlling ways. A lump lodged itself in her throat. Away from Travis.

A dull ache spread across her chest. All her life she'd dreamed of marrying Travis Archer. But he wasn't a dream. Not anymore. He was flesh and blood and just down the hall. Could she really give him up when he was finally within reach?

Travis hunkered down next to the broom and broke off a handful of straw from an already frayed edge. After selecting the pieces most similar in length — and tucking one of them inside the cuff of his sleeve — he strode back to the table.

"Everyone's agreed that this will settle the matter, correct?" Travis eyed his brothers and waited for each of them to nod. "Good." He tossed four pieces of straw onto the table. "Crockett, shorten one of the straws."

Crockett snapped about an inch off the end of one of the straws and tossed the leftover piece onto the floor. Then before anyone else could volunteer for the duty, Travis snatched the straws up and turned his back.

He arranged the straws in his fist, making sure each end stood at a height equal to the others. But instead of including the short straw, he withdrew the fourth long straw from his shirt sleeve and added it to the mix. A pang of guilt shot through him. He'd always demanded honesty from his brothers and never gave them anything less than that himself. Until now.

Not wanting to examine his motives too closely, Travis shoved the short straw into his sleeve and told himself what he was doing was for the good of the family. Then, with a deep breath, he spun around to face his brothers.

"All right. Who's first?"

Neill reached out a hand. "Here goes nothing." He closed his eyes and grabbed. When he spied the long straw, a crooked smile twitched across his face an instant before a more solemn expression crowded it out. "Well, it ain't gonna be me, fellas."

Travis's guilt eased at the boy's obvious

relief. He swiveled toward Jim next, and when he, too, pulled out a long straw, there was no indication of strong feelings one way or the other. He simply waggled his brows at Crockett and Travis, then propped a foot on the seat of his chair and leaned an elbow on his knee.

"Guess it's you or me, Crock." Travis extended the final two straws to his eldest brother, tightening his grip to ensure the fourth straw didn't escape when the third one was tugged free.

Crockett eyed both options and frowned a bit in concentration. Travis had to focus to keep his hand steady. Was Crock trying to pick the short one or the long one? Did he actually have feelings for Meredith? His offer to marry the gal earlier had seemed practical, not personal. But what if there was more to it than that?

Travis clenched his jaw, his thoughts growing defiant. What if there *was* more to it? Crock didn't share a history with Meredith, and he sure as shootin' wasn't the guy Meri had said she'd dreamed about.

"Loosen your grip, Trav," Crockett said, breaking into his thoughts. "I can't pull my straw out."

Heat climbed up Travis's neck. "Sorry."

Crockett shook his head and grinned as

he pulled the third straw free, but his smile faded as he examined his piece. "It's a long one."

"Guess that means Travis gets her," Neill proclaimed.

Crockett grasped Travis's wrist. "Let's see the straw first."

Panic shot through Travis. How was he going to make the switch? He needed a distraction — something unexpected, something . . .

"You're drawing *straws?*" Meredith stepped into the kitchen, her nightgown swirling about her ankles, her hair mussed, her eyes shooting blue fire.

Every male eye in the room locked onto the honey-haired virago. Travis had no idea how many seconds ticked by before he realized that Crockett's hand had fallen away. He quickly dropped the long straw, scraped his boot over it, and sent it skittering back toward the wall as he shook the short one down into his cupped palm.

When he looked back up, her anger pierced him. However, it was the hurt hiding behind the sparks in her eyes that made his heart ache. "Meredith, I —"

"Four grown men put their heads together," she said, cutting him off as she reached to the wall for support, "and *this* is

174

the solution you come up with? *Drawing straws?*"

"Jim wanted to arm wrestle — *oomph.*" Neill's explanation died as Jim's elbow connected with the kid's stomach.

Meredith speared the two of them with a quick glare, then dropped her hand to her side and stalked toward Travis. Crockett sidled out of range.

"So this is how you see to things, is it? How diplomatic of you to leave my future in the hands of chance. I'm surprised you didn't throw an extra straw in the mix for Roy Mitchell. Might as well give him a shot, too. But then he'd have my land, which would increase his determination to get his hands on yours in order to complete his enterprise, and you couldn't allow that. After all, the land always comes first with you. Isn't that right, Travis? The land and your brothers."

Somehow Travis managed not to flinch under the barrage of sarcasm. He held her gaze until she finally dropped her eyes from his face to someplace lower. Her hand closed over his. A shiver of pleasure mixed with dread snaked up his arm. She drew his fist up between them and gently extracted the short straw from his grasp.

"The land and your brothers," she repeated softly. "Of course you drew the short straw. How else could you spare your brothers from the burden of being shackled to me?"

"It's not like that, Meri." Travis reached for her hand, but she pulled it away the instant his fingers grazed her knuckles.

"I expected better from you, Travis." Her words hacked into him like an ax in a tree trunk, and he swayed a bit from the impact. The trust he'd grown accustomed to seeing in her eyes had dimmed to disappointment.

"I expected better from all of you." She stepped back, creating an invisible chasm between her and the men who had let her down. "Did it never occur to you that I might actually want some say in my future? Or did you assume I would meekly accept whatever the four of you decided and thank you for lifting the heavy burden of thinking for myself off my weak female shoulders?"

Silence smothered the room.

Travis swallowed the excuses he'd been feeding himself — the fact that she'd been asleep, that she was under his protection, that she'd seemed to welcome his assistance when he'd promised to see to things for her.

He knew what it felt like to have fate decide your future. If he had stayed home and watched over his brothers like his father

176

had told him to that day fourteen years ago, he never would have been caught in a thunderstorm. And if his father hadn't gone searching for him, he never would have been thrown from his horse when the lightning stuck. And if his father hadn't been thrown, he never would have incurred the wounds that led to his death.

Travis fidgeted as old guilt erupted to mingle with new.

Joseph Archer had extracted an oath from his son that day. An oath borne of desperation and a desire to protect the sons he was leaving behind. An oath that placed a heavy burden on the thin shoulders of a fifteen-year-old boy. But that boy took it on without complaint. Travis's dreams and plans no longer mattered. He had to atone for the damage his disobedience had caused. Guarding Archer land and the Archer family became his sole duty — his road to redemption.

Meredith's situation, however, had no root in disobedience. It was kindness alone that set her on this path. Unlike him, she didn't deserve to have her future wrested from her hands.

"You're right, Meredith." Travis shifted his weight and forced himself to meet her gaze. "We should have waited and discussed the matter with you."

"Yes. You should have."

"Would you like to discuss things now?" He held out his palms and took a cautious step forward.

"I'm not a spooked horse that needs to be placated." Her dry tone halted him in his tracks. He lowered his hands, a reluctant grin curving his lips.

He *had* been approaching her that way, hadn't he? Funny that he'd failed to recognize it until she called him on it. The gal was perceptive. And intelligent. Perhaps it was time to take the kid gloves off and treat her as he would one of his brothers.

Travis leaned his hip against the corner of the table. "All right, Meredith. No placating. No sugarcoating. Here's where we stand."

She crossed her arms and braced her legs apart like a warrior willing to talk peace while still prepared to battle should talk prove ineffectual. With an arched brow, she nodded for him to continue.

Travis ticked off his arguments on his fingers. "Your reputation is tattered. You have no home except for a house on a piece of land that Mitchell will do anything to get his hands on. You can marry Mitchell and live the rest of your life with a man you despise, or you can refuse his suit and see what vile scheme he concocts to steal your land from you. He could burn you out like he tried to do with us, or he could compromise you in order to force you to the altar. No matter how capable or careful you are, a woman alone has little chance against a man like him."

Meredith kept her head high and her face schooled, but the fabric around her knees wavered. Travis grabbed two chairs. Whether it was trepidation or her injury that was causing her to tremble, he didn't know. But he wasn't about to let her fall to the ground. He set one chair beside her and turned the other around and straddled it. Then he continued his assessment as if it didn't matter to him if she sat or not.

"Your only other option is to marry one of us." He paused. "Me." Travis suddenly felt the need to clear his throat. "This alternative would repair your reputation, give you a place to live, and provide the protection of four able-bodied men. Unless you have something else to suggest . . . ?"

"Actually, there is something else." Her quiet statement startled him.

"There is?" He glanced over at Crockett. His brother shrugged.

Meredith slowly lowered herself into the

straight-back chair, the fight draining from her. "I could leave Anderson County. I could go farther west to where the railroad is opening new towns, or head to a larger city where no one knows me." Her chin jutted upward. "I could find work. Make a clean start."

Leave Anderson County? Travis frowned. He hadn't considered that option. Didn't really want to, either. It was reckless. Dangerous. And for some odd reason . . . disappointing. Besides, he'd already settled his mind on this marrying business. No sense muddying the waters.

"You're a good man, Travis. An honorable man." Meredith plucked at her sleeve. "You drew the short straw, and you're willing to stand before a preacher because you feel responsible for me. But you're not. I made the decision to come here, and I'll deal with the consequences. You deserve to have a wife of your own choosing, not one forced on you through circumstances outside your control."

"It's not like that, Meredith. It's . . ." Travis sighed and rubbed his jaw. Why did she say nothing about what *she* deserved? He didn't know much about the workings of the female mind, but he knew one thing — she deserved a choice.

"I'm not going to force you, Meredith. If you believe leaving is the best option, I'll not stop you. But if you think you might be able to make a home for yourself here, with a bunch of unrefined men, we'd like you to stay. *I'd* like you to stay."

Stretching his hand across the space that separated them, he caressed her cheek with his knuckles, then let his arm fall away. "You're a fine woman, Meredith Hayes. You're strong and brave and kind. And should you decide to take a chance on me, I'd be honored to make you my bride."

14

Meredith gripped the edge of the chair seat with her left hand as a new light-headedness assaulted her. Travis Archer had just proposed. Really proposed. Sure, he'd made no mention of love, but he had only been in her company for three days — four if she counted the day she stepped in that trap twelve years ago. The man needed time to catch up. After all, she'd been in love with him since she was ten. She had a bit of a head start.

But did he really want her? What if his pretty words were just flattery? Travis didn't strike her as the manipulative type, yet if she agreed to marry him, she'd be risking her entire future on an idealized impression. What if she was wrong?

"Meredith?"

She blinked and refocused on the man in front of her. The man who could be her husband if she gave the word. The man she wanted more than any other. The man who could hurt her more than any other.

She bit her lip and glanced at the other Archers spaced about the room. All eyes lingered on her. Waiting. Leaving the decision in her hands.

How was she supposed to know what to do? If she married Travis and he never returned her feelings, she'd be miserable for the rest of her life. But if she ran away when there *was* a chance for her and Travis to find love together, she'd be running away from her greatest hope.

"Meri? Are you all right?" Travis's rugged features softened in concern. He lifted his hand as if to touch her cheek again, and Meredith bolted out of her chair. Out of his reach. Her head throbbed at the sudden movement, and the floor seemed to roll beneath her feet, but she couldn't let him touch her again. His tenderness would cloud her judgment.

Recalling how Travis had extricated himself from her uncle earlier in the day, Meredith took a shaky step backward and employed the same tactic. "I'll give you my decision in the morning."

Travis's eyes met hers for a long penetrating moment. Then he nodded. "Fair enough."

He didn't offer to see her to her room, and though a small part of her was disappointed, a larger part was grateful. He seemed to sense her need to exert what little control she had over her situation and respected her choice to do so.

She limped back to her bedroom, the air taking on more of a chill the farther she moved from the kitchen. Logic said it was the loss of the cookstove's heat, but Meredith feared it had more to do with walking away from Travis.

A solitary tear rolled down her cheek as she closed the door. She leaned her back against it and sucked in a quivery breath. Why was this happening to her? How had things become so complicated? All she'd wanted to do was help Travis, yet instead, she'd trapped him — trapped him in his own honor, an honor more ironclad than the steel trap that had closed around her leg all those years ago.

She should grant him his freedom. Just as he had freed her from the steel jaws of that trap, she should free him from his self-imposed responsibility.

Stiffening her spine and her resolve, Meredith marched across the room to the bed. But when her hand closed around the bedpost and she sank down to the mattress, both her spine and her resolve weakened. She opened her right fist and stared at the short straw in her palm. Out of all the brothers, Travis had ended up with the short straw. Was it a sign that she should stay? God's will?

Meredith pressed her forehead against the curved wood of the bedpost and groaned. Why did the choice have to be so hard? Why couldn't God make his will simpler to discern?

"Seek the Lord, and his strength."

Meredith lifted her head. Those words. They were from one of the Psalms her father had helped her memorize as a child.

"Seek the Lord, and his strength."

They ran through her mind again, eclipsing all other thought, resonating with her soul. The answer to her immediate dilemma remained as murky as before, yet a new clarity emerged. She'd been seeking answers within herself, not from the Lord.

No wonder none of this makes sense, God. Only you can see what the future holds. Therefore, only you can guide me in the direction that is best. Please make the way clear. Help me make the right decision.

Meredith tightened her grip on the bedpost and hoisted herself back to her feet. Travis had mentioned something about a

Bible he kept in his bureau when he brought her that book of western tales yesterday — in case she preferred it to the male adventure novel. She hadn't thought much of it since, but suddenly her spirit hungered for the wisdom it contained.

She found it in the second drawer she opened, next to a mahogany keepsake box. The black leather cover was well worn, with cracks running parallel to the spine and part of the gold lettering rubbed away from the bottom of the *H* in *Holy.* It fit comfortably in her hand, as if it belonged there, and for the first time since she'd awakened, a hint of peace fluttered about her heart. It didn't fully alight, but its nearness brought her a much-needed assurance that she was on the right path.

Clutching the Bible to her chest, Meredith petitioned the Lord again for guidance and understanding, then crawled onto the bed, propped the pillows against the headboard, and settled in for a long night of prayer and searching. Whenever a verse tugged at her memory, she'd look through the Scriptures until she found it. She'd read it and reread it, trying not to form conclusions but simply absorb what God's Word was saying. On several occasions, she dozed off in the midst of a prayer, yet when she stirred, her fingers still marked the passages the Lord had led her to. As the first hint of dawn lightened the room, she read back over the verses she had marked.

"Be kindly affectioned one to another with brotherly love; in honour preferring one another . . . Distributing to the necessity of saints; given to hospitality."

She flipped from Romans to Hebrews.

"And let us consider one another to provoke unto love and to good works: not forsaking the assembling of ourselves together, as the manner of some is; but exhorting one another. . . ."

Meredith turned a couple of pages to the next passage. *"Let brotherly love continue. Be not forgetful to entertain strangers: for thereby some have entertained angels unawares."*

And finally, the verses from First Peter that filled her with purpose. *"Likewise, ye wives, be in subjection to your own husbands; that, if any obey not the word, they also may without the word be won by the conversation of the wives."*

Over the course of the night, a growing sense of certainty had blossomed within her as she meditated on the verses the Lord had led her to. A thread of similarity ran through them all — a theme of service, of love, of hospitality. She had thought her decision hinged on what was best for her, but as the approaching sunrise tinted the sky with pink, she finally understood that, in truth, it hinged on what best fit in with God's plan. A God who was faithful, a God who desired his children to serve one another in love and to spur one another on to good works, a God who could use a wife to gently sway a husband to a life of greater faith.

Even when sleep claimed her during the night, she'd dreamed in images and ideas. The Archers imprisoned on their own land. The sign at the gate threatening away all visitors. Loneliness. Isolation. *"Love thy neighbour."*

She'd found no promises of any love more than brotherly love. She'd found no assurance of happiness beyond the joy inherently found in hope. But what she had found was purpose and a belief that God could work through her to bring about good for Travis. And the rightness of it resonated in her soul.

Meredith turned the pages back to Romans, to where she had placed Travis's short straw as a marker. Once again she read the precious promise written in the eighth chapter. *"And we know that all things work together for good to them that love God, to them who are the called according to his purpose."*

She inhaled deeply through her nose, and her eyes slid closed. "I don't know if Travis will ever love me, but I pray you will help me to trust in your promise, Lord. Help me to believe that you will work things out for our good so that I will not fall prey to bitterness or discontent. I'm leaping, Lord. Please don't let me fall."

Exhausted from the long night, yet oddly invigorated at the same time, Meredith climbed out of bed and padded over to the window to watch the sunrise brighten the trees. The dull ache in her head reminded her of her injury, but the floor respectfully stayed put instead of rising and falling as it had yesterday. She smiled and silently thanked God for small blessings. It wouldn't do for the bride to stagger around like a drunkard on her wedding day.

Travis stared at his jawline in the small square of mirror that hung in the bathing room and drew the straight razor down his cheek. He winced as the blade nicked the edge of his ear. Adjusting his grip, he rinsed the shaving soap from the razor and reached up for another stroke. His fingers trembled. Travis frowned. A lack of sleep combined with a prolonged sense of uncertainty had stolen his usual steadiness.

How was a man supposed to prepare for his wedding day when he didn't even know if the bride was going to show up? Not that he blamed Meredith for her indecision. A person needed time to settle something this big in her mind. It was just that he was accustomed to being the one who did the settling. He gathered input from his brothers, chewed over the ramifications, rendered a verdict, and put it into action. Simple. Direct. Practical.

Meredith, on the other hand, left him stuck in the chewing phase while she mulled through her problem without his assistance. He'd been tempted more than once to knock on her door and ask if she'd reached any conclusions, but good sense had prevailed and he'd left her alone. Now that the sun had crested the horizon and it was officially morning, however, the desire to know his fate had him back on edge.

The razor snagged a spot on his chin, and Travis scowled as a drop of blood beaded on his jaw. *Great.* With the way things were going, he'd end up with enough scratches on his face to have Meredith thinking one of the displaced barn cats had mistaken him for a mouse. Not exactly the impression one wanted to make on a woman who had yet to make up her mind concerning his worthiness as a mate. He'd dug himself into a deep enough hole last night without inviting more unfavorable scrutiny this morning.

"Coffee's on," Jim growled in a sleep-roughened voice as he plodded through the bathing room, the wire egg basket dangling from his meaty fingers.

Travis had never really noticed how incongruous a picture the big man made carrying the thin basket, since Jim had been in charge of all food chores and cooking duties since the time he was ten. But as Travis held his razor away from his neck and watched his brother exit, he couldn't help imagining what it would be like to have Meredith squeeze past him with the basket, her skirt brushing his pant leg, maybe a smile curving her lips as their eyes met in the shaving mirror.

The sting of the blade biting into his neck brought him back to reality. "Thunderation!" He hadn't been this clumsy with a shave since he was Neill's age.

"Nervous, Trav?" Crockett stood in the doorway, one shoulder propped against the jamb. The fellow looked far too well rested and chipper for Travis's taste, and the teasing gleam in his brother's eye rubbed over him like sandpaper.

"Worried she'll turn you down, or afraid

she won't?"

Travis glared at him in the mirror and swiped the razor under his chin for the final stroke. Ignoring the quiet chuckle behind him, Travis set the blade aside and rinsed the soap residue from his face before toweling dry. If he was lucky, Crockett would be gone by the time he finished.

He lowered the towel from his face and stole a glance toward the door. *Drat.* Luck never had favored him much.

"You know, I could stand in for you if you're not up to the task."

The words lit a fuse in Travis. He twisted to face his brother fully and jabbed his finger into Crockett's chest. "Leave it alone."

Tossing down the towel, he shoved his way through the blocked doorway and stormed over to the stove to check the coffee. As he reached into the cupboard to retrieve a mug, however, his conscience nudged him. Taking the cup in hand, he slowly reined in his temper. After a long moment, he reached for a second mug.

Travis poured two cups of coffee and motioned for Crockett to join him at the table. "Sorry I snapped at you."

Crockett shrugged and slid into a chair. "I

knew the spot would be sore when I prodded it."

Travis shot a glare at him. "Then why'd you bring it up? For pete's sake, Crock, we're in enough of a mess without you stirring up more trouble. The matter's been decided. If Meredith chooses to marry, she'll marry me. That's the end of it."

Instead of firing back, Crockett stared at him over his coffee cup as he sipped the steaming brew. The silent survey lasted so long, Travis grew uncomfortable and finally dropped his gaze, suddenly finding it imperative that he unroll his shirtsleeves and fasten the button at each cuff.

The sound of Crockett's mug coming to rest on the tabletop brought Travis's head back up. The sparkle he was accustomed to seeing in his brother's eye glowed once again.

"I needed to be sure Meredith was marrying the right Archer."

Travis raised a brow. "And?"

Crockett smirked and lifted his cup to his lips. "Let's just say my concerns have been addressed."

15

Meredith twisted from side to side, examining her appearance in the mirror above Travis's bureau. Some bride she made, dressed in faded calico. In her dreams, she'd always worn blue brocaded satin with lace at the neckline and cuffs. She'd imagined her hair done up in an elaborate style. Perhaps a pearl comb or a spray of tiny flowers tucked into her tresses, depending on the time of year.

But with over half of her hairpins missing following her run-in with Samson, the best she'd managed was a braided chignon low on her nape. Her bangs had lost most of their curl and frizzed a bit at her forehead. She wound a strand around her finger, counted to fifty, and released it, but the rebellious ringlet failed to hold its curl. Huffing out a breath that sent all her bangs fluttering, Meredith smoothed a hand over her tremulous stomach and lifted her chin.

So what if this wasn't to be the wedding of her dreams. She was marrying the *man* of her dreams. That would be enough. Besides, a wedding was only an event. It was the life together following it that truly mattered. *Grow up, Meri. It's time to start putting sensibility ahead of sentimentality.*

Her shoulders sagged a bit as she examined the worn navy housedress hanging from her frame in all its wrinkled glory. *Was it too sentimental to wish for a prettier dress to wear?* She sighed. At least it didn't smell like smoke. The green dress she'd worn the night of the fire stank of the stuff, and she worried she might not be able to get all the soot stains out. One thing was for sure — when she took over the cleaning duties around here, laundry was going to top her list.

A knock sounded on the door. The butterflies she'd willed into submission earlier burst forth in a flurry of batting wings.

"Meri?" Travis's voice. "Your breakfast is ready."

"Thank you. I'll . . . I'll be right there." She spun away from the mirror and gripped the bedpost a final time, more to steady her nerves than her feet. Closing her eyes, she mentally recited her version of the promise of Romans 8:28. *"All things* will *work together for good. All things* will *work together for* *good."*

Then, with a lift of her chin, she opened her eyes and strode to the door. She grasped the handle and pulled, only to find Travis waiting for her. He straightened from where he'd rested his back against the opposite wall, his widening eyes traversing from her face, down the length of her, and back up to her eyes. When his gaze connected with hers, the flare of male appreciation he failed to tame sent warm tingles skittering over her skin before he hid it behind a look of apology.

Meredith felt a blush warm her cheeks, but oddly enough, she felt no need for his apology. If anything, the look he'd given offered hope that, in time, there might be more than a relationship of duty between them.

"You're looking . . . better this morning," he said, breaking the silence at last. "How's your head?"

Meredith suddenly found it hard to hold his gaze. Her attention slid to the floor as she fidgeted with the edge of her sleeve. What was wrong with her? She'd been staring at the man just fine while he gawked at her, but now that he offered polite conversation, she turned into a mess of jumbled nerves. Really. It was too ridiculous.

She coughed softly and forced her chin up. "The dizziness is gone, so long as I don't move too quickly, and except for a dull ache behind my ear, my head is much improved." Darting a glance into his brownish-green eyes, she added, "Thank you for asking."

He smiled, then looked at the wall behind her. "I'm glad to hear it."

Now he was the one fidgeting. Meredith nearly giggled as the sole of his boot scraped back and forth over the floorboards. And what were those red marks along his jaw? The poor man looked like he'd been in a tussle with an angry chicken. She thought of one of her mother's laying hens that always used to peck at Meredith's hand. She'd been terrified of that bird until the day Mama finally tired of its antics and served it up for supper. Meri had never taken more delight in stabbing a knife into a chicken thigh than she had that night. Perhaps she ought to add roasted chicken to the Archers' menu this week.

"Did you . . . ah . . . arrive at any conclusions during the night?" Travis asked, lifting a hand to cover the red spot on his neck.

The chickens roosting in Meredith's mind vanished.

"I did." She fortified herself to look at him

and waited until his eyes touched hers to continue. "If your offer still stands, Travis . . . I accept."

She sensed him sigh, even though no sound or movement evidenced such an event. And while she wouldn't necessarily describe his demeanor as overjoyed, the way his mouth curved up at one corner combined with the slight crinkling around his eyes communicated a positive reaction to her response that stretched beyond mere politeness.

"Good." He nodded once and gestured for her to continue on to the kitchen. "Jim held back some eggs for you in the skillet, and if Neill didn't get to it first, you might be able to scrounge up a scrap of ham, too. I'm gonna round up some clean clothes while you eat." Travis pointed to her room and headed that direction.

Well, technically it was *his* room. Although after spending so much time there the last few days, it felt like hers. Meredith crossed into the kitchen and picked up the empty plate that sat waiting for her on the table. When her hand closed over the spoon handle to ladle up what was left of the scrambled eggs, however, a new thought froze her where she stood.

Would it be *their* room tonight?

Meredith blinked and reminded herself to breathe as she scraped the last of the eggs and a tiny square of ham onto her plate. Somehow coffee ended up in her cup and her rear ended up in a chair, despite the fact that she had no recollection of accomplishing those tasks herself. As she bent her head to pray, thankfulness for her breakfast didn't even cross her mind.

Lord, I'm not sure I'm ready to be a wife. It seems a lot more daunting now that it's staring me in the face. I thought I was prepared, that my affection for Travis would make things easier, but all those lovely daydreams seem so juvenile in light of what is truly to come. Please don't let me embarrass myself. Give me the courage to be the wife he needs.

As she chewed the lukewarm, overdone eggs, Meredith vowed to be like the biblical woman Rebekah. If she could enter Isaac's tent on the first day they met and become his wife, surely Meredith could manage the same feat after knowing Travis three times as long.

Although . . . Rebekah had ended up with twins.

The square of ham she'd just swallowed lodged itself sideways in her throat. Meredith grabbed her coffee cup and gulped down a swig of the strong, bitter brew in an effort to keep from choking.

Good heavens. Contemplating the realities of life with a husband was frightening enough. Motherhood could wait a bit.

At least she didn't have to worry about facing Travis's brothers yet. Meredith eyed the mound of dishes waiting for her in the washtub with a wry quirk of her lips. It seemed they'd already abandoned the house to her care. Either that or it was their custom to save the dish washing till the end of the day.

Maybe they drew straws for that duty, too.

Travis yanked on the too-short sleeves of his father's old suit coat and scrunched his shoulders for fear of tearing out the back seam. His dad had always been such a large figure in his mind, Travis never imagined that his coat wouldn't fit. The thing was as old as the hills and musty as month-old bread, but it was the only decent suit coat in the house. Travis and his brothers certainly had no need for fancy duds, living the way they did. Or they hadn't until today.

So much for dressing for the occasion. Travis shrugged out of the coat and returned it to the bottom drawer of his bureau, where it would probably sit unused for another couple of decades. At least he had a clean shirt to wear. Of course, it was the scratchy white cotton one that always made his neck itch, but it was probably more appropriate wedding attire than the dark brown flannel he usually wore. And he could dress it up with his dad's black string tie — the one part of the suit guaranteed to fit.

Travis took out his mother's keepsake box and ran his hand over the rose pattern carved into the top of the mahogany lid. After seventeen years without her, his memories had faded. He remembered her smile, the way her arms felt around him when she hugged him in the morning before sending him off to school, the way she fussed at him for tracking mud into the house. But he couldn't recall the particular sound of her voice, or the precise color of her eyes. He thought they might have been green, but perhaps they'd been more brown, like his.

What would she think of his marriage? Would she approve? He didn't doubt that she'd like Meredith. Mama had always been a fighter, even at the end when the childbed fever finally claimed her life. Meredith possessed the same quality, in spades.

Travis opened the mahogany box and fingered the hodgepodge within. His father's watch, a packet of old letters, the three-legged dog he'd whittled for her one Christmas. Then his hand closed over the slender band he'd sought. Plain and not as shiny as he would have liked, yet the ring warmed his palm as if the love his parents shared still radiated from within its circle.

He didn't have a proper suit of clothes or a white clapboard church to offer, but his bride would have a ring — a ring representing all he hoped their relationship would one day become.

Before closing the box, he snatched the black ribbon that wove in and out of the treasures and strung it through the center of the ring. After knotting the ends of the tie securely around the gold band, he shoved both objects deep into his trouser pocket. With his father's tie and his mother's ring on hand, he'd be ready whenever Mr. Hayes showed up with the parson. In the meantime, he had work to do.

Travis slid his brown wool vest over the scratchy cotton shirt, wincing as the stiff material pressed against his back. He did up the buttons and grabbed his hat, catching a glimpse of himself in the mirror as he turned for the door.

Meredith wasn't getting much of a prize in their arrangement. Travis frowned at his razor-nicked face and saddle-bum clothes and thought about how pretty she'd looked stepping out of his room with her hair done up and her eyes glowing shyly at him. Seeing her only in a shapeless sleeping gown the last couple of days, he'd nearly forgotten what nice curves she had. The faded dress she wore with its snug bodice and trim waist brought all those memories rushing back.

Meredith Hayes was a fine specimen of a woman. And sometime later today, she was going to be his.

A rogue with a devilish grin stared back at him from the mirror. Travis winked at his reflection, settled his hat into place, and fought the urge to whistle as he headed outside to tend to his chores.

Roughly two hours later, before the sun hung fully overhead, the expected sound of gunfire ricocheted through the pines. Travis looked up from the pile of scorched tack he'd been sorting through, his gut suddenly knotting. *This is it.*

The banging over by the shed where the boys were reinforcing the lean-to halted. Neill and Jim emerged from the west side, hammers moving from right hand to left as they reached for their gun belts. Even knowing who their guest would be, they were ready for any trouble that might be riding shotgun. Travis straightened, pride infusing his stance. His brothers were competent men — Archers through and through. Whatever came through that gate, they'd handle together.

And it was a good thing, for when Crockett finally rode into view leading their guests, Travis noted that the wagon Everett Hayes drove carried a passenger who bore little resemblance to a preacher. Jim's indrawn breath echoed loudly in Travis's ear, and one glance at the dazed look on his brother's usually stoic face confirmed that trouble had indeed ridden shotgun — and their normal defense tactics would be useless.

16

The minute Everett Hayes reined in his team and set the wagon brake, the young gal at his side shot to her feet and grabbed a handful of pink skirt as if she meant to leap to the ground then and there. Travis had never seen Jim move so fast. Usually the deliberate one of the bunch, Jim's movements blurred as he holstered his weapon and dropped his hammer to the dirt, all while hustling toward the wagon before the pretty little blonde could alight on her own.

"Why, thank you," she said as she rested her hands on Jim's shoulders and allowed him to lift her to the ground. She beamed a smile at him that must have blinded the poor fellow, for all Jim could do was blink at her after he set her down. "Are you Travis?"

Jim's head wagged slowly in the negative, his eyes never leaving her face.

Travis's eyes rolled in a sardonic arc at his

brother's absorption while he strode forward. Apparently an introduction was beyond Jim's abilities at the moment. He lifted a finger to his hat brim when he reached Jim's side and nodded to the petite lady with the china-doll face. "I'm Travis, ma'am. Travis Archer."

She examined his face and glanced over the rest of him, yet her inspection held such innocence, he couldn't exactly call her bold. Curious was probably a more apt description.

"A pleasure to meet you, sir. I'm Cassandra Hayes, Meredith's cousin." She turned one of those glaringly bright smiles loose on him, but his vision remained unaffected.

Oh, she was pretty all right, and there was something about the joy inherent in those smiles that made a man want to hang around and see how many he could draw out of her, but nothing significant stirred in Travis when she turned the full force of her sky-blue eyes on him. They were pale compared to the vibrancy of Meri's and didn't evidence the same depth of living.

"You *are* going to marry my cousin, aren't you?"

The young lady was certainly direct. Travis grinned and scratched a spot on his jaw with the back of his thumb.

"Cassie, dear," Everett Hayes murmured as he moved around the horses to position himself between his daughter and the Archer brothers. "We wouldn't have brought the preacher with us if there wasn't going to be a wedding."

Travis glanced past the pair in front of him to see Crockett talking quite animatedly to an older man climbing down from the back of a mule.

"Yes, Papa, but you only said she was marrying an Archer. You didn't specify which one."

When Jim continued staring at Cassandra, Everett Hayes scowled a warning at him, then took his daughter's arm and tugged her close to his side before smiling at her in a way that was so indulgent it bordered on condescending.

"It doesn't matter which one, darling. All that matters is that she marry."

Cassandra pulled her hand free and stared up at her father, tiny lines creasing her porcelain brow. "How can you say that, Papa? Of course it matters. Meredith has to marry Travis."

Everett's smile flattened. "Why?"

Travis tilted his head, eager to hear the answer himself. But before Cassandra could say anything, another voice rang out from the porch.

"Cassie?"

The distance did little to disguise the wonder on Meredith's face — wonder that quickly transformed into happiness so radiant that Travis wished he'd been the one responsible for it. Then she let out a little squeal and charged down the steps as if she hadn't just spent two days in bed after being kicked in the head by a mule.

Her cousin broke away from Everett and ran to meet Meredith, surprisingly unconcerned about the hem of her pretty pink dress dragging in the dirt. The two women embraced, and at once, Travis recognized the bond between them. Meredith loved her cousin the way he loved his brothers.

"How did you ever convince Aunt Noreen to let you come?" Meredith asked as she gently untangled herself from the embrace.

"I didn't ask." Cassandra waved away Meredith's arched look. "She never would have agreed, so there was no point."

"But she'll be livid about you exposing yourself to the scandal of the situation."

"I'm here with my father and a man of the cloth — surely that will protect me from any imagined taint. I couldn't miss your wedding. Not after all we've shared. I would have rented a horse and ridden here unescorted if I'd had to."

Meredith laughed softly. "You? On a horse? That would've been something to see."

Cassandra pulled a face and shuddered. "A horrendous sight, I'm sure. But I would have done it had Papa not relented and allowed me to join him in the wagon."

Travis's impression of the little princess bumped up a couple of notches. Perhaps there was a woman of character behind all the flirtatious smiles, after all. But the quick glance she darted toward Jim before linking her arm through Meredith's left no doubt that her being here still spelled trouble.

"The first thing we have to do," she said, as she steered Meredith toward the house, "is find you a different dress. You can't get married in that old thing."

"But I don't have —"

"Yes you do. I packed your trunks." Cassandra paused long enough to toss a softly pleading look Jim's way. "If one of these strong Archer men would be kind enough to bring them inside for us?"

In answer, Jim strode to the back of the wagon. Travis followed. It was only fitting that he help cart his future wife's belongings. Crockett could deal with Everett

Hayes and the preacher.

The women left the front door ajar behind them, and when he and Jim entered the house, the aroma of cinnamon and baking swirled around them. Jim twisted toward the kitchen and raised an eyebrow but didn't pause on his way down the hall. Travis, on the other hand, took a moment to breathe in the delicious scent. He hadn't smelled anything like it since his mother passed on.

Cassandra was showing Jim where to set the first trunk when Travis arrived at the bedroom, so he took the opportunity to sidle up next to Meredith. "What're you baking?"

"Cinnamon rolls. They just came out of the oven." She dipped her chin as if embarrassed, although about what he couldn't figure. "I hope you don't mind. I know it probably seems silly considering the unusual circumstances surrounding the wedding, but I thought it would be nice to have some way to mark the occasion. You didn't have much sugar left, so I decided against a cake. I found a tin of cinnamon buried behind the coffee and thought sweet rolls might be an acceptable substitute."

He grinned. "I can't wait to taste them."

She smiled back, and a little frisson of

pleasure coursed through him. Reluctantly, he stepped away and pulled the trunk off his shoulder to place it against the wall next to the one Jim had brought in. Travis turned back to Meredith, but before he could continue their conversation, Cassandra maneuvered between them and expertly shooed him out of his own room.

"Thank you, gentlemen. Why don't you show my father around while I help Meredith change?"

She closed the door before Travis could answer, which was probably for the best, since she was bound to dislike his response. There was no way he'd be showing Everett Hayes anything on his land except maybe the charred shell of his barn. The man was in business with Mitchell, and despite the ties he had to Meredith, he was the enemy.

"I have a surprise for you." Cassandra released the door handle and spun to face Meredith, her eyes glowing with secret glee. "Come see."

Meredith's tummy fluttered in anticipation as she followed in Cassandra's wake. Her cousin unbuckled the straps of the first trunk and threw open the lid with a flourish. "It's polished muslin instead of satin brocade, but it's blue and there's plenty of lace. What do you think?"

She twirled around, an Egyptian blue-and-ivory-striped gown pressed to her torso.

Tears welled in Meredith's eyes. "You're letting me borrow your courting dress?" Aunt Noreen had commissioned that dress from a local seamstress, and to the best of Meredith's recollection, Cassie had only worn it once.

"No, I'm giving it to you. Consider it a wedding gift. I let out the hem last night, so it shouldn't be too short." She slid an arm under the skirt and held it out for Meredith's inspection. "My stitches aren't quite as fine as the dressmaker's, but no one will be looking at your feet."

"Oh, Cass. It's b-beautiful." She barely got the words out before a sob lodged in her throat and cut off her ability to communicate.

Cassandra laid the dress on the bed and rushed to Meredith's side. "Now, don't start crying," her cousin admonished in a teasing voice. "You don't want your eyes to be all red and puffy when you exchange your vows with Travis." She reached into the pocket of her skirt and retrieved a handkerchief, then paused with her hand only half extended. "You *are* marrying Travis, aren't you?"

Meredith nodded vigorously as she wiped

her cheeks with the back of her hand.

Cassandra let out a hearty sigh and handed her the lacy handkerchief. "Good. For a minute there, you had me worried."

Meredith dabbed her eyes and blew her nose before setting the soiled handkerchief aside and lifting her chin. Cassie was right. Travis wouldn't want to see her all red-eyed and weepy. He'd told her he admired her courage and fortitude. He wouldn't want a maudlin bride. She drew in a deep breath and squared her shoulders.

Cassandra nodded her approval and gave her a gentle push toward the bed, where the dress lay. "Now, let's get you changed."

Meredith smiled at her cousin as she reached for the buttons at her neck. "So, dear fairy godmother, did you bring me glass slippers, too?"

Cassandra laughed. "Didn't you hear? Glass slippers went out of fashion last century. All the fairy godmothers are providing kid leather nowadays." She knelt down by the trunk again and rummaged around until she finally pulled out Meredith's Sunday button-up heels. "See?"

The two giggled just like they had as girls huddled together on Cassie's bed, reading Perrault's tale of *Cinderella*. Meredith's worries floated away on the laughter. She felt lighter than she had in days.

Stepping out of her simple work dress, Meredith reached for the blue-striped skirt of Cassie's courting costume. "You really are my fairy godmother, you know," she said in all seriousness, fitting the skirt over her hips. "I was trying so hard to be practical about this impromptu wedding, telling myself that little things like a dress and a cake and a bouquet of flowers didn't really matter, but deep down I ached over not having them. Then you roll onto the ranch with everything I need to make this day special. Including yourself."

Cassandra helped her with the fastening at the back of the skirt, and once it was in place, Meredith twirled around and wrapped her arms around her cousin. "Getting married without Mama and Papa is hard enough, but I was certain that Aunt Noreen would keep you away, as well. Having you here is like a miracle, Cass. A lovely miracle that gives me hope for my future."

The two hugged each other tightly for a moment, then separated. Cassandra reached for the solid blue polonaise with the striped trim that fit over the skirt and held it out so Meredith could slip her arms into the sleeves. As it settled into place with its elegant draping in the back, Meredith snuck a peek at herself in the bureau mirror. "I've never worn anything so fine, Cass. I feel like a princess."

"Well, you should." Her smiling eyes met Meredith's in the glass. "Your prince is certainly handsome. No wonder your infatuation lasted all these years. The Archer men are a comely bunch — those rugged physiques and the mysterious air surrounding them. Did you ever learn why they are so adamant about keeping to themselves?"

After twelve years, the Archers were grown men and no longer faced the dangers that threatened them when they were children, but even so, Meredith couldn't bring herself to share what little she knew. It seemed disloyal to Travis somehow, and if he was to be her husband, he deserved her loyalty. Perhaps if he grew to trust her, he would grow to love her as well.

Meredith turned away from the mirror and gathered up her shoes along with the button hook Cassie had dug out of the trunk. "I've been laid up in bed, Cass, recovering from an injury. We haven't exactly had time to delve into the Archer family secrets."

"I suppose not. More's the pity." She sat on the bed behind Meredith and began undoing her cousin's braids. "I guess I forgot about your injury in all the wedding excitement. You seem to be much recovered."

"The dizziness has passed, for the most part, but my head still aches a bit. Oh, and the area behind my left ear is rather tender," she warned as Cassandra tugged a hairpin free near the spot where Samson's hoof had collided with her skull.

Cassie's hands immediately gentled. "I'll be careful."

Once the braids were undone, she ran the brush through Meredith's hair and Meredith closed her eyes as the bristles massaged her scalp, sending delightful tingles along her neck.

"It's too bad we don't have time to roll your hair in rag curls," Cassie said. "You look so pretty in ringlets. But the wave from your braids will give us just the right volume for a lovely French twist. And I have ribbons to dress it up even more. Travis won't be able to take his eyes off of you when we get done."

Meredith allowed herself a smile as she submitted to her cousin's artful ministrations. She knew she was no great beauty, and the prettiest hair in the world couldn't hide her limp or make up for the fact that she was a bride of duty instead of love. But if Travis could look at her this morning with appreciation flaring in his eyes when all she'd worn was a faded housedress, perhaps seeing her in full bridal finery would dissolve any lingering regret he harbored from drawing that short straw.

She'd vowed to the Lord last night to do her best to be the wife Travis needed, but in her heart of hearts, she desperately wished to be the wife he wanted.

17

Travis paced along the front of the house. An hour. Meredith and her cousin had been closed up in his room for an hour. How long did it take a woman to change her dress, for pity's sake? He was going to be out a full day's work at this rate.

Crockett was doing his best to keep the visitors entertained. Well, the parson, at least. The two of them were sitting on the porch discussing sermon topics and spiritual flock tending as if they had known each other for years.

Jim and Neill had returned to work on the lean-to, promising to come as soon as the women were ready. That left Travis with Everett Hayes, a man he respected little and trusted even less. They'd run out of things to say to each other after the first five minutes. So now, Everett Hayes sat on the porch eyeing the Archer pines as if he were measuring them for his mill while Travis paced the yard in front of the house, tension coiling tighter in his gut with each pass.

By the time the front door finally opened, he'd wound himself so tight, he nearly sprang out of his boots.

Cassandra stood in the doorway, one of those dazzling smiles on her face. "Thank you for your patience, gentlemen. We're ready for you to take your places in the parlor."

As she slipped back into the house, Travis mumbled, "It's about time."

Everett Hayes had the gall to wink at him. "Better get used to it, Archer. Things are never the same after you install a woman in your house."

"That is true," the parson said as he pushed up out of his chair, his expression slightly censorious as he glanced at Everett. "But if the Lord is installed, as well, the changes can bring blessing to a man." He shifted his attention and peered at Travis. "Marriage is a sacred union, son, and not something to dread. As Ecclesiastes says, 'Two are better than one, because they have a good reward for their labor. . . . A threefold cord is not quickly broken.' Keep God woven into your relationship and this union will make you stronger. But if you treat it as a burden, it will become one."

Travis stared into the kind eyes of the preacher and nodded. This was not the time to fret over work going undone or to stew about Everett Hayes and his connection to Mitchell. This was the time to focus on family, old and new. For that is what Meredith would be after today — family. And as such, she deserved his consideration and his patience. The work would keep.

"You all go in," he said. "I'll fetch Jim and Neill."

Travis made his way toward the lean-to, and when his brothers came into view, he called out a greeting and waved them in.

Neill jogged over to meet him. "It's time, Trav?"

"Yep."

"It's sure gonna be strange having a girl livin' here." Neill leaned against the wall of the shed, his knees and elbows poking out at odd angles. "I reckon I'll hafta start pullin' on my trousers before I go use the outhouse at night, huh?"

Travis fought to keep a straight face. The boy looked seriously aggrieved by the inconvenience. "Yep, I reckon so. But at least you won't have to worry about the washing anymore."

Neill's face brightened considerably at that. "Jim told me that she'd be taking over the cookin' but he didn't mention nothing 'bout the washin'.'" He bounced away from the shed and gave a little hop toward the house. "C'mon, Trav. Get a move on. We gotta get you hitched!"

Travis chuckled. "Go clean up at the pump, scamp. I'll be there in a minute." Neill trotted off, and Travis turned to Jim. "You think the kid's glad to get off laundry detail?"

"He might change his tune when all his duds start smellin' like flowers," Jim groused.

"Why would they start smelling like flowers?"

Jim shrugged. "Just stands to reason that if a woman starts handlin' a man's clothes they'd start smellin' like her. And women smell like flowers."

"Meredith doesn't smell like flowers." Travis frowned. He remembered the rose scent the schoolmarm used to douse herself in. He'd never misbehaved in class for fear he'd suffocate if he had to stand in the corner next to her desk. Meredith smelled nothing like that. She smelled . . . well . . . like Meredith. Like cinnamon and sunshine.

"Cassie does."

Travis hadn't noticed anything particular about the way Meredith's cousin smelled, but he wasn't about to argue. Instead, he clapped his brother on the shoulder and quirked a grin at him. "We'll all have some adjustments to make — Meredith included. And no matter what our clothes end up smelling like, the woman's family, now. Remember that."

Jim's mouth curved slightly upward. Then he nodded and clasped Travis's arm, sealing the silent pact. Archers stood together, no matter what. Not even frilly-smelling laundry could tear them apart.

Jim released his grip and moved past. Travis pivoted to follow, but something caught his eye near the fence surrounding the garden plot behind the house. Near the gate stood a small brushy shrub, its branches intertwined with the wooden pickets. Most of the tiny white blooms that had dotted it earlier that fall had faded, but one section still blossomed. Travis altered his course.

Meredith might not smell like flowers, but that didn't mean she wouldn't like some. His mother had always kissed his cheek whenever he picked wild flowers for her. She'd fussed over them and put them in a jar with some water and told him what a thoughtful boy he was for bringing her such a pretty present. It seemed like a paltry offering now that he was older, but maybe he'd get lucky and it would make Meredith smile.

Hunkering down beside the fence, he took his pocketknife and hacked off the thick stems holding the largest clusters of flowers. The reddish centers of the calico asters stood out against the spiny white petals as he ordered and reordered the stems, trying to decide which arrangement looked the best. Not having a clue how to make such a judgment, he finally just shoved them together and pulled a white cotton handkerchief from his pocket. After the awkward job of rolling the fabric diagonally against his thigh with one hand, he wrapped it around the stems like a bandage around a wounded arm and knotted it off.

Travis shoved his hand deep into his trouser pocket to make sure his mother's ring was still there. He'd removed it from the string tie after bringing in the trunks and fashioned the black ribbon into a floppy bow under his shirt collar in anticipation of his imminent marriage. Only the ceremony hadn't been as imminent as he'd thought, so the thing had strangled him for the last hour. But his bride was finally ready to put him out of his misery and get the deed done.

Hating to be the last one arriving at his own wedding, Travis jogged up to the back porch and entered the house through the bathing room. He paused long enough to check the straightness of his tie in the shaving mirror, then inhaled a deep breath and strode through the kitchen and down the hall to the parlor.

The parson stood at the front of the room near the woodstove, an open Bible in his hand and a welcoming smile on his lips. His brothers stood in a line in front of the sofa, while Everett and Cassandra Hayes held places near the bookcase.

The one person he didn't see was Meredith.

Then a soft rustling from the corner behind him drew his attention. "It's not too late to change your mind, you know." Meredith's husky whisper met his ears before he'd fully turned.

A gallant denial sprang to his lips, but the moment he saw her, his ability to speak vanished. She was a vision. Her honey-colored hair was rolled against her head in thick, soft twists accented by loops of blue ribbon with long tails that draped along the side of her neck. Travis's fingers itched to follow the trail of those ribbons, to brush the tender skin at her nape.

Her lashes were lowered, and he wondered at her shyness until he recalled that he hadn't answered her comment. "Meri, look at me," he murmured in a quiet tone that no one would overhear.

Those thick, dark lashes lifted slowly, and the blue of her eyes, made even more vibrant by the blue of her dress, pierced his heart. Her teeth nibbled her bottom lip as she forced her gaze to hold his.

"I'll not be changing my mind."

Her shoulders relaxed and a tentative smile tugged at the corners of her mouth. His own mouth curved in response. Then he remembered the awkward bouquet he'd brought. Feeling a little sheepish, he raised his arm and held it out to her.

"It's not much, but I thought you might like them."

Her breath caught and for a moment she did nothing but stare at the rustic offering. Unable to see her eyes, Travis's doubts grew. "I know they're just a bunch of weeds, so don't feel like you have to carry them. It was probably a stupid idea anyway." As his mumbled excuses tapered off, Meredith's head snapped up.

"Don't you dare call them weeds, Travis Archer. They're glorious!" Her eyes glistened with moisture he didn't understand. "No bride could have a finer bouquet. Thank you."

The softness of her palm caressed his knuckles as her hand circled the stems, and the contact had an odd tightening effect on his chest. He offered her his arm and led her to the parson.

To be honest, Travis didn't remember much of what the preacher said during the brief ceremony. He supposed he answered at the appropriate times and vaguely recalled Meredith doing the same, but when the parson announced that he could kiss the bride, his senses came on high alert.

How did one kiss a bride he'd never expected to have, one he'd known less than a week? Thinking to buss her chastely on the cheek, he leaned forward. But he couldn't seem to pull his attention from the fullness of her lips or the way they parted slightly as she drew in a breath, and somehow his mouth found her lips instead. The kiss was brief, gentle, but exquisitely sweet. If not for the hoot Neill let out, he would have returned for another.

A pretty blush colored Meredith's face as she turned away to accept her cousin's congratulations, and Travis had to fight the urge to swagger when he approached his brothers.

"I guess this means you won't be bunking

with me no more, huh, Trav?" Neill snickered as he elbowed him.

More than ready to give up the cot in his brother's room, Travis scowled without any heat and shoved his kid brother's shoulder.

Crockett clasped Travis's hand and reached around to slap him on the back. When he stepped back, however, the knowing grin he wore communicated his thoughts all too clearly. "I'm sure he'll miss your snore terribly, Neill, but I imagine Meredith will distract him from the loss."

Travis felt his neck grow warm. "Leave it alone, Crock," he warned as he turned to accept Jim's hand.

In truth, he'd been so caught up with worries about Mitchell, the barn, and whether or not a wedding would even take place, he'd given very little thought to what would happen after the exchange of vows.

His gaze found Meredith across the room, the ribbing comments of his brothers fading from his awareness as he lingered over her profile. The curve of her cheek. The way the ribbons caressed her neck, inviting him to do the same. The slenderness of her waist. The curve of her —

Meredith glanced up at that moment, and Travis jerked his attention back to his brothers.

All right, so he *had* thought about it. Just not in any . . . uh . . . practical sense.

Instinctively, he knew that Meredith would not refuse him his marital rights. She would consider it her duty as his wife. Yet most husbands had first been suitors, courting their prospective brides with sweet words and gifts of affection. Except for the handful of weeds he'd presented her that morning, he'd given her nothing but a scarred leg and a dented head.

"What's got you frowning, brother?" Crockett jostled him with a shoulder to the arm. "You want me to hurry this party along so you can have some time alone with your bride?" His eyebrows wiggled suggestively, but Travis ignored the bawdy gesture.

He nudged Crockett aside and lowered his voice so the others wouldn't hear. Jim had already wandered into Hayes territory anyway, trying to get closer to a certain gal in pink, and Neill was smart enough to take the hint and turn his attention to the parson.

"Do you think I should give her some time to adjust before I move into her room?" Travis stretched his neck from side to side in an effort to rid himself of the kinks that suddenly arose.

"Shoot, Trav. It's *your* room, not hers."

"I'm serious, Crockett. It would be the

considerate thing to do, don't you think? This situation has been thrust on both of us without any warning."

The teasing light in Crockett's eyes dimmed, and his mouth stiffened. "Are you saying you're not attracted to her in that way?" His voice was tight. "You should have never gone through with this if you —"

"Of course that's not what I'm saying," Travis hissed. "Just look at her. A man would have to be blind not to be attracted."

Crockett's face relaxed.

"I just thought, maybe I should, you know, court her a bit first." Travis kicked at the edge of the rug with the toe of his boot. He'd rather she be a willing partner than simply a dutiful one.

"When do you plan to court her, exactly? While we rebuild the barn? Or maybe out among the cattle while we search out new places for them to forage, since half our fodder went up in smoke? Thanks to Mitchell, we have more work on our hands and less time to accomplish it with winter already knocking on the door." Crockett looked to the ceiling and blew out a breath before turning back to his brother. "I don't know what the right answer is, Travis. I've even less experience than you when it comes to women. Talk to Meredith. Decide together what is best for the two of you. And pray for the Lord's guidance."

"Travis?" Meredith's soft voice gave him a start.

He spun around. Had she overheard any of their conversation? He prayed not and schooled his features as best he could to keep his chagrin hidden.

"I thought our guests might like to eat those sweet rolls now." She spoke with hesitation, and her eyes had difficulty holding his, but her smile reached inside him and undid the knots in his gut.

Travis offered her his arm and called out to the rest of the room. "My wife informs me that it's time to eat. And I, for one, am eager to sample my bride's cooking."

"It takes a brave man to marry a woman without proof of her ability to keep him from starvation, Archer," the parson said on a chuckle as he bustled forward.

"Says the man in the greatest hurry to get to the kitchen."

Meredith giggled at his jest, and Travis smiled. He slipped his hand over hers where it rested on his forearm and enjoyed the feel of his mother's ring beneath her glove.

"I said *you* were brave, lad. Not me. I've tasted Miss Meredith's baked goods and know precisely what quality of treat waits for me in the other room. And I plan to snatch the largest roll." He broke into a bouncy jog as if afraid someone would beat him to the prize. The room erupted in laughter.

Emboldened by the man's high spirits, Travis leaned down and whispered in Meredith's ear. "If they taste half as sweet as the one who baked them, they'll be delicious indeed."

"Travis," she chastened in low voice, her lovely cheeks matching her cousin's dress.

He grinned unrepentantly and urged her forward.

He was going to enjoy this courting business.

18

Meredith winced as she straightened from the wash basket and lifted one of Travis's shirts to the line. Laundry day had always made her lower back throb with all the bending and heavy lifting required, but as she surveyed the neat rows of male clothing, sheets, and table linens flapping in the chilled air, a proud smile curved her lips.

These were her family's things. Her *husband's* things. Amazing how that simple fact took the drudgery out of the chore.

Smiling to herself, she tossed the shirt over the line for a moment, then pushed her palms into the small of her back and turned her face up toward the sun as she stretched. The sound of a door shutting brought her head around.

Jim clomped down the back steps, his stocky build making his stride heavier than Travis's loose-limbed gait. His hair was a shade lighter than her husband's, but his eyes were similar, only they didn't have the intriguing touch of green she saw in Travis's.

Meredith raised a hand in greeting as he walked down the clothesline. The taciturn man favored her with a lift of his chin but not much else. He was a bit of a curmudgeon, but she didn't let it bother her since he acted the same way around his brothers. The only one he didn't act that way with was Cassie. But Cassie had that effect on men. She could charm a rock into floating on water with one of her smiles.

"I've got some stew simmering for supper," Meredith called out as he passed. He stopped and turned, but instead of answering her, he grabbed one of the trouser legs from the line and held it to his nose.

Was he . . . *sniffing* it?

He released it with a grunt, one that sounded rather like the ones her father used to make when he'd find the answer he sought in one of his research books. Then he glanced up and briefly met her gaze.

"Stew needs salt." And with no further commentary, he strode on to his shed.

Meredith didn't know whether to be offended at his opinion of her cooking or pleased that he'd actually spoken to her.

Turning back to her task, she pulled a clothespin from her apron pocket and fastened one shoulder of Travis's plaid flannel shirt, the one he had loaned her, to the line. As she worked to pin the other side, a ray of sunlight glinted off the gold band on her left hand. Meredith paused to admire it.

A married woman. Her. Meredith Hayes.

No, she corrected, *Meredith Archer.*

Her smile widened as she reached into the basket at her feet and retrieved her nightdress. A sigh escaped her as she shook out the wet, wadded cotton — the virginal white fabric a reminder that she was not yet a wife in all respects, only a bride. She forcefully flicked her wrists, snapping the gown into its full length.

She'd spent her wedding night alone.

Oh, it was out of consideration for her feelings. Travis had explained all that. And in her mind she understood his kindness and even appreciated the time he was giving her to truly get to know him before their relationship became more intimate. But in her heart? Well, deep down his consideration felt a lot like rejection.

Had he not felt the pulse-stopping current she had when their lips met during the ceremony? She guessed not, since he seemed in no hurry to repeat the experience. Travis hadn't kissed her once since the wedding three days ago.

She'd waited twelve years for that kiss, and now that she'd had a taste, three days without one felt like an eternity. Maybe Travis was the one who needed time. Meredith tilted her head as she pondered that idea. Perhaps he'd suggested they wait to consummate their marriage because *he* needed time to adjust. It wouldn't be surprising, really. Her uncle had practically forced the man to the altar. Meredith let out a sigh. She supposed she'd have to be patient.

At least Travis didn't seem adverse to her touch. His hand had a tendency to brush hers when they passed food around the supper table. And when they'd shared the sofa yesterday during the worship service the Archer brothers conducted in their parlor on Sundays, Travis had held the hymnal and sat close enough to her that she could feel the length of his leg whenever she leaned to the side to get a clearer view of the page.

The Lord probably didn't appreciate her feigning nearsightedness in order to repeatedly lean into her husband when she should've been concentrating on the meaning behind the hymn she was singing. It was no doubt her shameful behavior that prompted his divine hand to intervene in the song selection. When Neill accidentally announced the wrong song number, he decided to lead the unplanned hymn anyway. After three verses of "Nearer, My God, to Thee," Meredith's vision miraculously improved.

She reached for another garment, the green calico she'd had to scrub three times on the washboard, thanks to all the soot stains. When she straightened, the tune from that convicting hymn found its way to her lips. As she hummed the lilting melody, she recommitted her priorities. God first. Husband second. Yet when the words of the refrain ran through her mind, they brought with them recollections of a verse from James. *"Draw nigh to God, and he will draw nigh to you."* Meredith couldn't help wondering if such a strategy would work on husbands, as well.

Two shots fired in close succession rent the air. Meredith startled and dropped the clothespin she'd just extracted from her pocket. Then she remembered the sound was her husband's version of a doorbell and ordered her pulse to settle.

"One of these days I'm going to convince Travis to get rid of that awful sign," Meredith muttered as her hand closed around another wooden pin.

Just yesterday, Crockett had preached a fine lesson on the parable of the Good

Samaritan. He'd kept looking at her with those twinkling eyes of his, leaving her to wonder if he saw her in the role of the Samaritan, performing a good deed in warning Travis of Mitchell's attack, or if he'd cast her in the role of the poor traveler who'd ended up half dead upon the road. Either way, Jesus clearly told the story to teach his followers to love their neighbors through acts of kindness and charity. How exactly did Travis think he and his brothers would fulfill this calling if they closed themselves off from anyone who might be considered a neighbor?

That sign had to go.

"Meredith?" Travis called out to her as his long strides ate up the distance between the shed and the trees that supported her wash line. "I need you to go into the house."

"I only have a few things left to hang. It'll just take a min—"

"Now, Meredith. Do as I say." The hardness in his voice surprised her, and the firm set of his jaw made it clear he expected her to jump to his bidding.

She *had* vowed to obey her husband, but she'd made no promise to jump like a scared rabbit every time he took to ordering her around.

Meredith lifted her chin. "Why must I go

into the house, Travis?"

"Because," he gritted out, "there might be a threat, and I want to ensure that you're safe."

"What kind of threat?"

Travis yanked off his hat and swatted his thigh with it. "Confound it, Meri. Will you just do as I ask?" He slapped the abused hat back on his head, then took her by the arm and pushed her toward the back steps. "I don't know what kind of threat, but I don't take chances. For all we know, Mitchell could have sent more men to convince me to sell."

"Or my uncle could have stopped by for a visit." Meredith didn't resist his forced guidance. His grip wasn't rough, just insistent. But she meant to make it clear that she didn't appreciate his high-handed tactics.

When they got to the back porch, he released her. "I know you haven't been here long, Meredith, but you're an Archer now, and you've got to learn how Archers do things. We always expect the worst. It keeps us alive. And when someone gives an order, you don't question it, you follow it. Explanations take time away from setting up our defense, and that leaves us vulnerable. Trust me to do what's right for you, Meri. It's for your own protection."

She frowned at him, letting him know she wasn't too pleased with his methods, but dutifully nodded her agreement. "All right."

Travis clapped her upper arm in a movement probably meant to convey his satisfaction over her compliance, but the hard lines of his face never softened. She would have preferred a smile. She'd have to make do with the brotherly thud on the arm, though, for he was already striding away from her, heading to the corral, where his mount waited.

"One of these days you're going to have to learn that the whole world isn't out to get you," she said softly to his retreating back, unsure if he heard her or not, even more unsure if she wanted him to hear. "You're keeping out more friends than foes with that gate, Travis." This last observation she whispered to herself.

She'd follow Travis's instructions and trust him to protect her, but she'd also follow the directives the Lord had placed on her heart. The Archers might be experts when it came to defense, but they were sadly lacking in their execution of hospitality.

Meredith marched through the bathing room and into the kitchen. After stoking up the fire in the stove, she took out a mixing bowl and scooped out three large portions of flour from the bin. She sprinkled a pinch of salt into the bowl, then cut in enough lard and cold water to make a dough. Taking the rolling pin from the drawer, she quickly rolled out the crust, not caring what shape resulted from her hasty efforts. Instead of reaching for a pie pan, she selected a large baking sheet from the cupboard and greased it. She cut the dough into strips, laid them in the pan, and dusted them with the leftover cinnamon-sugar mixture she had reserved after making the sweet rolls. While the crisps baked, she tidied the kitchen, then bustled back to her room to tidy herself.

If their guest proved not to be foe, as she suspected, the brave soul would be showered with neighborly hospitality. It was time the Archers were known for something other than seclusion.

Travis charged through the trees on Bexar's back, left hand on the reins, right hand on the butt of his pistol. Catching a shadowy glimpse of a wagon, he slowed the chestnut's pace and steered him off the path to take cover in a thicket of young pines. Crockett must have heard his approach, for the call of a white-winged dove floated on the breeze. White-winged doves rarely nested this far from the Rio Grande Valley, so when Joseph Archer taught his three older boys to imitate the call, they immediately turned it into a game of secret communication. Later, when they were on their own, it became an essential tool of stealth, allowing them to communicate to one another without being seen.

Taking his hand from his pistol, he patted Bexar's neck and waited for the second call that would signal all was well. When it came, the tightness in his chest lessened, and he drew in a deep breath. Strangers on his land made him tense at the best of times, but now that he had a wife to protect, fear for her safety intensified the usual concern that poured through him every time shots echoed from the road. At least he knew it wasn't one of Mitchell's agents. Crockett never would've admitted a wagon through the gate if he didn't know the driver.

Travis cupped his fingers around his mouth and returned Crockett's call. When the wagon drew abreast of his position, he urged Bexar forward with a touch of his heels and added his escort.

"Travis, my boy!" the bewhiskered driver boomed. "Good to see ya. I wondered where you were hidin'."

"I'd hate to grow predictable on you after all these years, Winston." Travis grinned at his father's old friend, the only man with a free pass onto Archer land.

"Shoot, that'd take all the fun out of it. Coming to see you boys is about the only excitement I get nowadays." He reached under his coat and scratched a spot on his chest with the three fingers left to him on his right hand. "Jim got my cabinets ready?"

"Yep. Finished the fourth one a couple weeks back."

Early on, the Archer boys had traded livestock for supplies — a cow or a hog, whichever they could best spare, in exchange for three months worth of flour, cornmeal, lard, coffee, sugar, and other necessities, like garden seeds, tools, and medicines. But when Jim started dabbling in woodworking and turned out to have a true talent for carpentry, Seth Winston quickly renegotiated their standing arrangement. They could keep their animals if Jim would fashion pieces Winston could sell to the local farmers' and ranchers' wives in his shop. Winston's general store and post office, along with a saloon and a church that doubled as the local schoolhouse, were the only buildings in the nearby tiny settlement known as Beaver Valley, but having the store situated on the market road between Palestine and Athens provided a place for the locals to congregate and therefore a steady trickle of customers. Customers who apparently appreciated rustic oak and pine furnishings.

"Can't wait to see 'em. Pansy Elmore's been badgerin' me somethin' fierce about that open cupboard I promised her. You know how antsy them women can get." Winston slanted a glance at Travis and let out a cackle. "No, I reckon you don't, do you?"

"Oh, he's learning," Crockett offered in a wry voice.

Winston twisted to eye the younger Archer. "Whadda'ya mean, he's learning? You four are livin' in bachelor heaven. You ain't even seen a female in fourteen years. Lucky dogs. Womenfolk're more trouble than they're worth, if you ask me. Always naggin' a man to death. I tell ya, there's been many a time I thought about holin' up out here with you boys just to get some peace."

"Your sister still pestering you to move down to Palestine and retire?" Travis asked, eager to veer the conversation in a different direction.

"As if I'd want to be surrounded by her clan. Nellie's brood is all girls. And not a one of 'em has up and married yet. I'd be

243

stuck in a house with five females. Five! Can ya imagine the torture? All that yappin' and carrying on. It'd drive me batty." His violent shudder made Travis smile. Seth Winston was a grouchy old cuss, but beneath all that bluster beat a loyal heart. If a person ever managed to find a way to his good side, he'd have a friend for life.

When Joseph Archer helped him rebuild his store after a twister tore off the roof, he'd landed himself on Winston's good side. And fortunately for Travis, Joseph's sons inherited the man's favor when their father passed.

"Yessiree. You boys are the smart ones. Protect what you got out here, Travis." Winston pointed at him with the trio of fingers on his right hand. "Don't let no woman come in and start changing things. She'll suck the freedom right outta ya."

They arrived at the front of the house right as he made that statement. Jim and Neill set aside their rifles and stepped down from the porch to help unload the wagon.

Crockett grinned and winked at Travis over the old man's head. "I think your warning came a couple days too late, Seth."

Travis shot him a quelling look, but Crockett just chuckled and dismounted, wisely staying on the opposite side of the wagon, out of his big brother's reach.

Winston squinted up at Travis, consternation furrowing his brow. "Tell me he's jokin', Travis. Tell me you didn't —"

The sound of the front door squeaking open stole the rest of his sentence. Meredith backed through the doorway, her arms occupied with a tray. When she turned, a cheery smile lit her face even as her eyes darted nervously between all the men assembled in the yard.

"Consarn it, Travis! What is *she* doin' here? Ya gone and ruined everything, haven't ya?"

Staying atop his horse so he could hold Meredith's widening gaze from the far side of the wagon, Travis tried to communicate his apology with his eyes. Her smile only slipped a little before her determination propped it back into place.

Man, he was proud of her.

"Seth Winston," Travis intoned, a touch of steel lacing his voice. "My wife, Meredith."

"Wife?" The man nearly shouted his outrage. "Good gravy, boy. It's worse than I feared."

19

Of all the sour-minded, pig-headed . . . Meredith breathed through her nose, careful to keep her smile in place. Of all the people God could send her to practice her hospitality on, did it have to be Seth Winston? The man had scared her to death as a child when her mother took her shopping in his store, always glaring at her like an ogre from one of her fairy-tale books. She hadn't seen the man since she started school in Palestine, and truth be told, she'd gone out of her way to avoid him even before that, so it didn't surprise her that no recognition flashed in his eyes. And that was fine with her. She'd take every advantage she could get in this battle. For a battle it would be — one she had no intention of losing.

It was time to slay the ogre. And though she longed for a sword, her weapons would have to be cleverness and kindness instead.

Meredith marched forward, head held

high. Until she noticed their visitor's gaze drop to her feet. It wasn't the first time her limp had garnered a rude stare, but it was the first time her imperfection reflected on someone other than herself. Not trusting herself to glance at Travis to gauge his reaction, she focused on the ground as she navigated the steps.

What was that verse from Romans? *Oh yes. "If thine enemy hunger, feed him; if he thirst, give him drink: for in so doing thou shalt heap coals of fire on his head."* She peered at her tray of cinnamon crisps, and smiled over the fiery coals waiting to be consumed.

Mr. Winston clambered down from the wagon bench and eyed her approach as if she were a bobcat looking for someone to sharpen her claws on.

"I know you," he said pointing a hand at her that lacked a couple of fingers. "You're Teddy Hayes's girl. The one with the bum leg."

"And I know you, Mr. Winston," she answered before Travis could say anything. "You're that cranky old store owner. The one with the bum hand." Unlike their guest's vinegarish tone, Meredith infused her barb with a thick dollop of honey.

The man blinked at her, his mouth slightly agape, as if he couldn't quite believe her audacity.

"You used to tell the most gruesome war stories when I came to your store with my mother," Meredith continued, her smile still in place as she swept past Crockett, Jim, and Neill without a sideways glance. "Even though they gave me nightmares, I couldn't stop myself from listening. You have quite a gift for storytelling."

She held the tray out to him when she reached the place where he stood. "Cinnamon crisp? They're fresh from the oven."

He didn't move, just stared at her as if she were an oddity he couldn't decipher.

Meredith continued holding the tray as if she had nothing better to do than ply the recalcitrant man with sweets. "You know, when I was a girl, Hiram Ellis nearly convinced me that Travis shot off those two missing fingers of yours when you trespassed on his land. I'm glad I didn't believe that nonsense. You've obviously been on friendly terms with my husband for quite some time." She emphasized the word *husband,* hoping to rile the grumpy cuss. Two could play at his game. "Why don't you come up to the house? You can entertain me with more of your stories while Travis and the other, younger, men unload the supplies."

Mr. Winston turned an accusing glare at Travis. "She fer real?"

Travis nodded, and a grin stretched across his face. He even winked at her before he dismounted. "She's real, all right."

"She know it's rude to insult comp'ny?" The old codger shot a challenging look her way before turning back to Travis, obviously thinking he'd bested her by excluding her from the conversation.

Little did he know that Meredith Hayes Archer never backed down from a challenge, spoken or not. "Oh, she'd never insult a guest, Mr. Winston," Meredith answered on her own behalf as Travis came around the front of the wagon. She moved to stand by his side. "Like any good hostess, she's sensitive to the preferences of her callers and is careful to address them in the same manner in which they do her. Anything less might make them feel ill at ease, and that would never do."

Someone tried unsuccessfully to stifle his guffaw. Probably Crockett. But Meredith dared not take her eyes off of Mr. Winston to verify her theory.

The man grunted, then snatched three of the sugared pie-crust strips from her tray and proceeded to bite the ends off all of them at once. Crumbs fell into his beard, but his mouth stayed closed while he chewed. It was more than she had hoped for from the ill-mannered fellow. And really, at this point he could have spat on her shoe and she wouldn't have cared. She had bested him!

Her smile grew as she watched him stuff her snacks into his mouth. She knew a delaying tactic when she saw one. He couldn't come up with anything else to say. The man couldn't even hold her gaze.

Then all at once, his jaw stilled, his eyes feasting on something behind her. He swallowed. Slowly. "So, Travis," he said, his voice deceptively pleasant. "You marry this harpy before or after she burned down yer barn?" He tossed the rest of the crisps into his mouth and chomped down, victory written all over his face.

"After." Travis couldn't resist; he was having too much fun watching their sparring.

Meredith's sharply indrawn breath roused his conscience, though.

"I did *not* burn down your barn, and you know it!" She shoved the tray into his stomach so hard he almost failed to steady the thing before all her little treats fell into the dirt. That would've been a crime. Jim had an able hand for making stew, but he never could bake worth a hoot. Meredith's desserts were precious commodities.

When Travis had all the goodies safely balanced, he glanced up and caught the vivid blue fire of his wife's eyes. "And I am *not* a harpy!"

With that dramatic pronouncement, she strode back toward the house, giving Crockett a censoring shove when he laughed. He managed to contain his mirth until the front door slammed closed behind her. Then it burst forth even louder than before. Neill joined in, and even Jim cracked a smile.

The woman had held her own against Winston like a seasoned verbal warrior. So why had one teasing word from Travis ignited her temper?

Winston clapped Travis on the back, unsettling the cinnamon things again. "That's one ornery spitfire ya got there, Travis." He grabbed another handful of pastries and ambled to the back of the wagon to lower the tailgate. "She just might make a halfway decent Archer yet."

If she ever let him near her again.

Travis blew out a heavy breath and headed for the house, passing the tray off to Neill as he went. This business of wooing one's wife was complicated. The pitfalls were so well hidden, a man didn't even know they were there until he'd fallen into one.

"Good luck, Trav." Crockett's voice wobbled on the end of a chuckle. Travis shot him a glare and pounded up the porch steps.

She wasn't in the kitchen. The bedroom, either. He checked the parlor and even peeked into the boys' rooms on his way down the hall. Nothing.

"Meredith?" He held his volume to a minimum, not wanting the others to know he'd lost his wife. He lifted his hat, scratched at a spot on his crown, and fit it back into place. She'd only been a minute or two ahead of him. She had to be somewhere in the house.

The only place he hadn't checked was the bathing room. Travis crossed the kitchen in six long strides and pushed through the unlatched door. "Meri?"

The room was empty, but cool air whistled through the back door, where it hung ajar. When he nudged it open, he spotted her stomping between the clotheslines as if she were squashing a wolf spider with every footfall.

Travis shook his head at the picture she made — arms swinging like a soldier, bonnet flapping against her back, pieces of hair coming loose and dancing about in the breeze. He took off after her and caught up just as she snapped the wrinkles out of a damp petticoat.

She had to realize he was there. He stood less than a foot away, for pete's sake, yet she refused to look at him. Her lips pressed together in a tight line as she jabbed a clothespin over the cotton garment.

Travis crossed his arms, his own temper rising a notch. "You gonna tell me what I did wrong, or am I'm gonna have to guess?"

"You betrayed me!" She spun to face him, and for the first time he noticed the tears behind the fire in her eyes. But the accusation she flung at him burned away any soft feelings that might have been evoked.

"Whoa, now." Travis uncrossed his arms and held up a hand of warning. "Archers don't betray their own."

"I must not be one of your own, then."

Travis stepped closer and glowered down at the woman daring to impugn his honor. "You agreed before God to take my name. Have you forgotten?"

"No, but it seems you have." She glowered right back at him. "I complied when you ordered me into the house. I even put together refreshments on the rare chance that someone might actually be welcomed onto sacred Archer land. Then when you did bring a guest to the house, he turns out to be the grumpiest woman-hater north of the Rio Grande. But did I shy away? No, sir. I faced Seth Winston head on. And I was making progress, too. Until you" — she poked him in the chest — "chopped the legs right out from under me."

He knocked her finger away. "One word, Meredith. One lousy word. You're getting all worked up over nothing."

"Nothing?" Her voice rose. "With that one word, you sided with the enemy. You as much as conceded that I had something to do with that fire and agreed that I'm some kind of ill-tempered harpy!"

He raised an eyebrow and stared at her until she realized the irony of the shouted statement.

At that moment the starch went out of her. She glanced away and kicked at the edge of the laundry basket with her shoe. "You didn't defend me."

His anger evaporated at the tremor in her voice.

Travis cupped his fingers under her chin and turned her face back up to his. "You didn't give me the chance." He stroked the edge of her jaw with his thumb. "Meri, you are my wife, a part of my family. I will never betray you." Her eyes stared up at him like a doe's in an early morning mist. Travis dropped his hand away from her chin and shoved his fingers into his trouser pocket, worried he'd pull her close and kiss her if he didn't. "The truth is, I was so blasted proud of the way you were handling Winston that I couldn't resist a little teasing. I fully intended to clarify that you had nothing to do with the fire, but you stormed off before I got the chance."

"I ruined everything, didn't I?" She sounded so forlorn. "I let him goad me into losing my temper. I shamed you."

"You did no such thing." Travis frowned down at her. "Did you not just hear me tell you how proud I was of you?" Compliments seemed to slip off his wife as if they were covered in grease. Nothing stuck.

"But that was before I started acting like a harpy."

"For pete's sake, woman, you are *not* a harpy!"

Her startled eyes darted to his. Then without warning, a giggle erupted. Travis felt his own lips twitch, and soon they were both laughing.

"Hey, Trav," Neill called from the back porch. "Winston wants to know if you want to add anything to your usual order since we got us a female on the place now."

Travis winked at his new wife, her cheeks

rosy from their shared merriment. "Tell him we'll be up there to discuss it with him directly."

Meredith moaned and turned to reach for the last item in her wash basket. "Do I really have to face him again, Travis? The man will be insufferable after besting me as he did."

Travis grinned and grabbed up the empty basket. "You can handle him. I've got faith in you."

He held his hand out to her after she finished pinning a second petticoat to the line. She glanced uncertainly at his offering, then slipped her palm into his. On impulse, he tugged her arm, causing her to stumble into him.

"We're Archers, Meri," he murmured as he tucked her briefly against his chest. "We can face anything if we do it together."

20

After five days of marriage, the shine was starting to wear off. Meredith grimaced as she stirred a bowl of cornbread batter. She'd cleaned the house from top to bottom, kept the men fed and their clothes mended — done everything a wife was supposed to do. Well . . . almost everything. And therein lay her trouble. Except for the quick hug he'd given her when encouraging her to face Mr. Winston, Travis had offered her virtually no affection, leaving her feeling more like a housekeeper than a wife.

She'd told herself he was being gallant when he suggested they take some time to get to know one another before sharing the intimacy of the marriage bed, but now she wondered if that had just been an excuse to avoid her. After all, he hadn't wed her out of love but rather a sense of responsibility.

"Quit being pitiful, Meri." She forced herself to stop pulverizing the cornmeal and poured the batter into a square baking pan. Love needed time to grow. It was unfair to expect her husband to blossom overnight into the idealized romantic hero she'd spent her adolescence mooning over. Besides, she was a woman now, not a girl, and she needed a man to stand at her side, not an imaginary hero.

But she still wanted that man to care for her.

With a sigh that was still far too pitiful sounding for her peace of mind, Meredith opened the oven door and slid the pan into the heart of the stove. It was then that she noticed the quiet. Travis and Jim were supposed to be tearing out damaged boards from the sections of the barn that were still standing, while Crockett and Neill checked the cattle out on the range and scouted new pastureland. There should have been voices, the crash of wood planks hitting the scrap heap, something. But even when she held very still, all she could make out was a faint chatter from the chicken coop.

Heart thumping in her breast, Meredith crept over to the bathing room and grabbed the broom. It seemed a particularly opportune time to sweep the front porch. If trouble was afoot, she'd surely see it coming from there. Wouldn't hurt to have the shotgun at hand, either. Meredith took a detour through the den to collect the gun and tuck a handful of shells into her apron pocket. She stood the weapon against the wall of the entryway, then opened the door to find Sadie blocking her path.

"Shoo, girl." Meredith nudged the dog's side with her knee. Sadie held fast, her ears pricked, her attention focused somewhere down the path.

Meredith angled herself over the dog's back, jutting her shoulders through the doorway in order to glance around the yard. No sign of the men. She pressed harder against Sadie's side. "Come on, now. Let . . . me . . . through." Meredith's greater weight finally prevailed as she displaced the dog far enough to squeeze past. But before she could take more than a step or two, Sadie scrambled around to block her progress once again.

"What has gotten into you?" Meredith stroked the dog's fur, hoping a friendly rub would restore the animal's usual good humor. Sadie refused to relax, however. Her back remained stiff and straight, her legs braced like a soldier on guard duty.

All at once the pieces clicked into place. "Travis ordered you to stand guard, didn't he?"

Sadie twisted her neck and looked at her mistress with eyes that seemed to reprimand her for being so slow in comprehending the obvious, then turned her attention back to the path.

Meredith straightened and peered in the same direction. The trees obscured her view, and the uncertainty of what was happening behind their cover set her pulse to thrumming. Whatever had lured Travis away had been urgent enough to preclude him from stopping by the house to warn her.

Had Roy Mitchell's men returned? What of Crockett and Neill? Had something befallen one of them?

Her hands tightened around the broom handle. *Please, Lord, keep my family safe.*

A flash of color tickled her vision, dodging in and out of the pines. Meredith dashed around Sadie to the far end of the porch and leaned over the railing to get a better view. The dog barked once in protest, then bounded to her side.

Meredith squinted, the railing digging into her stomach. She spied a man. No. Two men. One tall and large, the other slender. Both dark-skinned. The path took them behind another tree, and Meredith bit the inside of her cheek in frustration. The tall one wore an odd-looking feather in the band of his tan planter hat. Even from a distance, she could make out the black plume against the lighter-colored headpiece.

She'd seen a hat like that before. As the memory slowly awakened within her, the hard voice of her husband cut through the late morning quiet.

"Take one more step, and I'll shoot you where you stand."

Like a pair of ghosts, Travis and Jim materialized out of the trees, their rifles pointed directly at the man who had built her father's school.

"No!" Meredith cried. "Wait!" She shooed Sadie with her broom and managed to evade the animal long enough to gain the steps. Dropping the broom, she hiked up her skirts and ran toward her husband.

He didn't look too happy to see her. The glare he aimed her way was downright furious, as a matter of fact. But Meredith refused to be cowed. He could yell at her later. Right now she intended to broaden the stubborn man's horizons.

"Meredith, get back to the house." Travis called out the demand, then shifted his stance to match her angle of approach, putting himself between her and the visitors.

A stitch in her side kept her from answering at first, but she knew he'd figure out her refusal once she reached the gathering. She stopped a few feet behind him and struggled to catch her breath as she surreptitiously rubbed her right leg. The punishment of running on the shorter limb had set it to aching.

Travis would have to be deaf not to be aware of her presence, even with his back turned. Yet he paid her no heed, just continued on with his threats.

"You're trespassing on my land." Travis aimed the barrel of his rifle at the larger man's chest. "The sign at the gate warned you of the consequences. Now turn around and leave before I put a bullet in you."

The big man held his arms out from his sides in a gesture of conciliation, but he made no move to leave. "I didn't read no sign."

"That doesn't change the fact that you're trespassing."

The younger fellow, just a boy, really — he looked about the same age as Neill — backed a step away from Jim, his eyes wary. "Let's go, Pa. Mr. Winston was wrong. They don't want our help."

"That's cuz they don't know what we're offerin' yet." The man's face gave nothing away, but Meredith could feel the challenge hanging in the air.

"The only offer I'm interested in is the one where you offer to leave my land." Travis waved his gun in the direction of the road.

Meredith lifted a hand to Travis's shoulder. Her touch was light, yet he flinched as if she'd burned him. "Travis. Please. I know this m—"

"Strangers aren't welcome here," her husband ground out, cutting off her explanation. But the others heard.

Moses Jackson peered past Travis, and when his eyes landed on her, his composure fell away. "Miss Meri? That you?"

She smiled and stepped out from behind her husband. An answering smile began to crease Moses's face when Travis shoved her back behind him. In an instant, the black man's good humor vanished and the hands that had hung harmless at his sides balled into fists — giant fists that looked like they could fell a tree.

"You here against your will, Miss Meri?"

Jim and Travis both tensed, and Meredith's stomach plummeted to her toes. *Merciful heavens.* If Moses started swinging those fists, Travis was bound to be the first target. And if one of the guns went off? Well, it didn't bear thinking about.

Just as she had with Sadie earlier, Mere-

263

dith dodged around her husband's protective stance and dashed directly into the line of fire.

Travis immediately raised his rifle barrel into the air, but the look he shot her felt just like a bullet tearing through the flesh near her heart. She prayed he'd forgive her once she'd explained. There was nothing to do now, though, but brazen her way through.

"Travis Archer, may I present Mr. Moses Jackson? Mr. Jackson built the freedmen's schoolhouse a mile west of Beaver Valley, where my father taught for several years." Meredith watched Travis's face for signs of softening, but his jaw remained as clenched as ever as he stared down the large black man. She turned to Moses only to find his face equally implacable. "Moses, Travis is my husband. I am here quite willingly."

Finally, Moses surrendered the staring battle to glance at Meredith. He relaxed his fists, and a hint of a smile played about the corners of his mouth. "Your man ain't the friendly sort, is he, Miss Meri."

She laughed, her nerves getting the better of her. "Not at first. But he can be a trusted ally once you get to know him." Meredith peeked back at her husband. He still looked none too pleased, but his eyes were no longer shooting bullets at her. It was a start.

Travis tipped his rifle barrel onto his shoulder, pointing it harmlessly away from the visitors, but his right hand continued gripping the stock in a way that would allow instant readiness should the occasion call for it.

"Why'd you come, Jackson?"

"Lookin' for work. Heard ya had a barn what needed rebuilding."

"I've got three brothers." Travis jerked his chin in Jim's direction. "That one's even a carpenter. We'll manage the task."

Moses crossed his arms over his chest. "Before the next rain comes?" The question hovered for a moment, everyone knowing the answer. "My boy's good with a hammer, and I've built just about everything there is what has walls and a roof. With us working for you, you can cut yer building time in half."

Travis's jaw worked back and forth.

"We need a place to store what's left of the hay," Jim stated with flat practicality as he shifted his rifle, pointing it toward the ground.

Travis made no outward show that he'd heard his brother, but Meredith sensed the battle inside him. The hay would mold if rain came before they got a roof on the barn, and in Texas, the weather was harder to predict than a hummingbird's flight path. It could hold off for a month or a storm could roll in tomorrow. But having strangers on Archer land went against everything Travis had clung to since his father died.

"I can't pay in cash money."

Meredith held her breath. He was bending.

"I'd work for provisions, foodstuffs to see me and mine through the winter."

Travis frowned. "I can't spare much. We've already laid in provisions for the winter and won't receive more until spring. We hadn't planned on needing extra for barter."

Meredith considered offering to go to town should they run low on supplies, but figured she'd pushed her husband far enough for one day. Perhaps discretion would be the better part of valor in this instance. Her gaze seesawed back to Moses, praying he'd not refuse. Travis needed his help whether he admitted it or not. And not just with the barn. He needed a connection with the outside world, with someone other than that dreadful Seth Winston, someone who could help him see that reaching out to others was as important as protecting one's own.

Moses uncrossed his arms. "I'll accept whatever you think fair."

Silence stretched over the pair as they continued to size each other up. Finally, Travis thrust out his hand. Moses grasped it with his own, and the two shook. Giddy pleasure gurgled through Meredith, but she contained it behind a soft smile.

"One of us will meet you at the gate each morning to escort you in," Travis instructed. "You and the boy can take your midday meals with us while you're working and collect your payment at the end of the week."

"Yessir, Mr. Archer." Moses dipped his head in compliance.

"Call me Travis. If we're going to be working together, there's no need for such formality. That there's Jim," he indicated with a thrust of his chin. "Crockett and Neill are out on the range. You'll meet them in a bit when they come in to eat."

Moses shook hands with Jim and introduced his son, Josiah. Meredith stepped back and watched the whole thing unfold, pride in her husband seeping through every pore. She'd worried, just for a moment, that the color of Moses's skin might have played a part in Travis's reluctance to accept his help. But clearly that was not the case. Not with him offering the use of his Christian name. No, Travis would have treated any stranger with the same discourtesy.

A giggle tickled her throat. Oh, that's right — he had. She'd nearly forgotten about her own inhospitable Archer welcome. That day felt like a lifetime ago now.

"Jim, why don't you take Moses and Josiah up to the shed and show them the sketches you've been working on," Travis said. "Meredith and I will meet you at the house in a couple minutes."

Jim nodded and led the Jacksons toward the shed. Meredith waved to Moses when he tipped his hat to her, then turned a beaming smile on her husband.

"Oh, Travis," she gushed. "You won't regret this. Moses is a good man and a talented builder. I know the two of you will get along famously. Papa always held him in high esteem even though he and his older boy never came to the reading classes. Too busy sharecropping. That's probably why he didn't heed your sign. I don't think he can read. But his wife and younger son attended and were fine pupils. Why —"

"Meredith," Travis snapped and grabbed hold of her arm.

The well of frothy babble inside her dried up in an instant. She met his gaze, and her heart started a painful throb in her chest.

She'd experienced his irritation and even an occasional flash of true frustration, but never had Travis directed a look of raw anger at her.

Suddenly she very much wished she had let Sadie keep her penned in the house.

21

Travis glared down at the woman who'd nearly given him a heart seizure. Her blue eyes had gone wide. *Good.* Maybe he'd scare some sense into her.

"Don't you *ever* step in front of my weapon like that." He ground the order out between clenched teeth. "Do you understand me?"

Meredith gave a quick little nod, her chin quivering. Travis hardened himself against the urge to set aside the lecture and gather her into his arms. This was no time to be soft. Just thinking about what could have happened made his blood run cold.

"A bump against the barrel, an involuntary jerk of my hand . . . anything could have set the gun off, and then where would you be?" He let go of her arm and stalked off a pace before whirling around, his finger jabbing toward the earth, where he visualized her bloody, prostrate form. "On the ground, that's where. Dead."

A shiver passed through him, and he raised a hand to his face to try to rub away the torturous image.

"I trust you, Travis." Meredith took an uneven step toward him. "I know you would never harm me."

"Not intentionally, but accidents happen. You need to exert better judgment, Meri. Stop rushing in to help all the time."

"Stop rushing in . . . ?" She stiffened her posture.

A tickle of unease gathered in Travis's gut.

"It wasn't *my* faulty judgment that placed me in front of your rifle, Travis Archer. It was yours." Her index finger collided with his chest.

Travis frowned. If she thought she was going to turn this around on him, she could think again. *She* was the one who needed to learn how things were done on his land. *She* was the one who needed to quit putting herself in harm's way, conducting those good deeds of hers that always seemed to go awry. *She* was the one —

"I tried to explain who Moses was when I first came across your little welcoming party," she said, intruding on the satisfaction of his inner tirade, "but you were so set on driving him away that you rebuffed my

271

efforts. Had you simply listened, there would have been no need for me to get your attention through drastic measures. Perhaps I did put myself in harm's way, but only because you drove me there."

"I'm sure you could have found other, *safer,* ways to secure my attention." Travis crossed his arms. Let her try to refute that argument.

Meredith crossed her own arms. "Maybe, but none of those options would have put me between you and Moses. And that was precisely where I needed to be. Or did you fail to notice the way his hands curled into fists when he thought I might be in trouble?" She paused, as if daring him to comment. "He would have flattened you if I hadn't intervened."

"I would've held my own," Travis grumbled.

"Would you have shot him?"

Travis rubbed the back of his neck and stared at the tops of his boots. Meredith knew he'd never shoot an unarmed man, he could hear it in her voice. So why was she pressing him?

She took a step toward him and braced her hands on her hips. "One of these days someone is going to call your bluff, Travis, and you'll either have to take whatever they dish out or pull that trigger and live with the consequences. I didn't want today to be that day.

"Moses outweighs you by at least forty pounds." Meredith eyed him dubiously. Travis straightened to his full height and glared at her. "You might've been willing to take him on, but I wasn't willing to let you try, not when I had the ability to clear up the misunderstanding with a simple explanation. So I did what I had to do. I'm an Archer, remember? We protect our own."

He wanted to throttle her. He truly did. Throwing his words back in his face as if the crazy woman actually thought he needed her protection. It was his job to protect her, not the other way around. Yet hearing her declare herself an Archer filled him with such satisfaction, he chose not to correct her misguided notions.

For now.

"Just promise me that you won't put yourself in harm's way again."

She lifted her chin. "I promise not to intentionally put myself in harm's way . . . *unless* I deem it necessary to protect the well-being of another."

Did she have to make everything so complicated? Travis bit back a sigh. At least she agreed to comply with his dictate for the most part. That'd have to be good enough. He'd just ignore the obstinate set of her mouth.

Only he couldn't.

He stared at her lips. Watching them soften as her defiance faded. Imagining the feel of them against his own. Would she welcome a real kiss from him? Not another chaste meeting of lips like at their wedding, but a deep, intimate joining?

Travis jerked his gaze to the sky and flared his nostrils as he strove to subdue the stampede of desire thundering through him. He'd always found his wife attractive, but he'd not been prepared for this sudden ambush of cravings — to kiss her, touch her . . .

Could she read his thoughts? Was he frightening her? 'Cause he was sure as shootin' scaring himself.

"I don't mean to make you angry, Travis," Meredith said, her expression more stubborn than fearful, thank the Lord. "But I can't promise to do something that may violate my conscience."

Angry? What was she talking about? "I'm not mad at you, Meri."

Her brow furrowed. "You're not? I could have sworn you were counting to ten or something, trying to keep your temper in check."

Travis nearly laughed aloud. His sweet, innocent wife had no idea what he'd been trying to keep in check. And he wanted to keep it that way. At least until he learned how to control it a little better.

"I promise I'm not m—"

Meredith's gasp cut him off.

"Oh my stars!" Her panicked eyes darted past him to the house and had him reaching for his rifle to confront the threat. "My cornbread!" She grabbed a fistful of skirt and sprinted down the path and across the yard.

Travis let out a breath and watched her go, propping the unneeded rifle on his shoulder. She sure was a pretty thing. Feisty, too. And even though he hated that she'd put herself in danger, he had to admit that her courage and tender heart were the things he admired most about her.

Perhaps it was time he got serious about courting his wife.

Travis secretly schemed during supper, determined to wait for the right moment. When Meredith cleared away the dessert plates and the empty pie tin that earlier had been filled with sweet, flaky apple goodness,

275

he excused himself to go check on the stock.

If the woman was trying to sweeten him up, she was doing a right fine job of it. He couldn't remember ever tasting anything as delectable as that apple pie. It only made him more anxious to get his wife alone. When he carried his coffee cup to where she stood washing the dishes, he caught the faint aroma of cinnamon and apples clinging to her even after the pie had been fully consumed. He couldn't wait to see if the taste lingered on her lips, as well.

After checking that the horses had adequate feed and water for the night, he headed back to the house with Sadie trailing at his heels. The sun had already dipped beneath the horizon, and light quickly faded from the sky. The moon promised to be bright, though — the perfect backdrop for a courting stroll.

He bent to pat Sadie's head, but the sound of the front door opening urged him back to an upright position. Jim crossed the porch, an unlit lantern in hand.

"Heading to your workshop?" Travis strode forward to meet him at the base of the steps.

"Yep." Jim halted when he reached the ground and hesitated, as if waiting to see if any other conversation would be necessary.

"Whatcha making this time?"

Jim tipped the brim of his hat back and shrugged. "One of them chests womenfolk like to store blankets and such in."

"Oak or pine?" Travis asked, not concerned so much with the answer as in keeping the conversation going.

"Oak."

A question burned on the front of Travis's tongue, but he couldn't quite seem to spit it out. It was only when Jim started to move past him that the words tumbled forth.

"Do you think I did the right thing in hiring Moses and Josiah?" Travis peered into his brother's face, hoping for a sign of approval yet worried that Jim might confirm the uneasy niggling in the back of his mind that accused him of giving Meredith too much influence over his decision.

As always, Jim took his time answering. "The man knows building," he finally said. "And his idea about using stonework for the first three or four feet of the walls is sound. We'll be able to get more use out of the lumber we've salvaged from the original barn, plus the stone at ground level will be less likely to catch fire should a torch ever be tossed down beside it."

"You think he's trustworthy?"

"Dunno. But he and the boy are hard

workers. They sanded the scorch marks from about half the boards in the scrap heap after lunch and tested them for weak spots while you and Crockett checked the grass up by Horseshoe Rock. Said he'd bring along his own tools tomorrow, too, so he wouldn't have to borrow mine. Seems a decent enough fella."

"Good." One of the knots in Travis's belly loosened.

"I think Neill got a kick outta having someone his own age around. Once those two started yakkin', they hardly ever stopped."

Which could mean anything from swapping names and a pleasantry or two to jabbering like a pair of magpies. It was impossible to tell with Jim making the observation. To him, a sentence with more than two words qualified as verbose. He'd probably said more in the last two minutes than he had all day.

"Well, I'll look forward to seeing them in action tomorrow."

Jim nodded and headed off to the shed. Sadie padded after him, leaving Travis alone with the other knot in his gut — the tangle of anticipation and nerves.

Surely Meredith was done tidying the kitchen by now, and hopefully Crockett would be off in the den working on Sunday's lesson or taking Neill on in a game of checkers. The last thing Travis wanted when he asked Meredith to walk with him was an audience.

As it turned out, no audience waited for him in the kitchen, but then, neither did Meredith. Travis moseyed down the hall in search of his wife, trying to look as nonchalant as possible despite the porcupine rolling around in his stomach. He ducked past the den before Crockett could see him, figuring he'd look there last. No sense opening himself to a round of teasing if it wasn't necessary.

Her bedroom door stood open, but when he peeked inside, he found no trace of her. When he turned, however, he was treated to the sight of his wife's backside wiggling toward him as she struggled to pull Neill's door closed while clasping a wad of clothing in one hand and her sewing box in the other.

Travis reached around her to assist, enjoying the contact as his arm brushed against hers. She jumped into a straighter position, and the movement pressed her back snugly against his chest. He liked that even more.

"I didn't mean to startle you." Which was

true, but he sure didn't mind taking advantage of the results. He breathed in the scent of her as he rubbed the side of his jaw against her hair.

Meredith lingered a moment, then stepped away. Travis bit back his disappointment.

"I was gathering the mending," she said, her shy gaze not quite reaching his. "I didn't realize you were behind me."

"No harm done." Travis smiled at her, hoping the grin would pass for charming. Sadie was the only female he'd ever tried to coax into sharing his company before, and something told him gals of the two-legged variety might be a little trickier to convince. "Would you . . . um . . . like to take a walk with me? There's a pretty spot down along the creek that I've been meaning to show you."

"It sounds lovely." Her lips curved encouragingly, then fell. "Oh, but I told Neill I'd repair the cuffs on his favorite work shirt. One snag and the raggedy things are bound to tear clean off."

Hoping the regret he heard lacing her voice was genuine and not just wishful thinking on his part, Travis gently collected the sewing box and pile of shirts from her and tucked them under his arm. "It'll keep," he said.

He led the way to the kitchen, set the mending items on the table, and then took her cloak from the hook on the wall and held it out for her to step into. "Shall we?"

She hesitated, looking at the mending before reaching out to him again. But when she bit her lip and nodded, a spark of eagerness danced in her eyes that set his pulse to thrumming. Meredith reached behind her back to untie her apron, then slid her arms into the sleeves of her cloak and allowed him to fit it over her shoulders. His hands smoothed down the edge of her arms as she did up the top few buttons, and he fought the urge to draw her into a more intimate embrace.

Finally, she turned to face him, her smile sending that porcupine tumbling around inside him again. Bowing slightly, he offered his arm, and once her fingers settled near his elbow, he led her to the door.

22

As they left the yard to stroll along the path his parents used to take when they wanted to escape prying eyes, Travis felt more like a married man than he had since the day he took his vows. Moonlight lit their way, its soft glow adding a touch of enchantment to the pines and walnut trees that surrounded them. He took care to modulate his stride to accommodate her shorter one. The hitch in her gait didn't slow her down, but he found himself taking extra care to guide her around pebbles and uneven ground that he usually didn't give a second thought.

Travis tried to think of something romantic to say, something charming or witty to entertain his lady, but his tongue remained glued to the back of his teeth. The scenery would have to be poetry enough.

"Do you hear the music, Travis?" Meredith glanced his way, her eyes luminous. "The rippling water, the humming crickets, the leaves rustling in the breeze. It's like a lullaby I vaguely remember from childhood coming back to soothe me after a long day."

Travis grinned. It seemed his wife had enough poetry in her soul for both of them.

"My father and I used to sit on the porch when I was young and listen to the night sing to us. He said it was the best cure for a weary spirit. And he was right. I would curl up in his lap and listen to the sounds of the night while the steady beat of his heart matched the rhythm of the rocking chair. No matter what had happened that day, my worries fell away while we rocked."

Her voice had turned so wistful, Travis could easily picture her as the young girl she'd been when first they met, snuggled up in her father's arms, her head lolling against the man's chest as sleep claimed her.

"The last three years must've been hard on you without him."

Meredith stumbled to a halt and turned startled eyes on him. "How could you know that? That he passed three years ago?"

"That's when Christmas stopped." Travis smiled softly at his wife's scrunched expression. "Well, I guess Christmas didn't exactly stop, but that was the first year there was no gift at the gate."

"I don't understand." Something more

than confusion sparked in her eyes, though. Something deeper. A longing to regain a piece of what had been lost.

He prayed what little he knew would ease that ache.

"The first gift arrived the Christmas after I carried you home. A couple old primers, an arithmetic book, and *The Old Farmer's Almanac.* Christmas Eve night he fired off two shots by the gate and left the books for me to find. The only reason I knew it was him was because he had inscribed the front of the almanac with a note thanking me for taking care of his daughter."

Meredith's eyes grew dewy, but her lips turned up at the corners. "Do you still have it?"

Travis nodded, his smile matching hers. "I do. I can show it to you tomorrow."

"I'd like that."

Wrapping his fingers around hers where they still rested in the crook of his arm, Travis gently urged her back into their stroll.

"He surprised me with more books the next year. He always included some kind of schoolbook and the newest almanac, but then he started passing along back issues of the *Palestine Advocate.* On Christmas morning, Crockett and I would take turns reading the stories aloud to the others." A chuckle rose up in Travis's throat as he recalled how young Neill and Jim had been back then. It seemed like ages ago. "It became a tradition. We would all sit outside on the porch on Christmas Eve and listen for the gunshots. I would retrieve the parcel and the boys would swarm me before I could get off my horse.

"Sometimes there would be a novel, once there was a book on animal husbandry, and Crockett's favorite was the year we got a collection of Charles Spurgeon's sermons. There were twenty-seven sermons in that little book if I recall, just enough for Crockett to preach each of them twice to us over the course of a year. I think he did that for three or four years before he finally started writing his own."

"I never knew he did that," Meredith murmured. "I knew he put parcels together for the families of his students. I even helped wrap them in brown paper and tie the strings. But I never knew that one of those parcels ended up on your doorstep."

"Three years ago, even though most of us were grown men, we still sat on the porch waiting for those shots just like we did when we were kids. Only that year, the shots never came." Travis tried to tamp down a rising lump in his throat.

"We grieved that Christmas, Meri. Not because we missed the joy of the gifts, but because we knew something had happened to the giver. I think all along it was the idea that someone remembered us and cared enough about our education and upbringing to give the books rather than the books themselves that made such an impact on us. Your father was a kind man, and I am proud to be married to his daughter."

Meredith brushed the pad of her thumb beneath her eyes, but the smile she turned on him was glorious.

"Thank you," she said, her eyes glistening — the longing replaced by gratitude and something else that made his heart turn a flip.

The path widened as they approached the pool at the base of a small waterfall. The creek only tumbled a few feet over the rocky ground, but it was enough to create a decent fishing hole. And near the edge sat a large boulder where his father used to sit with his mother.

Travis had never forgotten the time he'd cut through the trees with his pole and jar of worms only to find his father lifting his mother onto the boulder before nestling in beside her. Travis had hid among the pines and watched his mother lean her head on

Father's shoulder. Joseph Archer had taken her hand and held it to his lips, then turned to his wife and whispered words that had made her smile and lift her face to accept his kiss.

Not accustomed to seeing more than a quick peck or two between his parents, Travis grew uncomfortable when that kiss stretched longer and longer. He'd quietly retreated and returned to the house, ignoring Crockett's teasing about his inability to catch a fish. He never told Crockett about what he'd seen. It felt too private. But from that moment on, the rock at the fishing hole had been dubbed the Kissing Rock in his mind. He'd never climbed on it since, promising himself that the next time he sat there, he'd have a girl of his own to kiss.

"What a beautiful place," Meredith exclaimed as he drew them to a stop by the rock.

"I'd hoped you'd like it." Travis watched her face as she took in the surroundings with wonder and delight. "I thought we could sit and talk for a bit, if you wanted."

"I'd like that." The mistiness had disappeared from her eyes, yet they continued to sparkle in the moonlight.

"This rock makes a good seat." Hearing the huskiness in his voice, he quickly cleared his throat. "I'll . . . uh . . . just help you up."

He fit his hands around her waist, his gaze mingling with hers. Then, not trusting himself to linger too long, he lifted her onto the rock and scampered up the side where smaller stones offered footholds. He settled close to her side, brushing his legs against hers and bracing his right arm behind her back. He stole glances at her while pretending to be as lost as she in the beauty of their environment. Her mouth drew his attention again and again, and he found himself desperately wishing he knew what his father had whispered to his mother to make her offer him her lips.

So consumed was he with thoughts of kissing, that when Meri opened her mouth to speak instead, it took a moment for her words to register.

"I studied to be a teacher." She turned her head and looked at him. "Did I ever mention that?"

As he tried to refocus his brain on conversation, she stretched her arms behind her to support her back and inadvertently rubbed her forearm against his bicep. His muscle twitched at her touch, and Travis had to work to keep his mind on their conversation. "No. I . . . uh . . . don't think you did."

A faraway look came over her, and her gaze shifted to hover somewhere above the creek. "After the Freedmen's Bureau shut down in '70, Father continued teaching at the freedmen's school. The students and their parents were so hungry for the education that had been denied them, they made great sacrifices to continue paying him a salary.

"When I got older, he occasionally took me with him, let me read to the little ones and help them with their alphabet. Before long I was as enamored with teaching as he was, and for the first time in my life, I felt . . . useful and appreciated."

She crossed her legs at the ankle and swung them out and back, her heels thumping quietly against the rock in an easy rhythm. "I attended the Palestine Female Institute and planned to sit for the teacher's exam, but then my parents came down with that fever." Her feet stilled for a moment. Then she sat straighter and swung them back into motion. "I had hoped to continue Papa's work at the freedmen's school, but Aunt Noreen wouldn't hear of it. She declared it unseemly to involve myself with such people and insisted it was too dangerous for a young woman to travel such a distance alone."

Travis hated to agree with anything the old bat had to say, but just the thought of Meredith traipsing about unprotected made his stomach churn.

"Seeing Moses again today awakened those old dreams." Meri aimed her blue eyes on him, hope glimmering in their depths. "I want to teach at the school again, Travis. Just one day a week. Saturday — when the largest number of students are able to attend. I would only need to be away from the ranch for a few hours. I could leave right after the noon meal and be back before supper. I promise I won't fall behind in my chores. You probably won't even know that I'm gone."

Her sentences flew at him in such rapid succession, they made him dizzy. And the churning in his gut intensified.

"Please say you'll let me go."

"No." Travis's throat closed over the word, as if an unseen hand were choking him. Her crestfallen expression pierced his heart, but he wouldn't be swayed. He tightened his jaw and looked up to the moon.

Leave the ranch? Alone? There was no way he'd let her do that. Anything could happen to her. Anything.

Her legs halted their swinging, and she twisted to look him full in the face. "Why?"

A buzzing expanded through his brain like a swarm of bees growing more and more agitated. "Archers don't leave," he ground out.

Meredith laid her hand over his. "Why?"

A muscle in his thigh jumped. Why was she questioning him? Why couldn't she just let things be? His leg twitched again and his arm began to shake. Her palm stroked the back of his hand as if to calm him. She'd noticed. She thought him weak. Afraid. But she didn't understand.

Travis jerked his hand out from beneath hers. He needed to leave. To escape. To run.

"Why do Archers never leave the ranch, Travis?" she persisted.

"A promise." The creek disappeared before him, replaced by a vision of his father reaching out to him from his sick bed, clasping his hand and making him swear. "I promised to keep them safe. Together. 'Don't leave the land, son,' he said. 'If you do, they'll take it from you. They'll split you up. Stand together. On the ranch, you're strong.'"

Travis blinked away the image of his father and turned to Meredith, his voice little more than a whisper. "On the ranch we're strong."

Meri lifted her hand and caressed his face. His eyes slid closed.

"You're strong anywhere, Travis. You all are."

Her hand felt cool against his cheek, and for just a moment he allowed himself to rest in her confidence. Slowly, he opened his eyes and found hers gazing back at him filled with trust and admiration — sentiments he wasn't sure he deserved.

"Your father was right to urge you to stay together and seclude yourself from others who would try to take advantage of your youth, but you're not boys anymore. Not even Neill. You're men. Strong Archer men. This ranch has been a haven for you for years, but if you're not careful, it will become a prison."

"It's not a prison." He pulled away from her touch and jumped down from the rock. "It's a home." He fisted his hands as if he could fight off her words.

The slide of fabric against stone whispered behind him, punctuated by a tiny grunt as her feet hit the ground. "A home where no one is free to leave? A home where all who come calling are treated like criminals? How long do you think the others will be content to live here in your shadow? Did you not see how hungry Crockett was to talk to the minister on the day of our wedding? He stayed at the man's side, throwing question after question at him about shepherding congregations and seminary and sermons.

"He has a gift for preaching, Travis. I can tell that after only one Sunday service in your home. God placed that desire on his heart and equipped him for the task, yet because of his loyalty to you, he has done nothing to pursue his calling."

Travis spun to face his wife, his accuser. "Maybe God called him to minister to his family. Or is that not grand enough for you? Perhaps you think a man can only serve God if he impacts hundreds or thousands, that three souls are not significant."

"Even one is significant."

Why was she looking at him like that? As if she were no longer talking about Crockett but about him. This wasn't about him. Everything he did was for his family. To protect them. To support them. And now this . . . this outsider who had known them for all of . . . what, less than a week? . . . had the gall to insinuate that he was trapping his brothers in some kind of prison, binding them with family loyalty, and stealing their freedom. She understood nothing!

Travis pounded up to the creek bank, barely containing the fury that burned in his gut. "You want to leave?" He spun around and marched back up to her. "Fine.

Take your horse and leave. You're not really an Archer anyway."

She staggered back, her right hand pressed against her middle as if staunching a wound.

All at once he realized what he'd said. Remorse nearly cut his legs out from under him. Travis rushed forward and clasped her free hand between both of his. "Meri, forgive me. I didn't mean it. I swear I didn't." He drew her hand to his mouth and laid kiss after kiss upon her knuckles, unable to look at her face.

Meredith tugged her hand free of his grasp and turned her back.

"I don't want to leave you, Travis. I just want to help others." Her quiet words flayed him. "But helping others isn't the Archer way, is it?" She pivoted, her delicate chin jutting forth like that of a soldier. "Archers hide in their trees, too scared of what *could* happen to risk reaching out to someone in need."

"I reached out to you."

"But only because you felt responsible." Her chin dipped a bit, some of the fight going out of her.

Was she right? Had he only married her because he felt obligated? If so, why did the thought of her taking him up on his insistence that she leave chill his blood?

Travis closed the space between him and his wife with a single step. "You think I'm scared, Meri? Well, I am. Scared to let you go. Scared that something will happen to you." *Like what happened to my father.* He lifted one hand to her face and stroked her cheek with his thumb. "I can control things to some extent on the ranch, but away from it? I won't be able to protect you."

"Oh, Travis." She shook her head at him, her mouth twitching into an ironic smile. "You do realize, don't you, that the two most serious injuries I've endured in my life have happened while on your property? Not by any fault of yours, of course, but one could argue that I'm actually safer off the ranch than on."

A groan vibrated in his throat, turning into a reluctant chuckle. The woman had a point.

"No matter how many precautions we take, none of us are truly in control. Only God can claim that kind of authority. All we can do is use the good sense he provides and trust him to guide us." Meredith stroked his arm from shoulder to wrist, then lightly clasped his hand. "If you want to protect me, Travis, prayer is just as powerful a weapon as that gun you carry."

Travis blinked, stunned by the simplicity of that statement. Did he believe it? When was the last time he'd prayed, really prayed, for the Lord's protection over his family? He'd been depending on himself for so long, he'd forgotten how to trust another with that duty. Even God.

Reaching for a faith that was more than just Sunday-deep, he inhaled a shaky breath and cleared his throat. "This teaching thing. It's important to you?"

She nodded. "Yes. But not more important than our marriage. If you don't want me to go, I'll respect your wishes."

He didn't want her to go. Not at all. Yet he couldn't keep her a prisoner, either. How would she ever come to love him if he stole her freedom?

"You're not to tarry. You hear me? Straight there and straight home. And you'll take a rifle. Prayer is all well and good, and I imagine I'll be sending a constant litany heavenward while you're gone, but I doubt a little earthly defense will offend our Maker."

She bounced up and down on her toes, her smile bright enough to rival the moon. "Thank you, Travis. Thank you, thank you, thank you!" Before he knew what she was about, she grabbed his shoulders and planted a kiss on his cheek.

His blood heated in an instant. He snaked

his arm around her waist and drew her firmly against his body. "If you're gonna thank me, Meri, do it proper."

Travis bent his head and captured the startled little sound that escaped her parted lips. His emotions were too raw, too close to the surface to contain, so he kissed her with everything inside him. Desire, fear, yearning, and a touch of desperation fueled his passion. He melded his mouth to hers, trailing his hand upward along her back until his fingers buried themselves in the hair at her nape.

He told himself to stop, afraid he'd frighten her, but just as he steeled himself to pull away, she moaned deep in her throat and wrapped her arms around his neck. Travis's pulse leapt, her response too sweet to ignore. He slanted his lips over hers again, deepening the kiss until he felt her tremble. Only then did he gentle his assault, loosening his hold as he softened his lips. He moved his hands to cradle her face and leaned his forehead against hers. Eyes closed, lips inches apart, their ragged breathing mingled in the air between them.

"You belong to me, Meri," he whispered hoarsely. "You *are* an Archer, but more importantly, you're my wife."

She said nothing, but he felt the slight bob

of her head as she tried to nod. Something deep inside him relaxed.

He'd not driven her away after all. Thank God. He wanted to kiss her again, and more. Much more. But he'd already taken enough backward steps tonight. He'd not rush things. Meredith deserved a proper courtship, and she was going to get one, even if it killed him.

And kill him it might, if it meant sitting back and watching her ride off to teach at that school of hers. But he couldn't imprison her at the ranch and expect to earn her loyalty. Nor her love. Such commodities had to be given freely. As did trust — something he'd have to learn to give more freely himself.

Keep her safe, Lord, he prayed as he pulled Meredith into his embrace and tucked her head under his chin. *Keep my wife safe.*

He didn't know how or when she had become so important to him, but as he stood there holding her, he was certain of one thing. He never wanted to lose her.

23

"Swear to me you'll be careful."

Meredith smiled at her husband's stern expression. Travis demanded the same thing every time she left. Of course, this was only her third Saturday to travel to the school, so perhaps he was still adjusting. Nevertheless, her heart gave a little leap every time she heard the protective growl that proved he cared.

"I swear it."

He took the flour sack that held Neill's old primers and tied it to Ginger's saddle, then checked the cinch for the third time. Meredith chuckled and laid a gentle hand on his shoulder.

"It's secure, Travis. You saddled her yourself, remember?"

He looked up, his eyes scanning her face as if trying to commit every feature to memory. She ducked her head as her cheeks began to warm.

Travis cleared his throat and kicked at the dirt. "You got the gate key?"

"Yes." Meredith lifted her hand to her chest in confirmation. The key hung from a chain around her neck. Its outline was barely discernible to her touch through the layers of her dress and cloak, but she could feel the metal press against her skin.

Knowing what question he'd ask next, she answered before he finished drawing a full breath. "Yes, the rifle is loaded. And yes, I'll come straight home after the last lesson."

"You better." His lips twitched as he struggled to maintain his serious mien. Then before she could react, he grabbed the folds of her cloak and pulled her to him. His lips came down on hers, possessive, demanding, and so intense her knees shook.

"Come home to me, Meri," he whispered, his voice husky and deep.

"Always." The single word was all she could manage just then, but she infused it with all the love in her heart.

He'd still made no move to come to her room, not even after that soul-stirring kiss they'd shared down by the creek. He and the rest of the clan had been so busy with rebuilding the barn and driving the cattle to wherever they could find undepleted pasture, that she rarely even spoke to her

300

husband except at meals. But on Saturdays he made a point to see her off. On Saturdays he kissed her. On Saturdays he gave her hope that their marriage could be based on something deeper than hastily spoken vows.

She adored Saturdays.

Travis laced his fingers together and bent to give her a leg up. Meredith reached for the saddle horn, placed her left boot in the stirrup, and put her right into her husband's keeping. He helped her into the saddle and patted Ginger's neck as Meredith gathered the reins.

"I'll be watching for you." His hat shielded his face from her view as he ran his fingers along the chestnut-and-white pattern of Ginger's shoulder. His hand reached the cinch, and she thought the daft man was going to check it a fourth time, but he skimmed over the strap and settled instead upon her ankle. The solid presence of his hand filtered through the leather of her boot top as he assured himself that her foot sat securely in the stirrup. It seemed an intimate, husbandly gesture, and Meredith's heart swelled. Then his thumb stroked upward and brushed against her stocking. Her breath caught.

He finally lifted his face to hers, and the heated look in his eyes left no doubt in her mind that the touch had been deliberate. "Hurry home." The words lingered as his gaze melded to hers. Then he stepped back and swatted Ginger lightly on the hindquarters to set her into motion.

The paint's bouncing trot demanded Meredith's attention. She turned forward in the saddle and took charge of the animal. Moses called down a farewell from where he and Jim were nailing shingles onto the barn roof, and Meredith raised a hand to wave at them as she rode past. Jim saluted her with a lift of his hammer — a gesture so typical of her stoic brother-in-law that it normally would have brought a smile to her face. But Meredith was too consumed with thoughts of Travis to pay Jim much heed.

Could it be her husband felt something more than protectiveness toward her? More than obligation? She'd let herself believe so when he kissed her, but even then the fantasy didn't completely dispel the hint of desperation she sensed in him. It was as if he needed to stake his claim on her before he could let her go.

What would it be like to have him kiss her simply out of desire? Out of love? Suddenly Saturdays seemed inadequate. She wanted to be kissed on a Tuesday. No special occasion. No threat to her well-being. Just a warm sharing of affection between a husband and wife. To see that heated look in his eyes again, as if she truly meant more to him than duty.

And what of your vow to be content in your marriage?

The thought brought a swift end to her self-pity.

Forgive me, Lord. I'm turning my mind in the wrong direction, aren't I? I became so consumed by what I didn't have that I forgot all about what I do have.

Just like those times when Aunt Noreen's caustic personality wore her down and bitterness started to leak into her soul. She had to take charge of her thoughts and steer them in a more positive direction. It was time to count her blessings.

One — she was married to the man of her dreams. Two — Travis had allowed her to continue her father's legacy by teaching at the freedmen's school. Three — she belonged to a family of godly men who would protect her with their lives. Meredith turned her gaze toward heaven and smiled, the burden on her heart already beginning to lift. She truly was blessed. Just thinking about how far her relationship with Travis had progressed over the last few weeks stirred songs of thanksgiving in her soul.

She could only imagine what strides they could make in the next few weeks.

Help me to be patient. To accept your timing.

Her grin widened as the gate came into view. Perhaps one day soon, she would unlock Travis's heart as easily as she was able to unlock the gate to his land. All she had to do was find the right key. Or become so trusted by him that he unlocked it himself. Wouldn't that be something?

Buoyed by hope, Meredith slid from the saddle and drew the chain around her neck upward until the gate key freed itself from her clothing. Humming a cheery tune, she made short work of the gate, leading Ginger through and carefully relocking it before climbing atop a nearby stone to remount.

Travis might feel safe behind all his fences and gates, but she aimed to show him that freedom was sweeter. Especially when founded on love.

Urging Ginger into a canter, Meredith leaned forward in the saddle and let the exhilarating rush of the wind tug at her hairpins and sting her cheeks with its frosty bite. If she arrived disheveled and chapped, so be it. Her students understood the significance of freedom. They'd not condemn her for indulging in a spirited ride.

But fifteen minutes later, when she reined Ginger to a walk in front of the schoolhouse, a host of concerned children swarmed from the schoolyard to surround her.

"What done happened to your hair, Miss Meri?"

"Didja fall off your horse?"

"Why was you ridin' so fast?"

"Was som'un chasin' you?"

"I'm fine, children," she assured them, laughter bubbling up to accompany her words. "I simply chose to give Ginger her head today." She patted the paint's neck.

When the children continued to press closer, Ginger halted. The horse didn't seem too perturbed by the crowding, just cautious.

"Get back, now, and give Miss Meri some air." Myra Jackson moved through the throng, shooing children back toward the schoolhouse. "How's she gonna teach us anything if'n she can't get off her horse?"

The children moaned but obeyed, filing off toward the schoolhouse to find their desks.

"Joshua, you stay and tend to Ginger. Rub her down real good, you hear?"

"Yes'm." Myra's younger boy stood at the horse's head, waiting patiently for Meredith to dismount.

Once her feet were planted on the ground, Meredith tossed him the reins. "Thank you, Joshua." She untied her supply bag and stepped aside.

As the boy led her horse away, Meredith sidled up next to Myra. "You know, I think he's going to catch up to Josiah soon. He's nearly the same height."

"Don't I know it?" Myra's mouth turned up in a proud motherly smile. "And him three years younger. The boy's got his father's hands, too. Big as fryin' pans they are."

Meredith grinned, remembering how Moses had curled those big hands of his into fists. Getting hit with one of those would probably feel a lot like getting walloped with a skillet. "Joshua seems to have inherited your love of books, though. Has he finished *The Last of the Mohicans?*"

Myra nodded. "Mm-hmm. Two days ago. He tol' me you promised to bring a new one this week."

"That I did." She opened her bag and pulled out her copy of *The Adventures of Tom Sawyer.* "I don't think you've read this one yet, Myra. It was only published a few years ago, so it wasn't among the books my father used to loan you."

"Joshua might have to fight me for it,

then." The older woman winked at Meredith and tucked the book under her arm.

Meredith laughed and followed her friend into the classroom. Myra Jackson kept the small building as tidy as herself, which was saying a lot since the woman's apron was always starched and pressed, her black hair always combed into a perfect knot, and her dress always so pristine that dust wouldn't dare approach its folds. Meredith reached a hand to her own hair and sighed. Freedom had more than taken its toll. No wonder the children had stared.

Taking a minute to repair the wind's damage, Meredith remained at the back of the class while Myra called the group to order and asked them to take out their primers. The worn books were the same ones her father had started the school with over a decade ago. They'd been well cared for, though. Unfortunately, there were never enough to go around, which was why she'd asked Travis if she could borrow Neill's old schoolbooks.

Taking the slender volumes from her bag, she distributed them to the adults who sat on benches at the back of the room. The surprised faces and reverent strokes of the covers warmed her heart. These parents hungered for learning even more than their children did, yet they insisted the younger generation have first access to the few books and other materials available. Such noble souls. She wished she could do more for them.

As Myra asked one of the female students to stand and read a passage aloud, Meredith moved to the front of the room and quietly began writing a series of arithmetic problems on the blackboard.

Despite a lack of formal training, Myra had done her best to continue where Meredith's father had left off, teaching the local children the basics of reading, writing, and arithmetic. And when Meredith mentioned to Moses her idea of teaching at the school, she'd made it clear she had no intention of supplanting Myra in any way. She only wanted to make herself available to assist.

Myra, however, responded as if Meredith's offer were a gift from above. The first Saturday they met, she pulled Meredith into a fierce hug and praised the Lord right there in the schoolyard. She'd been praying, she'd said, for the Lord to provide a teacher for her advanced students, someone capable of preparing them for future studies or for professions that would utilize their minds instead of breaking their backs. She dreamed of her students one day becoming teachers themselves, or shopkeepers, or even doctors. Education opened doors, and Myra was bound and determined to fling wide as many portals as possible.

So, for the three hours Meredith spent at Myra's school every Saturday, she taught advanced mathematics, grammar, and history to the half-dozen students who already excelled in the more elementary lessons. Joshua was particularly bright, and Meredith had high hopes of him continuing his studies at Wiley College up in Marshall. Her father would've been thrilled to have one of his former students attend the new school, and she couldn't deny that she, too, would be proud to have played some minor role in the boy's success.

But first she needed to help him master algebra.

Turning to face her group of students, Meredith caught Joshua's eye as he slid into his seat after seeing to her horse. She smiled and motioned him forward. "Joshua, would you please come to the board and work the first equation?"

"Yes, Miss Meri," he said, matching her quiet tone so as not to disturb the rest of the class.

And so it began. Each of the older children took turns working problems, and when not at the blackboard, they practiced on their slates. If one student made an error, another could volunteer to make the correction. Once the algebra problems had been completed, Meredith administered the oral quiz she had prepared over the Boston Tea Party. The students had only one history text between them, but they had worked out a system that allowed each person to take possession of it on a different day, and she was pleased by how much they had retained.

The students had just started reciting their grammar lesson when the light from the doorway abruptly dimmed. Meredith glanced up to see a large man standing in the entrance.

"Moses?" The concern in Myra's voice sharpened Meredith's attention.

Why had he come? Had Josiah been hurt? Or . . . Travis? Meredith took an involuntary step closer to the aisle, her heart thumping painfully in her chest.

"I need a word with Miss Meri." He pointed the hat he held in his hand toward her, his gaze finally leaving his wife to settle on Meredith.

"Finish your recitations, children," she murmured as she took her cloak down from the nail on the side wall. "And study lessons seven and eight for next week."

Her students nodded but did nothing to break the unnatural hush that had fallen over the schoolroom. The quiet only amplified Meredith's unease, and every time a floorboard squeaked as she made her way to the door, the echo frayed her nerves further. By the time she reached Moses and followed him outside, her hands were shaking.

Moses tried to lead her a discreet distance away, but she grabbed hold of his arm, needing answers more than privacy. "Has something happened to my husband?"

"No, ma'am." He turned to face her, his earnest expression spearing relief through her. "Everybody be fine."

She exhaled a heavy breath. "Thank heavens."

"But there sure 'nough be trouble of some kind, 'cause Mr. Travis, he done tol' me to fetch you right quick."

Meredith slipped her arms into the sleeves of her cloak and worked the fasteners. There was no question — she would return at once. Travis needed her. "Do you have any idea what the trouble is?"

"No, Miss Meri. But it might have somethin' to do with their visitor."

A visitor? Meredith jerked her attention

from her buttons to the grim line of Moses's mouth.

"I noticed a strange horse in the corral when I come in from the barn. It weren't wearing the Archer brand."

Meredith's pulse picked up speed again. Had one of Roy's men come to make more threats? For the first time, she realized how Travis must feel when things began spiraling out of his control. The horrible helplessness that swamped her at the thought of her family being in trouble while she was too far away to help made her ill.

"I need my horse." She rushed past Moses only to see Josiah leading Ginger toward her.

Moses came up behind her and lifted her into the saddle. Meredith thanked him and kicked Ginger into a gallop. This time the wind in her hair brought no feeling of freedom, only a growing urgency as she raced home.

24

When Meredith rode into the yard, she scanned the barn and outbuildings for any hint of what the trouble could be, but nothing seemed out of place. None of the men were in evidence, either, which sent a frisson of alarm skittering down her back. Meredith reined Ginger to a halt in front of the house and jumped to the ground, ignoring the twinge of pain that shot up her weak leg. She tossed the lead line around the porch railing and pounded up the steps.

"Travis?" His name echoed through the house as she threw the door wide.

The sound of muffled voices drifted to her through the parlor wall. Meredith hurried the short distance to the entrance and nearly collided with her husband as his form filled the doorway. He looked blessedly hearty, if a bit haggard. She laid her palms upon his chest, needing the solid feel of him to reassure her that he was indeed unharmed.

"You're all right?" The breathless whisper escaped before her mind could stop it. The man probably thought her a nitwit. Of course he was all right. He was standing right in front of her, for goodness' sake.

Yet something that flashed in his eyes dissolved her chagrin. He claimed her hands in his larger ones and gave them a gentle squeeze before a wail from somewhere behind him broke the spell.

"What on earth . . . ?" Meredith tilted her head to see around her husband's shoulder. A familiar set of blond curls peeked at her over the back of the settee. "Cassie?"

Her cousin pushed away from a beleaguered-looking Jim, whose wet shirtfront attested to the length of time he'd offered himself as a human handkerchief, and twisted to peer at Meredith.

"Oh, Meri. Thank the Lord you're home." Her reddened eyes and blotchy complexion spurred Meredith to her side. Cassie had been known to shed a strategic tear or two when trying to get her way, but Meredith had never seen her so distraught.

Squeezing onto the settee between her cousin and the sofa arm, Meredith grasped Cassandra's hands. "What happened?"

Cassie's face crumpled. "Papa's done

something awful, Meri. Truly awf-f-fullll." The last word ended on another wail as Cassie threw herself into Meredith's arms.

Wrapping her cousin in a tight embrace, Meredith glanced around the room at her brothers-in-law, questioning them with her eyes.

They all wore the same bewildered expression, offering no help whatsoever.

"We haven't been able to get much out of her," Travis said softly, his hands gripping the wooden trim on the back of the settee near her shoulder. "She insisted on waiting for you."

"Well, I'm here now." Meredith spoke more to Cassie than Travis. She patted her cousin's back a final time, then gently clasped her arms and sat her up straight. "Whatever Uncle Everett has done, we will deal with it." Meredith reached a hand to Cassie's hair and began rearranging the disheveled curls. "Now, let's get you presentable so you'll feel better. You really are quite a wreck." She smiled fondly at her cousin to take the sting from her words. Yet the delicate prick to Cassandra's vanity sparked the exact reaction Meredith intended.

Her cousin immediately set about putting her appearance to rights, wiping the tear tracks from her cheeks, smoothing her skirts, and straightening her posture. The quick self-conscious glance she directed toward Jim as he rose from the settee didn't go unnoticed, either. Cassie wouldn't be falling apart again — not in front of the men, anyway.

"I never thought Papa would steal from his own flesh and blood." Cassie gave a little sniff. "It's not like him at all, you know. But when Mama insisted it was the only way to save the business, he gave in." Cassandra placed her hand atop Meredith's, her earnest face pleading for understanding. "You must forgive him, Meri. His financial troubles are much more dire than I imagined. I'm sure he felt this was the only way."

"Cass, you're making my head spin." Meredith's forehead crinkled as she tried to make sense of the convoluted story. "What, exactly, has he done?"

"Before I tell you, promise me that you won't hold it against me. I want no part of this scheme. I said as much to Papa, but Mama slapped my face for talking back and said I'd do what was right for the family, that I'd been pampered long enough, and it was time for me to do my duty."

"Aunt Noreen actually struck you?" The shock of it pushed Meredith back against the arm of the sofa. Her aunt had always doted on Cassandra. Meredith couldn't even remember the woman speaking to her daughter in a harsh tone.

"Yes." Cassie's chin wobbled, but she fought to keep the tears at bay. "That's when I knew that I couldn't cajole Papa out of the idea. There was too much at stake. My only chance to escape was to beg you to take me in."

"You are always welcome in my home, Cass. You know that. But you really must cease all this beating around the bush and tell me what is going on."

Her cousin lowered her lashes as if too ashamed to meet Meredith's gaze. "Instead of signing over Uncle Teddy's land to you upon your marriage, as he and Uncle Teddy arranged, Papa plans to use it as a dowry. For me."

"He's stealing my land?" Meredith could barely get the words out, so deflated was she by the revelation. "The home I grew up in?"

A warm hand settled on her shoulder and stroked the skin at her neck. *Travis.* His quiet support kept her from shattering. But she couldn't look at him. What would he think? That land was the only thing of value she'd brought to their marriage. She'd hoped to pass it down to their children one day, just as his father had passed down the Archer ranch to him and his brothers. Her dowry had just been stolen from him to be given to another.

To Cassie.

Meredith stiffened. The only reason Uncle Everett would use the land as a dowry for Cassandra would be to entice a prosperous suitor into making an offer. A man who would value the land.

Meredith's stomach lurched. She prayed her intuition was wrong. "Who do they expect you to marry?"

Cassie finally looked up, her eyes twin pools of sorrow. "Roy Mitchell."

Tension speared through Meredith's shoulders beneath Travis's fingers. He tried to massage some of it away, but his own muscles had bunched so tight, he doubted it was very effective.

How could Everett Hayes be such a weak-livered dunce? What little respect Travis held for the man due to his relationship with Meri evaporated. Even if Hayes was fool enough to believe Mitchell innocent of the attack on Travis's barn, he should have enough qualms to prevent him from handing over the daughter he claimed to love

318

simply to boost his deteriorating business.

He glanced at each of his brothers, all of them wearing the same stony-eyed expression, and made his intention clear by moving to stand directly between the backs of the two women sitting on the settee. Travis slid his hands along the wooden trim of the sofa until his spread arms encompassed them both. Meredith loved Cassandra like a sister. That made her family. Archers protected family.

Crockett, Neill, and Jim all met his stare and gave their nod of assent. Jim held Travis's gaze the longest and took a deliberate step closer to their visitor as he clenched his jaw in determination. His meaning was clear. Jim had just staked a claim. And made himself responsible for Cassandra's welfare.

"You can't go along with it, Cass." Meredith shoved up out of her seat and started pacing, her uneven gait agitated and unsteady as she crossed the rug. Travis moved farther into the room, wishing he could spare her this latest betrayal.

Cassandra shifted to the edge of the settee. "I know. That's why I came here. You were obviously right about Mr. Mitchell. He must have only been after your land if the bride accompanying it makes so little difference to him. I can't marry someone who cares nothing for me."

"It's worse than that." Meredith spun to face her cousin. "He's dangerous. Or did you forget about him sending men to set fire to the Archers' barn?"

The younger woman tilted her chin at a quizzical angle as she slowly rose to her feet. "Papa assured me that was a misunderstanding. That it was one of Roy's competitors who set the fire."

"I heard him give the order, Cassie. There was no misunderstanding." Meredith crossed her arms over her chest. Instead of lending her a look of determination, however, the movement gave her an air of vulnerability, as if she strove to protect herself from another family member's disbelief.

"Papa wouldn't lie to me. I'm sure of it."

Travis strode to Meredith's side, the instinct to protect her driving him forward. His jaw tensed as he glowered at the young woman before him. "Your papa *wants* to believe in Mitchell's innocence because he needs the man's partnership." His words came out clipped and impatient even to his own ears. Little Cassie would just have to deal with it, though. He couldn't stomach another Hayes gainsaying Meri in order to make excuses for the man who destroyed his property and plotted to steal his land. "Money clouded his judgment, and he accepted the word of a stranger over family."

"Isn't there the slightest chance you misheard, Meri?" Doubt clouded the girl's features as she scrambled to keep her doting father from sliding farther off his pedestal.

"No," Meredith answered, her voice rich with compassion. "I'm sure of what I heard. But even if there *was* a chance, would you be willing to risk your future happiness on such short odds?"

Cassandra bit her lower lip and shook her head. Meredith rushed to her side and wrapped her arms around her.

"What am I going to do?"

Meredith smiled that brave smile of hers that always made Travis's chest puff with pride. "We'll think of something. For now, though, you're going to come to the kitchen and help me make supper."

"You know I can't cook."

Meredith tucked her cousin under her arm like a mother hen with a chick and led her toward the door. "Well, it's about time you learned, don't you think?"

Meredith twisted her neck to meet Travis's gaze before she swept out of the room. He felt her thanks without her having to say a word, and the fact that he could read her looks as well as those of his brothers made him pause. She was becoming part of him.

Once the women's voices receded, Travis turned back to face his brothers. They all gravitated toward the center of the room.

"What's the plan, Trav?" Neill asked.

"She ain't marrying Mitchell." Jim glared at Travis, daring him to argue.

Travis clapped him on the shoulder. "Cassandra will stay here under our protection until we decide what needs to be done. In the meantime, it might be a good idea —"

A pair of shots echoed in the distance, cutting Travis off. He instinctively looked to the window. Cassandra's father had made good time.

"Have you noticed that we've had more visitors in the last few weeks than we had all of last year? Maybe we should consider opening a hotel." Crockett's sarcasm earned him a punch in the arm from Jim.

Travis bit back a reply. He couldn't deny that things had started spiraling further and further out of control ever since Meredith showed up on their ranch, but even with all the trouble, he didn't regret her appearance. How could he? She was family.

A tiny seed of a thought surfaced in his mind, that perhaps she was even more than family, but he didn't have time to examine it too closely. He had an irate father to deal with and a brother to restrain from shooting said father. That was about all he could handle at the moment.

"Jim, you're with me. Neill, take position near the barn. Crockett —" he paused long enough to smirk at his oldest sibling — "you can man the Archer Hotel."

Crockett's chuckle followed him as he and the others filed out the front door.

25

Travis and Jim approached the gate from among the trees instead of using the path, taking the opportunity to observe their quarry before making their presence known. Everett Hayes paced back and forth beside the gate, muttering under his breath. The rifle gripped in his right hand gave Travis pause.

Perhaps his customary show of force wasn't the best course of action this time. The man had already worked himself into a lather, and with Jim's temper being riled, as well, things could get ugly fast. Meredith's warning about someone calling his bluff one day floated through his mind.

With a silent motion, Travis lifted his rifle from its ready position across his lap and angled the barrel into the scabbard attached to his saddle. He shoved it home.

"What are you doing?" Jim hissed.

"Put your gun away."

"Not a chance." He tightened his grip on the weapon and braced the stock against his thigh.

Travis frowned at him. "Do you really think that putting a bullet in Cassandra's father is going to endear you to her?"

Jim shifted slightly in his saddle.

"If Everett Hayes is foolish enough to believe Mitchell's lies, he's foolish enough to start something with that gun of his that we'd have to finish. And if one of us puts a bullet in him, we'll have to take him up to the house and let Crockett patch him up. Not the best scenario for keeping him away from Cassie, is it."

Jim said nothing, just eyed Everett Hayes through the trees, his jaw clenched. After a long minute, he expelled a full breath through his nostrils like a provoked bull, then flipped his rifle around and crammed it into his scabbard.

Thanking the Lord for his brother's co-operation and adding in a quick plea for Hayes to see reason as easily, Travis nudged Bexar out into the open and raised a hand in greeting to his wife's uncle.

Hayes started at the sight of Travis and Jim emerging from among the pines and snapped his rifle to his shoulder. "About time you got here." He glowered at Travis over the barrel of the gun with eyes that looked a little too wild for reasonable conversation. "I want my daughter back. Now!"

"Cassandra's safe," Travis said. He figured if *his* daughter ran away, fear for her well-being might make him a bit crazed, too. The least he could do was put that fear to rest for the man.

"Safe with *you?* Ha! The last female of my household that came to visit you unescorted ended up half dead with a soiled reputation. I'm not about to let Cassie share the same fate."

Travis leaned forward in his saddle, his brief flash of sympathy hardening to stone as he glared down at the older man from his position atop Bexar. "Put the gun away, Hayes, and we'll talk. Keep waving it at me, and you can forget about gaining my help with your daughter."

The man held his position, but Travis could see indecision playing across his face as he glanced from one brother to the other. Finally, he lowered his rifle and stepped closer to the gate.

"All right, Archer. Now let me in so I can fetch my daughter."

Travis stood in the stirrups and swung his leg over Bexar's back. Jim dismounted, as well, and the two strode forward. When they reached the gate, Travis hung both arms over the top of the highest crossbar and braced a foot on the lowest, trying to appear as friendly and nonthreatening as possible. Jim, on the other hand, stood as straight as a soldier and kept his gun belt within easy reach. Neither made a move to unlock the wooden barrier that obstructed the man's entrance.

"Cassandra will be staying with us for a while," Travis informed Hayes, the sternness of his voice belying his casual stance. "My wife is thrilled to have her company, of course, and will gladly serve as her chaperone."

"Impossible!" Everett Hayes blustered. "Cassie is coming home with me, at once."

Jim took a single menacing stride forward. "She's staying."

Travis brushed a bit of dust from his sleeve. "I'm sure she'll calm down in a day or two and see reason again." He shook his head and expelled a sympathetic chuckle. "The poor girl actually believes you plan to marry her off to Meredith's former beau. Can you imagine? I did everything I could to convince her that you couldn't possibly be thinking of forcing her into a union with that barn-burning, land-grabbing fiend, but she seems quite convinced. Even went so far as to gain my promise that I wouldn't let you take her away. So, unfortunately, I cannot let you in."

"Curse your lying hide, Archer!" Hayes seized the top rail of the gate and rattled it on its hinges. The rails shook with such violence that Travis had to step away to keep from having his chin pummeled. "You said you'd help me."

Travis held up a conciliatory hand. "Simmer down. I said I'd help you, and I will. I cannot break my word to Cassandra, of course, but I'd gladly deliver a note to her if you wish to clear up the misunderstanding. Surely after she learns she was mistaken, she'll be eager to return to her family."

"You're meddling in affairs that do not concern you." Hayes jabbed his finger at Travis over the gate. "If you won't bring Cassie to me, I'll take her myself." He leapt forward, intent on scaling the barricade, his rifle still clutched in one hand.

In a flash, Jim had his revolver clear of its holster, and the sound of the gun being cocked echoed loudly in the air between them. Hayes halted his climb.

"I wouldn't recommend trying to take her by force," Travis said. "We do have a policy about trespassers, after all, and I'm sure it would distress my wife if I let Jim put a bullet in you. Oh, and should you consider sneaking in after dark, I think it only fair to warn you that my hound is a fierce guard dog. She doesn't take kindly to strangers skulking about and is likely to take a piece out of your leg. I'd hate for you to become injured after I promised to help you and all."

Hayes swore under his breath and dropped down from the gate. Jim lowered his revolver. Travis grinned.

"Why don't you go back to town and get some rest? Give Meri and Cassandra a few days to visit, and when your daughter is ready to come home, I'll see to it that she is delivered to you safely. You have my word."

"I don't want your word. I want my daughter." Nevertheless, Hayes stomped off toward his horse. The animal danced sideways, unnerved by the hostility emanating from his master.

Hayes jerked the reins with a rough hand and hauled himself into the saddle. He steered his mount in a tight circle as he fought for control, then turned his attention back to Travis. "If Cassandra is not home in three days time, expect an armed posse at your doorstep. And I'll shoot any man or beast who tries to keep me from her." His narrowed eyes shifted to Jim and lingered for a heartbeat or two before he brought his horse's head around and dug his heels into the animal's sides.

Neither Archer spoke until the hoofbeats from Hayes's horse faded into the distance.

When the sound could no longer be heard, Travis pivoted away from the gate and faced his brother. "You think he'll follow through on that threat?"

"Yep." Jim holstered his gun and strode to his horse.

Travis's mouth settled into a grim line as he followed. "Me too."

Meredith and Cassie managed to have a simple supper of skillet-fried ham, mashed potatoes, and green beans ready when the men came home.

"Why don't you take the biscuits to the table while I whip up a batch of redeye gravy." Meredith nudged her cousin over to the counter, where the biscuits sat in a pair of towel-covered pie tins. Ever since Travis and Jim returned, Cassie hadn't been able to concentrate on any task for more than a minute or two. And no wonder. The men had been terribly tight-lipped over what had happened at the gate.

All Meredith had ferreted out was that

their visitor had indeed been Uncle Everett and that they had managed to convince him to allow Cassandra to stay for a few days. She hoped that once everyone sat around the table, Travis and Jim would give a more detailed accounting.

Meredith poured about half a cup of coffee into her skillet with the ham drippings and deglazed the pan, scraping every bit of ham from the bottom and sides that she could. As the gravy simmered, she glanced over her shoulder to check on Cassie's progress. The girl had gotten all the biscuits into the serving bowl, but the bowl hadn't quite made it to the table. Meredith hid her grin by turning to stir the gravy.

Cassie hovered at Jim's side near the doorway, the biscuit bowl in the crook of her arm. It was hard to tell if Cassie was attracted to the stoic man or if he just made her feel safe, but one thing had become abundantly clear — she preferred Jim's company to any of the others. Which Meredith found surprising. She would have guessed that Crockett's charm and gentle teasing would hold more appeal for the usually effervescent Cassie. But it was Jim who drew her.

While Meredith added salt and pepper to the redeye gravy, she spied Jim taking the biscuits from Cassie. He thumped the bowl onto the table and immediately put a hand at her waist to guide her to a chair — one that sat directly next to his.

Her cousin wasn't the only one smitten.

Meredith's gaze wandered over to where her husband stood near the head of the table. Was Travis smitten? Did he long to be close to her like Jim longed to be near Cassie? She inwardly pleaded with him to look at her, to assure her of his affection. But he didn't. He just kept jawing with Neill and Crockett about the barn roof. Oblivious.

Biting the inside of her cheek, Meredith turned her attention back to the gravy. Her elbow flapped as she stirred the drippings with a tad too much zeal. Foolish fancies. What did she expect? That he would read her mind and suddenly cross the room to take her in his arms? He was a man, not some kind of clairvoyant wizard. Unrealistic expectations would do neither of them any favors.

Yet . . .

Her hand stilled, and the gravy ceased its frantic whirl.

Travis had looked at her earlier today. *Really* looked at her. After he'd kissed her and held her tight against his chest, he'd helped her mount and caressed the base of her calf. A touch that still made her shiver when she thought of it. And the heat in his eyes as he'd gazed up at her? That heat had warmed her blood and stolen her breath. Oh, he'd looked smitten then.

Perhaps if they could find an opportunity to be alone . . .

Meredith removed the skillet from the stove and twisted toward the counter to pour the gravy into a small bowl. The ocean blue of Cassie's dress loomed up from the corner of her vision like a wave sent to dash Meredith's hopes. She couldn't exactly instigate a rendezvous with her husband when her cousin was sharing their room, could she? Now wasn't the proper time for that kind of thing, anyway. Cassie was in trouble. Her needs took precedence.

"Neill, grab the beans, would you?" Meredith called to the youngest Archer as she set the gravy near Travis's end of the table.

Travis stopped talking at her approach and finally turned. His eyes met hers, and though she sensed his distraction and concern over what had happened with her uncle, she also sensed a connection, as if her presence actually comforted him. It wasn't a heated look of attraction like the one earlier in the day, but it warmed her just the same — deep in her heart, where her most protected dreams dwelt.

Crockett moved past her to take charge of the potatoes, reminding Meredith of her duties. She scurried back to the stove and removed the ham platter from the warming oven. Travis stepped forward to carry it to the table. Meredith wiped her hands on her apron and double-checked the counters to make sure she hadn't missed anything. Then, praying the men would assume the stove was responsible for her flushed cheeks, she joined her family at the table.

The instant the blessing ended, the men tucked into their food with their usual gusto. Cassie, on the other hand, spent more time pushing her ham around her plate with her fork than actually eating.

Hoping to lighten the mood and perhaps spark her cousin's interest, Meredith leaned forward to see around Cassie and addressed her brother-in-law at the end of the table. "So . . . Jim. I've been meaning to ask you a question."

His jaw halted midchew. He glanced around the table as if looking for another man named Jim to respond. Not finding one, he swallowed what was in his mouth and scrubbed the back of his hand across his chin. "What?"

Cassie's head came up, and Meredith

secretly cheered. Straightening in her seat, she set aside her napkin and peered down the table. "Well, I've managed to figure out that all you Archer men have names connected to the Alamo. Travis" — she turned to smile at her husband at the head of the table to her right — "of course refers to Lieutenant Colonel William Travis, who took over command of the regular soldiers at the Alamo in relief of Colonel James Neill" — she pointed to the youngest Archer, across from Cassandra — "who had to leave San Antonio de Bexar to tend to a sick family member. Crockett most certainly is named for Davy Crockett, the famous Tennessean who arrived at the Alamo only two short weeks before Santa Anna. So, logically, I would have to assume that you were named for James Bowie, the commander of the volunteers. What I don't understand is why you are the only Archer who doesn't go by your hero's surname."

A dull red color seeped up Jim's face, and Meredith immediately regretted asking the question. She'd only wanted to distract Cassie from her troubles, not embarrass the poor man.

"Never mind. I didn't mean to pry. I —"

"You're not prying." Jim interrupted her

babbling. "You might as well know the truth."

Perhaps it was the sideways glance he darted in Cassandra's direction, but Meredith got the feeling he wasn't really aiming that last comment at her.

"Ma was real big on remembering the Alamo. And you're right. She didn't name me James. My given name is Bowie." He ducked his head and stabbed a bean with the tines of his fork, though he made no move to lift the vegetable to his mouth.

"And none of us can figure out why he doesn't like it," Crockett said, his eyes full of teasing. "It's not like it sounds like a hog call or anything. Boo-ie! No, wait. Soo-ie!"

Neill laughed out loud, nearly spewing mashed potatoes all over the table. Travis grinned and shook his head, a little huff of laughter puffing out his nose. Meredith couldn't resist a little smile of her own.

"I think Bowie is a wonderful name. It's strong. Heroic." Cassie's passionate defense brought Jim's head back up. His eyes focused on her with an intensity that left Meredith feeling as if she was intruding on a private moment.

"However, I can certainly understand your preference for a nickname." Her cousin blushed a bit under Jim's regard. "I myself prefer being called Cassie. It's so much friendlier and less pretentious than Cassandra, don't you think?"

Jim never took his eyes from Cassie's face. "I think they both fit you right fine. One is elegant and graceful, the other fun and lively."

Cassie's cheeks flushed a deeper red. "What a lovely compliment. Thank you."

After that, Crockett turned the conversation in a less intimate direction with stories of how the Archer brothers used to reenact scenes from the Alamo battle as boys. Jim had even whittled an imitation Bowie knife to use during their skirmishes, which sparked his interest in woodworking.

While Meredith cleared the dishes and refilled coffee cups, Cassie begged to see the knife Jim had carved so long ago. He offered to show it to her along with his carpentry workshop, and Cassie didn't hesitate. With an eager smile, she took his arm and allowed him to lead her from the room.

A look passed between Jim and Travis over the top of Cassie's head, and at once Meredith knew that Jim had just taken it upon himself to explain the situation with Uncle Everett to her cousin. Meredith glanced at Travis and deliberately reclaimed her seat at the table. The dishes could wait. Explanations could not.

26

Travis wrapped his hands around his coffee cup and stared into the dark depths. He could feel Meri as she lowered herself into the chair next to him, his senses attuned to her movements. He didn't have to turn, he *knew* she was there — knew she was looking at him, waiting for a recounting of what happened with her uncle. Waiting for a solution he hadn't yet devised.

Her gaze bore into him almost as fiercely as it had earlier when she'd been setting out the food. He still couldn't recall a word of what Crockett had said about the barn shingles. He'd just nodded and tried to look contemplative when all the while he'd wanted nothing more than to cross the room and wrap his arms around his wife.

My wife.

Heaven help him. He was past ready to make Meri his wife in truth. To hold her throughout the night and wake with her in his arms every morning. He'd plotted all afternoon how best to approach the topic with her that evening. After she'd kissed him with such fervor and even allowed — no, welcomed — the boldness of his touch on her leg, he'd been able to think of little else.

Now, thanks to Everett Hayes and his idiotic scheme, he'd have nothing but thoughts to keep him warm as he scrunched himself onto the too-short cot in Neill's bedroom again tonight. Travis closed his fingers around the crockery mug before him, wishing it were Hayes's throat.

"So, Trav —" Crockett made a grand show of finishing his coffee and plopping the empty cup against the tabletop — "what did Hayes have to say?"

Travis forced his fingers to relax their stranglehold on the mug and leaned back in his seat as he expelled a heavy breath. "We convinced him to let Cassandra stay for a visit." He hesitated, trying to come up with some way to soften the rest of the facts for Meri's sake.

"Spit out the rest of it, Travis." Meredith nodded to him, but he could see the strain around her eyes where tiny lines creased her skin. Apparently she didn't care about soft. She just wanted the truth.

Knowing the truth would be painful, he

worded a short, silent prayer, and then summed up the situation as succinctly as possible. "If Cassandra's not home in three days, Hayes will round up a posse and take her by force."

Meredith tried to muffle her moan, but Travis heard it. And the sound cut right through his heart. Not caring about what his brothers might think, he reached around the side of the table and grabbed one of the spindles on the back of Meri's chair. He dragged her to his side, the chair legs scraping against the floor in a loud racket, took her hand in his, and cradled her entire forearm against his stomach. She laid her head atop his shoulder and leaned into him.

Crockett tapped the edge of his thumb against his thigh. "Is he set on marrying her off to Mitchell?"

"Seems to be. He didn't come right out and say so, but every time I hinted at such a union being a mistake, he sputtered something about me minding my own business and not meddling in his affairs."

"Travis, she can't marry that man." Meredith raised her head and stiffened her spine.

"I know, darlin'." Travis hugged her arm closer. "We'll figure something out."

She looked past him for a moment, catching her lower lip between her teeth. When her eyes met his once again, determination glowed in their vibrant blue depths. "I'll go talk to him. Give him permission to sell the land to Mitchell straight out. No dowry, no need for a wedding. All Roy wants is the land, anyway."

Crockett shook his head. "I don't think it would do any good."

"Why not?" she demanded, jerking forward in her seat. "Roy gets the land, and Uncle Everett would have him in his debt. Both of them get what they want."

Travis stroked the exposed skin on the back of her arm from the wrist joint all the way to her elbow, where her rolled sleeve sat bunched against her bicep. "Your uncle wants a stronger tie to Mitchell, one that will ensure his business for years to come. A marriage contract would bind him more fully than a bill of sale."

"The homestead was supposed to be my inheritance. Maybe if I got a lawyer . . ." Her words died when Crockett shook his head.

"If the deed is in your uncle's name, I imagine he can do whatever he wants with it, even if it goes against your father's last wishes. Now if the land was specifically deeded to you . . ." He left the sentence hanging, a thread of hope holding it aloft.

She shook her head and snapped the tenuous thread. "No. Papa trusted my uncle to look out for my interests since I was not of age. Nothing is in my name."

Meredith slumped, and Travis tugged her back into his side.

"I just can't believe that Uncle Everett would do this. Papa trusted him. His own brother. He was supposed to oversee the property on my behalf, not sell it out from under me or give it to his daughter. And Cassie . . . Oh, Travis." She turned anguished eyes on him. "He's not just stealing my land, he's selling his daughter. How could he do that? He loves Cassie. I know he does. This doesn't make any sense."

Travis kissed her forehead and murmured into her hair. "Desperation can warp a man's mind. Keep him from seeing things clearly. Your uncle must be in a financial crisis."

"I don't care what kind of crisis he's in." Meredith drew back, a sob catching in her throat. "What he's doing is wrong!"

"I know it is, love." He gathered her close again, aching to fix what Everett Hayes's betrayal had broken. "We'll find a way to protect Cassie. I swear it."

"Already found one." Jim's deep voice rumbled in from the bathing room an instant before he and Cassandra stepped through the doorway into the kitchen.

Travis frowned. How had he not heard the back door open?

Cassie bounded forward, arms outstretched to Meredith. The smile Travis had noted during her first visit had made a miraculous reappearance. Reluctantly, Travis relinquished his hold on Meri, freeing her to clasp her cousin's hands.

"You'll never guess our plan," Cassie gushed as she slid into the chair next to Meredith. "It's perfect. And it was all Jim's idea. He's so clever." She smiled at her accomplice over her shoulder as he, too, reclaimed a seat at the table.

"What didja come up with?" Neill elbowed Jim, speaking up for the first time since dinner.

"It's the most brilliant plan." Cassie's enthusiasm bubbled over before Jim could shape his mouth into a response. Not that the fellow seemed to mind. Having someone do his talking for him was probably a dream come true.

Cassie released Meredith's hands in order to include everyone at the table in her gaze. "First, we're going to give Papa his three days. I'll stay here at the ranch, making my objection to his scheme clear. And perhaps with the six of us praying, the Lord will see fit to nudge him into a more rational stance."

Travis took a swallow of his coffee, hoping to hide his skepticism. Everett Hayes would need more than a nudge from the Lord to help him see the error of his ways. A wallop upside the head with one of the charred pine planks from the barn might be better.

"Then on Tuesday," Cassie continued, "I'll return home and tell Papa and Mama straight out that I will not be coerced into marriage. No matter how they plead, I will not be dissuaded." She lifted her chin in such a way that Travis had to smile. She looked so much like Meri. Brave and determined. Perhaps the princess had gumption, after all.

Crockett hunched forward over the table and scraped his coffee cup across the wooden surface as he drew it closer to his chest. "I don't mean to dash your hopes, but I highly doubt that a little time and stubbornness on your part are going to accomplish much. If your father is truly set on this marriage, all he would have to do is find someone to officiate who could be convinced to ignore your protests. And unfortunately, Mitchell's got enough money to bribe a man into forgetting his scruples."

"That's where your brother's cleverness comes into play." Cassandra's smile didn't dim for a second.

Travis raised a questioning brow at Jim, but the man made no effort to enlighten him, his face as stoic as ever.

"If Papa insists on the wedding despite my protests, then we move to stage three."

"What's stage three?" Meredith asked when Cassandra decided to pause for dramatic effect.

Cassandra rose from her chair, her eyes glowing. "Only the most brilliantly simple idea ever." She clapped her hands together beneath her chin and slid over to where Jim sat, his gaze centered somewhere between the table and his lap.

Travis's jaw began to twitch. He couldn't quite figure out where this was headed, but his gut told him he wasn't going to like it.

"Papa can't force me to marry Roy if I'm already married to someone else."

"Jim?" The single word clawed its way out of Travis's throat as he tried to convince himself he'd misunderstood Cassie's meaning.

His brother finally lifted his head, defiance glittering in his eyes. "I offered to be her groom should she find herself in need of one."

Travis shot up so fast his chair tipped backward onto the floor. "You did *what?*"

Jim slowly pushed to his feet and crossed his arms over his chest. "Why so surprised, Trav? I'm just following in your footsteps."

"Jim?" Cassandra's smile wobbled, and uncertainty clouded her features.

"Everything's fine, Cassie." Jim patted her shoulder, but his eyes never left his older brother. "Travis just doesn't handle surprises well. He'll get over it."

"Outside," Travis ground out between clenched teeth. "Now."

He rounded the table and strode down the hall, his arms throbbing with the need to hit something. When he reached the front door, he wrenched it open, not caring that it thudded against the wall with enough force to loosen the hinges.

What could Jim be thinking? He'd known Cassandra Hayes for all of about two minutes. How could he possibly make a decision that would affect the rest of his life on a . . . a whim? Travis paced the length of the porch, the heels of his boots pounding against the pine boards. He was on his second pass when Jim finally got around to joining him.

"You can save your breath," Jim said as he pulled the front door closed, "I ain't changin' my mind."

Travis stalked up to him, his hands fisted at his sides. "Think about what you're doing, Jim. You don't really even know the woman."

"I know enough."

"What do you know, exactly? That's she's pretty? Quit thinking with your eyes and try using your brain. The girl's been pampered her whole life. She can barely sit a horse, she can't cook, probably can't sew or garden, either. What happens when those pretty smiles of hers turn into pouts because she hates being a rancher's wife? Will you follow her to town?"

"Maybe."

Fear coiled in Travis's heart at Jim's dark expression. Would he actually choose town life with Cassie over the ranch?

Jim drew himself up to his full height and set his jaw. "Meredith's got a bum leg and a penchant for meddling, yet you seem willing enough to overlook her faults. It's no different with Cassie. I can teach her what she needs to know. And if there comes a time when she wants to return to town, I can handle that, too. I'm sure Palestine could use a new carpentry shop."

An invisible vise clamped over Travis's chest. His lungs refused to draw in a full breath. His heart throbbed as if his rib cage were shrinking.

Meredith's words came back to him, flaying his defenses like a skinning knife cutting away a hide. *"How long do you think the others will be content to live here in your shadow?"*

Would they really leave? All of them?

"Marriage is forever, Jim." Travis leaned a bent arm against the doorframe, needing its support. "You can't just jump into it on a chivalrous impulse."

"Like you did?"

"That's different," Travis sputtered. "I knew that I lo—" *That I loved her.* The shock of that thought sent him reeling. He pushed away from the wall and staggered over to the railing. His palms dug into the wood as he locked his elbows and braced himself against the truth swirling around him.

He loved her. He had all along. That's why he'd not protested when Everett Hayes demanded a wedding. That's why he'd rigged the straws. It wasn't to spare Meri's reputation or an act of brotherly duty. Nothing so altruistic. He'd wanted her for himself. Needed her.

Somehow, on a gut level, he'd known she was the one meant for him, and he'd made up his mind to do everything in his power to keep her.

Jim's quiet footfalls sounded behind him. "Look, Trav. It's a last resort. Neither of us plans to rush into anything. I might have a strong hankerin' for the woman, but if I marry her, I want her comfortable enough around me that I don't have to bunk with one of my brothers while she adjusts."

"Hey!" Travis spun to face his brother, fists clenched. But the half grin on Jim's face stole his ire. He thumped his fist against his brother's arm anyway, though he put no real force behind the blow. "Yeah, well, I'll listen to your advice when you actually have some experience as a husband. Until then, keep your thoughts to yourself."

Jim thumped him with his own fist, and Travis grinned as he staggered slightly to the side. Suddenly their problems didn't seem quite so dire.

"So would you really do it, if it came down to it?" Travis asked.

Jim raised a brow. "What? Marry Cassie?"

"No. Willingly tie yourself to a pair of in-laws like Everett and Noreen Hayes?"

Jim growled and lunged for Travis, but Travis sidestepped his brother and darted up to the porch, a chuckle vibrating deep in his throat.

Maybe he wouldn't have to worry about Jim moving into town after all.

27

Eager to get Cassie alone, Meredith shuffled her cousin off to the bedroom the minute the dishes were done. The men accepted her excuse of being tired easily enough. Heaven knew all the emotional upheaval they'd endured in the last few hours would exhaust the most robust of women. Yet in truth, sleep was the furthest thing from her mind.

"Will Travis need to come in to get a change of clothes?" Cassie asked as she laid her small satchel on the bed. "I can wait to undress until after he gathers his things."

"He has clothes set aside already. Don't worry about him." Heat suffused Meredith's cheeks at the awkwardness that lay in that conversational direction. She quickly focused things back on her cousin. "You just make yourself comfortable. It will be like old times, the two of us snuggled under the covers, telling stories. And believe me, I expect to hear all about how you and Jim concocted this plan. Are you really prepared to marry him?"

Cassie paused in the midst of her unpacking, the hairbrush she'd pulled from the satchel quivering slightly in her hand. "I am."

"Even though you hardly know him?" Meredith came up behind her cousin and started unpinning her hair.

"When you had to choose between Roy Mitchell and Travis, you chose an Archer. I'm doing the same. You don't regret marrying Travis, do you?"

Meredith took the brush from Cassie and gently tugged it through the blond waves. "I don't regret it. Not for a moment. But I've harbored feelings for him all these years. It will be different for you. Jim's a good man, but he's a stranger to you. How do you know you'd suit?"

"He kissed me," Cassie whispered.

Meredith stopped brushing, the shock of Cassie's admission slamming into her with the force of Samson's hoof. She dropped the brush onto the bed and took hold of Cassie's shoulders. Slowly she turned her cousin around to face her. "He kissed you?"

Silent, stoic Jim?

"Mm-hmm." Cassie nodded, her rosy face

glowing. "And it wasn't a little peck on the cheek, like the ones my past suitors pressed on me. It was strong and deep and . . . wonderful."

The sigh that escaped her held all the drama of a young girl's first love. Meredith couldn't help but smile. After all, she felt much the same about Travis, only her yearning had passed the early stages of attraction weeks ago. Her love for Travis had intensified to the point where she couldn't imagine her life without him.

Meredith blinked. When had her schoolgirl crush turned into this soul-deep need? She'd called her young infatuation *love,* but when she looked into her heart now, nothing there resembled those girlish feelings. Everything was so much richer and deeper — as if what had come before was simply an artist's preliminary sketch, void of detail and color, and over the last few weeks, that same artist had brushed the canvas of her heart with masterful strokes, creating a vibrant work that left her breathless.

"Do you think it's shameful for me to hope that Papa *won't* change his mind about Roy?" Cassie asked in a hushed voice, bringing Meredith's mind back to the matter at hand. "So that Jim will have an excuse to marry me? Not that I wouldn't prefer a proper courtship and time for us to get to know each other, but part of me worries that without the urgency, he'd stay out here on the ranch and forget about me altogether. The Archers don't have much use for towns, you know."

Meredith stroked Cassie's arm and gripped her hand in reassurance. "The Archers are honorable to the core, Cass. If Jim kissed you the way I think he did, the last thing you need to worry about is him forgetting you." Meredith gently steered her cousin around until her back faced her, then took up the brush again and resumed detangling her long tresses. "Besides, the Archers aren't as reclusive as they appear. They've just been secluding themselves for so long it's become a habit. I don't imagine Jim would let a little thing like a town keep him from calling on you. He's too smitten."

Cassie's head swiveled to the side. "Do you really think so?"

"Yes." Meredith grinned and nudged Cassie's chin back to the forward position. "The question is, are you smitten with *him?* Would you still want to marry him if the situation with Roy and your father didn't exist?"

Meredith expected a quick, affirmative response. Cassie wasn't known for having an overly contemplative nature, after all. But silence stretched between them. Meredith had set the brush aside and plaited a braid halfway down Cassie's neck before her cousin finally answered.

"I feel safe, cherished when I'm with him. He held me while I cried today and never once asked me to hush. In his workshop, he vowed to protect me from Roy and even my father if it came to that. And when he looks at me . . ." She pivoted to face Meredith, her eyes soft and dewy.

Meredith tied off the braid with a piece of ribbon, and the two girls sat on the end of the bed.

"When he looks at me, Meri, he makes me feel like the most beautiful woman in the world, as if he could gaze at me for a lifetime and never grow tired of my face. As if he sees not just who I am, but who I can become. And when I look at him, not only do I see a handsome suitor who makes my heart flutter, I see a solid, dependable man who can be counted on no matter how difficult the road may become. A man who wants more than a pretty ornament to dangle on his arm. A man who wants a partner."

Cassie dipped her head and traced the line of a fabric fold in her skirt. "It seems too soon to label what I'm feeling love, but whatever it is, it is more intense than anything I've felt for any other beau." She bit her lip, then finally raised her chin. "There is something strong between us, Meri. Something that promises to last. Would I marry him if we weren't in this crazy predicament? Yes. I believe I would."

Moisture gathered at the corners of Meredith's eyes. "Then that's all that matters." She clasped Cassie to her breast and hugged her tight.

Guide her in this, Lord. Work this out for your good and hers.

Once the two separated, Meredith rose to her feet and began removing her own hairpins as she strolled toward the bureau. "You know what this means, of course," she said, meeting Cassie's gaze in the mirror.

"What?" Cassie stood and unfastened the buttons of her dress.

"We're finally going to be sisters."

Cassie gave a little squeal, and Meredith barely had time to turn before she was assaulted by her cousin's spirited embrace.

The trials facing them seemed to fall away as the two cousins giggled and prattled like a pair of adolescent schoolgirls while they readied themselves for bed. Once they'd scrubbed their faces, changed into their nightclothes, and crawled under the covers, however, reality started to creep back in. At least for Meredith.

Curled up on her side, she stared into the darkened room, her thoughts centered on Travis. Somehow she'd imagined he'd be the first one to share this bed with her. Not Cassie. Scrunching her pillow to her face to muffle her sigh, Meredith closed her eyes and waited for sleep to rescue her from her discontent. But it didn't come.

Frustrated, she flopped onto her back, careful not to flail her arms. When Cassie wiggled closer to her edge of the bed, as if trying to give Meredith more room, the urge to confide in her cousin grew too strong to ignore.

"Are you awake, Cass?" Meredith whispered, promising herself that if her cousin didn't answer she'd just bite her tongue and roll back over.

"Yes."

A staggering relief flowed through her at the quiet answer — followed by a rush of nerves.

"Umm . . . Can I ask you a question?"

"Mm-hmm," came the sleepy reply.

Cassie made no move to roll toward her, and Meredith relaxed a bit. Staring at the dark ceiling somehow made it easier to voice her secret fears.

"When we were talking earlier, you said that if you had your preference, you'd rather have a normal courtship with Jim so the two of you could get to know each other better. But if you were to marry him tomorrow, would you still want that courtship? I mean, before the two of you . . . you know . . ." Meredith closed her eyes as mortification poured over her in a heated wave.

"I'm not sure," Cassie said, sounding decidedly more alert. "I enjoyed his kiss, so I'm pretty sure I would enjoy other aspects of . . . well, of married life, but I imagine it would be easier if we didn't feel so much like strangers." She fell quiet for a moment or two, then cleared her throat. When she spoke, her whisper was so low Meredith had to strain to catch the words. "What was it like with you and Travis?"

Meredith bit back a moan. "I can't tell you, Cass."

"I'm sorry. I shouldn't have asked. It's just that I don't know what to expect, and Mama surely isn't going to tell me anything. I'm not certain I'd trust her opinions on the matter, anyway." Her words tripped over themselves trying to cover up her obvious hurt. "I just thought that since you and Travis were in much the same situation when you married that you might be able to give me some advice, but it's much too personal, of course. I shouldn't have —"

"Stop, Cassie." Meredith rolled toward her cousin and laid her hand on her arm. "It's not that I don't want to answer your question. I wish with all my heart I could."

"What . . . ?" Cassie squirmed sideways until she faced Meredith. "What do you mean?"

Meredith nibbled her lip as she summoned her courage. "Travis sleeps on a cot in Neill's room."

"Oh, Meri." It was too dark to see, but it sounded very much as if there were tears in Cassie's eyes. "I know how much you care for him. How awful. Why, I have half a mind to storm into that room and kick his sorry hide off that cot and onto the floor. The dog. How could he treat you so cruelly?"

A chuckle escaped Meredith's lips as Cassie swung from sleepy little girl to sympathetic confidante to vengeful angel all in the course of a single minute.

"What are you laughing at?"

"You." Meredith smiled into the darkness. "Travis hasn't rejected me." Although it was harder to believe that when she lay alone in the big bed with nothing but a spare pillow to hold. "He is trying to be chivalrous. To court me first."

"So he's kissed you?"

"Yes." Meredith pressed her palm against her stomach as she recalled the heart-stopping kiss they'd shared by the creek.

"More than once?"

Warmth spread through her midsection as she thought about the kiss he'd given her that very afternoon. "Yes."

Cassie shifted to a sitting position an instant before her pillow collided with Meredith's face. "I hear that dreamy, besotted sigh in your voice, Meredith Archer."

Meredith grabbed the pillow and retaliated, smiling in triumph when it plowed into the side of Cassie's head. "No more than the way you sounded when you talked about Jim."

"But I haven't been mooning over Jim for half my life the way you have Travis. You're tired of the chivalry, aren't you?"

"Yes." She couldn't believe she'd just admitted it aloud. Although, truth be told, it was possible Cassie hadn't even heard her, so tiny was her whisper.

But Cassie *had* heard, for she sought out Meredith's hand and gave it a squeeze. "On Tuesday, when Jim takes me back to Palestine, I think you should find Travis and tell him that you're ready to be a wife to him."

"Just tell him straight out?" Meredith pulled her hand from Cassie's grasp and clutched at the neck of her nightdress as if trying to protect her modesty. "I couldn't do that. I'd die of embarrassment. It's highly improper for a lady to speak of such things. Why, there's no telling what Travis would think of me."

"Seems to me he'd be glad to know you'd welcome him in the marriage bed." Cassie's dry answer made Meredith cringe.

It sounded so simple. But what if she made her feelings clear and Travis still didn't come? She couldn't bear that. The rejection would be real then, and no clever argument could dismiss it.

The sheets rustled as Cassie settled back down on the mattress. "Do you have any married friends you trust enough to ask for advice? Seeing as how I have no actual experience in this area, it might be wise to seek another opinion."

Myra immediately came to mind. "There is one lady," Meredith admitted, her mind already spinning with ideas about how to convince her husband to let her leave the ranch on a Tuesday. "She's the wife of one of the men Travis hired to help rebuild the barn. They've been married for probably twenty-five years, and she and Moses seem devoted to one another even after all that time. I could ask her."

"Good," Cassie said, a yawn distorting the word. "That's what you should do."

As Cassie's breathing deepened, Meredith's mind continued to turn circles. Her heart told her it was time to take action. But *which* action was the right one?

28

Tuesday dawned gloomy and gray. Meredith shivered beneath her cloak as she stepped away from the house and received the full brunt of the northern wind against her side. Crockett led a pair of saddled mounts out of the barn while Jim bundled Cassie into one of his old coats. The thing nearly swallowed her, but the added warmth would be a blessing on the long ride to town.

When Jim turned to fasten a pair of saddlebags behind the cantle of his mount, Cassie buried her nose in the collar, and Meredith imagined her inhaling his scent.

Meredith came alongside Travis and slid her hand down the length of his sleeve to let him know she was there without interrupting him while he instructed Neill on where to check for strays. When her fingers reached the back of his hand, she thought to taper away, but he twisted his wrist and captured her palm against his. Then he laced his fingers through hers and tugged her into his side in a motion so natural, it felt like a well-rehearsed dance instead of a spontaneous improvisation.

Meredith leaned her head against the side of Travis's shoulder and looked toward the ground, not wanting to witness Neill's reaction to his brother's show of possessiveness.

Possessiveness. The thought struck Meredith hard, and a delightful little shiver worked its way up from her stomach to her heart. Travis *was* acting possessive, wasn't he? But did his behavior stem from a growing affection for her or was it simply an expression of his protective nature?

What she wouldn't give to have something more substantial than intuition to guide her. She was afraid to trust hers. Roy might have stepped out with her a time or two, but she'd never had a true beau. How could she possibly comprehend the workings of a man's mind? And now her only confidante was leaving. She had to see Myra today. She couldn't wait for Saturday. The uncertainty was driving her mad.

"You're awfully quiet," Travis said close to her ear. "Are you worried about Cassie?"

Meredith drew her head back, surprised

to see Neill had already mounted and was heading out to check on the stock. She hadn't even noticed him leave. Giving herself a mental shake, she turned her attention to her husband.

"Jim knows to set a slow pace, right? Cassie's not too comfortable atop a horse."

"He'll watch out for her." Travis rubbed the pad of his thumb over the top of her hand, but she sensed a strange tension coiling beneath the surface.

Meredith searched her husband's face as he turned to watch his brother make final preparations for the journey. A muscle ticked in his jaw, and all at once insight dawned. "You're worried about Jim."

Travis tightened his grip on her hand. He said nothing for a long moment, then dipped his head and spoke in a low voice. "None of us has left since Pa died."

"Except for you," Meredith gently reminded him.

He finally met her gaze. A small smile curved his lips. "Only because of a pretty little trespasser."

Warmth spread through Meredith's chest. She reached across her body, clasped his arm, and hugged it close to her side. She'd been so consumed with her own worries, she'd never even considered what this day would mean for her husband.

"I'm proud of you, Travis."

His eyes widened a bit at her words.

"I am," she confirmed. "Letting Jim go can't be easy for you, yet you never once tried to talk him out of it." A gust of icy wind blew across her face, whipping tendrils of hair into her eyes.

He dragged his finger along the edge of her cheek, collecting stray hairs and tucking them behind her ear. "You're the one who gave me the courage, Meri." He grew silent again, and Meredith simply leaned into his side, enjoying his closeness. Yet instead of relaxing as she expected him to, Travis stiffened. Meredith lifted her head.

"Pa died because I left the ranch." The stark statement hung in the air between them like the fog of their breath. "I was supposed to be at home watching out for my brothers, but I left. Snuck out to meet a group of boys down at the swimming hole. I don't even remember why now. All I know is a fierce storm blew in, and Pa came looking for me. A clap of thunder spooked his horse and he fell. He died later that night."

Meredith clung to Travis, blinking away the sudden moisture that blurred her vision. She wanted to weep for the young boy who had watched his father die, for the boy who carried such a heavy burden of guilt so unnecessarily.

Give me words to ease his burden, Father.

"He died because he fell from a horse, Travis. Not because you left the ranch."

Her husband tried to release her hand, but she refused to let go. "He wouldn't have fallen from that horse if I hadn't disobeyed him."

"It was an accident, Travis. A tragic accident. One you are no more responsible for than I am for the sickness that struck my parents."

"It's not the same."

"No?" She kept hold of Travis's hand but shifted her body to stand partly in front of him. "Why not? I disobeyed my parents many times. Maybe their death was my punishment, too."

"That's ridiculous." He shoved his hat back and rubbed the lines of his forehead.

"Yes. It is." Meredith stretched up on her tiptoes and laid a slow, tender kiss on her husband's tanned cheek. "God forgave you long ago, Travis. Your father, too, I imagine. It's time to forgive yourself."

As she settled back onto the flat of her feet, Travis's eyes met hers. The intensity shimmering in his eyes was so intense, Meredith couldn't move. Couldn't breathe.

He slipped his arm from her grasp and wrapped it around her waist, his hold so strong she wanted nothing more than to melt into him. Travis angled his head. His gaze shifted to her lips.

Meredith lifted her face to him, the love inside her swelling.

Then Crockett strolled up with Travis's horse, and cleared his throat. "You send Neill up to the north pasture?" he asked, completely unsuccessful in his feigned innocence. The rogue knew exactly what he was interrupting and wasn't the least bit repentant.

Travis cleared his throat and released her. He adjusted the way his hat sat on his head, angling it more sharply over his eyes. "I plan to join him out there in a bit," he said, gravel in his voice. "I didn't figure you and Moses would need me on the barn. With the roof done, all you'll need to do is bring in the hay and add those two extra stalls we talked about."

"I figured as much." Crockett handed Bexar's reins over to Travis and climbed aboard his bay. "I'll ride with Jim to the gate and wait for Moses there. He and Josiah should be along shortly."

The mention of Jim brought Meredith's attention back to her cousin. They'd already said their good-byes in the house, but Meredith couldn't resist one final word of farewell. As Jim gave Cassie a leg up into the saddle, Meredith quietly approached.

Seeing her, Jim nodded once and backed away, allowing them a private moment.

"I'm going to miss you." Meredith reached her hand up, and Cassie grasped it, her gloved fingers tightening around Meredith's bare ones.

Tears glistened in Cassie's eyes and her chin wobbled slightly, but she pulled her mouth taut and managed to keep her emotions under control. So proud of her, Meredith raised her other hand and cocooned Cassie's between both of hers. It was one thing to plot and plan when safely removed from a threat. It was another matter entirely to ride out to meet that threat. Yet her little Cassie was doing exactly that.

"Whatever comes, God will see us through." Meredith punctuated her words with a squeeze to Cassie's hand. "Trust him, Cass. Lean on his strength."

"I will." Her voice quivered, but when she pulled free of Meredith's grip, she sat erect on the rented livery nag and even found a tiny smile.

As Jim led her down the path, Travis came up behind Meredith. The welcome weight of his arm settled atop her shoulder. He didn't say anything, just hugged her to his chest and let her rest her head against him. As she watched Cassie enter the trees, Meredith sank into Travis's strength, comforted by his solid presence.

"Thank you for staying with me this morning," she murmured once Cassandra had completely passed from sight. "It would have been much harder to say good-bye alone."

He tightened his hold on her, and she felt the gentle pressure of his lips against her scalp as he pressed a kiss into her hair. Meredith's eyes slid closed.

"Travis?"

"Yeah?"

She turned to face him, his arms loosening to accommodate her movement. Immediately she missed his warmth. "Would you mind if I rode out to Beaver Valley to visit with Myra for a short while this afternoon? I won't be gone long. I promise. I just . . . Well, I feel the need of a woman's company. I think it would help me adjust to Cassie's leaving and give me a chance to talk to her about something besides teaching."

Something like husbands.

Travis stared hard at the sky. "I don't like

371

the look of this weather. It could turn nasty if the temperature keeps dropping."

"Or it could be sunny by noon. One never knows in Texas."

He resituated his hat and blew out a quiet breath. "Visiting with Mrs. Jackson is that important to you?"

No, having a marriage filled with intimacy and love was that important to her. But since talking with Myra was her best chance to achieve that . . . "Yes. I really think it will help."

"All right." He grumbled as if he would have much rather given a different answer. "But only if it's not raining. Rain can turn to sleet in an instant on a day like this, and the ice would make the roads treacherous. Promise me?"

Meredith nodded, unable to hold her grin at bay.

Never had she flown through her morning chores so quickly. So far the weather was holding, but the clouds were turning an ominous shade of gray. If she didn't leave soon, she might not be able to leave at all. After adding an extra flannel petticoat beneath her skirt, Meredith dug out her woolen mittens and matching scarf. She wrapped the scarf around her head to protect her cheeks and ears from the bitter wind blowing out of the north and fastened her cloak over her shoulders. The ride wouldn't be long, but she'd be facing the wind much of the way. Coming home would be easier.

Having told Crockett her plans when she'd taken sandwiches out to the barn a few minutes ago, she wasn't surprised to see Ginger saddled and ready at the end of the porch. With anticipation dancing in her chest, Meredith descended the steps and hurriedly untied the lead line from the porch pillar.

"Need a leg up?" Crockett emerged from around the corner as if he'd been waiting for her.

His sudden appearance startled her, but Meredith managed to greet her brother-in-law with a smile. "Thank you." She fit her boot into his laced fingers and soon found herself on Ginger's back. "I'll return in time to fix supper."

"If I were you, I'd return long before then." Crockett hesitated before handing her the reins. "There's a storm coming. It'll do you no good to be caught in it."

"I'll be careful," she assured him.

And she was. She held Ginger to an easy canter on the road and didn't even take the shortcut across Beaver Creek. She stopped by Seth Winston's store, but only long enough to give the crotchety old man a dozen of the oatmeal cookies she and Cassie had baked yesterday. He might have won their first skirmish, but she was determined to win the war.

"Ya tryin' to poison me, woman?" Winston grouched as he untied the knot on the napkin-wrapped treat.

"Nope, just sweeten you up some."

"Doggone women, always thinking they gotta change a man. Infernal creatures. A fellow'd be better off with a mule than a wife."

Meredith let the insults slide off her back, knowing she didn't have time to rise to his bait, and wished the storekeeper a good day.

Braced for the cold, she turned the knob and stepped outside, giving the door enough of a tug to allow it to close behind her. But the thud she expected never came. She turned to reach for the knob a second time only to find Seth Winston filling the doorway. The ornery old buzzard had followed her.

She offered a brief smile, then spun away and scurried down to the street to unhitch Ginger.

"Always thought them Archer boys was

too smart to let a female hog-tie 'em." Winston called after her.

"Guess that proves my gender's superiority over the male of the species," Meredith called back, unable to hold her tongue any longer.

"How's that?"

Meredith didn't respond until she was safely in the saddle. "Not only are we smarter, but we tie better knots."

With that, she reined Ginger around and touched her heels to the mare's flanks. She could have sworn she heard a bark of laughter from behind her, but that was impossible. It must have been the wind.

Since Myra only taught at the freedmen's school during the morning hours on weekdays, Meredith rode past the schoolyard to the small pine cabin that sat a quarter-mile behind it.

"Miss Meri? That you?" Joshua called out from beside the woodshed where he'd been splitting logs. "Everything all right with Pa?"

"Yes. He and Josiah were helping Crockett fork hay into the loft when I left. I just wanted to visit with your mother. Is she at home?"

"Yes'm." He leaned his hatchet against the chopping stump and rubbed his palms along his trouser legs. "Go on up to the house. I'll see to your horse."

Meredith smiled at the young man as she dismounted. "Thank you."

By the time she reached the cabin, however, her smile had twisted into a nervous grimace. Second thoughts leapt through her mind, causing havoc with her stomach. Marriage was a deeply private affair. Perhaps discussing her relationship concerns with Myra wasn't such a good idea.

But how else was she to figure out what to do?

A verse from Titus surfaced through the panic. A verse about older women teaching younger women how to love their husbands. Surely the answers she sought fell into that category.

Meredith inhaled a long, steadying breath, then raised her hand to knock. When Myra answered, Meredith blurted out the thought uppermost in her mind.

"I need you to help me end my husband's courtship."

29

"The cold musta done froze your brain, Miss Meri, 'cause you ain't making a lick of sense." Myra took Meredith by the arm and drew her into the house. "I got water on in the kitchen. I'll make some tea. Maybe once you thaw out, I'll be able to understand what in the world you're sayin'. I could've sworn I heard you say you wanted to stop your husband from payin' court to you."

"Yes, but that's not exactly —"

"Uh, uh, uh." Myra held up a hand and shook her head. "Not until we get that tea."

She bustled Meredith into the toasty kitchen, collected her cloak, and directed her into a chair, then reached into the cupboard and took down a tea canister.

Grinning at her friend, and a little at herself, Meredith dutifully kept her mouth closed as she unwound her scarf and slid her hands free of her mittens. The strains of a familiar hymn wove through the air, so quiet at first that Meredith couldn't tell if she actually heard them or if they resonated only in her mind. But when Myra turned to set a teacup on the table in front of her, the melody rose like the sun cresting the horizon.

"Father of Mercies." A stillness came over Meredith. Little by little, her frantic desperation dissolved as her mind filled in the lyrics extolling God's abundant blessings. She became so caught up in the prayerful attitude of the song, that when Myra stopped humming in order to pour tea into their cups, she had to blink several times to return her focus to her surroundings.

"Take a sip, Miss Meri. Then tell me what you come here to say."

Meredith did as instructed, then set her pink-flowered teacup back on its saucer and faced her friend. "I find myself in need of advice — from someone accustomed to dealing with a husband."

"I see." Myra paused as she lifted her cup to her lips. "Travis causing you trouble?"

"Not really, it's just that . . ." Meredith sighed. "We married under unusual circumstances, and Travis thought I deserved a proper courtship. So for the last few weeks he's been courting me."

"Honey, if you got yourself a man who's

willing to pay court to you even after the vows are spoke, you got yourself a treasure, not a problem."

"You don't understand. He's courting me like a suitor, not like a . . . a husband." Meredith dropped her gaze to the tabletop. She toyed with the corner of her napkin as she revealed the rest of it. "He sleeps on a cot in Neill's room. Not with me."

"And you're ready for that arrangement to change?"

Meredith bit her lip and nodded.

Myra set her cup on her saucer and scooted them both out of the way. "Miss Meri, if your man is attracted to you at all, I can promise you he's been thinkin' of little else than changing that arrangement. He's prob'ly just waiting for some kind of signal from you to let him know he'd be welcome."

"That's the problem. I feel like I've been signaling more than a flagman on the rails, but Travis fails to notice. I respond to his kisses, I come up with excuses to be near him, I never pull away from his touch. How many signals does a husband need?"

A mild laugh rumbled in Myra's chest. "Oh, Miss Meri. You gotta remember them Archer boys grew up with only themselves for comp'ny. They ain't been around womenfolk to learn how to interpret them quiet

379

signals of yours. You're gonna have to take a more direct approach, I reckon."

Meredith's hand shook as she reached for her teacup, setting it to rattling against the matching saucer. She managed to get the cup to her mouth without dribbling anything on Myra's tablecloth, but the brew did little to fortify her.

"How direct?" Meredith glanced around the kitchen to ensure they were still alone. She'd be absolutely mortified if Joshua were to overhear their conversation. The rhythmic *thwack* of a hatchet splitting wood outside, however, gave her the courage to continue, albeit in a whisper. "I don't want Travis to think I'm some sort of . . . loose woman."

Myra smiled, but this smile was different. Far from the friendly, open grins Meredith was accustomed to receiving, this one spoke of secrets — seductive secrets. "A lady can be direct and still be a proper lady, Miss Meri."

Meredith leaned forward. "How?"

"Have you ever been the one to start a kiss?"

Heat climbed up Meredith's neck. "Not really. I did kiss him on the cheek earlier today, but Travis has always been the one take the lead with . . . well, real kisses."

"Then the next time the two of you are

alone, surprise him. And not with some little buss like his ma woulda given him. Take his face in your hands and kiss him the way your heart tells you. Slow. Sweet. Full of all the love you been storin' up."

Could she do something that bold? Meredith ran her fingertip around the rim of her cup. Even if she could find the nerve, would she be able to find him alone? There always seemed to be another Archer around once the evening chores were finished.

"Even when you're not alone, you can make it feel that way," Myra continued as if she had read Meredith's mind. "Meet his gaze from across the room. Let down your guard and show him the truth of your feelings in your eyes. Men fear rejection, too, you know. Give him every reason to believe you'll say yes, and he'll find a way to ask you the question."

"But what if I can't get him alone or he can't read my eyes? Is there anything else I can do?"

"Honey, if the man is that dense, you can drag that cot he been sleepin' on into your room, nab his clothes, and lay in wait for him. When he comes lookin' for his things, lock the door and settle the matter once and for all."

"Myra!" Meredith gasped in shock, then

promptly started laughing at the picture that came to mind of a bewildered Travis searching high and low for his bed.

"You ain't got nothing to worry about, Miss Meri." Myra reached across the table and patted her hand. "From what Moses says, your man's got a good head on his shoulders. He'll figure it out. And if it takes him longer than you like, you can always let him *accidentally* see you with your hair down, or tangle your apron strings in such a knot that you need his help to undo them. Find excuses to touch him, even if it's just passin' the potatoes, and look him in the eye while you do it. Trust me, that cot will find its way back into storage faster than you can fold the sheets."

Myra winked at her, and the insecurities that she'd been dragging around for days finally lifted. She could do it. She could woo her husband.

Meredith sat a little straighter in her chair and finished off her tea, ideas churning in her mind. Myra stood to refill her cup, her secretive smile no longer quite so mysterious. With confidence blossoming, Meredith felt a similar smile stretch across her face.

Knowing she needed to get back to the ranch, Meredith downed her tea as quickly as politeness allowed. Myra didn't seem to mind. She just peered at her over the rim of her still half-filled cup, her eyes gleaming with a light that made Meredith's cheek warm.

"I'm sorry to rush out on you, Myra. I promised Travis not to stay long." Meredith stood and collected her mittens and scarf. "The weather, you know."

"Mmm-hmm," Myra murmured, that secretive gleam of hers only growing brighter.

Meredith ducked her head to hide an embarrassed smile. It was the middle of the day, for heaven's sake. She probably wouldn't even see Travis for another couple of hours. It wasn't as if she were rushing home to put their plans into action.

All right, maybe that accounted for *some* of her urgency. But the coming storm was cause for concern, too.

Just as she reached for her cloak, Joshua stomped through the back door, letting in a gust of wind that pricked her skin like tiny ice needles.

"Lord have mercy!" Myra inhaled sharply. "When did it turn so cold?"

Joshua closed the door behind him, but Meredith still shivered. She hurriedly donned her cloak and crossed her arms over her middle, trying to reclaim the heat she'd lost.

"It's been droppin' for the last hour, Ma," Joshua said as he moved closer to the stove. "And now it's rainin'. Ain't much more than a drizzle, but the water's freezing on its way down. I suspect we'll get snow overnight."

Myra jumped to her feet. "I had no idea." She tossed an apologetic look Meredith's way. "You *do* gotta get home. Joshua, saddle her horse for her."

"Already done it. Ginger's ready to go when you are, Miss Meri."

"Thank you, Joshua." Meredith stuffed her hands into her mittens and wrapped her scarf high around her neck. "I best be on my way. I don't want my husband to worry."

And heaven knew, Travis would worry. He'd specifically warned her about the freezing rain. If she didn't get home soon, he might not let her leave the ranch for the rest of the winter.

Myra helped fasten the buttons on Meredith's cloak, since mittens didn't allow for much dexterity. Meredith thanked her and pulled her friend into a brief embrace.

"I'd be lost without you, Myra."

"You and Mr. Travis will find your way through this," the older woman whispered fiercely in Meredith's ear. "I have no doubt."

Meredith followed Joshua outside, heartened by the woman's words and eager to get home to put some of Myra's strategies into practice.

Icy drizzle stung her cheeks, and the wind seemed to know the location of every crack and crevice in her clothing, chilling her instantly. Ginger stamped her hooves and twisted her head away from the wind.

"I know, girl," Meredith soothed, stroking the paint's neck. "Let's get you home to that new barn."

"Pa always takes the cutoff by Beaver Creek," Joshua said after helping her mount. "It could save you some time gettin' back."

Meredith nodded as she took up the reins and turned Ginger's head toward home. "Thanks."

Moses and Josiah usually traveled on foot, not on horseback, but Meredith trusted Ginger to handle the terrain. It wasn't truly raining, after all, just drizzling. The ground didn't even feel muddy when they left the road.

By the time she reached the edge of the creek, however, the drizzle had worsened into a light shower of sleet. Her soggy mittens only intensified the cold as the wind blew through the knit, leaving her fingers numb.

Meredith reined Ginger in and tugged her mittens off with her teeth. She tucked them into the pocket of her cloak, then lifted her hands to her mouth and tried to warm them with her breath.

"All right, Ginger," she said as she guided the horse to the lowest spot on the creek bank. "Home's not much farther. Let's get across."

The paint tossed her head but obediently trudged forward. The creek wasn't more than a foot deep, but the banks were getting slick as the rain increased. Halfway down, Ginger's back hoof lost purchase and sent her staggering to the right. Meredith grabbed the horse's neck, barely managing to stay in the saddle.

"Easy, girl." Heart thudding in her chest, Meredith righted herself and ground her teeth together as she urged Ginger into the water.

They splashed across without much problem, so Meredith relaxed her grip on the saddle horn. Then, as Ginger surged up the opposite bank, her hooves slid on the mud. Her hind legs buckled, and she fell hard onto her haunches. Meredith flew backward. She screeched and grabbed desperately for the pommel, but her numb fingers were too slow to connect. The reins tore from her hand, and she toppled end over end — right into Beaver Creek.

Meredith gasped. Frigid water slapped her face. Cold rushed up her arms and legs, her cloak offering little protection as she lay half submerged in the creek. She scrambled to her feet and quickly waded to the bank, but already she could feel the added weight in her skirts.

Wiping water from her face with the back of her hand, she searched for Ginger. The horse had made it up the small embankment, but the way she kept lifting her rear left foot sent a frisson of dread through Meredith.

After wringing what water she could from her petticoats, Meredith hiked up her skirts and planted her boot on a thick tree root protruding from the muddy bank. She grasped a handful of tall grass from atop the rise and crawled out of the creek bed.

"So maybe we should have taken the longer way around, huh, girl?" Meredith scraped her mud-caked boots on the yellowed grass and carefully approached Ginger. "We're definitely both going to need a bath after this." She collected the dangling reins and wrapped them around the pommel, then ran a calming hand down the paint's neck and shoulder. Slowly, she stroked her way back toward the mare's hind legs.

"Let me take a look, girl. Easy." Meredith ran her palm down Ginger's left leg, over the hock and down along the fetlock. Ginger tossed her head and snorted as if in discomfort, but otherwise submitted to the examination. Nothing seemed to be broken, thank the Lord, but something was definitely paining her. Hopefully, it was just a bruise. But it could be a sprain or even a fracture. One thing was for certain, Meredith wasn't about to risk causing her horse further injury by forcing her to carry her added weight. They'd have to walk the rest of the way.

Meredith unwound Ginger's reins and limped up to the animal's head. "It's only a couple of miles, girl. We'll be home in no time."

Unfortunately, that promise proved to be a bit optimistic. As the temperatures continued to drop, Meredith's pace slowed. With every step, shards of pain tore through the arch of her right foot and up into her calf and thigh.

"We . . . make quite a . . . pair, don't we, Ginger?" Meredith ground out as she bent to retrieve a dead branch to use as a cane. It didn't offer much relief, but a little help was better than none. "Two girls with bum legs limping home."

After another dozen or so excruciating steps, her weak foot came down on a stone hidden beneath a scattering of leaves and pine needles. Meredith cried out and crumpled to the cold, wet ground, her ankle twisting beneath her. As her knees hit, she released Ginger's reins.

Meredith drew in a few deep breaths and willed her mind to disregard the agony in her leg. She could rest when she got home — home to Travis.

Travis. Meredith concentrated on her husband, on her plans to encourage his attentions, to become his wife in truth. Gripping the oak branch with both hands, she levered herself to her feet again, a groan vibrating in her throat.

They were close, maybe only a quarter mile away. *I can do this.*

Ducking her head against the sleet that continued to pelt down on her head, she planted the walking stick firmly against the ground and lifted her right leg. The moment her foot came down and took her weight, however, the weakened limb gave way.

"No!" Angry tears filled her eyes as her hip collided with the earth. Why did her body have to be so feeble?

Ginger sidestepped her mistress and swung her head back around, her big brown eyes seeming to convey the truth Meredith was loath to accept.

Time to part company.

Meredith pushed up onto her good knee, blew out a heavy breath, and nodded. "All right, then. Go fetch the men, Ginger." She swatted the paint's rump with her walking stick. "Hyah!"

The horse trotted off, still favoring her back leg.

Using her arms, Meredith dragged herself over to a nearby pine and leaned her back against the trunk. Only then did she remember the key on the chain around her neck. The Archer gate would block Ginger's path.

She closed her eyes for a moment, her mind turning heavenward. *Help Travis find me, Lord. And don't let him worry too much. Or blame himself.*

The more she thought about Travis and the conversation they'd had that morning, the more Meredith's heart ached for her husband. *Don't let this accident reinforce his fears. Bring him beyond that, to the assurance that can only be found in depending wholly on you.*

Exhaustion pressed upon her and kept her eyelids closed. She'd just rest for a few minutes, regain her strength. Then she'd crawl home if she had to. Travis needed her.

30

Travis and Neill rode in from the range, rain and sleet sliding off their hat brims and oilskin ponchos. When the house came into view, Travis nudged Bexar into an easy lope. What he wouldn't give for a hot cup of Meri's coffee right about now. If he was lucky, she might even have some of those oatmeal cookies left over. Well, if Crockett, Moses, and Josiah hadn't already finished them off.

Those three had had it easy that afternoon, working under the cover of the barn roof. Nevertheless, Meredith had most likely packed up half the kitchen for Moses in payment, including the cookies. Travis couldn't begrudge the man the treat. He and Josiah had worked as hard as any Archer over the last couple of weeks. They deserved a healthy payment.

He'd come to respect Moses's abilities, his work ethic . . . shoot, the man himself.

He and Josiah were going to be missed now that the barn was finished.

Crockett must have heard their approaching horses, for he pulled wide the barn doors and allowed Travis and Neill to ride directly inside.

Josiah stepped out of a newly fashioned stall and moved forward to take charge of Bexar. Travis tossed him the reins as he dismounted, scanning the shadowy interior for Moses. He finally spotted him up in the hayloft, examining the ceiling.

"Any leaks?" Travis called out.

Moses grinned down at him, his white teeth glowing against his dark face. "No, sir." He patted the barn wall to his left. "She's holdin' together real fine."

"I suspected she would." Travis strode to the ladder and met Moses on his descent. "You've done well, my friend." He offered his hand.

Moses shook it. "Mr. Jim's the master carpenter. I just supplied some extra labor and a bit of experience."

"More than a bit." Travis winked at the big man, then pulled his soggy hat from his head and tried to reshape the brim. "We wouldn't have had the barn up in time for this storm without your help."

Crockett joined them at the base of the

loft. "Yep. It's going to seem strange not having you and Josiah around every day."

"I can still meet up with Josiah on Saturdays to go fishin', can't I, Trav?" Neill's raised voice drew Travis's attention to where the boys stood rubbing down the horses. The two had become fast friends, and Travis had no intention of forcing a separation.

"Absolutely. The Jacksons are welcome here anytime."

Neill nodded with all the cockiness of a young man coming into his own, but he couldn't quite stifle the grin that lit up his face. It was nearly as bright as the one he sported the Christmas they gave him his first rifle. Meredith had been right about the boy needing a companion his own age.

Meredith. The urge to see her spurred him forward.

"Why don't we walk over to the house and get you some hot coffee before you head out?" Travis clapped Moses on the arm. "I'm sure Meri's got a pot warming on the stove."

"Uh, Trav?" Crockett edged closer, his eyes uneasy. "She's not back yet."

Travis stiffened. "Not back? You mean you let her go out in this mess?" Fear-spawned rage flared with such unexpected force, he had his brother by the collar before he even

394

realized he'd moved. "I trusted you, Crock. If anything happens to her, I swear I'll —"

"Whoa!" Crockett brought his arms up in a sharp motion and broke Travis's hold. "She left two hours ago, before the storm hit. You're the one who gave her permission to leave as long as it wasn't raining. Don't go laying this on me."

Travis backed away, drawing a trembling hand over his face. Crockett was right. This was his fault. He never should have let her sway him from his better judgment. He should have —

"Josiah and me will check the path by the creek," Moses said, striding toward the barn entrance, buttoning his coat as he went. "Myra mighta sent her back that way when she saw the ice. It's shorter."

"Neill, go with Moses," Travis ordered, his mind racing ahead. "If you meet up with her, send up a couple shots. Crock and I will check the road."

Neill left with the Jacksons on foot while Travis and Crockett saddled fresh mounts.

"Sorry." Travis glanced over at his brother as he tightened the cinch. He didn't have time for a lengthy apology, but Crockett didn't seem to need one. He nodded his acceptance as he fit a bit into his horse's mouth.

"We'll find her, Trav."

Travis planted his foot in the stirrup and hoisted himself into the saddle. "We better."

Not waiting for his brother to finish, he set off at a canter and overtook Neill and the others before they reached the gate. The wind whistled in his ears, the wind and something that sounded vaguely like a horse's neigh.

Meri.

When he rounded the last stand of trees, Travis spotted Ginger's distinctive chestnut-and-white patches.

"Thank God," he breathed. But his relief lasted only a moment.

If Meri was at the gate, why couldn't he see her? It was possible she had just arrived and dismounted, but his gut told him otherwise. Travis slowed his gelding and leapt from his back before the animal came to a complete halt.

"Meri!" He called her name as he dug in his trouser pocket for the key he always kept there. "Meri!"

Travis shoved the key into the padlock. When it clicked open, he yanked the steel clasp free of the chain and tossed it into the dirt. Grabbing the middle rail of the gate, he pried it open with one hand, just far enough to squeeze himself through. He held out a calming hand to Ginger, noting the way she shied from putting weight on her left hind leg.

What happened? Had Meri been thrown? Was she even now lying hurt somewhere? Travis scanned the ground as far as he could see, cursing the trees he loved for obscuring his vision.

Turning his attention back to the horse, he captured the bridle and patted the paint's neck. Her coat was soaked. Ice crystals had accumulated in the dip of her saddle and in the dark strands of her mane. The ground had been churned into a muddy mess from her hooves.

God have mercy. Travis staggered back a step. How long had she been out here? How long had *Meri* been out there waiting for help while his locked gate kept Ginger from alerting anyone of trouble?

Stupid! Travis fisted his hand around the pommel and leaned his forehead against the seat. Meri had warned him about the gate, told him he didn't need it anymore. But did he listen? No. He knew what was best. He knew how to protect those he loved. Idiot!

He raised his head to the sky, not caring about the sleet that stung his face. "Help me find her, Lord. I need you. Please."

A firm hand on his shoulder brought his

head around. Crockett's determined expression reignited Travis's spirit.

"Send the paint back toward the barn, then follow me with the horses." Once again in control of his emotions, Travis handed Ginger's reins over to Crockett. "Moses," he called to the man crouched down a few feet from him, examining hoofprints in the mud. "Help me track her."

"Don't worry, Mr. Travis," Moses said as he pushed to his feet. "As long as the rain don't start pourin', we oughta be able to follow her tracks good enough."

The men advanced on foot, Crockett and Neill keeping the horses behind the rest to ensure the tracks were not obscured. Travis's focus remained glued to the ground, jumping from one hoofprint to the next as he half-jogged down the path.

"Here!" Josiah shouted from several yards ahead. "Mr. Travis. Over here. I found where the horse entered the road."

Travis lifted his head. "You sure?" The tracks were getting harder to spot as the rain wore them down. He couldn't afford to waste time following a false lead.

"That's about where me and the boy cut through to go home," Moses said in a low voice, assurance lending power to his words. "If she done took the shorter route, she woulda been headed here from that direction."

Careful not to tread on any of the existing tracks, Travis raced up to Josiah's position. The markings were harder to spot among the pine needles and leaves, but when he examined them, he had to agree that they were most likely from Meri's horse.

"Good work, Josiah." Travis braced his palms against his thighs and pushed up from his crouch. He peered into the darkness of the forest, his gut clenching. He should be feeling relief that they were getting close, but all he felt was an increasing sense of urgency.

He cupped his hands around his mouth and yelled his wife's name into the shadows. "Meri!"

No one moved as they listened for an answer. Nothing came.

"Neill, stay here with the horses." Travis motioned impatiently to his youngest brother. "Mark our place in case we have to retrace our steps. Moses?" He turned and pleaded with the man he'd come to trust. "Show me the way."

With a sharp nod, Moses took off through the trees. Travis followed on his heels, scanning the surrounding trees. He called out Meri's name every dozen steps or so, his heart pleading with his ears to capture a response over the rustling of their footfalls against the leafy ground.

When it came, he nearly stumbled.

"Hush!" he ordered. The men halted abruptly, their labored breathing the only sound beyond the wind and sleet.

"Meri!" He closed his eyes and willed the response to come again. *Please, Lord. Help me hear.*

A small sound carried above the wind. Soft yet distinct.

Thank you!

Travis sprinted past Moses and veered slightly to the right, something deeper than instinct guiding him. A tiny movement at the base of one of the pines caught his attention.

"Meredith." Immediately he changed course. He'd nearly passed her by, the dark brown of her cloak blending in with her surroundings. Thank God for white petticoats. If that ruffle hadn't winked at him from near her boot tops, he might never have seen her.

Travis dropped to his knees at her side. "Meri? I'm here, darlin'. Are you hurt?" He ran his hands lightly over her arms and down her legs, assessing for breaks. Alarm surged through him when he realized how wet her skirts were. Ice particles had collected on her clothing just as they had on her horse's mane, making the fabric stiff. Her limbs must be frozen through. She didn't even react when he touched her, as if she were too numb to feel his hands.

"I'm sorry, Travis." Her voice whispered over him, stilling his movement. He turned his face from examining her leg and watched the hood of her cape lift as she raised her chin. She was conscious. Yet her face was so pale, he feared that state wouldn't last for long. "The storm came up too fast . . . Ginger fell . . ." Meredith's eyes glazed. "I didn't want you to worry . . ."

Her chin slumped forward then, as if it required too much energy to hold up.

Travis levered his left arm beneath her legs and his right between her back and the tree trunk, pulling her tight into his chest. Close to his heart. He pushed to his feet and called to his brother.

"Crockett. The horses. I need to get her home."

Crockett dashed through the trees, hollering Neill's name. Travis followed with his precious burden, thinking to save every second he could by shortening the distance between him and the horses. Moses and Josiah shadowed him, their worried faces offering him little comfort.

Thankfully, Neill and Crockett galloped through the trees a moment later. Crockett dismounted and held his arms out to Travis. "Let me take her while you mount. Then I'll hand her up to you."

Travis didn't want to let her go, even for a moment, but he knew his brother was right. He gently transitioned her into Crock's arms, then mounted his gelding. Wishing he had the better-trained Bexar with him, he did his best to still the gelding with the pressure of his knees while he reached out for his wife.

"All right. I'm ready."

As he bent to collect Meri, his horse sidestepped, agitated by the weather and all the odd happenings. Instantly, Moses appeared at the beast's head. He took the bridle with a firm hand and ordered the animal to be still.

Travis solidified his hold on Meri and drew her up onto his lap. She burrowed her hands under his oilskin in search of warmth as she secured herself to his waist. Even through his flannel shirt, her fingers felt like ice.

"Get that gal home, Mr. Travis," Moses said as he released the bridle.

"Thank you, my friend. For everything."

Travis hugged his wife's half-frozen form to his chest and made for the ranch as fast as the storm and the extra weight on the horse's back would allow.

31

Meredith felt herself falling. With a tiny cry, she struggled against the lethargy that bound her and scrambled to reclaim her hold on the warm rock that was sliding away from her.

"Shh, Meri. It's all right," the rock said. "We're home. Let go for just a minute, sweetheart, so I can get down. Then I'll carry you inside."

But she didn't want to let go. Without her rock, she'd fall. She'd be alone in the cold again. "No," she murmured, tightening her grip.

Something soft and very unrockish touched her brow. It left a small circle of heat against her skin, like a promise. "Trust me, Meri." More warmth fanned across her cheek, warmth and familiarity. Strange how much her rock sounded like Travis.

Strong hands gripped her wrists and gently pried her away. Meredith whimpered but didn't fight. She trusted her husband's voice — whether he be rock or man.

As the rock shifted out from under her cheek, the hands returned, propping up her shoulders as she slumped forward. She tried to hold herself erect, but apparently her spine had turned to mush, for her body slumped to the side, following the hands as they edged farther down.

"I've got you, love."

The falling finally stopped as she came to rest against her warm rock once again. But when the rock began moving, her head jostled in a way that kept her from slipping back into the comfort of oblivion. Annoyed, she strained to open her eyes, just enough to glare a complaint. But the stubbled jaw that blurred in and out of focus a few inches from her face looked nothing like the rock she'd expected. Oh, it was set at a hard angle and clenched tight in concentration, but it was definitely flesh.

"Travis?" she croaked.

His chin dipped, and the brown eyes she loved so dearly caressed her face.

"I'm glad you're my rock." She knew it wasn't quite the right thing to say, but so much fog swirled in her mind, it was the best she could manage.

Travis's jaw softened a touch, and one

corner of his mouth lifted. "I'm glad, too."

A sharp gust of wind slashed across her face, bringing her mind into momentary focus. Cold. She ached with it. Everywhere. It ran so deep she feared she'd never be able to cast it out. She burrowed closer to Travis, but even he seemed to lack heat. The place she had laid her cheek against his oilskin during their ride had chilled.

"I'm c-c-cold." Shivers began coursing through her with such violence she worried she might shake herself free of Travis's arms. But he held fast.

"You'll be warm soon, Meri. I swear it."

As he climbed the porch steps, another horse pounded into the yard, two riders on its back. For once, Travis didn't bellow any orders to his brothers, he just continued on to the house. Meredith would have smiled if her teeth hadn't been chattering so shamefully. Her husband was learning to surrender control — trusting his brothers more fully, and perhaps God, as well. Dare she hope that one day he might even trust *her* enough to bestow his heart?

When he carried her across the threshold of her room, she could think of little else. Her eyes slid closed, and she imagined herself in the blue-and-white-striped dress she'd worn at her wedding, her husband's arms around her, his eyes full of love and laughter as he escorted her into their room. *Their* room. The room where they would belong solely to each other, where love would be shared and children conceived. A room where she could truly be a wife.

"Meri? Can you stand?"

Why did he need her to stand? Wouldn't it be easier just to lay her on the bed? Her dress would look so pretty fanned out around her. She could open her arms, and he could bend down and kiss her . . .

"I need you to try to stand, sweetheart. If I lay you down, you'll get the bed all wet."

Wet? Meredith scrunched up her nose. What an odd thing for a husband to say. It wasn't at all romantic.

"Come on, Meri. I need you to help me get your clothes off."

Meredith sniffed. That wasn't very romantic, either — all gruff and businesslike. Where were the sweet words a husband used to woo his bride? And why wasn't he kissing her? Everything would be so much better if he'd just kiss her. Then he could do whatever he wanted with her clothes.

She leaned forward to show him what she wanted, but for some reason, her lips missed their target and landed somewhere on his neck. At least it felt like his neck. Not that she'd ever kissed him there, of course. But it felt much like she expected a neck to feel. She thought to adjust her aim and try again. However, she couldn't quite summon the energy. Oh well, necks were nice, too.

"Meredith!" Travis's bark combined with a brief, jarring shake tore away the curtain of her delirium, leaving her exposed to the harsh light of reality.

She hung like a rag doll from Travis's arms, her feet dragging the floor, her face plastered against his neck. No wedding dress. Only mud-smeared calico and a soggy wool cloak.

"I need your help." This time she heard the fear in his voice. "Please."

The hovering darkness promised escape, but she resisted its pull. Travis needed her.

Meredith reached her hands up to her husband's shoulders and drew her feet more firmly beneath her. Bracing her weight on her good leg, she gazed into his eyes as she forced herself to stand. His eyes held hers, infusing her with strength.

Keeping one hand at her waist to aid her balance, Travis used the other to undo the cloak's fastenings. Once he had it undone, he helped her slip each arm through the sleeves and tossed the sopping garment into a heap near the wall. He had just reached for the buttons that ran the length of her bodice when a masculine voice intruded.

"How is she, Travis?"

Meredith twisted her head away from Crockett, feeling exposed and vulnerable.

"She's frozen, half delirious, and weak as a newborn kitten, but I think if we can get her warm, she'll be all right."

"I've got water heating for some tea and a pair of bricks heating in the hearth. I brought some toweling, too." Crockett raised his arms to indicate the small bundle, then walked into the room and set it on the bed. "Need any help?'

Meredith gasped. She thought the man wanted to be a preacher. How could he make such an improper suggestion?

"Yeah. Come hold her up for a minute while I get out of this slicker."

"Travis, no," she moaned.

His eyes widened slightly, then crinkled at the corners. "Don't worry," he whispered close to her ear. "I'll send him away before we undo any more buttons."

What on earth had possessed him to say such a thing? Travis stripped off his hat, slicker, and coat, tossing them to the floor. The woman was soaked to the skin, her teeth chattering faster than the rattle on a snake's tail. The last thing she needed was a flirtatious husband. Yet it *had* brought a touch of color back to her cheeks.

Travis took a minute to rummage through the bureau drawers and find one of Meri's nightdresses before he relieved Crockett. His brother stepped aside, then winked at Travis, careful to keep the gesture hidden from Meredith.

"A little different from last time, huh?"

Images of the two of them bumbling over Meredith's corset after her encounter with Samson scurried through Travis's mind. "Very," he ground out.

Thank the Lord Meredith was conscious enough to cooperate this time, for there was no way he'd let Crockett assist in her undressing. That duty belonged to her husband. And only her husband.

Crockett slapped him on the back and strode to the door. "I'll knock when the tea and bricks are ready," he said, all teasing gone from his voice as he grabbed the knob to pull the door shut. "Feel better, Meredith."

"Th-th-th-hank y-y-you," she stammered in reply.

Travis gently tugged her head toward him until it lay against his chest, and then he ran his hands briskly up and down her arms, trying to ward off her convulsive shivers. His own legs were cold inside his rain-soaked trousers, but his comfort could wait. Meri's couldn't.

Together, they managed to get her dress, petticoats, and corset off. But when Travis started to toss the pink, lacy undergarment on top of the pile of wet clothes, Meredith shrieked and grabbed his arm with more strength than he would have given her credit for.

"Drape it over the b-b-back of the ch-chair."

He figured it was safer not to argue with her, so he did as she instructed and hurried back to her side, grabbing the toweling off the bed as he went. He wrapped her in the dry cloth as if it were a shawl and urged her to lean on him as he rubbed her back and arms. So focused was he on getting her warm that it wasn't until he was kneeling before her, running a second towel up and down her calves, that he realized how well her damp chemise and drawers clung to her curves.

Travis immediately turned his attention to her feet.

After a moment of carefully regulated breathing and a stern internal lecture, Travis stood and faced his bride. "Do you think you can handle the nightdress on your own?"

She gave a jerky little nod, and he exhaled in relief. Her shivers had calmed somewhat, but she still looked unsteady on her feet.

"I'm going to turn around to give you some privacy, but I'll be right here if you need me. All right?"

Another nod.

Travis turned his back and immediately started naming the books of the Bible in his head. Then the twelve apostles, thirteen if one counted Matthias, which he did because he needed all the distraction he could get to keep himself from imagining what was transpiring behind him. He added Paul in for good measure, too, and then started on the twelve tribes. Although, really, there were thirteen there, too. What with Joseph's descendants split into two tribes and named after his sons, Ephraim and Manasseh. But then again, the Levites didn't inherit any land, so —

A muffled cry banished the Israelites from his brain. Travis spun around to find Meredith bent sideways clasping her calf through the white cotton of her nightdress. He was at her side in an instant.

"What is it?"

"Cramps," she whimpered. "In my w-weak leg."

He picked her up and carried her to the bed.

"I sh-shouldn't have put any weight on it. I know b-b-better."

Travis pulled the covers back and laid her on the sheets. "What can I do?"

She squeezed her eyes shut and rolled toward him, curling up into a ball. "It'll p-pass eventually."

That wasn't good enough. Travis tucked the blankets up to her chin, knelt on the rug that ran alongside the bed, and reached for her leg — the leg his trap had weakened all those years ago, the leg that had brought this incredible woman into his life.

Meredith groaned and tried to ease the limb away from him, but he wouldn't allow her to retreat. Using a light touch at first, he worked his way up her calf to just above her knee, then back down to the arch of her foot and even her toes. Gradually he increased the pressure of his massage, working the knots out of her muscles until she finally began to uncurl from her protective posture.

When Crockett's knock came, Meri's eyelids had relaxed, and though she continued to shiver slightly, her breathing had evened enough that Travis suspected she might have drifted off to sleep. Slowly, he drew his hand down her calf, over her ankle, and across her foot, enjoying the feel of her skin one last time just for the pure pleasure of it before rising to answer the door.

"How is she?" Crockett asked, lowering his voice to a whisper when he noticed her lying in bed.

"Better, but she's still shivering. I'm worried she might have caught a chill."

"Yeah, well, I'm worried *you're* going to catch a chill unless you get some dry clothes on yourself. Go change while I try to get some of this tea into her. Neill's gathering the bricks now. We'll have her warm in no time."

Travis glanced back at Meri, reluctant to leave. But Crockett was right. He'd be no good to her if he was ill.

"I left a mug of hot coffee for you on Neill's dresser."

"Thanks." Travis strode down the hall, determined to change in record time.

His wet trousers made the going slower than he would have liked, clinging to him like woolen leeches. He eventually succeeded in peeling them off, along with his drawers and socks. The dry clothes went on much easier, and within minutes, Travis had gulped down his coffee and was helping Neill arrange the cloth-wrapped hot bricks under the sheets at the bottom of Meredith's bed.

Crockett got about a cupful of tea into Meri before she waved him away. Her haggard expression elicited Travis's protective nature, and he immediately shooed his brothers out of the room. Meredith inched her way back down in the bed, no doubt drawn to the heat of the bricks, but once there, she still curled herself into a ball, as if the added warmth failed to penetrate her.

"Are you still cold?"

"Mm-hmm," she mumbled against the pillow.

Travis could think of only one other way to help her get warm. He walked around to the opposite side of the bed and lifted the covers. His heart throbbed against his ribs. After more than a month, he was finally going to share a bed with his wife.

The mattress took his weight, and Travis tentatively shifted closer to Meri. As if someone had shot off a starting gun, she rolled over and burrowed into him with such haste that he barely moved his knees in time to avoid a collision. Her legs tangled with his while her arms folded up between them. Frigid toes rubbed against his calf where his trouser leg had bunched up, shocking him with the sheer cold that continued to cling to her despite the blankets and heated bricks. He sandwiched his legs around her feet, hoping to speed their thaw. Her hands eventually wiggled their way beneath his untucked shirt, and when her icy fingers found his bare chest, she let out a tiny sigh that made his heart flip.

One thing was for sure. Crockett needn't worry about him catching a chill tonight. With Meredith touching him like she was, he'd be lucky not to go up in flames.

32

Travis woke before the sun, pangs in his stomach prodding him to rise and make restitution for skipping supper the night before. But he resisted. Contentment lay over him like an extra blanket, so foreign yet utterly captivating that he didn't want to move for fear it would dissipate. Then it shifted, blowing a warm puff of air against his neck. Travis's mind sharpened in an instant.

Meri.

Travis opened his eyes and turned his head, ever so slowly, so as not to disturb the woman whose face lay in the crook of his shoulder. She was so beautiful. Her long lashes resting peacefully against the creamy skin of her cheeks, her hair cascading behind her, finally freed from the confines of its pins. As he watched her sleep, he couldn't resist the urge to stroke the deep blond tresses, their softness quickly becoming an addiction to his fingers.

He wanted nothing more than to gently kiss her awake and finally claim her in the way God intended. But as he leaned forward to touch his lips to her sleepy eyelids, he noted the faint smudges of exhaustion still evident beneath her eyes and pulled away. She needed rest.

Turning his gaze to the ceiling, Travis exhaled. He might as well get up. Sleep was well beyond his grasp now, and Meredith would rest better without him tossing and turning beside her. But, oh, how he hated to leave. One thing was for certain, though, if she would have him, he'd be spending all future nights in this bed with her. Their courting had gone on long enough. It was time to begin their marriage.

Careful to disturb her as little as possible, Travis cupped the back of Meredith's head as he slid his arm out from under her cheek and eased away. Her mouth puckered into an adorable little pout as she grumbled her displeasure in her sleep before resettling. Tenderness welled inside him as he smiled down on her. What a precious gift he'd been given.

A gift he'd nearly lost yesterday.

His smile faded as he padded on bare feet over to the window and looked out over the predawn landscape.

How am I supposed to protect my family, Lord?

Twice now the measures he'd taken had come back to haunt him, and both times Meredith had been the one to pay the price. She could have lost her leg the first time, and yesterday she could have frozen to death waiting for him to find her.

All my life I've striven to protect those you've entrusted to my care. Yet no matter how hard I try, my efforts are never enough. What do you want from me?

As the first hint of light softened the sky, a verse from Proverbs illuminated his heart. *"Trust in the Lord with all thine heart; and lean not unto thine own understanding. In all thy ways acknowledge him, and he shall direct thy paths."*

Conviction speared through him, and Travis had to place a hand against the wall to steady himself. He'd been shouldering the burden of guarding his family since his father charged him with the duty fourteen years ago. And all that time he'd trusted only himself to take care of them. Rarely had he sought the Lord's guidance. His father had always said that God gave man a mind and expected him to use it, but perhaps he had taken that admonition too far.

Travis glanced back at Meredith. *Show me how best to take care of her. How to be a good husband, provider, and protector.*

Hungering for direction, he crossed the room on silent feet and eased open the dresser drawer where he kept his Bible. Then he crept out to the kitchen, lit a lamp, and settled into a chair at the table. His brothers would be up soon, but right now the morning was quiet — a good time to listen for the Lord.

Not sure where to start, Travis thumbed the pages open to Proverbs. For much of his life, he'd clung to the wisdom of a particular verse in chapter 27. He ran his finger down the page until he found verse 12: *"A prudent man foreseeth the evil, and hideth himself."* That's what he had been doing the past fourteen years, trying to predict what evil might threaten his family and taking steps to hide away from it. But the disquiet in his soul made him wonder if perhaps the season for that tactic had passed. He and his brothers were no longer vulnerable boys who needed to hide. They were grown men who could fight for what was right.

His gaze drifted over the page, not truly

focusing, until the word *brother* caught his attention, just two verses up from where he'd been reading.

"Thine own friend, and thy father's friend, forsake not; neither go into thy brother's house in the day of thy calamity: for better is a neighbour that is near than a brother far off."

Don't forsake friends. Depend on neighbors. Your brothers might not always be at hand when trouble comes. Travis rubbed his brow, bracing his elbow against the table. Friends? Until Meredith had talked him into letting Moses help rebuild the barn, he hadn't had any. Seth Winston might count as a friend of his father, but the old man only came around four times a year.

And neighbors? He recalled a few schoolmates who'd had farms in the area, but he had no idea if their families were still around or not. Hadn't Christ said that except for loving God, the most important command was to love one's neighbor? Kind of hard to do that if he didn't even know who his neighbors were.

Another verse floated into memory, one about not only looking out for one's own interests, but also to the interests of others. Travis began flipping pages toward the New

Testament, but before he found the verse, something stuffed between the pages in Romans caused him to halt.

A straw. A broken, short straw.

She'd kept it.

He wasn't quite sure why that fact make his heart jump around in his chest, but it did. His hand even trembled slightly as he moved to take it out of the book's crease. The brittle piece felt thin and delicate in his rough fingers. He stroked its length with his thumb and thought of the wife it had brought him.

Meredith deserved better than a reclusive life. Whenever she talked about teaching on Saturdays, her whole face lit up. Myra and the children brought her such joy and gave her life a sense of purpose beyond daily chores. And she'd been right about his brothers, too. No matter how badly he wanted to keep them tied to the ranch, he knew the Lord had planted ambitions in them that could one day take them away. Jim had his carpentry and his newfound attachment to Cassie. Crockett had his preaching. And Neill? Well, the kid had an entire world of possibilities to explore.

"Travis?"

He swiveled toward the sleepy voice. Meredith stood in the doorway, her nightdress floating about her legs as she squinted into the lamplight.

"Is everything all right?" Her fingers clenched nervously at the shawl she'd wrapped around her shoulders.

Travis got to his feet. "What are you doing out of bed? You should be resting." He closed the distance between them, thinking to lead her back to the bedroom.

"I missed you." The hushed admission froze him in his tracks and drove all other thought out of his head.

She missed him? Beside her? In bed?

His gaze flew to her face to gauge if perhaps he'd misunderstood, even while his heart raced with the hope that he had not. She dipped her chin away from him, a delightful shade of pink coloring her cheeks.

"I . . . I was cold." She still couldn't meet his eyes, and he prayed it was because his heat wasn't the only thing she missed.

Travis moved his hands up her arms to her shoulders, his fingers digging through her hair. "You know," he said, probing her gently. "Now that winter's here, you're apt to be cold often. I'd be willing to help you stay warm on a more regular basis. If that was something you wanted."

She angled her face away from him and nibbled on her bottom lip.

"Meri?" He forced himself to breathe slowly as he waited for her to turn and look at him. When her lashes finally lifted, the longing he read in her blue eyes matched the desire pulsing in his chest. "Is that what you want?"

"Yes."

Tightening his grip on her nape, he drew her to him and slanted his lips possessively over hers. He stroked her jaw with the side of his thumbs and urged her to deepen the kiss. A tiny moan escaped her, and she melted against him. He was about to sweep her into his arms and take her back to his room where they could make good on the promise passing between them, but the creak of one of the hall doors brought him back to his senses.

Reminding himself they had years to be together, Travis gentled his kiss and then pulled away. The fact that Meredith didn't seem to want to stop nearly derailed his good intentions, but he managed to disentangle himself from her hold on him, pleased by her reluctance to let him go.

"The others are starting to rise, Meri," he murmured low in her ear. "Why don't you go back to bed? The boys and I can fend for ourselves this morning."

"I don't mind seeing to things, Travis. I can —"

"Shh." He placed a finger on her lips. "With all you went through yesterday, you need to rest. Besides, I have a special project I thought you might like to help me with later this morning. You won't be able to help if you're too worn out."

Her eyes lit. "What sort of project?"

"I thought we could dismantle the front gate. Oh, and those warning signs, too. Something tells me we don't really need them anymore."

A beatific smile blossomed across her face as she clasped his hand and drew it to her middle. "Oh, Travis. Do you mean it?"

His chest expanded as he returned her smile. A man could get used to his woman looking at him like that.

"Yes, darlin'. I mean it. I think it's time for the Archers to rejoin the world."

Meredith stretched up on her tiptoes and touched a kiss to his cheek. "You *are* my world."

Her husky comment made his gut clench, but before he could do more than blink, she released his hand and trailed away from him. Which was probably a good thing seeing as how Crockett was standing right outside the doorway trying to look inconspicuous.

Meredith bundled her shawl more tightly around her shoulders before ducking her head and scurrying past his brother. Travis knew he probably looked like a lovesick pup just standing there watching her go, but he didn't care. Crockett even came into the room and stared into the newly emptied hall alongside him, obviously trying to taunt him out of his stupor.

"So when are you finally going to tell her that you're insanely in love with her?" Crockett asked, only a hint of teasing in his voice.

Travis rubbed a hand over his whiskery jaw, reaching his fingers up to the place she had kissed. "Tonight. Definitely tonight."

33

Meredith whistled and danced her way around the kitchen, drying the lunch dishes and wiping down the stove, her happiness too large to contain. Had there ever been a finer day? Yesterday's storm had passed, and the blue sky left in its wake portended a bright future.

Wouldn't Myra be surprised to learn that all their plotting had proved unnecessary? A tiny giggle bubbled out of Meredith as she returned a stack of clean plates to the cabinet shelf. She hadn't needed to use even one of Myra's suggestions in order to get Travis to stay with her last night. Of course, she'd slept through nearly the entire experience, but there were enough lingering memories of his scent close to her face, his chest beneath her hand, and his touch at her waist to reassure her that it hadn't been a dream.

And this morning? Meredith sighed. Her

hands stilled as she stared at the doorway where Travis had kissed her. She recalled the way he'd looked at her afterward, the possessive heat in his eyes, the way his lips quirked slightly as if eager to return to hers, the touch of his fingers through the sleeve of her gown. At that moment, all her self-doubts had vanished. She'd actually felt beautiful. Desired. Not at all like a woman who'd been foisted upon a reluctant bridegroom.

Could it be that Travis no longer saw her as simply a responsibility but as something more? Had duty deepened to . . .

Meredith couldn't quite bring herself to name the emotion, not even in her thoughts. The disappointment would be too keen if his affection didn't prove to be as deep as such a name would imply. His fondness for her had already grown so much. Getting greedy now would only risk halting their progress. Better to let the words come naturally. In their own time.

As she tried to convince herself that she was patient enough to wait however long it might take, pounding hoofbeats approached from the direction of the road, seizing her attention.

After working close to the house that morning, Travis had left after lunch to help

Crockett and Neill assess the damage the storm had done to the herd. With cattle scattered all over the northern pasture, she didn't expect him back until suppertime. Meredith reached for the loaded shotgun she'd propped against the wall near the back door, having sworn to her husband that she wouldn't leave the house unarmed, and moved to the front room, where she could get a better look at the rider.

Catching a glimpse of her brother-in-law's scowling face as he leapt from his horse's back, rifle in hand, sent relief spiraling through her — quickly followed by new alarm as she tried to guess what unseen foe had him so on guard.

Jim climbed the porch and positioned himself with his back to the door, his rifle aimed across the yard.

"Travis!"

Meredith jumped at the sheer volume of his yell. Heavens! The man was louder than a grizzly. Ordering her heart palpitations to cease, she moved to the door, intending to inform the bear of his brother's location, but the instant the hinge squeaked, Jim crouched and spun, bringing the barrel of his rifle in line with her chest.

Meredith's heart stopped altogether then. Her shotgun clunked to the ground as her breath hitched in her throat.

"Confound it, woman. I could have shot you!" Jim yanked his rifle out of her direction, but he scowled at her as if the mishap were somehow her fault. Then he noted the shotgun at her feet, and his irritated expression immediately turned wary. He placed himself in front of her and began scanning the yard again.

"Where are Travis and the others? Did Mitchell's men attack?"

"Everything's fine, Jim. Truly." Meredith stepped from behind him. "They're all out checking the herd. Why would you think Roy's men had returned? Unless . . ." She grabbed his arm. "Did you see someone on the road?"

His brow furrowed. "No. But the gate was down. Travis never leaves that gate open. I figured something must've happened."

Meredith's breath released in a soft whoosh. "Something did happen," she said, a grin stretching across her face. "Your brother decided to rejoin the world. Travis and I took the gate down this morning."

Jim's jaw hung slightly slack as he stared at her. "Travis took the gate down? *Travis?*"

She nodded, pride for her husband nearly unbalancing her as she rose up onto the balls of her feet. "He took the warning signs down, too. Did you notice? No more scaring away the neighbors at gunpoint, I'm afraid." A laugh escaped her, but it died when Jim's frown refused to abate.

"What about Mitchell? Didn't Travis think that removing the gate would make us more vulnerable?"

Meredith tilted her head a bit as she considered Jim's uneasy stance. She'd thought he would be more pleased about the change, seeing as how it would aid his courting plans with Cassie, not to mention being good for his furniture building business. Then again, the locked gate had been a symbol of security to this family for the majority of their lives. It was only natural that such a change would require some adjustment.

"Travis and Crockett discussed it at length this morning. They agreed that if Mitchell's men are bent on causing mischief, a locked gate won't stop them. The night of the fire proved that. All the gate does now is keep neighbors out and Archers in. With the four of you grown and fully capable of handling whatever comes down the path, Travis figured it was time to stop living in isolation."

The grunt Jim gave in reply was hard to read, so Meredith changed the subject.

"How's Cassie?"

Jim's mouth thinned, and a fierceness emerged in his eyes. "She assured me everything was fine. Said her father had given his word not to force her to marry Mitchell. She promised to come to me if he changed his mind." He worked his jaw back and forth. "You don't think they'd lock her in, do you? I watched her house last night and again this morning, and nothing seemed off. Her ma stormed out of the house early in the morning, but I saw Cassie before I left, and she said that except for an ugly argument between her folks, things were normal. She insisted I come home in case Mitchell stirred up trouble for Travis. I told her I'd check on her in a few days."

Meredith nibbled the inside of her cheek. Cassie had always been able to sway Uncle Everett to her way of thinking, but Aunt Noreen was another matter entirely. God had never made a more hardheaded woman. Hearing that she'd gone out early was a bit worrisome. The woman never took idle strolls. But what trouble could she possibly stir up without her husband's support?

"I've never known Uncle Everett to break his word to Cassie," Meredith said, trying to reassure herself as much as Jim. "If he's promised her not to force the marriage, he won't."

Jim made a noncommittal sound.

"Why don't you get cleaned up, and then come in and let me fix you something to eat?"

"Nah." Jim strode away from her and clomped down the steps toward his horse. "I need to talk to Travis."

She thought about stopping him, about mentioning that Travis had expected him to keep an eye on the house once he returned from town, but she held her tongue. Jim's stoic features gave away little; nevertheless, Meredith sensed how the situation with Cassie ate at him. The Archers always handled their problems together. This time shouldn't be any different.

Besides, it wasn't as if she needed a guard, she reminded herself as Jim mounted his horse. She had Sadie. And if the old girl slept under the porch most of the day, what did it matter? Meredith had periodically stayed alone for days at a time at the old homestead. She could certainly manage a few hours at the Archer ranch.

And if Travis didn't like the idea of her being unchaperoned for the duration of the afternoon, he could just come home and watch over her himself.

"You'll be all right here?" Jim turned in his saddle to face her, the tightness around his mouth testifying to his sudden indecision.

"Of course." Meredith's lips curled into a secretive smile. An afternoon alone with her husband? She couldn't get rid of Jim fast enough.

An hour later, Meredith had dusted the parlor, swept the kitchen, and chopped a pot's worth of vegetables for the stew she planned for dinner — a pretty remarkable feat since she spent nearly as much time peering out the window for Travis as she did working.

Surely he would come soon. Unless Jim had trouble locating him. She'd never ridden the north pasture, had no idea how large it was or how wooded. Perhaps finding Travis was more difficult than she'd imagined. And even then, Travis wouldn't leave without at least having a conversation with Jim.

As Meredith poured water over her potatoes, onions, and carrots, another thought struck her. What if Travis felt no urgency to return? What if he had full confidence in her abilities to handle things at the house? Meredith frowned as she set the water pitcher aside. She wanted Travis to trust her, to have confidence in her abilities. But what she wanted even more was for him to jump at the chance to be alone with her.

And wasn't that a muddled mess. Meredith rolled her eyes in exasperation. The man had a ranch to run, for heaven's sake. The last thing he needed was a love-struck wife making demands on his time during prime work hours. They'd have other opportunities —

The sound of a rider approaching banished all practical reasoning, leaving her head swirling and her stomach jumping as she rushed to the bathing room to check her appearance in the shaving mirror.

Travis had come after all.

Anticipation fluttered in her chest as she untied her apron and tossed it onto the table. She pranced down the hall, eager to greet her husband. But when she reached for the door handle, the sound of Sadie's growl stopped her. Caution reasserted itself. Meredith released the knob and instead reached for the shotgun propped nearby.

Whoever was in the yard, it wasn't her husband.

34

Travis guided Bexar through the muddy terrain left from yesterday's storm, methodically working his way back to the ranch. Jim had been none too happy to see the gate down and had given him an earful about how it didn't make sense to reduce security around the house until things with Mitchell were settled. And though Travis still believed that taking down the gate was what God had called him to do, hearing his own doubts voiced aloud left him uneasy.

I'm trying to trust you, Lord. But I feel like I'm fighting against nature. Common sense tells me to lock down, not open up. To protect those I love with every tool at my disposal.

What if he had misunderstood God's intention? What if his actions today were putting his family in danger?

"Is it too late to lay out a fleece?" Travis quipped, tilting an eye toward heaven. "A

little confirmation would sure be appreciated."

The more he thought about that fleece,
though, the more he remembered what the
Lord had demanded of the man who'd laid
it out. He'd demanded trust beyond what
common sense dictated. God whittled Gideon's army from three thousand men to
three hundred, then sent him into battle
against an enemy whose troops were too
vast to be counted. Gideon purposely made
himself vulnerable, ignored his instincts,
and put the welfare of his people into the
hands of another. And the Lord rewarded
him by granting him victory.

Travis squinted into the distance, sighting
in on the trail of woodsmoke that marked
the location of the ranch house. Was God
calling him to do the same?

Bexar ambled into a clearing as Travis
pondered. Then from out of the quiet, two
muted cracks — gunfire — set both man
and horse on alert.

Meri!

Travis kicked Bexar into a run. The animal
leapt to his command, his hooves eating up
the damp earth as they raced forward. The
frantic pace made them reckless, but Travis
drove on, his mind focused on only one
thing — getting to his wife.

I trusted her to you! his soul cried as trees blurred past.

Shoring up his faith, he held on to the knowledge that she had to be relatively safe in order to fire the signal shots. But even that did little to calm the anxiety raging within. He needed to see her, touch her. Only then would he be able to breathe.

The barn came into view. Travis slowed Bexar with a touch of the reins and yanked his rifle free of the scabbard. His gaze scoured the trees, searching for the threat. Meredith didn't spook easily. She wouldn't have fired those shots without reason.

When he found nothing suspicious behind the barn, he used his knees to steer Bexar into the main yard. That's when he spotted her. Sitting on the porch rocker, the shotgun near but not gripped across her lap, Sadie lying at her feet. She looked safe. Beautiful.

Something wound tight inside him uncoiled a bit.

He could tell the moment she noticed him. She pushed slowly to her feet, as if needing to verify his identity before taking any deliberate action. Once she did, she scrambled down the steps, picked up her skirts, and ran toward him, her limp exacerbated by her hurry.

Travis couldn't yet see her face clearly,

but there was a desperation to her movement that twisted his gut. She wasn't just relieved to see him. Something was wrong. Urging Bexar forward, he crossed half the yard in the time it took her to get to the corral. Once he was close enough, he slid from the horse's back and rushed to meet her.

His hands gripped her arms when he reached her, and his gaze roved over her, searching for proof that she was indeed unharmed. "What happened, Meri? Are you all right?"

"It's not me, Travis." Meredith bent her arms and grabbed hold of his elbows, her fingers pressing through the thickness of his coat. "It's Cassie."

He looked over at the house. "Your cousin's here? Jim said he left her in town."

"She's not here. She's at the old homestead. About to marry Roy Mitchell."

His attention snapped back to her face. "What?" Jim was going to be livid. "I thought your uncle gave his word not to force the union."

"Aunt Noreen must've interfered somehow. She hates to be thwarted, and in her mind, Cassie's marriage to Roy is the best way to preserve their livelihood." Meredith was rambling so fast, Travis struggled to keep pace. "She must've warned Roy of Uncle Everett's change of heart, not realizing what measures he would take to ensure he didn't lose the land he'd been promised."

Meri's vivid eyes locked with his. "I think he kidnapped her, Travis. It's the only thing that makes any sense. Mr. Wheeler tried to make it sound like everything was amicable. But I know Cassie, and she'd never —"

"Wait a minute." Travis's eyes narrowed. "Wheeler was here?" That was the man who'd tried to convince him to sell out, and no doubt one of the riders responsible for setting fire to his barn. He'd been here? Talking to Meri?

She nodded. "Roy sent him to deliver the invitation."

"Did he touch you?" Travis shoved the words past clenched teeth. If that snake had so much as laid a finger on her . . .

"He didn't even get off his horse." A gleam shone in Meredith's eyes. "Between Sadie's growls and my shotgun, we managed to welcome him in true Archer style."

Travis grinned. Here he'd torn down gates and disposed of warning signs — things his wife had encouraged him to do — and now she was the one welcoming strangers at gunpoint.

Sadie barked, and for the first time, Travis noticed the dog standing a pace behind Meri. He reached down and stroked her behind her ears. "Sounds like my girls had things well in hand." The old bird dog barked again in appreciation of his approval.

When he straightened, Meredith's eyes were scanning the woods beyond the barn. "Do you think the others heard the shots? Jim will want to know about Cassie. We'll need to strategize, and we don't have much time."

"Don't worry. They'll come barrelin' out of those trees any minute." Especially Jim. The man was already edgier than a new razor. "But for now, I think you better start at the beginning and tell me exactly what Wheeler said."

"There isn't that much to tell." Meredith shivered slightly and rubbed her arms. Her shawl must have slipped off when she left the porch. Funny how she hadn't noticed the cold until that moment.

Travis shrugged out of his work coat and settled the heavy garment on her shoulders. Tenderness softened his face for a moment as he fidgeted with the collar. But when he finished, the hard lines returned. "What did he say?"

"He said that Roy and Cassie were on their way to my father's old property along with my aunt and uncle and a handful of guests. Knowing how close Cassie and I are, Roy asked Wheeler to ride ahead and extend a personal invitation to us. For Cassandra's sake, he asked that we set aside any hard feelings over previous misunderstandings and attend the wedding. It's supposed to be in the cabin at five o'clock tonight."

Travis's eyes widened. "Tonight? That can't be more than a couple hours from now."

"I found that pretty suspicious, too." Meredith pushed her arms through the sleeves of her husband's coat and crossed them over her belly. "I told Mr. Wheeler that when I saw Cassie yesterday morning, she'd had no intention of wedding Mr. Mitchell. He just smiled and said she'd changed her mind."

Meredith searched Travis's face for some clue as to what he was thinking, but his stoic mask gave nothing away. She'd expected outrage or a promise to mount a rescue effort or something. Yet all he did was scowl and stare into the empty space between her and the corral.

"We *are* going to help her, right?" Meredith tried to claim Travis's gaze by searching out his eyes. "I know Cass. She'd never willingly marry that man. Roy must be threatening or manipulating her somehow."

"Of course he's manipulating," Travis growled. "And not only your cousin. He's attempting to manipulate me, as well. Which is why we can't rush off without thinking things through."

Travis twisted his neck back toward the woods. Only then did Meredith hear the sound of riders coming in.

"Mitchell needs both our properties to solidify things with his investors," Travis said, turning back to her. "If we play into his hand, we risk giving him exactly what he wants. We need time to figure out what game he's playing before we can hope to beat him at it."

"But —"

"We'll talk about it more when the boys get here."

Travis strode away from her to signal his brothers, and Meredith couldn't help but feel a little abandoned. Her mind insisted that anticipating Roy's machinations was the wise course, but her heart wanted a take-charge hero ready to ride to the rescue.

Forty-five minutes later, all the Archers stood in the center of the barn, still arguing

443

over the best plan of action.

"What if you're wrong, Travis? I won't take that risk." Jim refused to back down, and Meredith, for one, was glad.

"We don't even know for sure that Mitchell has her," Travis insisted. "More likely it's a ploy to lure us away and leave the ranch open to attack. Only this time, they'll raze everything, not just the barn. It's the only hope he has of driving us off the land. Either that or he has an army of men waiting to ambush us at the cabin. Dead men can't protest an illegal sale, after all."

Crockett pushed away from the post he'd been slouching against. "You did say Cassie was fine when you left her this morning. Right, Jim? Wheeler arrived barely an hour after you did. Mitchell would've had to abduct Cassie and her family, find a minister willing to perform a forced ceremony, and set out for Meredith's cabin in that same time frame. I find it hard to believe that he could pull that off in under an hour with no advance warning."

"He could if he had help." All eyes turned to Meredith. "You forget that Jim saw my aunt leaving the house before he left. She wants this union. She believes it's her family's financial salvation. In her eyes, Roy Mitchell is a saint. I imagine she went directly to his office this morning and probably even aided the man in kidnapping her daughter."

Jim stalked up to Travis and growled in his ear. "If Mitchell had Meredith, you'd go after her. You know you would."

She could tell by the way the two eyed each other in challenge, that Jim's statement hadn't been intended for her ears, but she couldn't stop herself from hoping it would be persuasive. Cassie was in peril. It was time to send in the cavalry.

Jim finally stepped away and let Travis mull over all that'd been said. The quiet ate away at Meredith, but she held her tongue, praying that the Lord would give her husband the wisdom necessary to make the right decision.

"Before Pa died, he made me swear to protect our family and our land. I won't leave the ranch unguarded or let the three of you walk into an ambush without proof that Cassie is truly in danger."

Jim made to protest, but Travis stopped him with a look. And in that moment, something shriveled inside Meredith. The land always came first with Travis. The land and his brothers.

"However," Travis continued, "I agree that we cannot risk Cassie's life, either."

Meredith inhaled a shaky breath. *Please, Travis. Please let us help her.*

"Therefore, I think the best course of action is to let Jim scout out the cabin. The rest of us will stay here in case Mitchell attacks. One man will be harder to spot, but you'll also have no one to watch your back."

Jim nodded, obviously eager to take on the task despite the risk.

"Once Jim determines if Cassandra is in fact at the cabin, he'll return and alert us to the situation — how many men Mitchell has, where they're holding her, and so forth. If she's there, we'll go after her. If not, we'll stay here and elude Mitchell's trap."

It wasn't exactly the cavalry charge she'd been hoping for, but at least it left the door open for a later one.

"I can go with Jim," Meredith volunteered. "I know the property. I can show him the best way to get close to the cabin without being seen."

Jim seemed to be considering her offer until Travis glared the consideration right out of him.

"Not a chance." He turned his glare on her. "If Mitchell got his hands on you, there's no telling what he would do. At the very least he'd use you to get to me. We can't afford that."

"Because it would put your precious land in jeopardy, wouldn't it?" Hot tears threatened to fall, but she forced them back. Any affection he felt for her ran a distant second to his loyalty to the ranch. She'd been a fool to think there could ever be more. "The land always comes first. Doesn't it, Travis?"

Unable to hold the tears at bay any longer, she sprinted past him, her only thought to escape. She headed for the house, but before she reached the porch, strong arms latched onto her from behind and spun her around.

Meredith tried to pull away, but when she saw the pained look in his eyes, she ceased. Even with his callous, overly rational behavior, she loved him too much to hurt him.

"Meri, honey. I know you're worried about Cassie. I am, too." Travis's face hovered above hers, his dark eyes sincere. "But I'm also worried about Jim and Crockett and Neill. We have to take precautions."

She said nothing.

He sighed and loosened his hold on her arms in order to cup her face. His thumbs stroked her cheeks, rubbing away the moisture there with such tenderness it almost set her to weeping again.

"I can't let you go with Jim. It's too dangerous. If something happened to you,

447

I . . ." He glanced up to the sky. His fingers trembled slightly against her face.

Meredith trembled, too. Waiting. *I couldn't bear it,* she imagined him saying. Or . . . *I would be devastated.* How she longed to hear words that would prove her wrong, to prove that his heart was truly engaged.

Travis's eyes lowered to meet hers. She held her breath.

"If something happened to you, Meri, I'd never forgive myself."

Meredith exhaled, and her hopes leaked out with the used air. He still saw her as a responsibility, a duty. Perhaps a pleasant one, but a duty nonetheless.

"I need to know you're safe," he continued, passion firing his words. "I'd give my life to keep you safe."

"I know you would," she said, a sad smile turning her lips upward. Her warrior. So protective. So honorable. He'd no doubt feel the same ardor for anyone under his care.

Placing her hands on his shoulders, she lifted up and touched her lips to his. Just for a moment. A sweet, achingly wistful moment.

Then she stepped away. "I'll be in the house."

"Thank you," he whispered.

As Meredith climbed the porch steps, she knew what she had to do. Travis wasn't the only warrior in the family. No, she had her own protective agenda. Cassie was more a sister to her than a cousin, and though she couldn't explain how she knew, Meredith was certain that Roy had not been bluffing about the wedding.

Cassie needed her. And right now that need outweighed everything else.

35

Meredith watched at the kitchen window until Travis disappeared into the depths of the barn to continue plotting with his brothers. When she could no longer see him, she snuck out the back door and crept down to the corral. Clicking her tongue, she called to Ginger and eased the corral gate open just enough to squeeze the horse through. Darting glances back toward the barn entrance every few seconds, Meredith led her paint around the house and into the woods.

A saddle was out of the question. Too many Archer men around the tack room. She used to love to ride bareback around the homestead as a kid. Surely she could still manage the feat. Meredith found a stump and used it as a mounting block, then urged Ginger toward the road at a fast clip, keeping to the trees.

She didn't have much time. She had to

get back to the house before Travis did. If he discovered her missing, the men would divert their attention from defending the ranch to finding her — which could mean Jim would be delayed in going after Cassie. No, it was essential that she be back at the house when Travis came in from the barn. Then, once he and the boys took up positions around the property, she could duck out the back, wind her way down to the creek, and follow it up to the road. She'd have to climb through the barbed-wire fence, but an extra blanket tossed over the barbs to keep her skirts from snagging should help her squeeze between the wires.

It was a sketchy plan, but it was the best she had at the moment.

Meredith steered Ginger out of the trees in order to pass through the newly ungated ranch entrance, then cantered a few strides down the road before dismounting. She led the mare back into the trees and tied her lead to one of the fence posts marking the property line. An observant rider would be able to spot Ginger's white patches through the sparse cover, but she imagined Jim would be too focused on his destination to look back toward the ranch.

Grateful that the house was only a quarter mile from the road, Meredith picked up her skirts and retraced her steps at a jog. A stitch in her side slowed her down about fifty yards from the house. Pressing a hand to her waist to battle the ache radiating there, she walked the remaining distance, stretching her stride as wide as possible.

If Travis was his usual, incredibly thorough self, she might be fortunate enough to return to the house before the men emerged from the barn. She doubted he would release them until they'd considered every eventuality and gone over their respective duties at least twice. However, Jim would be hard to corral for long, so she couldn't count on more than fifteen minutes. And she was pretty sure she'd already used at least ten.

The house finally came into view — along with the men. They all stood gathered around a mounted Jim. Their hats were off and their heads were bowed. Her conscience twinged at the sight of the Archer brothers taking the time to pray over their brother's safety and the situation at large, but she ignored it for the moment and took advantage of their inward focus and closed eyes to dash around the rear of the house unseen.

Once inside, she breathed a sigh of relief, or would have if her corset-laced lungs hadn't already been panting from her brief trot through the woods. Meredith strode through the bathing room and immediately grabbed the half loaf of bread left from lunch and began slicing it into thick pieces. The easiest way to disguise her intentions was to have Travis find her where he expected — in the kitchen. The vegetable soup she'd originally thought to prepare for supper would have to wait for another day, but she could throw together some scrambled egg sandwiches for the men to take with them on guard duty.

She had just cracked the seventh egg into the skillet when the front door opened. Heavy footfalls echoed in the hall. Meredith whisked the eggs frantically with her fork, then moved the skillet directly over the firebox to speed the cooking, hoping that Travis would attribute the perspiration on her forehead to the stove's heat and not comment upon it.

"Jim's on his way, Meri." Travis's quiet voice carried over the sizzle of the frying pan.

Meredith kept her back to him as she stirred the eggs, afraid Travis might somehow discern her subterfuge in the lines of her face. "I'll have these done in just a minute. You and the boys can take sandwiches with you."

He made no comment, but she could sense him nearing.

"I'm sorry I didn't have these ready before Jim left. He's going to be hungry."

Strong hands cupped her shoulders. "He'll be fine."

His touch felt good. Too good. Meredith stepped out of his loose hold and started heaping eggs onto the bread slices she'd set out. Head down, she built the sandwiches, trying to ignore her husband's presence. Which, of course, was impossible. She'd never been more attuned to another human being in her life.

"Meri, stop."

Her hands stilled as she wrapped a napkin around the third and final sandwich.

"Look at me, sweetheart."

Slowly she turned. His light brown eyes shone with a depth of emotion that made her heart pound.

"I swear to you, Meri — the minute Jim confirms that Cassie is at the homestead, we'll all ride out like the devil himself is on our heels. We won't leave her to face Mitchell alone."

He meant every word. She could see it in his face, hear it in his voice. But another voice echoed in her mind, as well — one asking what would happen to Cassie if Jim failed to return. How long would Travis wait before leading the charge?

Tears burned at the back of her eyes. She didn't want to defy her husband. Truly she didn't. It could destroy the trust between them, destroy the chance of love ever taking root in his heart. But she had no choice. She couldn't sit uselessly in the house under Travis's protection when her knowledge of the homestead could mean the difference between success and failure for both Jim and Cassie.

And with Jim's head start, the longer Travis stayed in the kitchen, the less time she'd have to make that difference.

In a desperate grab at the happiness that seemed to be slipping from her grasp, Meredith seized her husband's face between both her hands and kissed him with all the love she'd stored up for him since she was ten years old. It only took a moment for Travis to recover from his shock and respond with equal fervor. Yet when she felt his arms wrap around her back and start to draw her close, she forced herself to tear away.

"Here," she said, shoving the sandwiches at him as much to hurry him along as to keep herself from walking back into his arms. "Make sure your brothers eat."

Then, before he could say anything else,

she dodged around him and dashed down the hall to her room. Thumping the door closed behind her, she sagged against the wall and brushed a stray tear from her cheek while she waited for the telltale sound of Travis's boots against the floorboards.

They came down the hall and paused. Meredith squeezed her eyes closed. *Just go, Travis. Please.*

After a long moment, the sound began again, this time fading as Travis crossed to the front door and finally exited onto the porch. His deep voice carried through the walls as he called to Crockett and Neill.

Regret ate at Meredith, and second thoughts flashed through her mind. Then a picture of Jim crystallized behind her closed lids — a picture of him falling to the ground, as still as death. Her eyes jerked open, and her throat closed on a gasp. He was in as much danger as Cassie, heading alone into what was sure to be a den of vipers. She might not be able to bring the cavalry, but she could at least supply him with enough inside information to help even the odds a bit.

And she could watch his back.

Meredith grabbed her cape from the wardrobe and moved to the window. *Lord, keep him safe until I can catch up. Direct my steps and give me the courage to do what must be done. Guard Cassie and . . .* She paused and shifted the curtain just enough to peer out into the yard, where her husband and his brothers were dispersing to their assigned positions. *Help Travis forgive me.*

She released the curtain and turned to leave the room, but when she passed the bureau, she remembered the small tablet of paper Travis kept in the top drawer along with his watch and other odds and ends. After digging out a stubby pencil, she scribbled the few words her raw heart demanded she say, then grabbed an old blanket from the chest and hurried through the house to the back door.

Once outside, she made for the creek without a single backward glance. Regrets were a luxury she could no longer afford.

36

The old game trail was still where she remembered it being. Meredith urged Ginger off the road a couple hundred yards short of the main entrance. The path was almost imperceptible, completely overgrown with brush, but Ginger obediently followed her mistress's silent instruction and plowed through the oak saplings.

Meredith followed the landmarks she recognized more than the path itself, and when she reached the pine she'd long ago dubbed *The Survivor,* she drew Ginger to a halt. Not long after her accident with the trap, lightning had struck the tall, elegant tree. Half of the tree turned brown and brittle, too damaged to support life, but the other half remained green and healthy, flourishing with a will to overcome the adversity thrust upon it. Meredith stared up into the glorious green boughs on the east side and absorbed the hope they had always offered.

As a young girl, the tree had encouraged her to persevere and not let her own injured limb hold her back. Today, though, it inspired strength and fortitude. Meredith breathed deeply, inhaling the scent of the pine and allowing it to solidify her purpose. Time to find Jim.

If Jim had followed the usual Archer strategy of shadowing the road, he should be somewhere in the pines to her right. She'd made up some time by taking the game trail, but there was still no way to guess his precise location. If only there were a way to signal . . . The birdcalls! Neill had been teaching her the distinctive Archer call before the last storm hit. She'd not yet perfected the warble, but she could match the swooping pitch fairly well.

Meredith licked her lips, then cupped her hands around her mouth and threw her cooing voice as deep into the surrounding woods as she could. She waited a moment and repeated the signal, aiming her call more directly toward the cabin.

The silence stretched out for long minutes. Either Jim hadn't heard her call or he'd been unable to answer. Had he been captured? She prayed not. As she tried to determine her next strategy, a rustling to the south of her hailed a man's approach. Only then did she realize that she might have given her position away to one of Roy's men instead of Jim. The crunch of dead leaves grew louder, and Meredith's pulse throbbed harder.

Gripping Ginger's reins tightly between her fingers, she prepared to flee. The muscles in her thighs grew taut. Her heels twitched. Every instinct screamed at her to race away. But just as she began turning Ginger's head toward home, an answering call floated to her ear, one with a beautiful, well-practiced warble.

"Thank heaven," she whispered, releasing her hold on the reins as Jim emerged on foot between a pair of scrubby post oaks.

Her brother-in-law didn't appear nearly as relieved to see her as she was to see him. The hardheaded man was actually scowling at her.

"What are you doing here?" he hissed.

Meredith dismounted and squared her shoulders. Jim wasn't one to dance around a subject, so she got straight to the point. "I can help you get to the cabin unseen."

He narrowed his eyes at her. "Travis know what you're doing?"

"I left a note." She glared back at him in

challenge.

The man let out a breath and rubbed the back of his neck, but in the end, his desire to help Cassie trumped his reluctance to defy his brother.

"I've scouted the perimeter. No obvious guards are posted at the cabin, but I saw evidence of at least four men at the edge of the woods near the house. I think they're patrolling, so it'd be hard to know their exact position at any one time. I imagine Mitchell's got even more inside."

Meredith grimaced. It was a good thing the game trail lay deeper into the woods than Roy's men had penetrated. "So Travis was right. It *is* an ambush."

Jim shrugged. "A trap at least. Hard to know if they plan to pick us off or just ensure our cooperation."

Which would mean either loss of life or loss of land — both options equally heinous to an Archer.

"Have you seen Cassie?"

"No. Haven't been able to get close enough." Jim's gaze shifted, targeting the rooftop of the old homestead barely visible through the trees. "Heard the shrill voice of that mother of hers, though." He twisted his head to face her again, his dark eyes tortured. "She's here, Meri. I'm sure of it."

Meredith touched his arm, a similar dread flowing through her own heart. "Travis needs proof before he'll come, and you can't take on all of Roy's men by yourself." She squeezed his forearm and lifted her chin. "I'll get you to the house."

He didn't ask how or pester her for details. He simply nodded and pointed down the trail. "Show me."

Thankful, for once, for Jim's taciturn ways, Meredith looped Ginger's reins over a low branch and trudged ahead. Lifting her skirts and folding them close to her body to eliminate excess rustling, she kept her eyes to the ground and avoided as many twigs and pinecones as possible.

The trail wound closer to the cabin before forking. The main path led to a watering hole deeper in the woods, but a narrow shoot darted toward the left rear corner of the homestead — the corner that housed her childhood bedroom.

Meredith halted and peered into the thinning cover that separated them from the house. She looked to the right, then to the left. No one. At least, none that she could see.

"Have you spotted any of Roy's men?" she whispered to the man behind her. "I can take you closer, but I don't want to draw the attention of one of the guards." She stared at the foot of her weak leg and winced. "I cannot walk as quietly as you."

"Just tell me what I need to know." Jim came abreast of her, his rifle at the ready.

"If you stay to the left, the pines will give way to a stand of broad oaks. They shade the house in the summer, and since no one's trimmed their branches the last few years, a few limbs stretch all the way to the roof." She watched as understanding dawned in his eyes. His jaw hardened, and he strode forward, but Meredith stopped him with a hand to his arm.

"There is not as much cover near the house, so you'll have to be careful. You might be able to peer through one of the back windows from within the branches of the tree, but if you need to see into the main room, you'll have to crawl over the roof to the front of the house. It's risky, but hopefully none of the men will expect trouble from above."

Jim slid his arm from her grasp and took her hand in his. "Thank you."

She nodded. "Be careful." The earlier vision of his lying upon the ground came back to her, raking a shiver over her skin.

"Stay out of sight," her brother-in-law ordered. "Travis will kill me if anything hap-

463

pens to you." He released her hand and soundlessly moved past.

Meredith prayed over every step Jim took, her throat seeming to constrict at each sound that echoed in the trees. When he rounded the first oak and disappeared from her view, her breathing nearly ceased altogether. This wasn't right. She was supposed to be watching his back. She couldn't do that from this distance.

Taking extra care with her uneven gait, she crept forward, staying in the shadows of the trees until she stood behind the largest oak. Meredith spied Jim between the branches of the tree nearest the cabin and finally breathed easier. His rifle slung over his shoulder, he climbed higher, his footholds secure. The only trouble was the way the brittle winter leaves rattled with his movements.

Jim stretched himself across one of the thicker limbs that reached toward the roof, and began scooting along its length on his belly. Then all at once, he froze.

A twig snapped. But it wasn't from Jim's tree. It echoed lower. Closer.

Meredith silently gathered her cloak more tightly around her and drew the hood over her hair as she tucked her face against the coarse bark of the oak at her side. If she could have climbed beneath the bark itself, she would have.

A rough-looking logger emerged between the trees that she and Jim occupied. His heavy brows scrunched against his eyes as he scanned the area, his ear cocked in Jim's direction. Instead of a gun, the burly fellow carried an ax.

A gust of wind blew across the tree limbs. Meredith's gaze darted to Jim. The branch swayed. Jim's face contorted as he struggled to keep his back perfectly flat so his rifle wouldn't shift and knock into the leaves surrounding him.

The logger jerked his face toward the cabin, as if he sensed the intruder. He slapped the wooden handle of his ax against his left palm and stalked closer to the tree. All he had to do was glance up. . . .

Meredith scoured the ground near her for something she could use as a weapon, but all she found were decayed branches and pinecones. Nothing that would even slow the man down. But maybe she could draw the man away somehow. If she were to dart back toward the Survivor tree, he'd hear and follow, giving Jim time to lay eyes on Cassie and leave. All she had to do was outrun a bear-sized man for the short distance to Ginger. Shouldn't be too hard, right? She'd have a head start and was more familiar with the land.

She inhaled a deep breath and grabbed a handful of skirt. Then, just as she prepared to take flight, a saner idea took shape. Meredith released the fabric of her cape and scooped up a large pinecone. Taking careful aim, she hurled it behind the oaks, back into the forest. It cracked against the trunk of a small pine, and the sound brought Mr. Bushy Brow's head around. The man set off with a determined stride, and Meredith sagged against the trunk of her oak.

Thank the Lord for timely inspiration.

Once the logger disappeared into the woods, Meredith waved Jim toward the roof. The ungrateful man glared at her and jabbed his finger as if ordering her to retreat, but there was no time for a pantomime skirmish. If Jim didn't go now, he might not get another chance. Fortunately, the Archers were an intelligent lot. After a final jab in her direction, Jim resumed his belly crawl and soon lowered himself silently onto the cabin roof.

Shrinking into a crouch, he crossed to the peak. There, he laid flat and peered over the edge. Meredith fisted her hands in the fabric of her cape as he slid out of her view to the front side of the cabin. He seemed to be gone for an eternity. The roof's slope wasn't too steep, but even then, Jim would have to hang upside down from the eaves to see in the front window. What if someone saw him? What if he fell? He would have never been on that roof if she hadn't suggested such an idiotic scheme.

What have I done? Her soul cried out to the only one who could rescue them. *Protect him from my folly, Lord. I should have trusted my husband. I should have trusted you.*

All her big talk to Travis about trusting God to protect his family, about not letting fear dictate his actions, and here she was doing exactly that which she had so adamantly preached against. She should have sought the Lord's will from the very beginning. Instead she'd proceeded with her own plans and only once she was in the midst of them did she think to ask for God's blessing. And even then her mind was set on her own course of action. What if the Lord had inspired that vision of Jim as a warning to her that she not go, but because of her own willfulness, she chose to use it as justification for her actions?

Meredith bowed her head. *I surrender.* A tear trickled down her cheek. *I surrender. Only you can make this right. Show me what to do. Whatever sacrifice is required, I'll make it. Just, please . . . spare Jim and Cassie.*

When she lifted her head, there was Jim, slinking back over the peak of the roof and scrambling toward the tree. Her heart surged in gratitude. *Thank you!*

He had made it as far as the main trunk when the logger charged out of the shallow woods. The bushy-browed henchman ran full out as if he planned to leap into the tree like a cougar after its prey. Jim was too high to drop to the ground without breaking a leg. He struggled to find a defensible position among the branches. He needed his rifle, but his hands were too busy keeping him in the tree to reach for the weapon.

Meredith sprinted toward the logger, her eyes locked on the arm that wielded the ax.

Roy's man latched onto a branch, the soles of his shoes bracing his weight against the trunk. With a roar, he swung the ax in an upward arc, the blade aimed at Jim's flesh.

Meredith vaulted off her good leg mid-stride and caught the logger's beefy arm as it circled behind him. The logger tried to shove her aside, but she held fast to his right arm and threw what little weight she had to sway him. She had to give Jim time to escape.

She twisted and writhed, kicked out with

her legs, anything she could think of to slow him down. The shouts of other men echoed behind her. Reinforcements were coming.

A rifle cocked nearby, and for a split second, both Meredith and the logger froze. Meredith spotted Jim from the corner of her eye. He was on the ground with his rifle aimed at the logger!

He jerked his head to the side, urging her to move away so he would have a clean shot, but a beefy arm locked around her waist, holding her in place.

"Run, Jim!" she shouted between grunts as the logger renewed his efforts to wrench his right arm free of her grasp, no doubt hoping to hurl his ax at his foe. "Get Travis!"

For once Jim didn't scowl at her. His eyes had a desperate look to them, as if he were the one trapped. She knew he didn't want to leave her, that his protective nature demanded he stay and fight. But when the others arrived, he'd be finished.

"For Cassie, Jim," she pleaded. "Go for Cassie."

A yell from the other side of the cabin made his decision for him. He spun and ran.

The instant Jim's rifle was no longer pointed at him, the logger shifted to free his arm. But she hung on — all of her energy focused on keeping him from using his weapon.

"Blasted female!" The logger raised his ax. "Let" — he slammed his arm and hers into the tree — "go!"

Pain ricocheted past her elbows from the force of the collision, and her hands opened against her will.

The logger shouted orders to his compatriots and pointed in the direction Jim had run. The other guards rushed past them, pistols and rifles in hand. Meredith tried to slide away from her captor, but the logger had no intention of relinquishing his prize. He snatched up a handful of fabric at her neck and hauled her upward.

Her hands instinctively circled about his meaty fist, but she had no strength left to pry free of his hold. His dark eyes promised retribution. He gave her a shake as if she were an oversized rag doll and ordered her to cease her fighting. Since he no longer posed a threat to Jim, she obeyed and stumbled along beside him as he made his way to the front of the cabin. He kicked the door in with his foot and dragged her across the threshold.

"I brung you another guest for the wedding, boss."

A movement to her right drew Meredith's

attention. Roy stood near the hearth, a shotgun looped casually through his bent arm, the barrel pointed at Uncle Everett, who sat on the floor against the wall with his wrists bound.

She'd heard of shotgun weddings, but never one in which the groom held the gun on the father of the bride.

"Meredith, my dear." Roy smiled, and her stomach recoiled. "So glad you could make it."

37

Travis tucked the butt of his rifle into his shoulder and sighted down the barrel from his position among the pines nearest the old gate. The quiet rumble he'd noted a moment ago had grown louder, more distinct. Hoofbeats. A rider approached. And fast.

Inhaling a cleansing breath, he forced his pulse to calm. He needed a steady hand and a clear head to deal with whatever came down the path. His mind turned heavenward for an instant — not long enough to form a complete thought, but long enough to connect.

Finger hovering over the trigger, Travis peered into the shadows. Before man or horse came into view, a shrill whistle pierced the air. *Jim.* Travis blew out his tension and lowered his rifle. Expecting the hoofbeats to slow, he was unprepared for the second whistle or for the sight of his brother's mount racing past him.

New urgency speared through Travis, and he took off at a dead run for the house. Jim knew their positions. He would have stopped or at least slowed to call out his findings unless a threat existed that was too imminent to spare the time.

Cassandra must truly be in danger. Travis pumped his legs faster, his lungs burning with the sudden heavy intake of cold air. He leapt over a small gully and pushed forward, his energy solely focused on getting to Jim. The others were positioned closer to the house, so they'd be waiting on him. Thankfully, their horses stood saddled and ready in the corral. They could be on their way in minutes.

By the time he sprinted through the clearing, Jim was giving orders from the saddle. Travis overheard him sending Crockett into the den to collect extra pistols. Neill was hustling to the corral to gather the mounts. Travis pulled up so as not to startle his brother's horse. Between heaving breaths, he asked Jim for a report.

"Cassie and her folks are being held at the cabin," Jim said, his face grim. "Mitchell has Mr. Hayes tied up and at gunpoint. The women are under guard, as well, but not restrained. He's got at least four men patrolling. Two more inside. They're armed and don't seem too hesitant about attacking."

"Then we ride." Travis caught his breath and straightened his shoulders. "I'll tell Meredith and be back in a trice." She'd be beside herself with worry, but he couldn't keep it from her. Cassie was like a sister to her.

He had just cleared the porch steps when Jim's voice stopped him.

"She's not there, Travis."

He turned to face his brother, not comprehending his meaning. But when he saw the discomfiture etched into Jim's features, the regret in his eyes, his gut turned to lead.

"I tried to send her back, but she refused to go." Jim stiffened in the saddle then, as if ready to do battle. "I wouldn't have gotten a look in the cabin without her help, Trav. She saved my life. Twice. I'm not sorry she came. Just sorry I couldn't get her out before Mitchell's men swarmed us."

Meredith at the homestead? How could that be? She was in his room. Waiting for him. Safe. Wasn't she?

Holding down the bile that threatened to erupt, Travis spun back to the house and threw open the door. It crashed against the wall as he shouted his wife's name.

"Meredith!"

He ran down the hall, his boots slapping

the floorboards. It was a mistake. She was there. Safe in his room.

Travis burst through the door. The emptiness hit him like a sledgehammer to the chest. He scanned every corner as if she might be hiding somewhere. He even wrenched open the wardrobe in desperation.

"Meri." The anguished whisper fell from his lips. This couldn't be happening. She told him she'd be in the house. How could she leave the ranch when he'd expressly forbidden it? How could she leave *him?*

In a daze, he pivoted back toward the door. He took a step, but something about the room whispered to his subconscious mind, something out of place. His attention shifted back to the bed, then the dresser. He blinked, sharpening his focus. There. The tablet. Travis pounced on the paper. His eyes devoured the words.

Travis,
    I love you with all of my being, but I love Cassie, too. And right now she needs me more than you do.
Forgive me.
Meri

She loved him. The wonder of the statement seeped into him, but the joy that should have accompanied the knowledge faded beneath his growing frustration and fear. How could she possibly think that anyone needed her more than he did? She was his heart, his very life. If anything happened to her . . .

Travis tore the top page from the tablet and hardened his jaw. He'd just have to make sure nothing did happen. After all, if a wife was going to tell her husband she loved him, she ought to do it in person. And he aimed to see that she did precisely that. Right after he kissed the living fire out of her and showed her exactly how much he truly needed her.

Stuffing the note into the shirt pocket beneath his coat, Travis dropped the tablet on the bed and stormed out of the house. Crockett met him on the porch and handed him a second revolver. Since he only had one holster, and it was already full, he stuffed the gun into his waistband at the small of his back. He collected Bexar's reins from where they hung over the railing and mounted in a single motion.

Travis shared a look with Crockett and Jim and turned to Neill. "I want you to ride into Palestine and fetch the sheriff. All you have to do is head south once you hit the road. If you push your mount, you can be there before sundown. We can't afford to let Mitchell get away this time. We need the law on our side." And *he* needed Neill out of harm's way. The kid could handle himself well enough, but if things went badly, he didn't have the experience necessary to improvise. And if things went really badly, Travis wanted to ensure that at least one Archer lived to see another day.

"Archers stand together, Trav," Neill spat impatiently. "Isn't that what you always say?" He looked from one brother to the next. The errand was a pretense, and he knew it. "Y'all are already outnumbered. Why give Mitchell a bigger advantage? You have a better chance with me riding with you."

"Maybe, but someone's got to get the law involved, and you're the logical choice."

Neill opened his mouth to argue further, but Travis cut him off. "We're wasting time. You have your orders, Neill. Carry them out, like the Archer you are." Travis nudged Bexar past Neill's mount, effectively ending the conversation.

"Boys, I believe we've been invited to a wedding," Travis said, steel lacing his tone. "Let's not be late."

■ ■ ■ ■

Meredith clasped her cousin's hand as the two girls sat huddled together on the settee. The dreadful Mr. Wheeler loomed over them, legs braced apart, gun in hand. But it was the way he looked at her that frightened Meredith most. That wolfish gleam in his eyes, and the way his gaze kept traveling down her body as if he could see right through her clothing. He'd smile after perusing her in such abominable fashion, and the leering promise on his face turned her stomach.

"Should we start the ceremony now, sir?" A man standing in the back corner of the room posed the question. His black suit and white preacher's collar should have offered reassurance, but his bored expression as he scanned the room full of armed men and hostage women only served to confirm his complicity. There would be no help from that quarter.

"Not yet," Roy said. "Although I'm anxious to wed my lovely bride, I believe we're due to have a few more visitors soon, and I'd hate for anything unpleasant to interrupt our nuptials."

"Very well, but I'm charging you for the

extra time." The preacher, if the mercenary little man could be called by such a title, leaned against the wall and slid a silver flask from inside his coat. He unscrewed the lid and imbibed a large swig.

Cassie's grip tightened on Meredith's hand. "I hope he chokes."

"It would be a rather poetic form of justice," Meredith agreed softly. And such a lovely wrench to throw into Roy's plan. But then she remembered the logger going after Jim with that ax and decided it might be better for all concerned to keep Roy happy. At least for the time being.

Aunt Noreen paced across the carpet and glowered at Roy. "I don't approve of liquor, Mr. Mitchell. It's bad enough that my daughter's wedding is not taking place in a church, but I refuse to have a drunkard officiate her ceremony."

Roy's lips thinned as he peered down at the woman before him. "Let me remind you, madam, that I was only too happy to sponsor a church wedding, but Miss Cassandra would not consent. Hence our current predicament. If you feel the need to complain, kindly take it up with your daughter."

"But *you* were in charge of finding the minister. This one is unsatisfactory." She

479

folded her arms and frowned at Roy as if he were one of the ladies on her civic beautification committee who had failed to follow her instructions.

"Noreen . . ." Uncle Everett murmured her name in warning from his position on the floor across from her.

"Hush up, Everett. None of this would have happened if you hadn't given in to Cassandra's whining. The girl can't see past her nose. She's just young enough to think that some flutter in her heart is worth more than financial security. You should have taken her in hand. But, no. Like everything else, you bowed out and forced me to deal with it. You've got no backbone. That's the real reason the mill is failing. I probably should have taken that over, too."

"Mama!" Cassie gasped. But the woman paid her no heed. She'd built up too much steam.

"And as for you . . ." Aunt Noreen pivoted back to face Roy and jabbed his shoulder with her finger, apparently too full of her own agenda to notice the anger brewing in his eyes. "If you want to be my son-in-law, you had best find a minister who isn't incapacitated with drink! I won't allow —"

Roy backhanded her across the mouth with enough force to send her crashing to the floor. "You're not in a position to disallow anything, madam. You might flay your husband with that sharp tongue of yours, but turn it on me, and I will bite you back."

Aunt Noreen glared up at Roy, not all of her fire extinguished. "How dare you raise your hand to me!"

In a flash, Roy had the shotgun cocked and aimed directly at her head. "You know, it just occurred to me that married life would be much easier without a harpy for a mother-in-law."

"No!" Cassie lunged to her feet. Wheeler immediately grasped her arm.

"Please," she cried out to Roy, struggling against Wheeler's hold. "I'll marry you right now. Willingly. Just leave my mother alone."

Roy pulled the gun back. "Such an ardent declaration, my sweet. How could I refuse?" He stepped toward the settee and clasped Cassie's hand, his gentlemanly veneer back in place. Wheeler released her arm, and Cassie lifted her chin.

As Roy led her toward the hearth, Meredith pushed to her feet. There was no way she was letting Cassie face this horror alone.

"Where do you think *you're* going, darlin'?" Wheeler's gravelly voice grated against her nerves. Then his arm snaked around her waist and pulled her roughly against his side.

"I intend to stand up with my cousin, sir," she ground out between clenched teeth. "Release me."

Roy glanced over his shoulder and smirked at her. "Let her come, Wheeler. But keep a firm grip on her. She has a bad habit of starting trouble."

"I'll keep her under control," the man said as his arm tightened around her, nearly cutting off her air.

She stumbled past Aunt Noreen, who seemed to be in a state of shock, numbly letting Uncle Everett loop his bound arms around her and scoot her back against the wall.

The parson gulped down another swig from his flask, then pulled a Bible from his coat pocket and made a great show of flipping pages as he stepped out of the corner to join Roy and Cassie at the hearth.

"Dearly beloved," the man droned in a ponderous, self-important tone. "We are gathered here —"

The front door crashed open.

Meredith's head swiveled.

"What is the meaning of this?" the parson sputtered.

"Found these two riding up the path."

Her ax-wielding "friend" waved to his cohorts, and they shoved two dust-covered men, the obvious recipients of some very rough handling, into the room. One fell to his knee, his arms tied behind his back. The other, though also bound, managed to catch himself and halt his forward momentum before tumbling to the floor.

Meredith's heart recognized them the instant they came through the doorway. And when the man in front lifted his head and met her gaze beneath the brim of his hat, she instinctively stepped toward him.

"Travis."

Wheeler jerked her back against him, a wicked chuckle echoing in her ear. Travis's face hardened in an instant. He surged forward only to be brought up short by a shotgun barrel in the chest.

"Nice of you to finally show up, Archer." Roy tugged Cassandra behind him and nodded to the logger, who muscled Jim back down to his knees before he could fully regain his feet. "For a while there, I thought you decided to decline my invitation."

38

The metal gun barrel dug into his chest, but Travis barely felt it. All his energy was focused on Mitchell.

"I've come for my wife." The words rumbled out of him like thunder gathering in the distance, low and ominous.

The guards had confiscated his rife and gun belt, but the hidden revolver itched against his back, begging him to take it in hand. Never before had he actually wanted to shoot a man. But now it was all he could do not to reach for his weapon.

Mitchell's lips turned down in a mock pout. "I'm devastated. And here I thought you'd come to offer your felicitations."

Travis glared his disgust at the man.

"I assure you, Mr. Wheeler is taking very good care of our dear Miss Meredith. Aren't you, Louis?"

"Indeed I am, Mr. Mitchell. Indeed I am." The man tightened his hold on Meri, his arm deliberately pressing against the under-side of her breasts. Meredith clawed at his sleeve until he lifted his right hand and stroked the side of her face with his pistol. "Easy now, kitten." Meri stilled. "You might not want to jostle me too much. It'd be a shame if someone got hurt."

Rage steamed through Travis. Wheeler had just etched his name on one of the bullets in Travis's gun.

Gritting his teeth, he forced his focus away from Wheeler and settled it again on the man behind the shotgun. "I know you designed this meeting, Mitchell. Why don't we skip all the small talk and get down to business. What do I have to do to ensure Meri leaves this cabin unharmed?"

"Not much." Mitchell smiled that ingratiating smile of his that made Travis want to slam his fist into his face. "All I need is your signature on a little document I had my attorney draw up." He gestured to the table that stood on the opposite side of the room near the cookstove. "Should only take a minute. Then you and your bride will be free to go. Unless, of course, you'd like to stay for the wedding."

"Fine," Travis growled. "Bring me a pen. And get one of your men to untie my hands."

"No, Travis," Meredith gasped. "You can't."

But he could. He'd give up anything for her. Without a moment's regret. What he couldn't do was look at those big blue eyes of hers without getting distracted. So he set his jaw and marched toward the table, tipping his head so his hat blocked his view of her.

As he moved, he tallied Mitchell's men. Mitchell and Wheeler made two. The thug with the ax wrestling with Jim was three. And the two fellows who had trussed him and Jim up were loitering outside the door; he could see their shadows through the front window. According to Jim's earlier count, that left only one for Crockett to track down and disable before returning to the cabin. Their plan to draw the men out of the woods had worked. Now they just had to figure out a way to get Jim's hands untied and take out five armed men without endangering the women. He was still working on that part.

Meredith watched with swelling dread as Travis made his way to the table. He couldn't sign away his land. He just couldn't. That land was everything to him. If he sacrificed it for her, it would kill whatever hope they had of making a love-filled marriage together. Oh, he'd never voice his regrets. He was too noble. But he would grow to resent her. How could he not? Because of her, he was breaking his deathbed promise to his father and forfeiting the one thing he treasured above all else — his land.

She bit her lip. He'd never even looked at her. Not since Roy named his price. And that more than anything ate away at her hope.

"You mind untying my hands, Mitchell?" Travis twisted sideways, aiming his bound arms at Roy. "I can't exactly sign your papers with my hands behind my back."

Roy hesitated a moment, then nodded to the only man on his payroll without a gun in his hand. "Parson? Some assistance, please."

"All right," the man huffed. "But it will —"

"Cost me extra. I know." Roy glared at the minister. "Just do it."

The man pulled a blade from his boot and sawed through the rope at Travis's wrists. When her husband was finally free, he rubbed his chafed skin and immediately took up the pen that lay beside the document on the table. He only spared a moment to glance over the words before inking the nib and scratching his name across the bottom of the page.

A silent sob caught in Meredith's throat. It was done.

"A pleasure doing business with you, Mr. Archer." Roy nodded his head toward Travis in a mockery of a bow. "You and your wife may leave if you wish."

Travis strode toward her, but his narrowed eyes focused at a point above her head. Wheeler pressed the side of his pistol against her chin and forced her head around. Then before she knew what he was about, his mouth crashed down on hers. A sound of protest reverberated in her throat as she struggled to free herself from the violation.

From somewhere behind her, Travis shouted, and Cassie cried out for Wheeler to stop. Meredith could hear her husband's pounding footfalls, but right before he reached her, Wheeler yanked his horrible mouth from hers and threw her into Travis, nearly knocking them both to the ground. His wicked chuckle echoed through the cabin as Travis's arms closed around her.

Meredith scrubbed the vile man's taste from her lips with the back of her hand, wishing she could crawl into Travis and hide.

"Go outside and get on Bexar," Travis whispered close to her ear. "Ride for home."

Meredith stiffened. "I can't leave Cassie."

"Jim and I will take care of Cassie." There was no soothing in his tone. Only command. "I need you to go."

How were he and Jim, who was still bound as far as she could tell, going to take care of Cassie? It made no sense.

Travis's grip tightened on her arm ever so slightly. "Trust me, Meri."

The words cut through her. She'd not let him down a second time.

Meredith nodded and slowly stepped away from him. He released her arms, then staggered forward as if her moving had thrown him off-balance. She turned back and grabbed for him, but he'd already recovered. He found her hand within the folds of her skirt and slid a small cylindrical object into her palm. Her eyes widened, and in an instant he glanced toward Jim, let her go, and gave her a little nudge toward the door.

Not only was he asking her to trust him, he was trusting her in return.

Not knowing exactly how to fulfill her mission, Meredith exacerbated her limp so she had an excuse to slow her pace. Stomach fluttering, she made her way to where the logger was kneeling with a knee against Jim's hunched back near the doorway.

"Would you mind letting him up," she asked the man, struggling to minimize the nervous quiver in her voice. "I'm afraid I'll trip over his legs if I try to step over him."

The logger muttered something about "worthless cripples" but did as she requested, hauling Jim to his feet.

When the man was holding Jim only by the elbow, Meredith seized her chance and slid up against Jim's side, reaching for his hands as if to assist him in gaining his feet.

"Get away from there." The logger scowled at her and jerked Jim away from her grasp. But the transfer had been made.

"Sorry," she mumbled, praying he hadn't noticed anything. "I was just trying to help."

She turned back to the door, intending to leave as she'd promised, when one of the outside guards burst into the cabin, sending her skittering back toward Jim.

"We got comp'ny."

39

Roy cursed. "What is it *now?*"

Meredith flinched at his harshness.

"There's about a dozen townsfolk coming down the path, screechin' and carrying on with drums and washboards and such. They look like a bunch of crazies. What do you want me to do?"

"What I want you to do, Mr. Elliott," Roy answered through gritted teeth, "is to go out there and dissuade them."

"Dis . . . what?"

Roy slammed his fist onto the table, rattling the ink bottle Travis had used mere moments ago. "Scare them off, you idiot!"

Mr. Elliott recoiled from the shout and backed away. "Y-yes, sir." He spun around and lumbered past Meredith, leaving the cabin with all possible haste.

Meredith darted a glance toward Travis. Her husband seemed as surprised as anyone by the guard's announcement. The distraction was buying Jim some much needed time, though.

He'd gotten the penknife open and was working on the ropes at his wrists. Meredith maneuvered her way closer, using her body to shield Jim's hands.

The logger moved to the window and reported, "They're mostly darkies. Women and men. Only one feller looks like he'd be worth much in a fight, but even from here I can see a big stupid grin on his face. They're more nuisance than threat."

Could Moses be the man he referred to? A little thrill shot through Meredith. Perhaps the Lord had sent them assistance. The sound of drums, shakers, and other crude noisemakers grew louder as the group advanced on the cabin.

Then she heard the man called Elliott yell out a warning. "You're not welcome here. Turn around and go on home." His rifle boomed, but the oncoming noise never lessened.

"We heard Miss Cassie done got herself hitched," a strident female voice called out. *Myra.* "We come to give her a shivaree, and we ain't leavin' until we give it."

Roy shoved the paper Travis had signed into the pocket of his coat and stomped to the middle of the room, where he grabbed hold of Cassie. "Of all the ill-conceived, dimwitted — We're not even married yet!"

The logger turned a questioning glance to his boss. "What do you want to do?"

"Bar the door," Roy ordered. Then he turned back to the minister. "Get the deed done, Parson."

The door slammed shut. If Moses and Myra were out there, it was possible Crockett and Neill were, too. She had to find a way to let them in.

The preacher began the rushed service, mumbling the words more to himself than the bride and groom as his finger ran down the page of his prayer book in search of the vows. ". . . signifying the mystical union betwixt Christ and his Church . . . not to be entered into unadvisedly . . . If any man can show just cause why they may not be lawfully joined together, speak —"

"I've got plenty of cause." Jim's deep voice brought the clergyman's head up.

"Shut up, you!" The logger brought the handle of his ax across Jim's jaw, knocking his head against the wall beside him.

The penknife clattered to the floor. Meredith leapt forward to cover it with her boot and dragged it under the hem of her skirt. But before she could figure out how to retrieve it and get it back to Jim, her brother-in-law let out a mighty roar and snapped free of the weakened ropes. He lunged at the logger and tackled him.

Travis rushed Wheeler in the same manner.

Roy shouted.

A gun fired.

Cassie screamed.

Meredith's heart froze.

All she could see of her husband was a tangle of arms and legs. She wanted to run to him. See if he'd been shot. Help fight off his foe. But she forced the desperate urge aside. The help he truly needed stood on the other side of the door.

Kicking the penknife into the corner, she moved to the door and threw the latch. The swarm had overtaken the guards — Crockett and Moses at the center, throwing punches and wresting away rifles. Myra's iron skillet got in on the action — and was that Seth Winston clobbering Mr. Elliott with a washboard?

Josiah and Neill brought up the rear.

The cacophony of the shivaree drowned out the noise of the fight but also made it impossible to call out to her friends and neighbors, so Meredith waved her arms above her head until Neill caught sight of her and began steering the mob toward the house.

Meredith stayed at the door to ensure the portal remained open until Seth Winston hustled forward to relieve her of the duty. "Get on over by the horses, girlie." His raised voice barely carried over the din. "We'll cut the heifers out of the herd and let the steers fight it out." He frowned at her when she hesitated. "Go on, now. It's what your man would want."

Travis.

The old man was right.

With a prayer on her heart and a fingertip hold on her faith, Meredith walked away.

Fire burned across Travis's side from where Wheeler's bullet had creased him, but he spared it little thought as he grabbed for the man's gun hand and pounded it into the plank floor. Wheeler's knee surged into Travis's gut, stealing his wind, but he held on. He crushed the man's hand down again, this time aiming for the clawed foot of one of the settee's legs.

Wheeler let out a cry. The pistol fell from his grasp. Travis reached for it, but something hard slammed into his shoulder blade. His arms collapsed, and he fell fully atop Wheeler. The man wasted no time in kicking him aside. Travis thumped onto his back with a groan.

"It's over, Archer," Mitchell said as he switched the grip on his shotgun. The stock that had felled Travis twirled back toward Mitchell's shoulder. "You've been a thorn in my side long enough."

Mitchell took aim, pointing the double barrels at Travis's chest. Travis tightened his jaw and stared at his nemesis, refusing to cower. His only regret was that he'd never told Meri he loved her.

Then, as he inhaled the breath he fully expected to be his last, men and women, neighbors and friends poured into the cabin, carrying on with their blessedly ridiculous shivaree. Old Seth Winston guarded the door as the rest of the company wound through the room like a snake, whoopin' and hollerin'. Travis caught Moses's eye and then spotted Crockett, who moved to casually assist Jim with the ax-wielding logger as the rest of the parade wandered deeper into the house.

How had they known to come? What miracle had brought them at just the right time? Travis struggled to his feet, cradling his aching side, and spied the answer to his question. Neill. He ought to strangle that boy for disobeying his instructions, but he grinned at his kid brother instead. Apparently Neill wasn't too young to improvise after all.

Ever aware of his reputation, Mitchell tried to shoo the crowd away without violence, but when one of the women took Cassie's hand and started maneuvering her toward the door, he snapped. He fired his shotgun into the rafters, and the resultant *boom* and debris shower succeeded in silencing the revelers.

"Unhand my bride, madam. Now!" Mitchell lowered his weapon, the dark-skinned woman his new target.

She obeyed, slowly lifting her hands into the air. Then she darted a glance at Moses. Her chin twitched to the side.

As if he'd been waiting for the signal, Moses launched himself at Mitchell and knocked him to the ground. "Get outta here, Myra!" he ordered as he fought to separate Mitchell from his shotgun.

Pandemonium broke out. Women scurried for the door. Men brought out weapons.

"Wheeler!" Mitchell screamed as he fought to defend himself against the larger Moses. "Get the girl!"

"There's a window in the back room," Everett Hayes called out to his daughter.

"Remember, Cass?"

"Come on, Mama," Cassie urged her mother to follow them, but the woman never moved, her blank expression unnatural.

Wheeler lunged toward Cassie.

"Go!" Travis yelled, as he grabbed Wheeler's arm.

"Now, Cassandra," Everett demanded. "I'll stay with your mother."

Finally, Cassie turned and veered toward the small room visible off the kitchen. Myra followed. At the same time, Wheeler tore his arm free and smashed his elbow into Travis's side.

Travis cried out. Pain stabbed through him like a sword's blade as Wheeler moved toward the back room. He'd catch the women before they could get the window open.

Travis reached behind his back, hissing at the pain. His fingers dug beneath his coat and fastened around the handle of his revolver. He pulled it from his waistband, brought his arm around, and squeezed the trigger.

Wheeler fell.

Neill and Josiah charged past Travis and seized Wheeler's arms. He moaned at their treatment, and relief washed over Travis at the knowledge that he hadn't killed the man. He craned his neck to survey the rest of the room, his blood still pumping with the turmoil of the fight. A member of Moses's band crossed his line of vision, pulled a hunting knife from its sheath, and set about freeing Mr. Hayes. Crockett had a knee in the logger's back where he lay sprawled on the floor, and Seth Winston was tying the fella's wrists. Roy Mitchell hung unconscious over Moses's shoulder, and the preacher was beating a hasty exit out the door.

Travis's eyes slid closed, and he sagged against the floor. It was over.

After a moment, the sound of steady footsteps brought his eyes open. Jim stood over him, his hand extended. Travis took it and let his brother haul him to his feet.

"I thought you might want this," Jim said, holding out his other hand.

Travis stared at the paper, his signature glaring up at him from the bottom of the sheet. His chest clenched. Something wet pooled in his eye. He blinked it away and cleared the clog out of his throat.

"Burn that for me, will you?"

Jim grinned and strode toward the hearth. He reached to the mantel, took a match from the iron holder, and scraped the head against the striker. Fire flared at the tip, and Travis watched as Jim hunkered down before the hearth and lit the bottom corner of the paper. While his signature shriveled and turned to black ash, something deep in Travis's soul shouted in triumph.

Then a longing, equally deep, rose within him — a longing to share this moment, this triumph, with the one person who meant more to him than any other.

Meri.

40

When Meredith spied Cassie and Myra coming around the side of the house, she bolted from her spot by the horses, desperate for word of what was happening.

"Did you see Travis?" she demanded of her cousin without preamble. "I heard gunshots. Is he all right?"

"I think so, but I can't be sure. I was too busy climbing out your bedroom window when the second shot went off." Cassie clasped Meredith's arm, her eyes sympathetic. "I'm sure he's fine, though."

Meredith nodded, yet her heart wasn't as sure as her mind. She turned back to the cabin door. Things were quieter. Was that good?

Her stomach roiled. The waiting was killing her.

Finally, someone exited the cabin. Jim crossed the threshold, scanning the yard. "Cassandra?"

Cassie dropped Meredith's arm and hurried toward him. "I'm here!"

Jim pounded across the yard and embraced her with such ferocity her feet left the ground. It was joyous to watch, yet it left Meredith hungry for her own reunion and, at the same time, scared that even if Travis were well, he wouldn't be as happy to see her.

Myra came up behind her and laid a hand on her shoulder. "Our men'll be next. Don't you worry."

"I pray you're right."

When Moses did emerge, the sight of the oh-so-proper Roy Mitchell draped insensible over his shoulder brought a startled smile to Meredith's face.

"Didn't I tell you?" Myra patted Meredith's shoulder and stepped toward her husband. "I better send Josiah to fetch the wagon. Looks like we'll be needing it to haul all the sorry hides we collected."

Meredith actually giggled at that, and the release felt wonderful. Surely Moses would have given top priority to any of their men who had fallen during the melee. If he was carting Roy around, that must mean none of the injuries were too severe on the Archers' side.

She took a step toward the cabin, needing

to see her husband, to gain that final re-assurance that all was well.

A second step. Then a third. She walked as if in a dream.

Crockett marched through the door, dragging the logger behind him. Seth Winston followed with the man's ax. Her uncle hobbled out next, Aunt Noreen tucked under his arm. Meredith's pulse throbbed. *Where is Travis?*

So intent was she on looking for her husband that she didn't notice that Uncle Everett had paused in front of her until he spoke.

"Forgive me, Meri." His head hung low, his gaze meeting hers only for a moment before dipping back toward the ground. "I want you to know I'll be heading to the bank first thing in the morning to deed the property over to you and Travis, like I should've done right after your marriage."

Meredith nodded, unsure what to say. However, when he shuffled past, a burst of compassion rose up within her. She called his name softly and waited for him to glance back.

"If you allow Cassie to select her own husband," she said, thinking of Jim, "I'll give her the homestead as a wedding gift. Perhaps you and the man she chooses will be able to work together to revive your mill."

Uncle Everett's eyes misted, and for a moment he didn't move. Then he gave his own silent nod before ducking his chin and urging Aunt Noreen forward.

Pivoting toward the cabin once again, Meredith picked up her pace. Another shadow loomed in the doorway. Her feet slowed. Three men moved into the light, none of them Travis. Meredith swallowed her disappointment. Josiah and Neill carried a bloodied Mr. Wheeler down the steps between them.

The last of the men filed out as she reached the edge of the porch. The ones she knew from the freedmen's school smiled at her as they passed. Meredith thanked them for their aid, knowing she should say more, but her mind seemed unable to manage more than a simple thank-you with her heart so focused on locating her husband.

Taking a deep breath, she climbed the steps and entered the dim interior of the cabin. Travis stood near the hearth, his gaze focused somewhere inside the stone opening. He looked so solitary standing there, one hand braced against the mantel. Her heart longed for him with such acute need her chest ached. Yet she held herself back, not sure if he would welcome her intrusion.

Not sure if he would welcome *her.*

So she drank him in from afar. His long legs, wide shoulders, the sandy hair at his neck that needed a trim. As she continued her inventory, a frown drew her brows together. His right arm lay curved against his side as if protecting it.

"You're hurt," she said, her reticence dissolving as concern for his health eclipsed all else.

His head came around. "I thought you'd left for the ranch."

She dropped her gaze to the floor as she walked, ostensibly to avoid the hazards of wrinkled rugs and overturned furniture, but in truth she was afraid to meet his eyes — afraid of the disappointment she would read there.

"I stayed with Bexar, intending to ride out if the trouble moved outside, but then Cassie and Myra showed up and people started exiting the cabin. I . . . well . . . I figured the danger had passed."

Travis's hands closed around her shoulders. "I'm glad you're here." Something gruff rumbled in his voice. Something emotional and sincere.

Meredith raised her chin, but she had no time to judge what was in his eyes, for his lips descended upon hers and immediately demanded her full attention. His palms stroked upward to cup her face, and the tenderness in his touch banished her insecurities and planted new hope in the soil of her heart.

Her hands wandered over his ribs, pushing beneath his open coat, circling toward his back. But when her left hand rubbed against his side, Travis flinched. It was only for an instant, and his lips never broke from hers, but it was enough to bring Meredith back to the reality of the moment. She pulled away from his kiss.

She lifted the flap of his coat and grimaced at the sight of torn fabric bloodied from a wound. "I should get Crockett. You need to have that tended." She pivoted and tried to move away, but Travis grasped her arm and refused to let her go.

"It's not serious," he said, stepping close to nuzzle her neck. "You can tend it for me later."

Shivers danced across her skin as his warm breath caressed the lobe of her ear. "I don't understand," she murmured, trying to make sense of what was happening. "I thought you'd be angry with me." His teeth nibbled on her ear, nearly scattering her thoughts. In desperation, she twisted away from him. "Stop that."

Travis straightened and peered into her face, confusion etched across his brow.

Her voice grew scratchy. "How can you kiss me? You didn't even want a wife, Travis. You only married me because your bad luck stuck you with the short straw. And now because of my foolish actions, you've forfeited your land." She closed her mouth against the sob that rose in her throat, but a tear escaped her lashes before she could blink it away.

"Is that what you think?" He loosened his hold on her arm, but only enough to allow his hand to slide down and capture hers. "You think I married you because I lost when we drew straws?" He chuckled softly. "Oh, Meri. Sweetheart. I *won* the straw draw. I didn't lose it."

She stared at him, not comprehending the difference. "What are you saying?"

Travis grinned. "When we sat around the table that night, we didn't decide to draw straws because *none* of us wanted to marry you. We drew straws because *all* of us wanted to marry you."

Meredith blinked up at her husband. Could it be true? Had she been a prize, not a chore?

"And I'll tell you something else." He dipped his head and lowered his voice, his grin turning downright mischievous. "But you gotta swear not to tell the others."

She nodded.

"I rigged the contest."

"What?"

"I made sure that I was the one who ended up with the short straw."

Meredith's pulse quickened. "Why?"

Travis shrugged a bit, and if she didn't know better, she could have sworn his skin pinkened a bit under his tan.

"At the time I told myself that you were my responsibility. That because of our previous encounter, I should be the one to marry you."

A responsibility. Of course. Meredith forced her chin to stay raised and her back straight despite her yearning to curl up into a protective ball.

"But I was fooling myself." Travis's gaze met hers, and she caught her breath. The way he looked at her, it was . . . was . . . "Even then I was falling in love with you."

It was love.

"I couldn't stand the idea of one of my brothers marrying you. You belonged with me. I knew it. I couldn't explain it, but I knew it. And over the last several weeks, I've only grown more sure. I love you, Meredith. I thank God every day for bringing you back into my life."

Her heart felt as if it would burst, so full was her joy. But there was one issue she couldn't ignore. "What about your land?"

Travis squeezed her hand and tugged her into his side, then laid a kiss on her forehead. "You're worth more to me than any pile of dirt. I'd give up the ranch again, in a heartbeat, if it meant keeping you safe."

"Wait . . . again?"

He smiled at her and pointed to the blackened remains scattered across the floor of the hearth. "Mitchell was in no condition to protest when Jim reclaimed the deed paper work."

"Oh, Travis! I'm so pleased."

He returned her smile, but then his face grew serious, his voice unsure. "Meri? Did you mean what you wrote in your note? Have you truly come to care for me?"

Meredith bit her lip, her emotions swirling. "More than anything," she vowed. She reached a hand to his cheek and stroked his strong jaw. "I've been in love with you since that day you rescued me from that steel trap. Only now, I love you with the fullness of a woman's love — deep, abiding, forever."

Travis clasped her to him, his lips once again covering hers. But before Meredith could lose herself in the passion he inspired, a throat cleared. The sound echoed loudly in the nearly empty room. She jumped away from Travis with a start, a blush heating her cheeks.

"Sorry to . . . ah . . . interrupt," Crockett intoned from the doorway. "Wanted to see if we could borrow Meredith's horse. Noreen refuses to ride in the same wagon as Mitchell and his *criminal army,* even if the men are all tied up in the back. And she's declared their mounts equally repulsive. Jim fetched Ginger in hopes of appeasing her, but when she saw there was no saddle, she nearly had a fit of apoplexy. He's giving her his own saddle now, and she stopped screeching, so we thought we'd better head out while the gettin' was good."

Meredith shook her head in sympathy. "I don't envy you the long ride to town with her. But if having Ginger makes it easier, I am more than happy to lend her out."

"Do you have lanterns for after night falls?" Travis strode forward, keeping hold of Meredith's hand as he went. "You'll only have a half moon to light your way."

"Yep. Moses thought to bring a few along. He'll be riding with us to deliver Mitchell and the others to the sheriff while Jim sees Cassie and her folks home. Neill and Josiah wanted to ride along, too, if that's all right with you."

"I don't see why not," Travis said. "After all, it was the boy's job to fetch the sheriff in the first place. Might as well let him finish the job."

Meredith stilled as she did the math. That meant . . . she and Travis would be alone at the house. All night.

Travis turned to look at her and heat flared in his eyes as if he had read her thoughts. "I'll . . ." He cleared his throat and turned back to his brother. "I'll see you off."

Meredith trailed behind, a warm, sunny feeling blooming as she watched her reclusive husband reach out in gratitude to all the men and women who had offered their help. Relationships had been formed today, bonds that would last well into the future. No longer would the Archers be isolated from their community. They now stood among them as neighbors, as friends.

"Moses," Travis said, holding his hand out to the big man. "I can't thank you enough. This day would have ended very differently without you."

Moses clasped his hand. "I's just doing unto others like the Good Book says. Helpin' out is what neighbors do. Bearing each other's burdens, and all that."

"When it comes to burdens, Travis is good at the bearing part," Crockett said, slapping his brother on the back. "It's the letting-others-help-with-the-ones-*he's*-carrying part that needs some work."

Meredith opened her mouth to defend her husband, but Travis responded before she could do more than inhale a preparatory breath.

"You're right," he admitted, his humility so dignified it instantly unruffled her feathers and filled her with quiet pride. "But I think that's going to change after today."

"I believe it will, brother," Crockett said, all teasing gone from his tone. "I believe it will."

As the parties prepared to set off, Meredith hugged Cassie and Myra, then returned to her husband's side to wave her farewells. Once everyone had departed, she found herself wrapped in Travis's arms as the two of them rode double atop Bexar back to the ranch.

The short distance didn't allow for much conversation, but words weren't needed. Meredith simply leaned into her husband and let the sway of the horse's gait soothe away the strain of the last few hours.

Travis loved her. Nothing else mattered.

When Bexar halted, Meredith lifted her

head. Travis cupped the side of her face and placed a soft kiss on her lips. It was tender and brief and, oh, so sweet, yet when he pulled away, the tilt of his smile and the heat in his gaze promised more to come.

"I need to see to the horse," he said as he circled her waist with his arm and lowered her to the ground. "But I'll be in soon."

"I'll help you."

He raised an eyebrow at her but made no complaint as he dismounted and led Bexar into the barn. Meredith followed. She needed to be close to him. This was their first night to be completely alone together, and she didn't want to waste a single moment.

Travis removed Bexar's saddle and blankets while Meredith hung up the bridle. She checked the feedbox and water and found them both adequate for the night. Travis came up behind her, his hat brim bumping her head as he nuzzled her neck.

She giggled and danced away, feeling playful yet oddly shy at the same time. Travis gave chase, his husky laughter blending with hers as the two of them darted out of the barn. When they neared the porch, he grabbed her about the waist and lifted her off her feet. Meredith squealed.

"You can't escape me," Travis murmured

in her ear as he gently settled her back on the ground.

Meredith turned in his arms to face the man she loved. "I've no desire to."

His eyes darkened, and for a moment she thought he would kiss her. But then he scooped her into his arms and carried her up the porch steps. The front door proved more of a challenge to conquer. Travis had to juggle his hold on her a bit before he could get the latch open. Meredith laughed in delight, endeared by his awkward efforts. Once the door was cracked, he kicked it wide with his boot and carried her over the threshold.

"Welcome home, Mrs. Archer."

Welcome home. As if their marriage had just taken place and he had brought her home for the first time. Meredith's smile trembled as she met her husband's gaze. He was offering her a new start, offering a marriage based on love.

He carried her through the hall until they reached the kitchen. There he set her down and slowly undid the fastenings on her cloak. A shiver tingled against her skin wherever his fingers touched. His eyes held hers as he slid the garment from her shoulders, breaking contact only when he turned to hang the cloak on a hook.

While his back was to her, Meredith discovered a boldness she didn't know she had, and reached for the shoulders of his coat. She eased it down the length of his arms, admiring the play of his muscles beneath the flannel of his shirt. Placing his coat on the hook next to hers, her shyness returned.

Travis nudged her chin up with the edge of his hand. "Will you be my wife tonight, Meri?"

She bit her lip, her heart fluttering so fast she felt light-headed. But she knew what her answer would be. "Yes, Travis. Tonight and always."

No longer was she a short-straw bride, Meredith thought as she took her husband's hand and allowed him to draw her down the hall to their room. With the gift of Travis's heart, she'd been transformed into a well-loved wife. She couldn't imagine a greater blessing.

ABOUT THE AUTHOR

Karen Witemeyer holds a master's degree in Psychology from Abilene Christian University and is a member of ACFW, RWA, and her local writers' guild. She is the author of *A Tailor-Made Bride,* which was honored as one of the Best Western Romances of 2010 by the Love Western Romances Web site, as well as being nominated for a RITA Award and the National Readers' Choice Award. *Short-Straw Bride* is her fourth novel. Karen lives in Abilene, Texas, with her husband and three children.